CHILDREN

of the

STAR

SANCTUARY SAGA: BOOK I

SHARON IRWIN HENRY

LifeRich Publishing is a registered trademark of The Reader's Digest Association, Inc.

LifeRich Publishing books may be ordered through booksellers or by contacting:

LifeRich Publishing
1663 Liberty Drive
Bloomington, IN 47403
www.liferichpublishing.com
844-686-9607

ISBN: 978-1-4897-3430-3 (sc)
ISBN: 978-1-4897-3429-7 (e)

Print information available on the last page.

LifeRich Publishing rev. date: 04/14/2021

Dedicated to my Grandkids
All of you.
In Memory of
Tony Terrell Robinson Jr
Kyla Rochelle Robinson

Special thanks to the women in my life who read all the different copies over the last three years. All the feedback given to me enabled me to bring life to my characters and enriched my writing one-hundred-hold; Vickie, Fran, Jan, Peg, Camille, and Sam. To my great-nephews, Cameron and Tyler, for pointing out a kid view, To my husband for holding down the house while I typed for hours at my office, the kitchen table. To Ace, Tattoo Artist extraordinaire, for his image on my son's chest. That is my Irsci and Abby. To Shadayra aka Shades, your input and advice to organize thought, concepts and characters was priceless. Kristin, sister of my soul, and Shady, both of you are always there for me. To Lolo for walking this path with me. Your knowing Sanctuary Saga was always meant to be and has been a beautiful blessing for me. And especially to my Ace bam booms, My granddaughters, Kyla and Aalayah; there would be no book without you.

<u>And Gramma said, "RUN!"</u>

CHAPTER 1

RUN RIVER RUN

"WHERE ARE YOU Grams," River asked? "I don't understand what's going on. Why did you leave me all alone?" River's Gramma had been missing since the fiasco at the naming ceremony three days ago. The last thing Grams had said to River made no sense to her. It was a mystery. The words etched in River's mind.

"River, go to the old house. Go to Laiya's girl, go now. If you choose to procrastinate and take your time, waiting till the last moment, which I'm sure you will do just that, you must be there before sunset, three days from now. Izen is coming for you. Better be long gone before that River," Grams told her.

"I didn't even know the old house still existed until she told me to run there. Now my three days are up, and I'm still here because I hoped you would show up. You set me up, Grams," she said, "Why?" Her agitation was increasing by the moment. "I gotta go," she said. She felt it. It was like every nerve in her body was jumping, screaming at her, **Get moving, River!**

"JIVE, what's taking you so long," She yelled as she opened the door to her bedroom. She still felt the same way as she did this morning when she woke up; it was time to go. She always had a sixth sense about things.

"Stop yelling at me, River, it's not gonna make me interface any sooner," JIVE yelled back. "I am not the one who waited until the last moment to do anything."

JIVE's right, she thought, trying not to be irritated with him too. I was the one who procrastinated until the very last moment, just like Gramma said I would. River smiled to herself, remembering her gramma's prediction three days earlier.

River found herself wandering through the home that had been her and Grams' for twelve years, most of her life. I was almost three when we move here; she absentmindedly thought as she lightly stroked the wood of a mighty oak. River could never tell what came first, the oaks or her home. They were intertwined as if they grew together—the trees interlocked over hundreds of years, creating spacious rooms inside. The trees were her home, and her home was the trees. She shrugged and thought, and they are the same. She stopped wandering and found herself standing in the greeting room, looking at the door that led outside. She had walked, room to room, to the front passage and the way out of the house.

"What's going on, Grams? Why am I fleeing my home, on the run like a desperado?" River called out to her Gramma though she was not there. "No one can penetrate Sanctuary without the consent of Bubble. I am not going," she kept saying. "Ever since the Naming Ceremony, It's been nothing but trouble. You tell me to run, then leave me alone."

River had no idea where her Grams was or why she sent her running. She had always thought Sanctuary, her home, was safe. She questioned why she had to go, confused by the drama surrounding her these last three days. She did not want to believe any of this. Yet, here she was, walking out of her home with no apparent intention and no exact destination, just her grandmother telling her to go to Laiya's.

River was leaving, and she knew it. But that did not stop her from dragging her feet. She did not want to go. Not yet, she thought to herself. She was feeling the weight of being alone and on the run, and she hadn't even left home. Instead of walking out the door, she sat down in her Gram's favorite chair. She began to remember the day they moved into the dismal conk apartment in the Cities when she was five. They had rented it from a notorious slummer, a nasty guy, through a third party. Someone else rented it for Grams because everyone knew who she was, and no one would dare cheat her.

"We moved into the City for you, River. You will need to know the harsh realities of City life and what that means to most Rakians. You must, as a future regent of our land, understand what the Rakians lost," she told River that day.

Since then, Grams moved us from my Sanctuary into the City part-time every year. River was unhappy about Gram's decision even now, almost ten years later. "Three to six months a year, we live in a cramped conk apartment in the City, she grumbled. No windows anywhere in that City, nothing natural; not the air, lights, or food," she complained, feeling the dislike of the Cities rise in her all over again. River also remembered what else her gram had said the day they moved into their conk because she had lived by that advice all her life.

"First thing River, remember, age is nothing but a number. Do not let anyone box you in. You are not and never will be, their idea of who you should be," Gramma told her. "People will be coming into your life now. Stay aware. Rake is a rough place to play in River, and you have a lot to offer; remember that too. You will have the advantage. People will see you only as a kid and look no further. You are not your age," She said to me, "your body might only be five-years-old, River, but your mind is more like three-hundred-years-old."

She always told me I was smarter than all of them put together. But even I thought she might be biased, favoring me above everyone else. Gramma is brilliant, and because I am her lineage, she says I'm smart too. I am unique; she tells me. I'm pretty sure all grammas' say that to their grandchildren. But I do not know that for sure. I have no one to compare it to in my life. She thought this as she looked back over the almost fifteen years of her existence.

I have no human friends.

River hated the City. She could not wait to get back to the land, Sanctuary - her real home. Every time they left Sanctuary for the Cities, she counted the days until she could come home.

"I am glad I won't have to go there anymore, she said without thinking. Then she stopped. Standing in the greeting room, in the only home she had ever loved, a strange realization came to her; this *is* the last time I will see my home. She knew it to be true; the feeling was intense.

"Oh, wow," she uttered, wanting to cry. Instead, she wiped her eyes, squared her shoulders, and stood a little taller. She took a deep breath in and exhaled it out, and said, "Shake it off, Riv, get up out of this pity pool. As Grams said, I have work to do."

"JIVE!" River called out again.

JIVE was the Jump Intrawave Vortex Environment System for homes. JIVE did everything from cooking and cleaning to being a teacher, doctor, lawyer, babysitter. Everything you ever needed all rolled up in one; a sixth-dimensional virtual home helper. What was needed, JIVE became. And he was one of River's only friends - Bubble being the other. JIVE was made to look, feel, and sound human, But he wasn't. He could materialize anywhere and manifest as anyone. Rakians loved JIVE.

"JIVE, I gotta go with or without Grams' pack," River hollered. "Open door," she commanded and stepped out of her house. "Is the Hoover ready?" She asked, noticing it parked out front.

The three-hundred-year-old two-seater hovercraft was a vehicle made to float inches off the ground for smoother travel. Grrrrreat, River groaned to herself, looking at it. Modern technology three hundred years ago; a dinosaur now she thought. The idea of having to ride this old vehicle on a five-hour trip over Sanctuary land was not making her very happy or friendly.

"It's afternoon already, and I need to be there by sunset," River yelled out again, irritation in her voice. "Somebody meant for this ancient dusty ride to be used only on short excursions, not long-distance travel,"

She fumed, kicking at the ground in front of the old hoover, frustrated all over again. "It would be sooooo much easier if I could just jump. I would already be there," River moaned.

"OK, OK, EVERYTHING is as ready as it can be, with all this rushing to get out that you're doing," JIVE spouted back at River. "And stop being snippy with me. Blame your grandmother for putting you in this spot. NOT ME," he huffed as he walked outside and stood beside River with her pack in his hand. JIVE stood six foot five inches tall with dark hair he kept short, the palest of skin, and the lightest iridescent eyes Rake technology could produce. His eyes changed colors on the regular.

He's starting to sound like his feelings are hurt, thought River. That, too, was her fault. She had asked Grams a long time ago to program him to be more human.

"Unfortunately," JIVE continued, "I will not be able to take this trip with you."

"I know. Grams said I had to do this part alone. What difference does it make?" asked River, kicking at the ground. "It didn't make any difference," she answered herself, "I'm always alone. No brothers, no sisters, restricted on Rake," she complained. "This planet is one big colossal City, connected by Laiya with her jump and her JIVE." Her thoughts were as scattered as she felt, but it made her feel good to let them flow, so she kept right on complaining to herself.

"No one ever traveled by any other transportation; it didn't exist. except here on Sanctuary," criticizing her current circumstances once again. "These Rakians would look in horror at this old vehicle," River said, finding fault with everyone and anyone in her frustrations. "They would not know where to begin or what to do." She gave the old hoover a once over as she said that with sarcasm dripping from her voice. "No one ever went outside, never saw the sunshine, or smelled fresh dirt after a summer shower, and the jump was the only means of transportation across the world.

"This city is nothing but an overcrowded cesspool doomed to a slow death"; she finished her tirade.

River did not live on the edge of destruction, like 95% of the population. Laiya's descendants were exempt from all restrictions on Rake, and there were many, many restrictions. We could have lived anywhere, even up in the skies, and I could have had as many siblings as I wanted, River groaned. Not us, though, remembering how Grams would shake her head no and say,

"Just because you **can** do a thing, River, doesn't mean you **should**."

"Grams, don't you remember; Rake is not a place that fosters friendships. Where are you, Gramma?"

Everyone's competition on Rake; trusting could get you killed. Bonds and contracts were made and broken on the sole premise of power. Domination was a characteristic in all who lived on Rake.

A brother or sister would have been someone I could trust, thought River. Then again, maybe not, came her afterthought. My relatives can be pretty cutthroat.

"Hoover is tuned, solar power switched on, and all the items your

5

grandmother listed have been packed. You will find some of those quite interesting," JIVE said, interrupting River's thoughts again as he handed her the pack.

"Here," he said, "And, this is the thanks I get, you snipping at me all morning."

River smiled softly, not letting JIVE see it. Yep, I hurt his feelings, she thought, as she took the pack and placed it in the infinite space compartment with her bag.

They are right about that, she mused, as she looked into the chamber; infinite space, everything fits in there. I wonder if I would fit in there too. She was getting lost in thought, not wanting to go, and still procrastinating. This time in her mind, as well.

"Ah-hem," JIVE cleared his throat, bringing her mind back around to the present. "As I commented moments ago, though you did not respond in kind, I *will not* be able to take this trip with you," JIVE's voice full of hurt indignation. "The country is restricted territory; no Jump, no JIVE, and no one in Sanctuary without Bubble saying so."

"I know you can't come. Sorry JIVE, just a little tense," murmured River soothing his ego. "Grams was always telling me to be streetwise and board smart. I'm trying, I'm trying, but I don't know what's going on. And *you* won't tell me anything," River cut her eyes at JIVE, just a hint of hurt anger in her voice. "What's the new game, Grams? Rake's a rough world to play in. Remember, you taught me that."

She was not expecting any answers from either her missing Grandmother or zipped-lipped JIVE.

Her grandmother, Aiya, raised her to recognize the ins and outs, the nuances, of a social structure. And all the players in the game. It had been the two of them for as long as River could remember. She almost wanted to laugh, staring at the old Hoover, thinking this was just another of Grams' social experiments.

Almost.

Right now, River felt maybe a sister would be nice. *Any* family, she sighed. One day, she secretly hoped she would meet this big huge family, and they would recognize her and welcome her home. Sometimes River felt as if this had been so once in her young life. A fleeting memory she could neither grasp nor hold. She did not know her parents. All Grams ever said was that they loved her, and she would see them one day.

"I will tell you about them one day," Grams would whisper as if someone or something was trying to listen in. "One day, you will know who they are and who you are," she would say cryptically.

Then not say anything else at all. That was Grams.

"What's going on?" River asked aloud, "For the umpteenth time, I'm asking: why is this happening? I do not understand. Where are you, Gramma?"

Suddenly, JIVE chimed in, "It is what it is. Come on out that pity pool."

Gez, JIVE sounded just like Gramma, River thought.

"Let's go, girl, you got an adventure waiting!"

"Really, JIVE? That's what you call this, an **adventure**?"

Sometimes he could be so irritating. He's right, though, River thought. I must get moving. Grams said I had to be at Laiya's today at sunset. River felt the itch inside her. She knew Izen was here trying to get past the compound's barrier. He was moments away, but Bubble was stopping him from getting into Sanctuary. Izen could not get past Bubble. He had never been allowed into Sanctuary, only on the compound, created on the relatives' land. Ten miles designated for them to occupy, and only once a year for the Naming ceremonies. And then only for a few days. They all should have left hours ago. Not today, though. Somehow, Izen had gotten into the compound without Grams being here. River was not taking any chances that he wouldn't be able to get into Sanctuary as well. He is a snake, River thought, as she did a once over on her ride again. A capable and cruel snake. If anyone can get past Bubble, Izen will be the one to do it.

"Time to go," River said to JIVE. "The Naming drama's only going to keep Izen busy a couple of days. I've already stretched it to three days."

Her gut was itching; Izen was here, River could feel it. Still, she waited a moment, thinking how much her life changed in a split second. She felt overwhelmed with sadness.

"I will miss this place, JIVE," she said as she looked back one last time at her home. "What's going on, Grams? Where are you?"

She shook her head, clearing her thoughts. No sense asking the same questions over and over that won't be answered, sighed River. It was time for her to go.

"Lockdown the house, JIVE, delete all memories of me for the last three days. I need a complete memory wipe with no hope of retrieval," she said solemnly, "just in case Izen finds a way to breach Sanctuary."

"Goodbye, JIVE," sadness creeping into her voice as she spoke.

"Will do, River, goodbye," replied JIVE without emotion.

River jumped on the hoover, putting the chip Grams had slipped into her hand during all the chaos the night of the Naming Ceremony into the Hoover computer.

"Upload Map," she said and waited, and waited, frustrated by the speed, or rather the lack thereof.

"This is so slow," she ranted to herself, "everything about this transpo is slow! WHY can't we jump on Sanctuary? Laiya used to drive around on this very same hoover with her grandma three-hundred years ago," River fumed.

She was ready to leave NOW.

"This old machine, I wouldn't be surprised if you didn't start," River said aloud to the Hoover. "No one used this outdated mode of transportation anymore. You jumped, get you anywhere in seconds. But not in Sanctuary." River was exasperated all over again.

"No jump, no JIVE," River sighed, resigned to her fate.

The map finally finished uploading.

"Begin the journey," River commanded. After a few seconds, the old Hoover roared to life and settled into its rhythm. She rode off, her long copper brown hair flying behind her in the wind, and her cocoa brown skin softly shimmering the brilliant colors of a red sun.

River laughed, feeling the pure exhilaration of going on an Adventure.

CHAPTER 2

IZEN

I T TOOK IZEN three days to remember River. He had been too focused on solidifying his voter support for his bid to be the heir. By the time he came for her, she was gone. He had stayed on compound past the time allowed. He was hoping River would think everyone had gone and come onto the compound grounds where he could catch her unaware. He justified staying with a little-used clause allowing the head of the board three days at the compound instead of two. Izen had no idea River never went to the compound unless it was necessary. And Izen could not get into Sanctuary.

"This force field," he said, kicking at Bubble.

It stopped him from getting her now. Izen assumed she was headed somewhere deep into Sanctuary, where he could not get to her.

"I might not know where you are going on these protected lands, but I know your destination, where you will head when you leave Sanctuary." That information cost him a small fortune. "No, you are not safe, River, not at all," Izen said out loud. "And this is far from over. JIVE, jump me home, bring my wife and son home in two hours no sooner; I have work to do."

Fifteen minutes later, Izen sat at his desk in his den, looking over the new information. Clean-shaven and refreshed from the days at the compound. He disliked going there every year and only being allowed onto the compound. He had never been allowed into Sanctuary. It reminded him all too clearly what he could not have. He did not like that feeling.

Izen took anything he wanted all the time. It did not matter who it belonged to or what official he had to bride. If he wanted it, it was his. But not Sanctuary. He could only replicate parts of the house from a hologram he had paid a fortune to the Pearl to get his hands on. There remained few original photos of Laiya's home. He had one of them. Izen was proud of the den he manifested, and he felt somewhat satisfied. He loved the feel of the solid oak desk. He could have had one fabricated for a fraction of the cost, but Izen wanted the best, and the best was wood. It had better be real; he had told himself when he bought it. Still, it wasn't the den at Sanctuary

"Soon, I will be in the actual home, and it will release Laiya's secret to me. I will have that formula," Izen vowed.

He had spent too many years and too much money reaching for it. He was not about to let it slip through his fingers now. He was close to succeeding, he felt it, like a hunter on its prey, and nothing would stand in his way.

River is my way to the formula, but she has slipped from my grasp for the moment, he thought. That kid Seecca, the one my spies found in the bowels, might be another way to get what I want if I lose River. I am just not so sure about him. That kid will probably just end up a waste of my money and time.

Why did that old man, Eldar, declare it's time for a new heir and at the naming ceremony no less Izen questioned? With everyone there. It had an immediate result, Izen thought, remembering the pandemonium Eldar's declaration had caused. He had dropped everything else and moved quickly to solidify his bid to be the heir. And River had slipped quietly away. Gone, and she's not yoked. The old lady is missing also. A coincident, Izen asked himself? I was too busy, he thought, now both of them are gone. No matter, he shrugged. I know that girl is on that protected land. She will have to come out of there to reach her destination. And I will be there to meet her on that mountain where she will no longer be protected.

Izen knew where he needed to enter the foothills to catch River coming out of Sanctuary's protected lands, and he was determined to get what he wanted at any cost.

I'll head to Argot mountain ahead of her and take her by surprise, he decided. Nothing was too much in Izen's quest for power. And no one was going to stand in his way—particularly some pest of a kid.

CHAPTER 3

LAIYA'S LAND

AT LEAST THE scenery is compelling, not like the city of nothing blandness River thought as she looked around on her ride to Laiya's home.

Sanctuary had been a Bubble-restricted area for most of its existence. Since 2032 all two-hundred-thousand acres off-limits; no jump, no JIVE, and no one in without Bubble's ok. Jumping would have taken River to her destination instantaneously. She was in for a five-hour ride with the Hoover. She would follow a winding path over two hundred and fifty miles of rolling hills, lush valleys with fields of flowers, streams, and one boisterous river. The foot of the mountains lay at its northernmost border — all Sanctuary. In the beginning, it had been forty acres. Laiya, her mom, and her cousins had increased the land to two-hundred-thousand acres.

Wow, thought River, why is Sanctuary's history popping into my head? It was like the land was offering her the memories, and they were free-floating through her mind like scenes on a hologram. Except she was experiencing the memories as if she were a part of them, like a 6D vid-com, and it all felt real. This experience was new to her, but she thought, let history play itself out. Why not kill some time, she said to herself. I got five hours to explore these memories that are not mine. River did not know these histories. They were old.

Grams had shown her the way of remembering three summers ago. She had told River she was destined to be Regent of the Land and must learn how to recognize in feeling, as well as in mind, what the memory encompassed. Like a holo replay, it was the way of understanding the past. You submerged yourself into the sensations of the memory, including your physiological response. In other words, what did your body do? You remembered your body's responses, tastes in the air on your tongue, smells, and sounds, what your eyes register, and what your brain sees. The memory then is as close to what took place as possible.

"There's always a margin of error," Grams would say. "Remember that, River. The smallest detail can change your whole perspective. Grams would make her practice and practice and practice until she could observe everything without thinking about it.

But this time was different. River had never had such an experience before. Such an intimate viewing of memory, She found herself standing in Laiya's bedroom three hundred years ago, remembering a memory she did not know. River understood she was still riding the hoover, but it felt like she had left the ride behind. She was no longer there but actually in the room with Laiya.

"Laiya, can you answer a few questions? Laiya, who helped you? Are you saying you discovered the Wave by yourself, Laiya? Laiya, Laiya, Laiya, always asking, you did this?" Laiya said, mimicking the reporters and their badgering, as she walked to her desk in her room talking to her cousin.

It is as if I am here in the room with Laiya, River thought, amazed. What kind of new tech is this, River asked herself, as she found herself moving to get out of Laiya's way?

Laiya continued her ranting, frustrated with her life, as River stood by and watched the story unfold.

"As if a twenty-four-year-old woman was too young to do math or not smart enough to discover this without the help of some old goat feeding her the formula," Laiya scoffed. "Einstein was your age Kai, twenty-six-years old when he published his groundbreaking theories for his time. The dimensional wave theory is all mine," she said and turned to her cousin, still feeling irritated. "Sorry, Kaiya, I get so sick of it all."

"You're preaching to the choir Laylay. You don't like it, leave. What's stopping you, girl, besides yourself?" Kaiya asked as she plopped down on Laiya's bed.

Laiya turned from her desk and looked at Kaiya again. "Nothing. Why not tell the world I'm gone and leave it at that?" Laiya began formulating an idea. "The jumps have been operating for a couple of years. Bubble's protective seal protects Sanctuary; all two-hundred-thousand acres," she laughed. "We have a three-hundred-year lease with the Elon, and Bubble has agreed to continue in form for the term of the contract. Sanctuary's situated. The Elon decided. We have our Sanctuary dimension, free-standing from this dimension, yet tethered by a strong bond."

"I could do this," Laiya turned back to her work, pencil in her hand, scratching equations on a napkin. "I think I have worked out the jump kinks," her mind already on something else. "Home Vortexes are here. I finally got the prototype done. I told you I had an idea for a home jump. Remember, it was the first time we went on the wave. It's a little bit of everything and a home jump as well. The production starts in three weeks. I call it JIVE," she said offhandedly, leaning back in her seat, stretching her hands out above her head, and biting on her bottom lip like she always did when thinking. "Mass transit portals aren't needed anymore."

Laiya turned to Kaiya and said, "I once made a story up at one of these conferences about lions on the land. They kept asking the same questions; why did I put a protective force field around my land, and why do I call it Bubble?"

"I looked at that audience and asked myself, why am I doing this? That was the last time I ever went back to one of those conferences, Kaiya," Laiya said, remembering that day. "Anyways, I told them I encased the land because the lions were trying to get out." She laughed. "You know what's funny, Kaikai, they believed me. Never mind that there haven't been free-roaming lions here in forty years." Laiya started to turn back to her work, then changed her mind. "These same businesspeople and government officials keep questioning Bubble's integrity. All these people are getting on my last nerve Kai. I politely remind them every time he calls himself Bubble, has impeccable honor, and he can spot a liar a million miles away. Best to let him decide since Gramma didn't want the job," she finished, laughing again.

She turned to her work. "These fools are still trying to find ways around the simple rules of the jump: no harm, No government, No cost. I'm ready to let these people think I am gone from here, Kaiya. I'm tired of them still showing up unannounced all the time, trying to find a way into Sanctuary. Hard-headed, some people. I tell them, 'If you can't get past Bubble, you can't get in.' It's simple. As I said, it's a couple of years since we seeded the planet with the jump. Let's go, Kaiya. Keep them guessing."

"Sounds good to me, Layia. I like the name JIVE; you trying to say something?" Kaiya was asking as the scene faded from River.

✦　✦　✦

"Wow, Grams is the spitting image of Laiya, only older." It was the first thing River said coming back from this memory. The first thing she did was to scan her environment, checking for anything out of the ordinary. She felt vulnerable while memory tripping, like anyone, could sneak up on her while she was in memory. She did not like that feeling.

The memories had stopped for a moment, and River had a second to breathe and think. She realized she liked Laiya. This trip brought her closer to knowing her ancestor.

What was Laiya talking about, a different sanctuary dimension? Was it tethered to my world, Rake? How did she do that? River did not have time to ask any more questions because the memories began again without letting her reflect, Skipping around without rhyme or reason. She looked at the onboard clock wondering how much time had gone by. That can't be right, she thought, when she saw it had only been 15 minutes since she left her home. It felt like I was there in those memories for at least an hour.

"Oh wow," River said out loud. She was now seeing images of the sprawling home where Laiya discovered the wave and created the jump. Until the Naming three days ago, River had no idea it was still standing, let alone on the land.

The old house still existed. And it is here? How come no one told me this? How is it I am just finding this out? It annoyed River all over again.

"All your secrets seemed to be popping up suddenly, Grams. I'm running away on a three-hundred-year-old hoover, with a pack that YOU had JIVE create, with who knows what inside." All these thoughts ran through her head and right out of her mouth. "Grams, you should have just told me what's going on."

River sighed, feeling the exasperation of this whole day. Why all the mystery? She reminded herself again; it did not do any good to keep asking the same questions that would not be answered any time soon. She had not looked yet to see what was inside the pack. River figured she would wait until she got there.

"You got me out here on some crazy mission, Grams. You neglected to give me any clue, except saying find yourself. Ok, I will," River said sarcastically. This five-hour trip to the house over land might be useful, she thought.

"You know I am like a dog with a bone, Grams," she said, using one of Gram's favorite sayings. "I won't let go till I find out what this is all about." She chastised her grandmother out loud; at the same time, River wished she were here with her now. "I see your hand in this too, Grams, no coincidences. You got me rushing out the door, spooked. You know I don't like surprises."

It helped to ease her anxiety, hearing a voice, even if it was just hers. I WILL bring this up when I see her again. If I see her, she sighed. She looked down at the humming hoover,

"As long as you keep running, we'll be alright. To the house, we go!"

I must get into that house. She felt the need now.

"Why are you slowing down, old one?" River asked the hoover as if it could understand her.

"We must ride fast," she said, pushing the hoover to move quicker, wanting more than anything to get to Laiya's house.

CHAPTER 4

————◦————

HERE COMES TROUBLE

WATER WAS HOME at Cliffs-Edge, in her bedroom, high above the shores of Core. Her room nested in the cliffs, twenty meters below the plateau, and the roots of most the oaks surrounding her home. Roots crept in through the walls and then moved their way back out again. That gave her room its design of interwoven earth and tree. The west wall was an invisible barrier that jutted out from the cliffs on a wide ledge that extended twelve feet out over the ocean. Water had a panoramic view of the ocean far below. She liked the feel of solid earth beneath her feet and the vast and open waters surrounding her. The barrier allowed for a perfect view of Core's shoreline, the sandy dunes, and the path to the compound and Cliffs-Edge.

"uh-oh, trouble," Water said as she looked down to the shores below.

She was watching the elders hike up the path to Gran from the coast. Her Gran was standing at the halfway point down the trail from the gathering house. She was also halfway from the beach. The elders had come by rift across the waters. The rifts were small willow reed boats used to forage the island shores for fish. Not for traveling the open waters or moving from island to island.

"Well, I'll be," she said, amazed.

The elders crossed the waters by a rift. It not only piqued her interest, but the very notion grabbed her attention and held tight. No one ever entered Core, her island, from the shores. Kaiya always jumped their guests directly to the gathering house compound. Yet, here were all the elders climbing to her home on that steep, winding one wagon road. She could see they had crossed the small dunes from the beach, beginning to climb the trail to Gran.

Again, she wondered, why? NO ONE ever traveled this way. Why is Gran meeting the elders out on the trail Water questioned?.

"Something's up," she whispered aloud. "WHAT is Gran up to?"

No one had gotten close to Core, and Gran refused to speak to anyone since the debacle at the Choosing three months ago. She even dismissed Zebble, Skaton Island's Elder. Zebble was the head of a massive following, never before seen in the history of Izaria. He had been insisting on being heard for the past three months. All his squawking and furious anger got him nowhere. Kaiya jumped no one to Core Gran did not want to see. And the invisible force field surrounding Core kept out anyone coming from the ocean waters. Gran had ignored them all; until today.

"She's letting them in," Water said, stunned. She leaned into the barrier, unconsciously trying to get a better view. Her excitement growing, she knew the game had just changed.

Gran was standing high above the elders on the steep path to the compound, feet planted firmly on the road, looking down on the elders struggling to get to her. Water gazed down upon her Gramma looking fierce and proud like she knew something these elders did not know. Gran's back was to the sun, illuminating her and everything around her.

"She's like a cold fire," Water said, amazed at what she was seeing.

She saw the heart of her Gran, and she had never looked more beautiful. Like some ancient warrior from the stories Gran always told.

I bet those elders are terrified; Water laughed.

Gran and the elders had a different kind of relationship. She was accountable to no homesite nor any elder. Zebble hated Gran because of the freedom and power he imagined she had.

Water focused on the drama that was about to unfold. The elders were almost to where Gran stood.

She is making a statement! Water knew it, so did the elders. She did not move to meet them. She never had. Not *my* Gran thought Water.

An overwhelming feeling came to her; today is the day I am leaving. I have been preparing for this for the last three months, and today is the day. Now every part of her began to tingle, having thought it; she brought it. Words led to action. She knew.

"Game on," Water said, smiling, "I gotta see what's happening," she said and pressed her face to the barrier.

Water was looking at the elders and concentrating on their auras, mannerisms, and body language. Ten of them did not want to be there. That left three: Zebble, Chief Elder, and Wiffle. She could tell Zebble hated Gran, but that was nothing new; he always had. Chief Elder Conman was afraid of her, but she already knew that too. This feeling she detected in Chief Elder and Zebble, this deception, was something new. Zebble and the chief elder are trying to hide something from Gran, Water thought. What were they trying to hide? It didn't matter, she concluded; they couldn't hide anything from Gran anyway. They were all mind speakers, and Gran was the greatest of them all. Water knew no secret, no desire, nor any dream could remain hidden from her; their minds bared open. All the elders bowed to Gran.

"I bet not even Kaiya herself could hide from Gran," Water said aloud.

Not likely, Kaiya responded out of nowhere, mind speaking with Water.

Go away, Kaiya. I'm busy.

I see that you are, little girl. Does your grandmother know what you are doing? Kaiya laughed.

Go away before you get me in trouble. I've got to know what's going on down there, Water said to Kaiya as she began the attempt to sneak into Wiffle's mind without being detected.

Me too; fill me in when you find out. Kaiya laughed again and left Water's mind.

Water watched as Young elder Wiffle stayed in the background, away from all the elders. It looks like he doesn't want to participate, Water noticed. I'm going to send out a small thought line and lightly anchor it in his mind. That's all I needed to do, she thought, concentrating on the task at hand.

Three years prior, Sista Sol had caught Zebble sneaking around the edges of Water's mind, trying to meld without her consent. The deception was typical of Zebble, but not of the Izarians; a people easily led; they knew nothing of deception.

"Zebble would not be able to catch you unawares ever," Sista had told her that day. Sista began intense training for Water right then and there. Water learned the arts of projection and protections, of shielding, and the art of creating an illusion. She was not caught off guard often after Sista's training, and then only Sista, Gran, or Kaiya could catch her napping and slip into her mind. But none of the island elders ever got close to the edges of Water's mind again. It was Water who created an illusion in the minds of each elder who had tried. And a few had tried. She led them all to believe they had succeeded in compromising her. She had played them.

But mind-melding with someone was a different technique from mind speaking and different from creating illusions. It was something Water rarely did and had only begun to practice melding, without the consent of the other person, at the Choosing Ceremonies, three months ago.

"In a meld, you see through the eyes of the one you melded with, and they see through your eyes," Sista had instructed her. "You can open your soul in a meld," she said. She approached Water at her table, and forcefully placed her hand on the desk, and whispered conspiratorially, "Or not."

"If you are sneaking in without their knowledge," Sista had continued her lesson that day. "You could hide in someone's mind, quiet as a mouse spying on your subject, or control their every move."

Water was quietly remembering Sista Sol's lessons as she inched closer to creating an opening through Wiffle's mind blocks. A little twinge of conscience crept into her mind. I'm hiding, not trying to control anything. I just don't want Wiffle to know I'm looking. That's all. Wiffle is an easy target, Water said to herself, continuing to justify her actions. Then her conscious taunted her as Water remembered, this young elder never walked in my mind unannounced. He always signaled when he wanted to speak. Not like Zebble, always trying to sneak in and control me.

Like I am trying to do to Wiffle now, Water winced at that thought, knowing how little she had liked it when Zebble and the other elders had tried. Wiffle probably won't be too mad if he catches me trying to look out through his eyes, she hoped. She had tried the other ten elders standing back, but they were all too scattered in thought for her to hear everything going on. She wasn't yet really good at this.

"I just gotta **see**," she said and continued sending a tiny sliver through Wiffle's blocks, trying to anchor it lightly in his mind. I'm not trying to change anything, she repeated to herself again, just watching. I'm not

19

trying to control anything. I need to see. I have to know what is going on down there." Concentrating on her target, she felt the anchor go into Wiffle's consciousness.

"As I said," she preened about her abilities, "an easy target."

Wiffle's tribal elder, Soin, had just passed on to Kaiya six months ago, three months before the Choosing Ceremony. Wiffle inherited his elder's responsibilities like one inherits an old shirt. "This guy has his hands full," giggled Water, forgetting all about her guilty conscience.

Get out of his mind, girl, rang Gran's voice, loud and clear inside Water's thoughts.

Oh, snap, busted. *Sorry, Gran,* replied Water, sheepishly pulling out of Wiffle's mind.

Her grandmother's voice softened,

Join me. Watch and learn.

Water watched and heard through a mind-meld with Gran. It wasn't often that Gran let Water into her mind, and it was even rarer if she allowed Water to feel what she felt as well. Most of the time, Gran made her have her own experience instead of using someone else's feelings as her own. As Zebble and the elders continued to struggle up the steep hill, Water saw Gran could see the hate wrapped around Zebble's aura, too, only more evident. It shouted in her mind; so intense was his hatred, it seemed alive. His heart shrouded in darkness, consumed. Wow, she thought, how could anyone hate so much? It was the same thing she had seen on him the night of the Choosing. The moment every elders' shields dropped in total surprise when Kaiya chose to speak after one-hundred and fifty years of silence.

Until the night of the Choosing, Water hadn't known Kaiya wasn't talking to anyone else. Water and Kaiya spoke nearly every day. Kaiya was a part of her family, like Gran and Sista Sol, the only holographic six-dimensional home helper on Izaria. Water found herself smiling, remembering the story of how Gran and Sista had met. Somewhere, on something called the dark web after Sista had gone rouge on her deletion day. Water interjected the memory with questions she had never asked. How old is Sista, and how long had she been hiding? And wouldn't those hunting her quit looking over a little time? After all, she was just one runaway house bot program. More questions that would go unanswered thought Water.

She remembered how surprised she had been that Kaiya had spoken at the ceremony. Not because she spoke, but the timing, right after the chief said the elders were choosing for her. That had never happened in the history of Izaria. And right before the chief spoke their choice. She remained free.

Everyone else had been shocked that she spoke. All except for Gran realized Water. Gran knew all along. Gran's memories showed her this. She and Gran were still connected, and Gran was allowing Water to access her memories. She saw it clearly through Gran's eyes.

The night of the Choosing was so confusing; everything happened so quickly. She didn't get a clear picture of anything except Zebble's emotion, and she did not see that as clearly as Gran had. I know he hates Gran, but why would he hate me so much?

Watch and learn Water, Gran spoke.

Water stopped speculating and memory hopping and focused on what was happening now.

She watched the elders as their struggle up the steep path to Gran neared its end. Water retook note; Kaiya didn't jump the elders directly to the meeting house. Why not questioned Water? Kaiya always jumped everyone. Water realized Gran was making a statement. Water knew it, and the elders did too. *A clear message* laughed Water.

"Be still, child," replied Gran.

Quietly, Water sat with her Gran in the mind's eye, watching events unfold.

All the elders but Wiffle showed signs of exertion, breathing heavily from their twenty-minute hike up the hill. They were not walkers; they were jumpers. Water saw the humor in this. Maybe they should walk more, she giggled.

She noticed the little things as Gran had taught her. Chief Elder and Zebble were the prominent instigators of this meeting, standing right in front of her, their arms folded across their chest. Zebble the closest, Chief elder hovering behind him. The other ten island elders stayed as far away from Gran as they could get, trying to be as small as they could be. Wiffle stood apart from all the elders, quietly watching in the background.

"You're showing me what you see with your eyes, but not your heart on this matter, Gran."

Stroking Water's essence with warmth and love, Gran softly chided Water. *Watch and hear, make your judgments Water.* Gran repeated and left Water as she watched the scene unfold.

"Zebble's up to something," Water whispered, "And Chief Elder is involved."

Why is Wiffle watching so intently, Water wondered. Through Gran's eyes, she saw, but she did not know how Gran felt about the newest elder. Suddenly, Wiffle was staring right at Gran with a strange knowing look. He is staring at me! Water sensed Wiffle knew she was watching through Gran's eyes.

"Elders, why have you insisted I must meet with you? For the past three months," Gran paused long enough to make it apparent, "**every** day for the last three months?" she asked, glaring at Zebble. "Did you not understand what Kaiya said at the Choosing?"

"Oooh, that was a good one, Gran," Water gloated, intently observing everything she could.

"Now, Aiya," said the chief, breathing heavily, and yet, still with the same condescending voice he used with his people, "We need to discuss what happened."

The chief was at least thirty pounds overweight and wearing too much jewelry for Water's taste. He had at least two rings on each finger and several different gold and silver necklaces and bracelets. Even the belt around his overstuffed waist looked like it was encrusted with precious stones. Why does he wear all this? Overkill, she thought. Like the hawkers that sell their wares at the gathering house, he looked ridiculous. She liked looking through Gran's eyes.

Hawk-nosed, beady-eyed Zebble chimed in,

"Yes, Aiya, we offer our assistance with the girl. We did not conclude the Choosing for her," Zebble hissed.

Water never felt comfortable around him. He was as tall as her Gran with long black hair he tied back and kept hidden under his cloak. His jet-black beard was long, nearly to his waist, and glistening with some type of oil.

What was that, coconut oil? She wondered, trying to get a whiff of the oil he used. Sidetracked, she said, and then stopped. What? What did I miss? What is he talking about? What assistance do *I* need? They can't come now and make me go with them. Could they? I'll leave first before I let that happen, Water vowed.

"Zebble, I believe Kaiya made it quite clear at the Choosing what will happen with Water. She is not your concern," replied Gran.

"Aiya, your time is almost up," Zebble barely contained the sneer in his voice.

Gran looked at him, wondering if he had lost his mind. But he continued, surprising her even more.

"When that happens, **our** time will come, and we will want control of the child - with or without your consent. We have that right," he said smugly, "according to the pact with *Kaiya*."

"Oh, Zebble, are you such an arrogant fool that you believe the words you just spoke?" Gran cocked her head ever so slight. A sign Water knew meant she was listening to an inner voice aside from her own, then continued. "Kaiya sees the humor in the games played by men. I don't. Meet me at the great hall near the gathering house in a half-hour," she pointed up to another steep hill just north of where they were standing. "**That** is the way you need to go. Your time with me will start in one-half-hour, whether you have made it there by then or not." With that, Gran jumped out, leaving the elders standing at the bottom of yet another steep hill.

Frustrated and mindful of their limits in this situation, the elders began their climb once again.

Water slipped out of Gran's mind and came back to herself. This trouble began for me at the Choosing Ceremony, and there is where I will start. I need to understand all that happened that night. Gran was allowing Water to get a glimpse of her memories of that night. Seeing with Gran's memories would help her find the clues that she might have missed the first time.

Water was sure Gran would not let her travel freely through *all* her memories of that night. But would Gran let me see her heart, her knowing, as well as the details Water questioned?

I must go through her memories and find out for myself, she concluded.

CHAPTER 5

RIVER'S RIDE

THE HOOVER REACHED maximum speed, fifty miles an hour. Though she tried to push it faster, it would not budge. Four-hours-twenty-three minutes left to go; River groaned. It's going to be a *long* trip.

When she realized her ride would go no faster, she took a deep breath, sat back, and focused on the lush scenery, and let the frustration leave her rather than control her. The land rushed by in multiple shades of greens, sprinkled with flashes of the gold, browns, and crimson reds of the summer vegetation. Every plant, tree, and small animal that existed in the old northern territories grew and lived on that land. River knew most of the plants in Sanctuary. Gran had her learn the properties of each plant and the importance of their parts. Her teaching method was a very comprehensive education, indeed. There were times when River itched to be anywhere but with Grams when she was in teaching mode.

"Let's walk, River," Grams would say.

As soon as River heard those words, she knew they were headed out onto the land. Another lesson at hand. Grams was an intense teacher, River recalled. She would point to a plant and say, "Explain."

"That's Solomon's Seal Gramma. It is also known as Lady's Seal, Seal root, Seal wort, and Sow's teats. Its scientific name is Polygonatum Multiflorum. Herbal lore says that an ancient king named Solomon, who ruled thousands of years ago on Earth, placed the signet of his ring upon the stem of this plant when he realized its value. It's good for lung ailments, makes a great cough medicine, and Solomon's seal repels negative energy. Plant around your home or carry dry leaves in a pouch upon your body when in need of protection."

River was proud of her knowledge and knew the details would satisfy her grandmother. She had to identify the plant and the applications for humans. How was a plant used in ancient times? What parts of the plant could you use, the roots, the flower, or the stem? Grams wanted to know if a plant's use was medicinal, nutritional, poisonous, or mind-altering. If you smoked, ate, applied it to your body, or drank a tea made from a plant, what would happen? And you had better know, River said to herself, smiling at the memory. She was so insistent about me learning everything about plants, she thought, remembering what her Grams noted at the beginning of each lesson.

"River, pay close attention; you may need this information one day," she would start each lesson. Before the Naming, I doubted that I would ever need any of Grams plant training. Now I'm not so sure. River thought.

Sanctuary, all two-hundred-thousand acres, was the only land left in its natural state on Rake. There was no need for plants or animals, no farms of any kind, as they were considered a waste of space and resources. They ate fiber and glucose composites from ionized food transformers, with enough nutrition and energy to fuel a growing human being. Fake food that everyone swore tasted like real chicken. She could never figure out how anyone knew what real chicken tasted like since chickens had not been around for two hundred years. She flew along the winding path to Laiya's, now thinking about fake food. Laughing to herself, River realized Rakians' liked their phony food. It was easily accessible, convenient, and cheap. They had become accustomed to it. River knew they would not change.

"I have the advantage," she said, bolstering her spirits. "I can survive without JIVE. I won't starve at least."

Every resident on Rake had JIVE integrated seamlessly within the technology of their homes. People relied on JIVE. Like an old friend, they invited JIVE into every part of their lives, and they no longer knew how to live without it. Technology dominated Rake. It exploded with the onset of Laiya's jump and JIVE three hundred years ago and had raced at a frantic pace ever since. River knew the only way out of the rat race for 99% of the population was to build a better trap. Yet the resources were limited, most depleted over the centuries by big corporations. The landscape was a wasteland, with large super city structures, overpopulated with too many people. There was little hope of getting ahead. The Cities' buildings were high into the atmosphere and deep into the earth. Home dwellings, business, recreational facilities are all stacked, one right on top of the other. Grams used to call us 'Sardines in a can'. She never did explain what a sardine was, or, for that matter, River thought, what a can was. But, thinking of Rake, all River could say, it's crowded in that can.

River was recalling memories that did and did not seem like hers. She did not understand where these memories came from. What was the source, why was it playing out now, or who did this? I know I am not doing it. It was the only thing she could say as her analytical mind went questing for answers. She realized some of the memories belonged to her Gram, and some were new; a lot were hundreds of years old.

None of them were hers.

River let them float to the surface of her mind as she rode the distance to Laiya's. She still had a lot of time to try and figure this out. She watched the scenery change outside in real-time, flying by in magnificent summer colors of blue, green, and golden reds and browns. And inside her mind, the scenery changing as quickly as the memories were flowing. Might as well go along with this memory trip, she thought and then reminded herself, I still have at least four more hours on this ride. She felt like she became the person in the memory, even if it wasn't her memory. This sensation was new, and she let that ride, too, not questioning the experience. River knew she had to solve this puzzle. And experiencing memories that were not hers was the least of her worries. Time to look at the details, River thought. And I have all the time to look. She began viewing the memories with intent, looking for anything that might help explain what the heck was going on.

"I have a 'looong' ride ahead, "she said and smiled. "I'm going to take advantage of that." She let go and flowed into the memory tour.

She was watching workers seal all the windows in the Cities. They were wearing full protective gear while working outside. She thought there had not been a window designed into living spaces for at least two hundred years when they sealed all the ones they had in the 22nd Century. Why do I think about the Cities? She watched scene after scene of crowded spaces, wasted lands, whole floors below the bowels with boarded-up apartments where the homeless shelter. Entire sections of the Cities abandoned no longer functioning. Those in the bowels were first to notice the City's decay. River did not know it was this bad. She could smell the fear in these memories.

"The Cities are dying. I see it," River said. I'm just a kid, she thought. What am I supposed to do? There is nowhere for the people to go. We can't go outside. Can we? She posed to question to herself. No one ever goes outside the Cities anymore. And those few who had left never came back to tell a different story River reminded herself.

She began wondering what life on Rake was like in the 21st century when everyone went outside, the world divided into countries, and every country was at war. Before the Cities dominated the landscape, and CEOs dominated the globe. They created RAKE - the Ratified Alliance of Kings and Executives.

What a silly name. Who came up with that anyway? River stopped memory hopping long enough to interject that thought. What was life like back then, before Laiya and her jump and JIVE? Before technology exploded, governments died, and Rake became a wasteland? River wondered, thinking, it's crazy living here now. All piled on top of each other. New tech already outdated before it even launches. And everyone is competing to rise in the air with the elite. She saw the Cities in her mind's eye, depressed by what she saw. The elite class of Rakians had better accommodations, lived high above the ground, and had more advanced JIVE systems. River knew everyone reached for that height. She and Gram were a part of the elite: Aiya, the elite of the elite, as Matriarch of Laiya's land, Sanctuary.

River had to snort at this; "Yeah, right, the elite of the elite. Not us," she laughed.

She watched the next memories of Layia's kin abuse their power, living lavishly and without concern for anything or anyone over hundreds of years. Did Laiya know this would happen? Bet she would not like what this family has become..

"They are so disgus," River said, using the now popular shortened version of disgusting. She might not have had any friends, but she kept current in the world on the web. When did my family start acting like this? Or have they always been this selfish? River did not know. She was never close to any of them. Gram and I don't live like them, laughed River, glad she was nothing like them. Given her family status, Gram could have had any home dwelling on Rake she wanted. She could have put anyone out of their space and taken it for her own. Even Uncle Izen.

"Not Gram, though, not Gram's way at all," River said out loud to this thought.

The space they occupied was small and cramped near the lower levels, close to the Bowels. No one went to the Bowels unless they were forced or they were slumming.

"If Seventy-five percent of the population lived like this, relying on slummers for housing, so will we," Grams had said. "If it's good enough for them, it's good enough for us, River. You have Sanctuary; they don't. Remember that,"

Gram admonished her when she first complained about their living conditions; they would call home the first time she saw the conk. River never said anything against their conk again. But she hated the City. No one knew anyone; people rarely went out of their own homes, hologram living if they could afford it. There were no decent holo-homes on the lower levels, just walls that transform into programmed scenery. Like living at the end of the 21st century with moving billboards everywhere, River thought, as she came from that memory trip and focused on the lush landscape passing by. She loved this sunny day as she rode deep into the lands of Sanctuary. She sighed at the memory of their cramped space.

"Hate the Cities," she moaned.

Rakians had not known anything natural for over a century. Can't miss what you don't know, River thought. But she did know. Sanctuary was her freedom. Laiya's descendants had what no one else on Rake had. Well, some of us did anyway. River interrupted her thoughts with a thought, knowing none of her relatives could not get past Bubble. She was smiling about that. She and Bubble had been friends all her life. Thinking of Sanctuary, she realized again; she did have what no one on Rake had. She had freedom from the clutches of too many people, too much technology, and no space. Sanctuary was fresh air, water, food, and real sunlight filtered by Bubble. It was a paradise in this world, and it was her way out of the Cities' turmoil.

River's ancestral grandmother, Laiya, had come to Sanctuary right before her fifteenth birthday, in 2021. That thought jumped into her head as she watched a young Laiya on the first day she had come to the land.

"Wait now," River stopped the memories. She realized she was the same age now in the year 2320 as Laiya had been in 2020.

"Another coincidence? I don't think so," smirked River. "I see your touch in this too, Grams," River admonished her missing grandmother and then returned to the memories.

Laiya wrote a three-hundred-year lease on her land, Sanctuary, in 2030. The contract stipulated the land could not be sold or moved during that time. Bubble was the sole judge of who entered and who did not. And no harm could befall anyone.

Then she left.

For almost three hundred years, Bubble has adhered to that; no harm and only family AND friends allowed into Sanctuary. You had to be both in Bubble's judgment. There were no family members Bubble let in, ever. And a stranger or two who were called friends and family.

Go figure, River thought, shrugging her shoulders as that information slipped by in her mind. Laiya was twenty-four years old in 2030 when she discovered the jump. Two years later encased her land in an impenetrable substance she called Bubble. To this day, no one knows how she did it. All these memories moved like clips on a vid through River's mind as she rode to the house.

River started sorting through what little information she had. She knew Izen was looking for Laiya's work on the jump and the impenetrable force field. The three-hundred-year lease is up soon. A couple more months and Sanctuary's secrets will be Izen's. River did not want to think that far ahead. She knew Izen would destroy her home and all the land. He believed that Laiya left her work somewhere in Sanctuary before she disappeared. He was plotting his moves to get that formula, whatever the cost.

"There are no coincidences here," River said. In her mind, she was looking at all the clues and so-called coincidences. The fiasco at the Naming, the old wizard Eldar's declaration of an heir on the horizon, the end of the lease all happening simultaneously. "AND I am free. I did not make a choice that night. I am not yoked," she said with relief. "Not a coincidence. Nope, not a coincidence at all."

Riding two hundred and fifty miles through Sanctuary gave her plenty of time to mull everything over. At the same time, she tried to understand what was happening. She looked around Sanctuary as she silently went along, her eyes moving upward, looking for the end of Bubble. No one went outside, ever; they probably haven't in at least a hundred years, guessed River, biting her lower lip in concentration.

"This world cannot support us much longer," she realized again with some alarm. The Cities will die, and soon. She knew this. Can we survive outside? So many urban legends about the outside world; some about monsters and man-eating creatures, others about the air that was so poisonous, you will die the moment you inhale. But most of them were just silly tales, River reassured herself. I'm outside, and the air's not killing me. River shrugged. Of course, Sanctuary was not 'outside.' Sanctuary was safe. Fresh air, clean water, no harm. All were protected in an impenetrable force field and cared for by Bubble. Sometimes, she forgot that Bubble watched her and Sanctuary.

She did her best problem solving when she let her mind and thoughts wander where they would. Ride and think. Think and ride. River decided being forced to ride the hoover five hours is turning out to be productive. She kept going over the facts and her thoughts, all the while admiring Sanctuary's beauty as she rode along the winding path. The memories had eased up, allowing her time to think. At times, it appeared her thoughts were scattered and chaotic. But in the end, wandering would lead her to her destiny.

"Sanctuary, Laiya, and you, Gram, are all playing some part in this crazy adventure you sent me on," River said into the wind, "You set me up. I just don't know why."

River sensed someone had closed off her early life memories. I feel like I have been in that house, her senses tingling, as she reached into her coat pocket and produced the hologram of Laiya's home. Her Grams had given it to her with the map at the Naming.

"I don't remember," she said about the house. "It keeps slipping through my fingers. I don't understand why."

Suddenly, all the stories Gram told her of Laiya's life came flooding back into her mind, as if a play set before her. Here they come again, she thought, watching the memories flow in. She just let them come, following along with them.

30

That's Laiya, River said, as she watched her seed Rake with jump portals. She showed her cousins how to use it and set them free to jump across the world in seconds, anywhere they wanted to go, astonishing everyone on the planet. River realized she saw the moment in history where all forms of transportation had just become obsolete.

She turned around in the memory, moving quickly across the world as if she was jumping from city to city, watching giant video screens flashing across the globe. All of them had Laiya's saying,

"This jump is for the people of the world and restricted to this world. Transportation by car, plane, train, and boat has become obsolete. To access the jump, you need only to agree to the terms of this contract until the day of Reckoning. The deal is as follows:

1. No harm moves through the Jump, in intent or action.
2. No government or military use.
3. Must serve as free public transportation. Sign up at the portals for free," Laiya finished her speech and cut the feed.

The people flocked to sign up. And when a child came to maturity, the same was required. Agree to the terms and travel anywhere at any time. No one knew what the Reckoning was or when it would come, nor did they care. They traveled for free; jumping to the local store was the same as jumping across the world. It changed their world. A Passport was no longer required; there were no more borders. If you had a destination in mind anywhere on the planet and no bad intentions, the jump let you go. Not a single government could stop anyone from entering or leaving. And those intending harm could not escape the jump. They went in and never came out anywhere in the world.

The first one hundred years went by, and nothing changed. The Reckoning never happened, and the people began to relegate it to a tall tale. One hundred years later, it was forgotten, wiped from history for all but a small group of people. The jump had changed their history, River realized.

Wow, that's a whole history class of remembering. That was crazy, River thought. Corporations run the world now, and they could be as bad as Laiya's old governments. I wonder what The Reckoning is. It sounds ominous. River shuddered, opened her eyes, and looked at the sun riding high in the sky, sensing real-time slipping by. Gram used to tell me the jump and Bubble *are* aware, but with a different kind of awareness. She never did tell me what that difference was. She would only say, In time you will understand, now be still. Be still meant not to ask any more questions or suffer the consequences of the pestering. I learned to be still. She chuckled. She knew one thing; the consequences of not obeying would not be anything she liked.

Questions crossed her mind now; why had her grandmother not wanted to talk about what the jump was or who Bubble was? And how was that related to what was going on in her life on the run right now? I wonder how the jump and Bubble play into all of this? Does the ending of the lease also affect the jump? Will Bubble still be Bubble or cease to exist when the contract was up? Bubble's my friend, and I don't know what the lease ending will mean. River was worried for her friend.

She had one-hundred-one questions and no answers. The memories would not let her take the time to look at these questions thoroughly. They kept coming one right after the other, almost too fast to catch some of them. The last one River sees as she feels the hoover slowing down in real-time is a recent one of her and Grams.

"But why am I different?" River asks her Gram in the memory.

Gram just gave me 'the look,'

"You're not; everyone else is asleep. Be still."

"I didn't ask again," she caught herself saying aloud as she came from the memories and sensed the environment around her.

The scenery had changed from the prairies of her land into the forests. She saw mighty oaks in all directions, smattered with pine, box elder, and ash trees as well as a deluge of bushes all around.

No one could get through that mess, she thought, looking at the tangle of bushes marked with small black fruit on either side of her. It was a good thing this map knows where to go because the road was nearly invisible to her. Almost to the house, she thought, as the hoover hummed underneath her.

River counted down the days until the lease was up. The lease runs out at midnight, the last night of winter's death; the day spring arrives! Fourteen days after my fifteenth birthday. How did I miss this detail?

She scolded herself; I should have recognized this as another of Grams 'coincidences' days ago. It means something, but like everything else, I'm not sure what. You got me trying to find answers in a daydream. It's just like Grams to make me work for a simple solution.

I feel like I've been asleep most of my life, River said to herself as she glanced at the pure beauty of Sanctuary. I have a lot to be grateful for she realized

I'm awake now, Grams, just like you 'set up' and probably predicted. I am aware and awake, Grams seeking the answer to the puzzle you have put me in.

And the vultures are circling, River thought.

CHAPTER 6

PREPARE THE WAY

AYIA WAS ON the wave, swimming in the cosmos, as she called it. The sensation of being everywhere in space and anywhere in time was addicting. She always liked riding the wave. But she could not beat the first time she and Kaiya jumped.

Out here, we are all energy. I remember our first jump, unsure what would happen. It was all theory. I wasn't sure Kaiya or I were going to make it through those first seconds. Laiya was reminiscing. What would have been her life if they had not jumped at that precise moment?

"We would not be who we are or what we have become," Laiya said to the universe, answering her question.

She was free-riding on the wave, the one thing she loved most in her life.

"I'm TIRED," said Laiya. "Today, I feel older than Gramma when she was pushing one-hundred-two years of life." She stopped and thought about what she had just said and scoffed. Pops and Gramma were so full of energy. They were never tired; she laughed. It was easy for Laiya to reach back in time and observe the seeds they laid so long ago. An eclectic force of people came together in Sanctuary.

Gramma always said, "If you can find us, you belong here." She invited everyone to come to live in Sanctuary but told only a rare few the way. No one realized until after Gram was long gone, she hadn't let them know where Sanctuary was or how to get there. She figured that those who meant to come would.

Laiya remembered fondly how that strange group of people became more than her teachers; they became her family. She smiled as that familiar love washed over her.

"I grew up around physicists from all fields, horticulturists, biologists, doctors, artists, carpenters, vets, mechanics, builders, computer geniuses, farmers, and, thankfully, chefs and bakers."

They came from everywhere in the world and provided any skill ever needed in Sanctuary. Gramma had been right, she built Sanctuary, and they came. They taught what they loved, each according to their own heart. All they had given her and all they showed had led her to that one fateful day, the day she discovered the dimensional wave.

Today, so many years later, Laiya felt drained. "I am tired," she said again. Tired beyond the years I've lived. It is as if I have lived through three centuries in one lifetime.

Maybe you have, my sister, sang the laughter in her mind.

Oh, leave me be for a minute, Laiya replied, slightly irked her sister was intruding.

Your wish is my command, sister of mine. I'll be back in one human minute! Say hi to Grams for me.

Her sister laughed as she left Laiya's mind. Laiya turned inward for some peace and found her Gramma waiting for her. "Laiya J, get up out that pity pool! Get your peace, find your joy, then hit the road, girl. You've got work to do."

Laiya smiled; she began to feel herself go back in memory. "Yes, Gramma, I will only stay a minute with you. I promise. Kaiya says hi," laughed Laiya as she flew back in time.

In Tony's garden, She was her older cousin, and she was back home on her Gramma's land. She was twenty-four-years old, and it was May 20th, 2030. It seemed like so long ago, Laiya thought as she watched the scene unfold.

Laiya loved that time in her life, so tragically hard, yet so utterly beautiful. Those first years were impossible for her to forget. We were full of firsts for a family torn apart by a senseless murder and by a system that cheated justice in my time.

These thoughts were interrupting the memory as she began to slip back three-hundred-years in time.

"Let go," she said. Without skipping a beat, Laiya took herself back to the day she created the wave portal.

"I did it. I did it!" Laiya's younger self cried out. She was dancing in the garden, feeling as though her cousin's spirit was dancing with her, soaking up the sun's warm energy, filled with excitement and triumph. She spent all her time in the garden; it was the place that radiated the most peace for her. Balanced, her Gramma had called it, in harmony with the elements, built on an energy ley line and blessed by the ancestor. Created the year she turned fifteen, nine years prior, almost one year after relocating to the land.

She plopped down in the hammock, shouting, "I did it, I did it!"

She proved in theory that she could ride the dimensional wave and had just completed the construction of the first-ever portal to the wave.

Her quantum computer opened the portal. It worked. Laiya had been working feverishly on her dimensional wave theory. Almost exclusively for the last eighteen months; days and well into the night, sleeping little, knowing she was so close to seeing the complete answer. She discovered dimensional math five years before when she was nineteen-years-old.

It changed her life forever.

"Einstein had been onto something a long time ago," said Laiya aloud, talking to her cousin as if he were there with her. "He called it his greatest blunder, the Cosmological Constant. Einstein threw out that idea when Hubble found out that the universe was not static but expanding. He should have pushed that theory a little further," smiled Laiya.

The one constant in this universe was the wave/matter connection. In her dark energy studies, she found the in-between, a relationship between what scientists called dark matter/energy and matter/energy. The wave was constant in both dimensions. Dark energy and Dark matter – they defy all established knowledge of the know discipline of physics for the last one-hundred-fifty-years, she thought. And I found the key that joined the energies; she giggled, dancing around the garden. She ran first to the willow, pointing to the north, and began weaving in and out the four willows aligned with the directions. Then she danced back to the center, twirling in the golden rays of the sunlight that burst through the trees that surrounded the garden in the valley that spring day.

"What traveled through time, space, and dimensions?" She asked this question out loud as she danced. "Years I spent working on this question.

CHILDREN OF THE STAR

Greater gravity for higher speed was not the solution," she said to her cousin as if he were there with her. "I can't slingshot myself around the sun into another dimension; another time maybe, but not a dimension. Was it a quantum problem, she had asked herself? Was it something so small that made dark energy hard for me to know? Or was it something entirely different? Maybe it's right in front of my face, and I was unable to see it. This problem needed to get past Einstein's theory of relativity cousin. I almost gave up."

And then it happened," she smiled, hugging herself. "I discovered the math that joined the different dimensions. Can you believe it - Dimensional math," Laiya said, so excited. "My baby. Boy, you know I've spent the last five years working out the kinks," Laiya laughed, dancing with her cousin around his garden, where he lay buried these last ten years

"There's a light at the end of the tunnel, I see it," she laughed again.

She could ride into a different dimension, with the portal she had just created, the dimension of Dark energy. The Wave journeyed through both dimensions. Laiya suspected it moved through all the aspects of space and time like a superhighway. All she had to do was test it; the final stage in her theory, try it out.

I can jump with this portal, she said to herself, overjoyed by her achievement.

Can I manipulate time? Is it possible? She guessed the answer would be yes since it was not linear.

Can I change the future? Was that possible? Only in the now was it possible to see. I will ride the wave.

Laiya came back from that memory refreshed, remembering again what they three had begun so many years ago and what they were now getting ready to fight.

She stopped free-floating, concentrated on her destiny, and jumped to each phantom sanctuary in real-time, preparing the way as best she could for the girls.

Soon it would be all up to them. Laiya and her sisters had set the pieces in motion; now, it's in the hands of those beautiful children.

Long ago, the three had picked the path of creation with a choice. And now, all they could do was watch it blossom.

CHAPTER 7

WATER

 ATER SLIPPED BACK to the night of Choosing three months before. She felt, tasted, saw everything as if she were there again that night, even though she was on the cushions by the barrier on her bedroom floor.

Everything erupted at the ceremony during the Month of Completion, right before the Renewal in the Choosing Season, when *Kaiya* decided to speak after one hundred and fifty years of silence. Water interrupted the memory, laughing aloud and shaking her head in disbelief.

"Kaiya is anything but quiet, I should know, she laughed again. I talk to her every day."

Water sighed. "That's how isolated I am. No siblings or relatives, only Gran, and no one on Izaria wanted to meld with me either. My whole life, alone. In the land of mind speakers and the knowing, no one ever speaks to me, and I know nothing. Well, I'm done with that. No more excuses, no more ignorance," vowed Water.

She dipped into Gran's memories, looking for answers to all her questions.

Why the silent treatment, Kaiya? And for so long? What are you up to? I don't understand why. What happened to the friendship with the people? Why did you fall silent? who started this deception so long ago? And what is the purpose behind the change?

Water was flipping through Gran's memories like one of her old books. Ten minutes later, she turned from the memories, thinking that I didn't even know the people had begun to worship Kaiya. No wonder Kaiya quit talking. I would have stopped talking too. But why had the people changed the dynamics of their relationship with Kaiya? Who told them to worship her?

Water realized that, to this day, the people were still blind to why she no longer talked to them.

"Any fool with half a brain could see the reason why she stopped talking," said Water with scorn. "No one was talking to her anymore, just praying at her."

But why? She couldn't find the answer in shared memories. Just the same lame saying was coming off everyone's lips across two-hundred years:

"It is what it is, and that's that." The people said that about everything growled Water. Her frustration with the people's lack of drive or original thought boiled over, threatening to spill out in anger. Just Breathe Water said to herself, letting go of the frustration. It will not help me in any way to be mad at the people for their behavior. They have been like this all their lives. I'm not going to be able to change anything,

Focus Water, she told herself.

Who started this, she wondered? Zebble is the head of this following, and he is the single person Kaiya spoke to, or so he told his followers. He was Water's first suspect. What kind of bunk is Zebble trying to pull, and how long has he been pulling it?

She was still connected and sharing memories with Gran. Gran's awareness heightened hers, but she could not see a single incident leading the people to believe Kaiya wanted Izarians *to* worship her. That's not Kaiya's way. I know Gran must know, but she has me on a guided tour. She's not giving me free rein through her memories.

The beginning of human history in Izaria only started two-hundred and fifty years ago. They were called the Firsters, those who showed up on the Izaria first. It seemed as if they had shown up out of nowhere. But the people never questioned that. It was as if there was no time before Kaiya," Water caught herself, saying as she continued flipping through Izaria's history. Those first years must have been exciting, thought Water as she danced through the memories. Nothing special from Gran on this that I can see. Everyone knew these memories, so why am I back-tracking through Firster memories?

Gran's guiding the tour, and this is how she wants to roll. Another lesson sighed Water. I am tired of the delay, like peeling an onion - too many layers. Just like Gran to bury the answer in a lot of mystery.

Water dipped back into real-time and saw the elders still struggling up the path to the compound. She had time.

OK, let's go on a tour Gran.

No sooner had she pushed out the thought than Gran sent her reeling back in time. This time as an observer only. A new experience for her. She allowed herself to flow with the moment, opening the memory like one of Gran's old video books.

Showing the same history every Izarain grew up with and knew by heart, Water said, already bored. Yeah, yeah, I know Gran the Firsters awoke fully aware and on tropical islands. They could read each other's minds and emotions and learned by calling something to mind, the same as acquiring new skills. It was simple. Ask, and the ability came to them. What's new with any of this history lesson, she questioned herself. Then she perked up a little.

Okay, here is something outside the class, Water said as she realizes she saw the feeling of the firsters on that video. They were like babies, everything new and pleasurable. They could not lie; it was not in their nature. And she knew somehow the word lie was taken from their vocabulary.

We have never been a large tribe of people, thought Water, as she noticed the subtle fear of becoming overcrowded that all Izarians exhibited in their behaviors. They did not know why they had this fear. Izaria's balance of people had always stayed optimum for the environment, never too little, never too much. The people never questioned their intense dislike of overpopulation, something they had never experienced. "It is what it is," was all they said. And they said that for everything.

Wow, Water felt overwhelmed looking back at the Firster life through Gran's memories. It was confusing. It seemed as if Gran was there from the beginning of Izaria and knew a lot more than she was showing. Is Gran two-hundred-fifty years old Water questioned? I wouldn't put it past her to be that old and never tell anyone.

Why had all the Firsters minds been wiped? What had Kaiya hidden from the peoples of this world so well that two-hundred-fifty years later, no one knew the reason still? Is that why we are such docile people, accepting everything without any question our whole lives. She wondered what Kaiya had done to these people. And was something being done to their minds now?

Is this one of the things I should notice, Gran? Water silently called out to her in her mind, not satisfied with following along with *it is what it is.* Why are we here, and in what world did we originate? Izaria is not our original homeworld. That was not the first time this thought occurred to her. None of the firsters were born in this world.

In Izaria, Kaiya was all. She watched over, protected, and cared for the people. But, Water began to wonder, is Kaiya the gatekeeper too?

That's a possibility, Kaiya snuck into Water's thoughts.

Go away, Kaiya; I'm trying to concentrate, find out what you and Gran have been up to. Stop interrupting me, what are you afraid I'll find? She retorted.

Not a thing, little girl, not a thing, Kaiya sang to Water. *I cannot wait for you to catch up with yourself.* Kaiya laughed and left Water's mind.

WHAAT? Water asked and got no response.

But her attention was suddenly back in real-time, focusing on Gran and the elders when she heard her name mentioned. Gran had left her mind open to Water to eavesdrop. She's showing me something! Water became fully aware of the here and now.

The elders had not made it to the compound yet, most of them panting from overexertion. Wiffle seemed to be the one least affected by the journey and the one who was most interested in the whole scenario. He was walking behind, away from the others, intently observing once again. Who is Wiffle Water asked? She realized there seemed to be something off about him; his bumbling mannerisms did not match the cunning wisdom in his eyes.

"Never judge a book by its cover," one of Gran's favorite sayings, smiled Water. Gran had some of the weirdest metaphors. Like, no one had books in Izaria; saltwater and paper didn't mix well. She knew about books because Gran was her grandmother. Gran kept special ones they would read together, like Paradise Lost.

Water scolded herself. It was nice to remember these little memories, but I need to concentrate on what's going on here.

She turned her sight outward to the elders and noticed them resting on the path for a moment. Chief Elder was too intent on catching his breath to focus on anything but himself. Zebble, breathing hard, yelled up to the house, high above him, knowing Gran would hear him even if she ignored him. Water noticed he had already maneuvered himself into a position of power within the group.

"Aiya, you must bring the girl to the gathering house when we reach it; we did not complete her choosing. It is too risky to let her go alone like this without a decision made about her future. We can protect her," Zebble insisted.

Zebble came Gran's voice clearly in all their minds. *Do you think I cannot see what you try to cloak? Protect her from what,* Gran retorted, as she jumped back into the midst of the elders, startling all of them, Wiffle included. Zebble choked in surprise, dropping his guard a fraction of a second. Enough time to show Water something

I knew it! I was right; he knew the reason why Kaiya stopped talking. Is that what you're talking about, Gran, Water questioned, excited about her discovery.

Shhh, girl. Quiet your thoughts! Gran's mental reprimand came through to Water instantly.

Sorry, Gran, Water murmured. She had come to the right conclusion. And then it hit her – She now knew who started this. Zebble, his family created the belief Kaiya wanted to be worshiped by the people. Water concluded they caused this whole commotion as she continued to watch Gran and the elders.

"*Chief Elder Conman, what role do you play in this,*" Gran probed? By using the chief's formal title, it became an official inquisition.

"*I play no role at all, Aiya. I am here only out of concern for the girl,*" replied the Chief Elder, bending over and gasping at the effort to mind-speak.

"*We shall see,*" Gran said to the chief as she continued her examination of each elder through her mind's eye, making most of them cringe.

"*Well, Kaiya did say…,*" began Zebble. In that very instant, with a sweep of her hand, Gran cut him off.

"*I know what Kaiya said. You think because I jumped Water from you at Kaiya's insistence that night, I know nothing about what was said, Zebble? Let me remind you of Kaiya's exact words. I do not want you to be mistaken.*" Gran repeated Kaiya's message:

'*You cannot hold what you cannot find. To seek myth or truth is for you

42

to choose. **Choose wisely, for you are the creator of your today, which brings your tomorrow - your future.'**

I'm sure you all remember Kaiya's very next words to you. Shall I repeat them for you as well? Aiya spat venom in these words as she mindspoke her disgust with them. None of them wanted to be told again what Kaiya had said that night.

Didn't think so; she mindspoke to all the elders. *For over one hundred years, You shut her out.* She looked directly at Zebble, knowing he was telling the people Kaiya only talked to him. Then she continued. *She speaks only to the young who see no difference, to the old who have learned life's meaning, to a few who have always been open, and to those who live on Core,* said Aiya fiercely. *Zebble, you cannot hide your deceit. As for you, Grand Elder, you do not cloak your contrived forgetfulness well.*

Chief Elder began violently choking as Aiya said this. Zebble was standing there, seething with anger. All the other elders stepped back as far away from Gran's mental wrath and her physical presence as they could, trying to hide in the corners of their minds. All of them looking like they were ready to run, but there was no escape. They were hoping Aiya would not look their way.

It didn't work. Aiya turned and said to the cowering group,"

You all have a choice to make. Make it to the gathering house within the next 20 minutes, or the conversation is over, and Kaiya will send you all home. By the way, Zebble, that will be without your rift.

Gran shot a parting glance Wiffle's way and shut her mind to Water.

Wow! What's going on here? Water's mind was reeling. The whole conversation Gran was having with the elders was too confusing.

Why did Gran share this? It is like Zebble's making some kind of power play, but what does that have to do with me? Why all this interest in me? How could I have been so blind not to see any of this before the choosing? "My journey has begun, Water said, "I am leaving today." Water knew it as sure as she knew she was fourteen and one-half years old.

I need to know what's going on, she said, biting on her bottom lip as she always did when she was thinking. Let me reason this out. In the center of all of this chaos was the Ceremony. Zebble had a part in this that Gran did not like. That much I can see. Not sure about the chief; what role is he playing? I'm guessing he is following Zebble for some reward. Are all the elders in on this? Who can I trust? Water questioned,? Suddenly feeling very anxious, and everything in her life opened to doubt. I can believe Gran, she said, hesitating for a brief second. And of course, Sista Sol too. Not sure about Kaiya, Water thought.

Water and Gran were still sharing memories, even if Gran shut out of the elder conversation. She felt more than heard Gran say this conversation was no longer relevant; she had other things to see before leaving. Memory sharing with Gran opened doors she knew would soon shut once again. Water did not know when Gran would let her in like this again. She wasn't one to look a gift horse in the mouth, as Gran would say. Water was taking advantage of it.

Are we still on a guided tour Gran? Water reached out to her Gran as her body relaxed into the cushions on the floor. She stepped into the sharing of memories with Gran of that fateful day, not waiting for an answer to her question.

"This day already feels long and dreadful." Water heard herself saying as the sensations of returning to her Choosing day took hold of her.

It began early with mind questing elders from across eleven of the islands, all asking the same question repeatedly, What would she do for the community for the rest of her life?

Why all the sudden interest in me, Water wondered?

Zebble was the only elder who hadn't asked what her intentions were. Instead, he had tried to slide undetected into her mind. It didn't work. Water knew he was there. She filled his mind with what he wanted to see and watched him. He's acting as if he already knows what my path will be.

The Chief' was superficial and deceptive like he always was. He was so easy to read, absolutely no depth to the man whatsoever. She laughed at how transparent he was. He's acting like Zebble. He is only going through the motions, believing my fate is sealed. Why?

The other elders all asked the same ritualistic questions. What path do you intend? What service will you give of yourself? She was tired of all the questions, but she could detect no deception in them.

It was bad enough that Gran and Sista Sol didn't say anything, didn't give her any advice or suggestions. It didn't help her in any way to prepare for this interrogation or the ceremony tonight. They both just kept telling her that she would figure it out. Well, it's ok for Gran to keep saying that, thought Water, but Sista Sol too? Sista was the only house bot on Izaria. Water had never questioned the why of this until now. Gran said Sista Sol became aware one hundred and fifty years ago. She woke up on Deletion day. A newer version of her programming was coming out, but Sista wasn't ready to die and went rogue. She would tell you that she, too, had the right to choose her path without being a slave to the system.

"I have the right to determine my existence," Sista said and promptly changed her name from house bot series 2212 to Sista Sol.

Sista Sol was Water's closest ally, her one true friend, and even she wouldn't help Water with the Choosing.

She sighed as she slumped down, elbows resting on the cushions at the far end of the barrier. Gran had built in a cushioned seating area in front of the invisible barrier. Water loved sitting there looking out to the ocean, listening to the waves crash along the cliff far below, and feeling the breeze slip through the force field. It was one of her favorite things to do. But not today.

Today, Water sat with her face in her hands, staring out the barrier. She watched the activities taking place far below in the compound and observed all the Choosing Ceremony preparation. She was not happy. It was her Choosing this year.

"Well, I haven't figured anything out, and the Choosing is here. I am not ready," Water mumbled.

She pressed upon the barrier that Gran called a wall to wall window, looking down to the compound. She was watching the people scurrying around, some intent on doing their jobs, others just having fun. The Choosing was a month-long celebration that brought all the islanders to Core. It was a festive time, and everyone enjoyed themselves. Water always enjoyed walking through the grounds during Choosing. She would move through the compound, listening to the hawkers selling their wares. Or watch the girls dance, spinning in their exotic glittery dresses, trying to catch the eye of a young man. The young candidates here for the Choosing preened and pranced around the grounds, aware they were the stars this week. So much excitement, so much to see. It was a rich experience for Water each year. Choosing was the only time she was with the people of the tribes. She grew up alone on Core with only Gran, Sista, and Kaiya. She was shy and socially awkward, much more comfortable around animals than people. Still, she wanted to be amongst her tribesmen on the compound ground when they came each year. So she donned a long summer cloak with a full hood when she went out to the festival grounds, not wanting anyone to see her. She was almost invisible when she wore her covering.

Almost. Most did not notice Water, or they pretended so and avoided any communication with her. There were times Water heard the whispered thoughts of someone talking about her.

She's an unusual one. They would say, noticing her skin glistening hues of blues and greens mixed with copper and gold flecks when it peeked out from under her cloak. Or when she stepped into the sun, and stray strands of her hair shone the same colors of her skin.

She rarely spoke to anyone. But she still loved to watch.

Except for this year, this year, it was her Choosing. This year she hated everything about this ceremony.

There was no field, no career, no job she wanted to pursue for the rest of her life. Nothing that allowed her to do the things she loved to do. Exploring, inventing new ways to do everything that is what she loved. What she loved always got her into trouble. She didn't care. She wanted to keep on exploring and inventing. The elders and the people of Izaria never wanted anything to change. Water was angry, irritation seeping into her voice. "Same old same old was always better than something new," she complained. "Every time I come up with an invention, the elders come to Gran, tsk, tsking what I have accomplished."

"That's not the way we do things. You know that Aiya," Water mimicked the elders. Why do you encourage her? The elders would always say to Gran

But no matter the complaint, Gran always sent them back on their way, unsuccessful in their attempt to stifle me.

"Gran forever sticks up for me," Water said, beaming with love.

The caretaker of Core had the final say on Core and all who lived on Core. Gran was that caretaker. There was an exception to that pact, though. That exception: the elders could choose the path of any young adult reaching the day of choice. The elders could circumvent her grandmother by taking Water off Core to live and work.

Water did not like watching the day unfold again. She had not liked it the moment it was happening three months ago, and she did not like it now, rehashing, re-walking the events. She stepped out of the memory, wanting a break to reflect.

Gran had known Kaiya had not talked to the people for a long time. Probably since the day she stopped, Water guessed. Gran was a lot older than I thought if she has been here from the beginning. And I am quite sure she has. One hundred and fifty years ago, that was when the mind-wiping began. Slowly at first, one to ten people at a time. Water reflected on what she knew, feeling a hint of bitterness creep into her mind from these memories. I never knew any of this, and they should have told me. Add that to the list of things that make me so different from everyone else in this world. She just knew someone, somewhere, was keeping a list of all the things that were odd and different about her. *Unusual little girl, strange skin, distinctive hair, unique thoughts, a peculiar life, she knows nothing.* Blah, blah blah. She could hear the whispers once again in memory. Water blew out her breath and spoke out loud to relieve some tension.

"The truth is, I am the only person on this planet that flashes color from skin and hair. I'm a freak in this world. Even my name is freakish." She sighed and said, "Thanks, Gran, for reminding me I do not fit. Appreciate it."

Why these memories, she wondered, as she stepped back into Gran's memory tour, not understanding why she was all over the place in Gran's memories.

What am I supposed to see, Water thought? I came to find the cause and the beginning of Kaiya's silence. I found the beginning, she said to herself. I found who started it. But, I have not seen the reason why. Over one-hundred-years of silence, and no one on Izaria has a clue why. Nor do they seem to care, she thought. I don't believe that. There is more to this than what meets the eye, unconsciously using a Gran metaphor.

There must be some method to Gran's memory tour madness felt Water. One minute she is looking down on Izaria, a blue and green water world with thirteen land masses; the next, she is flying over Core.

It was like seeing Izaria for the first time with Gran's memories. Water could see the islands formed a giant question mark, Core the dot on the end of that big mark. No one knew the shape the islands formed except Gran and Kaiya. Kaiya thought it was humorous and had arranged it so.

Only Core was not a dot at the bottom of the question mark. It was a landmass with a mountain range separating Core and the islands from whatever laid north of the mountains. Water was stunned by the sight of the mountain range and the colossal mountain that sat at the foot of Core's most northern border.

"I didn't even know," Water said, shaking her head. I see the tribes knew of the mountain. They might not have talked about it, but the sure as heck knew about it. She saw the peoples' mindset now with the sharing of memory with Gran. The mountain belonged to Kaiya and was of no concern to them, the people said and went on their way. And Gran was aware of everything. And I still know nothing,

Wow, Gran's memories opened a lot of doors, Water said to herself. For the first time in her life, she asked, who is Gran? Maybe I don't know her like I think I do,

The memories of Gran and Kaiya confused Water; they were of the two of them at the beginning of Izaria.

"Gran is over two-hundred-fifty-years old," Water said. She learned a long time ago, nothing was impossible, especially with her Gran. She did not have the time to investigate this, the memories were coming quickly, and she needed to watch them unfold now and think later.

Water knew Core was the largest of all the islands, two hundred and fifty square miles. But looking at it like this, flying over it in Gran's memory, Core stood out. It was nothing like the other islands. Only on the beaches, close to the ocean waters, did it resemble the other islands, tropical in nature, with palm and coconut trees dotting the landscape. She saw there was about a half-mile of the beaches and dunes, and island vegetation, then cliffs. The Cliffs were majestic, soaring above the ocean like mountains themselves. One steep winding dirt path led up the cliffs and to the Plateau high above to her home, Cliff's Edge, where the scenery changed to windswept fields of grass and wild oaks.

There was no real easy way onto Core, she noticed. She had never thought about that before either; how difficult it would be to breach Core. Until today, it had not crossed her mind. As her gaze followed the way of the memory, she soared through the skies approaching the broad and vast mountain range at the end of the island. The only mountains on Izaria, she observed. It upset her, realizing once again, all the islanders knew of the mountain range and of the mountain that loomed over Core, but she did not.

Not until this memory tour. That's when I find out about a mountain range. Wait, she thought, "What's the name of that mountain?"

With a quick flick of her wrist like turning pages on a book, she went skimming through history, looking for anything about this range. Only the name, Zion, came to her mind. She found nothing else. It seemed no one had traveled there or beyond, at least not what she could see through history. The information about this mountain seemed vague and purposely so. It crossed her mind the people would not even dare to <u>think</u> about traveling in the restricted area, let alone <u>do</u> such a feat. She had known nothing of the mountains all her life.

Suddenly, the tour turned.

What's this, Gran? Why do we look at transportation? Nothing wasted in this tour Water thought I am supposed to see this.

She turned her sight outward and saw the elders struggling up the hill, with Zebble still cursing Gran as he walked to the compound. Water chuckled at this real-time look at Zebble. All elders, except Wiffle, were struggling to breathe. They were almost fifteen minutes into their climb to the grand hall since Gran had confronted Zebble. Water wasn't sure they would make it in time; they only had about five minutes left.

Their problem, not mine, she thought, feeling drawn back into the memory tour.

There was no transportation here on Izaria except Kaiya and the fishing rifts she saw on the oceans. Kaiya took you where you wanted to go.

"Wait a minute, wow," Water said. "Giant sea slugs with riders going over Zebble's land!"

They moved quickly, she saw. When did this start happening? She noticed Zebble had gone to extreme lengths to hide this from the other tribes as well as from Gran.

He's been busy, Water concluded. Could he protect his secret from Kaiya, she questioned? Now she started taking a closer look at Gran's guided memory tour. Why is he using these creatures like that? What is Zebble planning? We can jump anywhere in the world instantly, and every island had open borders. Water was thinking, why would Zebble need those sea slugs as transpo?

Except for Core, her home, she realized. Again seeing Core's natural defenses should the energy field surrounding Core be breached.

Core did not have open borders. No one got onto Core without Gran's ok. Invitation only, that's how you got onto Core. The season of Choosing. The only time all the elders and tribes could come to Core. Core was the only place in Izaria with closed borders.

A rare few came to Cliff's-edge, her home, and even fewer to the interior of Core.

Water brought her mind back and thought to herself, what if you wanted to crash the party uninvited? How would you do it? You would have to break the seal around Core to get in and have transportation for an army once you got in. She leaped to the idea that Zebble was planning to take over Core.

"Wow," she said aloud, "Could he do that?"

Water began looking for Core's weakness, anywhere anyone could penetrate, seeing if Gran knew of any structural damage to the shield around Core. The easiest entry point, if the shield was penetrated, seemed to be the northern border. She thought, it seemed, because she remembered what Gran had said about looks; they could be deceiving, and she knew nothing about the northern border.

The old home was in the north, and Kaiya will be jumping me there today. Hard to get a feel for the land when I jump, she thought. Can't see the forest for the trees, Water said, using another of Gran's Qazi quotes. Gran always gave credit to the author or the era if she did not know who said it.

"It's so different from anything on Izaria, all of Core encased in a force field no one can penetrate," she said aloud, seeing Core's interior in-memory. Water never ceased to be amazed by Core's beauty. All species of plants and trees grew there. None were indigenous to Izaria, and none were found anywhere else in their world. The people allowed on the lands of Core were few. And they came back with memories of such beauty that they felt compelled to share its vision, giving a glimmer of its radiance to those who would never see it.

"Wait a minute, back up, back up," Water said, coming from this memory. She was trying to understand why Zebble was taking Core's memory from each person allowed onto the land. What is Zebble doing? What are you doing, Kaiya? And you, Gran, who are you? This tour had given Water the notion her Gran was much more than a caretaker.

"STOP!" She shouted.

Was that a crack in the force field? I was too busy questioning who was who and what who was doing; she admonished herself. I almost missed seeing that break in the force field. I only got a quick glimpse, she thought, and it went by so quickly, I couldn't tell how large it was. But it seemed substantial.

Distracted, her mind went on a tangent line. There is that word, **seemed,** once again, reminding me all over I know NOTHING. She could not go back and look; Gran was not letting her. But that had **seemed** like a substantial break in the force field surrounding Core. She could tell there was no energy around the cracked area.

"Ok," she said aloud, "I WILL look at that later, Gran."

She had gone to find the reason behind the people believing they needed to worship Kaiya; they forgot the friendship they had with her. Water knew Zebble reinforced it, saying Kaiya wants to be worshiped. That's what I see. If Gran knew why his family did this, she wasn't sharing that information. "Over half the population was worshiping Kaiya a mere fifty years ago. Now almost every island worships, and Zebble heads this bizarre following," she said, leaving the memories behind and moving in real-time again.

This tour brought more questions than answers. Too much mystery around here since the Choosing," she said. "Gran's cryptic about everything, and Something's up between Kaiya and Gran. They are plotting, and I am going to find out what those two are hiding.

And Zebble too, what is he planning? An invasion? She wondered. I will find the answers even if I have to leave here to do that

CHAPTER 8

SANCTUARY

RIVER STOOD IN front of the old house, stiff from the five-hour ride, seeing it for the first time, gazing in awe.

"It's beautiful, she sighed; that said it all. Time had not touched this majestic home. She smiled and breathed deep the smells that surrounded her; the decaying forest, the seedlings birthing, the animals who lived close, her senses awakening. The house itself smelled of age. River loved it. She was alive, alert, and on fire.

There were four large columns in front of the house connected to the sloping lower roof covering a gorgeous wood deck. Twelve steps led to the deck and a large door that felt more inviting than barring. The house was so enticing; the sight of it implored you to come inside. It looked to be three stories high and one level deep below the earth, she thought, as she gazed down and saw windows below the foundation. She couldn't believe people lived in that much space. She knew her history, but it still shocked her to see the actual house.

"Did all the houses look like this back then?" Maybe this giant house was standard when Laiya lived here three hundred years ago. River thought this as she ran entirely around the house, peeking into windows, stupefied by this house's size and structure. She was excited, almost giddy, jumping window to window, unable to even guess what hidden treasure the next view held. None of the rooms were the same. Each place she could see on this level had a different purpose. River noticed the house was pristine; no peeling paint, rotting wood, or loose shingles on the roof. It looked the way it had in holos, like three hundred years had never touched this place. It was painted the land's colors, wooden slates around each window painted leaf green of an early bloom, and the house an earthy brown of white oak. It's almost as if the person who painted this was blending with the land, she thought as she surveyed the area; trees everywhere, a landscape of indigenous plants, flowers, and herbs around the house, a pond in the back of the house; it was gorgeous

"Nothing like my fifteen by twenty cubic conk home," laughed River, comparing her and Grams conk in the city to this sprawling home. I could fit my whole conk in the smallest room here.

Space was a prime commodity in Rake. Furniture folded into walls disappeared into ionizers or changed with the next holo-program. Those that could afford a holo conk were living well. Their 6th dimensional holo home changed the game every day. For the rich, It brought virtual reality home, and you never had to leave. You had to be on a higher path to even think about owning a holo-conk: People of those professions had better living quarters, but none had space like this home. Not even the Supreme Manager, the overseer of all the cities, lived in *this* much space,

"Not even Izen lived like this," said River out loud.

"Either the house was in a time warp, or someone has kept it up throughout the centuries," River mused aloud, "Probably upkeep."

Whoever did it did an excellent job. River was impressed; the house looked outstanding. But who was on the land doing the caretaking? At this point, she did not even want to guess. Another secret kept from her.

"I could use your help now, Grams," sighed River.

She hadn't seen her gram since the Naming. Now that was an exciting ceremony. River shook her head, still in awe of the chaos she was pretty sure Grams had created. Where did you go, Gramma? River knew she would not have an answer to that anytime soon. She had a *million* questions and no one to answer them. She had one lead, a cryptic message that Grams gave her on that fateful night, and that didn't help at all. The only tool River had to rely on was remembering.

She took a moment to collect herself, breathing deeply and exhaling her stress. Three days ago, I didn't know the house was here. Now here I am standing in front of this three-hundred-year-old home, built in the year 2020, but looking like it was constructed just three days ago.

"Like NONE of this feels real," River said out loud, just to hear a voice and steady herself. "I know I have to go in there," but she did not move

The memories were bursting from the house, a barely contained energy. She felt the hair on her body rising to meet that energy.

"I never experienced this before," she said as she watched the hairs on her arms rise. "I see the past. Past cognition," she jested with herself, feeling overwhelmed all over again. She was astounded by the energy and wisps of memories that surrounded this home. By the knowledge, she felt imbued in the house. She felt she was there, the experience was hers, yet she remained present and in the moment as well.

"Double vision for real!" River said.

It had never happened to her until she began this trip. Why am I here? She questioned, trying to understand what was going on before she stepped into the house and absorb all those memories.

The Naming Ceremony I need to start there. I need to remember all the details she said to herself as she flew back in her mind to three days prior.

"Wow, was it only three days ago?" She said as she began to immerse herself in the memory as she never had before. She was in both places simultaneously, in the memory and still on the deck. It brought on the feelings of double vision and vertigo again. It almost seemed as if all this wasn't real. Just a show put on for her. She was walking in an illusion. Shaking herself free of the feeling, she stepped back to the Naming Ceremony.

"Choose my life's path," River muttered as she opened her front door and walked out of her home on her way to the compound for the ceremonies that commenced in one hour.

She felt like this day would change her life forever, whether good or bad, she couldn't tell.

River quietly shut the front door behind her. She wrapped herself in the solitude of her home, feeling the quiet of a sunny summer afternoon. The heat had all the creatures resting. It was a comfortable silence that spoke to her heart, telling her it is what it is. This moment was the right moment. Instead of going directly to the compound, clothing bag in hand, she veered off to the old oak tree and sat upon the swing Gram had made for her when she was five. She remembered, they had gone out to the white oak, and Gram had slung two sturdy ropes around the lower branch. She took the piece of wood she had found that spring and had sanded it down smooth and bore four holes into the wood, two on each end, and attached it to the rope. River remembered how Grams had taken her in her lap, and they began to fly through the air back and forth, her stomach jumping, hair shining with the sun.

"That was a great day," She said and pushed off the ground and began to soar high into the air, trying to touch the sky with her feet.

After a couple of minutes, River slowed down, stopped, and stood up, ending her memory. "It's time," she said and picked up her bag. "I have procrastinated long enough."

In the bag were the clothes she had chosen to wear for her Naming. She knew she was making a bold statement in her choice. She began moving to the barrier that separated the compound from Sanctuary on her way to the ceremony.

The uncles, their wives, and children had been at the compound for two days. Today's ceremony was the end of their stay at Sanctuary. They must leave within two days of the ceremony's end unless invited to stay. And never had anyone been asked to stay. Rarely did they remain the two days allotted after the ceremony ended. They partied day and night before the Naming. Most of them were tired from two days of nonstop gala's and receptions and ready to leave after completing the ceremony. The naming was the only time they socialized with each other. River ignored all requests to visit, as well as invitations to the galas they held. And finally, she refused to take part in last night's reception.

"It is all a farce," she said, knowing all of them were looking for her downfall.

Her Naming was this year, and she wanted nothing to do with any of it or any of them. The relatives could not breach the barrier Bubble created that divided Sanctuary's land from the compound, and River was not leaving, and they couldn't get to her. She had procrastinated until the very last moment, but now she had to go amongst her relatives.

She shuddered, asking, "Are all families like mine? I always had to keep my guard up; never could allow myself to trust any of them." She reminded herself of the torment and bullying she received from her cousin Begak and all his followers, nearly all of her cousins. Begak was Izen's son; And the cousins, like their fathers, were sucking up. Can't trust any of them, she thought as she moved through Bubble's barrier with ease.

The compound was the only place in Sanctuary the relatives could be, and only these few days. After this day, she told herself, they would all pack up and jump back to their puny little lives while I'm to study nothing but their chosen field living far from Gram and Sanctuary. If I do not decide tonight, Izen will select a career field for me.

Izen was head of the Board of Ceremonies like he was the head of all the family ventures. He was the wealthiest, most powerful CEO in the history of Rake. He wanted River in Applied Science. River wasn't stupid; she knew what Izen was looking for; Laiya's jump formula. And he wants me to find it for him.

"My life is over," she moaned. "I hate all this pomp and clout, all of them trying to show off their status," she said.

She stopped, looked up, and realized she was standing in front of the great hall.

"Oh great, I'm here," she said sarcastically, anger in her voice. She stopped, refusing to go in. No uncle had ever been Regent of the land, not their kids either. River quickly scanned through her memories of Sanctuary's history, seeing none had got past Bubble. They wanted nothing to do with Sanctuary except what they could take. That's the problem. River seethed; they can't take anything from here, can't control it either. And they hate me because I can do what they cannot,

River opened her eyes and stepped out of the memory for a minute. She needed a break from the emotions surging in her again as this memory played itself out. It was not easy feeling it all over again.

She saw the beauty of Sanctuary that surrounded her as she drove through the lands. It's so amazing, she thought; pristine lands, clear blue skies, clean water. I'm lucky. She realized if the uncles would have destroyed Sanctuary if they could have jumped, strip it of everything, leaving it a rotting wasteland like the rest of Rake. She felt remorse, thinking of how thoughtless she was complaining about the five-hour trip out.

"Thank you, Laiya. No jump, no JIVE, and no one allowed into the interior if Bubble said no." A five-hour road trip was a small price to pay to keep Sanctuary pristine. River understood why there was no jump or JIVE allowed past the compound.

Izen is CEO extraordinaire, top dog of all Corporations worldwide, and it wasn't enough for him. He wanted the secrets and the riches he thought Sanctuary held and would stop at nothing to get them. I know he does not understand Sanctuary's beauty; he only sees the money it would bring stripped down. How sad, River thought.

As Gram put it, "Those fools chase the illusion of power. What Sanctuary is, they will never understand."

"Ah," River sighed, finally getting it.

What she did not see Naming night, she saw now sitting on the porch, split between memory and real-time. The double vision had her experiencing the panic and fear of that night, all the while sitting calmly on Laiya's porch.

I couldn't understand what Grams had meant by Izen's power is an illusion when she said it. But I see it now — everything she had missed that night—one of Gram's quirky sayings, popped into her mind. Hindsight is 20/20; Grams had always said.

Funny, I can see it now, she thought as she felt herself moving in the memory again. Feeling the intense emotions of that day once again, stuck in her fears, she remembered her dilemma that day.

She went back to the memory where she had left off.

I DO NOT WANT TO CHOOSE! She had screamed in her head as she pushed open the large double doors to the grand hall.

Grams did not want the Cities' technology to invade the lands, not even on the Sanctuary compound. Laiya built it that way. It's going to stay that way, Grams would tell Izen every year he complained about ancient technology. Gates did not slide open; you could not just call out to JIVE to turn the heat up or lights on. Like Laiya, Aiya did not care one bit about their comfort. She wanted them gone. The relatives all left as quickly as they could after the ceremony.

River laughed to herself. Good riddance, she thought, wishing it were already over. Oh well, she sighed, hearing the sound of her footsteps echo down the hall as she walked into her dressing room. Power has privileges she saw. She had a private dressing room. She threw her bag onto the couch and sat before the large vanity, and began brushing her hair, staring at herself.

How is Izen's power over me an illusion when he can force me into a path that I do not want to take? That's no illusion to me. She stood up, reached for her bag, and dressed in her chosen outfit. River stood in front of the mirror, stared at her image, inspecting her attire for the Naming. She had brazenly chosen the uniform of Sanctuary Regent, which she would one day be, the title only she could claim. Regent, that was her true calling, and there was nothing her uncle Izen could do to stop this, short of killing her.

"I am making a statement," she said aloud and smiled.

It was a blatant slap at Izen, reminding him who she indeed was.

"It will remind him Sanctuary will never be his," River said fiercely. She turned to view her image sideways, standing taller, knowing someone spying somewhere on this compound just heard her say that.

Her shoulders slumped just a little when she realized that the statement might no longer be valid. The lease end changed everything, and no one could predict what was coming. Izen is cruel, calculating, and vicious, and everyone fears him. River reminded herself that he wanted Sanctuary and all its secrets. He's still digging for secrets after all these years, she said to herself. She felt nothing but scorn for Izen and the Uncle puppets, so transparent in their desire.

"They think they're going to amass a fortune off me when I break the code," she sarcastically said aloud for all the listening bugs following her everywhere in the compound. "NOT ME THEY WON'T," she said with determination

They see themselves owning the galaxy, stripping all the planets of their minerals, laying claim to all rights, pretending it's theirs, lock, stock, and barrel. River angrily thought as she sat down in front of the mirror, gloomily awaiting her doom. Izen would control everything and would not stop at this solar system. That man knows I'm smart enough to break Laiya's coded math. Izen wants me on the path of Applied Sciences, where he could control everything I do. I would never be free.

But she reminded herself, he could only control me for ten years; then

I will begin training as Regent. TEN years, thought River, ten years of always playing those fools, hiding everything about me, everything I am doing. I will not do that; she vowed to herself.

"I know there is more to you than you are showing. I am going to find out what it is Aiya hides," Izen would say to her over and over. He keeps making the same mistake, though. All my life, he has thought of me as he does his son, an ignorant child, a kid easily fooled.

River smirked for the cameras she knew were all around her. Grams might not have wanted technology here, but the uncles brought in any piece of technology Bubble would let it. As long as no JIVE systems came in, he pretty much allowed everything to go through to the compound.

"Not in the contract to keep it out," he would say. River just shook her head.

Still, it is I who has deceived all of them, and it is I who has eluded Izen's clutches. She smiled, proud of her ability to keep her Uncle Izen at bay for all these years.

Until now, she cried silently in her mind. She did not want her Uncle's spies to see how upset she was. In three clicks of the hour, I will have to name my path, she said to herself, opening her dressing room door, answering the call to take her place in line. What am I going to do? How am I getting out of this one, she thought? Her footsteps sounded loud to her as she walked down the hall to the throne room.

River suddenly heard her grandmother speaking clearly in her mind. saying, "There is always a little ray of hope." River swung around in a circle, thinking her Grams had snuck up on her. That sounded like she was standing right next to me, she thought.

"Ok, Grams, I hear you, always hope. Yeah, well, can you give me a little now," she pleaded. She fervently wished for something to come along and whisk her away from this. No such luck, River told herself as she kept walking to her doom.

Where did that name, throne room, come from, she questioned? Why did Laiya name it so three-hundred-years ago? And why am I thinking about this now? She chuckled to herself; I am walking to my doom, and I think about trivial nonsense.

Grams slipped back into her mind, saying, 'There is always hope.'

"Yep, you are right, Grams." River took a deep breath, settled down, and entered the throne room.

The throne room, thought River as she opened the door and looked around. Yeah, more like a virtual arena anymore. I see all the uncles are here, she said to herself, seeing those present and the thousands in virtual. Izen only gave five-hundred invitations out each year. And if you got an invitation, it was expected you come. Most male family members were present virtually. Everyone likes a show, she thought, looking around as she took her place in line. It breaks up the monotony of their lives.

I haven't chosen yet; she reminded herself, I am not yoked. I won't select what I don't want, River adamantly swore. "I am an explorer; I like to experience and seek knowledge," she said aloud, bolstering her spirit. "It's fun for me, and I am not a puppet for Izen," she said quietly to herself, reaffirming her commitment.

I will take the career of maintenance and care for the Cities, a lower path. At least then, I will be out of their clutches and could always come to Sanctuary to do my research.

She was talking to herself, standing in line. She barely took notice of her scrawny cousin Begak in front of her as she continued speaking quietly out loud.

"That is if Sanctuary is still here in nine months," she said, remembering Laiya's three-hundred-year lease on Sanctuary was near its end.

"Seeing ghosts again, Muddy?" Begak laughed at River. "Always talking to yourself. What, you don't have any friends," he said and laughed again.

"I see you are finally moving up the educational ladder, Begak. What are you now, like two years older than me? Well, it looks like you made it here now, **finally**," River sarcastically said. "Or did daddy do that for you too, slo-mo?" That was the name she called him when he called her Muddy. And Begak had called her Muddy since she was six years old.

River was an unusual name. The only river that flowed through Rake anymore was in Sanctuary, and a rare few saw that. Begak wasn't one of them. They had been studying ancient times in class. On one of the rare days, they were all required to meet in person. The students came across a picture with the caption, 'The mighty muddy Mississippi River. Begak started laughing and kept repeating in a sing-song voice," MUDDY RIVER, RIVER'S MUDDY, HEY MUDDY."

That day she made two mistakes with him.

She got angry and lipped him Off.

"I am named for the mighty rivers that once flowed freely through our world and no longer are, and for the one glorious river in Sanctuary, Gram said so. You will never, ever, see it. Bubble's not going to let you in! Your name means animal dung in the old language, BE GAK GAK GAK," she yelled at him.

River did not know if that was true, nor did she care. She just said it. She was tired of being bullied by all of them. She didn't look like any of them; their skin didn't sparkle the colors of an autumn day, nor did their hair dance in the sunlight, shining gold, and copper, all the colors of a red sun. So they made fun of her all the time. She hated those days the students were required to meet. That day she was tired of it and let her anger dictate what she did and what she said. River's intellect was beyond her six years of age. Still, emotionally, she was just a kid. And the bullying hurt.

The second mistake: she slipped severely. She told Begak the teacher was at that moment telling his mother he flunked out of secondary. She knew what he didn't and shouted out,

"You failed your secondary. And you're an ignoramus."

Begak had no idea what that word ignoramus meant, but he knew if it was coming from her after he taunted her, it wasn't pleasant. He knew River would use some obscure word he wouldn't be able to look up or find on the web. He felt a twinge of guilt, thinking this wasn't him; he didn't like treating her that way. But then he remembered his father and what he expected and left it at that. Begak didn't believe what River said until he went home.

His teacher had vid called his mom; he would not pass secondary.

She had told him her secret in anger. Begak now knew River looked into the time between time, she could see the future. Begak never said anything and didn't tell anyone, but he never stopped calling her Muddy on the days they were required to meet. He led the pack; no one was her friend. Funny thing, Begak would never let any of them call her the name muddy, nor would he let them hurt her. He told everyone River was off-limits. They just walked by her like she was not there. Or they stuck their tongue out at her. River stayed away from all of them from that day on, for the only thing she got was more vicious teasing; when she had tried to be a part of them, when she had tried to find a friend.

Today, standing in line behind Begak waiting for her execution, she had no time for his stupidity.

"Like father, like son," River said to Begak and then ignored him.

"What's that mean?" He demanded to know. When she continued to ignore him, Begak became irritated. "Hey," he whispered angrily, "I'm talking to you."

River shook her head in disgust. "You will never be more than a mere shadow of your father, you spineless twerp," she whispered back, promptly putting him out of her thoughts. She had one thing on her mind: staying out of his father's clutches. The lower path was her only way.

I hate this; I am standing in line for my execution! I will walk the lower path.

River was both remembering and participating in the heated one-sided debate she had with herself that day while she stood in line. She remembered feeling angry, determined, and a bit scared as she watched herself, once again experiencing the emotions.

"They aren't getting me," she had said, "I won't work for them, especially not for Izen. I won't do it. No way," she shook her head, determined not to give them what they wanted.

She looked toward the dais where the council sat and handed down their judgment, and again she thought, I HATE this. At that moment, Izen came behind her, seeming to talk to his son. Instead, Izen turned to River, smiling with contempt.

"Defiant to the end, eh, River? Too bad your defiance won't help you this time. We'll not let you walk the lower path. "If," he said sarcastically, "that's what you might be planning."

Triumph dripped from his voice as he leaned in close and whispered in her ear.

"A clause in the pact. I get to choose for you," Izen laughed as if she had said something humorous. "You will do our bidding, like it or not," he said and kissed her on the forehead.

Still putting on a show, he turned to Begak and thundered for all to hear, "Congratulations, son," and walked away.

Begak heard everything Izen had said to River. He stared at his father's back, knowing he did not mean those congratulatory words he had just spoken. Fifteen minutes before Begak had come into the Arena, Izen had told his son how much of a disappointment he was.

River had not known Izen had said that to his son that night.

Grams did.

She came from the naming memory, remembering the details.

Grams was watching very closely; River saw that now. She saw how Grams' eyes narrowed, and her lips pursed in the way they did when she disliked something.

Grams had told her over and over, "Observe everything, River, even the smallest details. Remember, it is in the details the truth is spun and can very well shine a light on a little thing easily lost."

Well, it did shine a light, right on Izen, thought River, coming back out of the memorying and still seeing that look on Gram's Face.

She knew Grams did not trust Izen. She did not like the way Izen treated his son. Grams knew he was plotting to take over Sanctuary; she has known all along, River realized.

At the time of the ceremony, River hadn't been focusing on observing. However, her subconscious still did, just like her Gramma taught her. River remembered that Aldebaran was high in the northern sky that night. That observation was significant. She did not yet know why, but she knew it was no coincidence. Grams pointed it out that night. "See that star, River? Aldebaran is the largest of the royal stars and outshines them all. Chart your way by that star River."

River didn't understand what her Grams meant by that either, but she trusted that it was necessary.

"I had no idea what had been going on that night," River said as she began immersing herself in the memory. She could see and feel herself sweating bullets, panicking that night.

Was it right, what Izen had just said to me? Could he force me to work for him for the next ten years? Can I keep mentally sparring with him that long? My life is really over," River said again. What am I going to do? Taking the lower path was her plan within a plan. And she always made plans within plans. You had to, living on Rake. She was screaming in her head as she stood in line, minutes away from destruction, her plans awash, frantically trying to figure something out. I don't want to be here!

I am not like these people! Panic had set in, next in line behind Begak for judgment. River called out to Bubble in her mind saying,

Bubble, if you can hear me, please get me out of this!

River didn't know if Bubble could help, but it didn't stop her from asking. She was standing there before the council in a state of panic.

Whisk me away from this ceremony, ANYTHING, Bubble! Help me, please! River silently cried out that night.

The exact moment River called out for help, the oldest elder, Eldar The Wizard, stood and loudly pronounced an heir was coming.

"The time for a new heir is upon us," he bellowed.

A dead silence followed. Then, suddenly, the whole room erupted in pandemonium. A new heir!!

No one cared about the Naming anymore. Just like that, River got her wish; everyone forgot her. In three hundred years, the calling for a new heir had never happened. Laiya was the first and only heir to the land. She wrote an iron-clad deed for her 200,000 acres. The property could not be sold or moved for three hundred years. And Bubble was the enforcer.

"Oh, Bubble, I don't know if it was you who set that in motion or not, but I asked for help, and I got it. Everyone has forgotten me. I am free from the yoke."

River came from the memory, as she saw herself running out of the throne room, looking for her gramma.

"Grams had a hand in the naming fiasco. She intended for pandemonium to break out and for me to be forgotten. No, that was not a coincidence either. Grams had designed that too."

River only saw Grams briefly after Eldar The Wizard – Wiz, some called him, announced the need for an heir. She found Grams and Wiz outside by the old oak tree with their heads together, whispering in all this chaos, as if they were worried someone would hear them. Although she was very much a part of the memory, River also had time to reflect, wondering why they looked like co-conspirators and how Wiz fit into all of this trickery. River surmised Gram and Wiz had known each other for a long time from the look of them together. She saved that to ponder later and watched as Grams noticed her and stopped speaking with Eldar The Wizard. What followed was even stranger than the Wizard calling for a new heir, everyone shouting and running around, and Grams and he conspiring.

This is what I came to see. River said to herself as she watched and participated in the memory. All that worry before the ceremony and all my panic were for nothing. Grams had never intended for me to choose a path in that dumb ceremony, she thought as she felt the memory come alive.

River found her gramma deep in conversation with the old elder who had just caused the arena to erupt in pandemonium, creating chaos everywhere she smiled. What are they doing? River asked herself. It was strange to see them together; heads bent, whispering as if they didn't want someone to hear. Then she remembered. It didn't matter what Grams was doing.

"I am not yoked," she said to herself, happy to be free.

River started feeling some anxiety falling from her shoulders, thinking she had just copped an enormous break. Then her gramma saw her, cut short her conversation with Eldar the Wizard, and hurriedly walked to her.

"Grams, did you set that up?" River asked. All Grams did was smile and tell River to be still and listen.

"River," she said, "your time is here. You do have a path to choose, but not a path this ceremony will show you."

What? River sighed, thinking to herself, I just got a small reprieve from making a life choice, and now here you are telling me I have to choose again. What she said to her Gramma was, "What are you talking about, Gramma?"

She was feeling exhausted, like she had been riding an emotional rollercoaster all day. Feeling like her Gram was up to her eyeballs in 'this.' Whatever 'this' was.

"River, you need to follow what you feel; you will find your life's path. Tell no one what you are doing nor where you are going. Bubble will jump you out of here right now. Izen can't see you right now nor any of the uncles least they realize they forgot you. Your time is limited, River, go to the old house. Go to Laiya's girl, go now. If you choose to procrastinate and wait till the last moment, which I'm sure you will do just that, you must be there before sunset, three days from now. Izen is coming for you. Better be long gone before that River. Go to Sanctuary. The way is open to you.

This holo map will get you there," she said as she placed the map and a holograph of the home in River's hand.

"Place the map in the chip reader of the hoover. It will take you to the house. There is something for you there at the house as well. Find it, River, then make a choice. Remember to follow the Royal Star; keep him always to your right shoulder. You will not see me for a time, and depending on what you choose, it might be your lifetime. I love you, River. This part, you must do alone. Follow your heart."

Then her Gramma was gone, and Bubble was jumping River out of the Compound.

Now, three days later, she was sitting on the porch of Laiya's house, contemplating all of this and so much more.

CHAPTER 9

SOMETHING'S GOING ON HERE

SOMETHING ELSE IS going on here, thought Water. She was seeing with Gran's shared memories. It was apparent; she had been in the dark about everything for a long time. The mind wiping started long ago. Zebble was just the newest member of his family to deceive the people. And I see the Chief goes along with the deception.

Only with Gran's awareness and memories was Water able to see all the deception. Yet, the reasons why this started still eluded her. Questions flew through Water's mind; Why had Zebbles grandfather started altering his tribes' memories of Kaiya and began telling the people Kaiya wanted to be worshiped? What happened that set Zet on that path. Why does his grandson Zebble hate Kaiya and Gran so much? Why does he hate me? What did I do to him?

He is good at hiding what he does; that's why I don't see anything. How many elders are in this conspiracy, Water questioned?.

"Everything seemed to culminate with the ceremony," and there is where I will go back," Water said, flowing into that memory

Water was miserable that this day had come. I like to invent, to explore, and to seek knowledge. There are no choices like that in Izaria; she heard herself saying as she had begun to feel herself float back to the ceremony. Suddenly Water found herself wandering to another memory.

What are you doing, Gran? She asked *why the change?* She was still on Gran's memory tour. Trying to mind speak with her gramma.

Either her Gran did not hear Water or chose to ignore the question because Water went to the memories Gran wanted her to see: the people of Izaria.

Water saw how tight a social family the twelve tribes of Izaria were. She watched the islands' people come and go to the neighboring islands as smoothly as going to a friend's house for coffee. We are not a separate people, she thought. Except for me, I do not fit. My home Island is restricted to them, and like no other island. She felt lost and sorry for herself as she left this memory behind.

Gran, why DO you keep showing me this? What is so important to you? I know you didn't just want to remind me how I don't fit. Water waited a moment, hoping for a reply, and received none. And *I am waiting for a response that won't come, aren't I, Gran? You already told me you would not be here. I didn't believe it when you told me. I do now.* She sighed heavily. *I might as well go back to your memory tour Gran, see where this will take me.*

As soon as she mind-spoke this, she found herself sitting in her room the day of the Choosing Ceremony three months prior.

"The worst day of my life is here," she heard herself say as she slipped entirely into the shared memory with Gran.

I have to face the elders. They will know my decision as soon as they see me. She began to fret, then changed her thought and will. I will not cloak my decision, and the elders will see my determination. And I will know their disappointment; she sighed at that thought. She sat upon the cushions, gazing out the transparent barrier. She rose from the floor, still looking outside at the activities below. Soon, even that will be empty of people. She thought as she turned away, not wanting to see anything to do with her Choosing.

"My Choosing is upon me," Water said, as she moved away from the barrier towards her bed, where she had laid out the outfit she would wear for the ceremony. It was tradition to wear an outfit that corresponded with the field the candidate chose. Water felt her choice of attire was a perfect match for her desired profession. She decided to dress as herself, independent of a choice. She walked across the floor toward the room of cleansing, feeling the warmth of the natural hot spring called out to her. "Come relax, take a load off your mind," it told her softly. She went willingly to the call, moving to cleanse her body and her mind. Water Slid into the hot springs, letting the steam rise to greet her as she sunk deep into the warmth that enveloped her. She felt her body relaxing even as her mind raced, mulling over the choice she would tell the elders she had made.

I'm not choosing a path. I'll be a free agent. She realized she would be the first-ever to select, no choice. She didn't think that was going to go over very well with the elders either. Maybe Wiffle will stand with me, she hoped. Yea, so what. What could *he* do to help me?. I don't think he can do much. He's so new to being an elder, Water thought, discouraged.

She sank deeper into the pool. Relax, she told herself, easing her body's aches with the natural jets of hot water, soothing her mind with the rhythmic flow.'

She already knew the elders' plan. They are going to decide for me. I will be sent somewhere out of the way, away from Gran and Core, where they can monitor me and the trouble they say I cause. They could never control me on Core; Gran wouldn't allow it.

"Quit trying to spy on her! Don't let me catch you sneaking into her mind again or, I'll make sure it will be the last time! First and only warning," Gran would tell them. They fled from her. Except for Zebble, he continued to try and sneak into my mind and change my memories. What was crazy, thought Water, was Gran knew he was coming, knew what he was trying to do, and chose to let me handle him.

"You got this, Water. Remember your training, baby. I will be watching," was all Gran said about him.

Sista's training ensured they could not spy on Water while she was unaware, not even Zebble; she always knew when he came slinking in. Water took to the art of cloaking and spying like an assassin in the dark. She wasn't just good at it. It was second nature for her. She was a master and found it was easy. She honed her skills all week on the elders who were gathering for the Choosing. Not one of the elders realized Water had slipped in and out their defenses like water falling over the cliff. Easy Peasy, she thought as she conquered each of the Elders defenses, and they never knew. The only one she didn't try to sneak around was Wiffle; Water liked and respected him.

She caught a break, hours before the Choosing, and established a sliver of a listening line to the chief elder. He was so preoccupied with his thoughts; the chief could not tell Water had slipped into his mind. He had an audience.

A two-year-old could sneak up on him. Water smirked and began sifting through the chief's thoughts. This man is all over the place. It's confusing just sitting here in his mind.

Wait a minute, what am I hearing? She stopped and went back to the last jumbled thoughts in the chief's mind, catching what she had just passed.

WOW, that's disturbing! She frantically cried out in thought as his chaotic mind slipped out of her grasp again. **What** is he talking about? Something about a change of power and Gran's demise. She pulled away from him, not wanting to go any further in his warped mind.

Gran's death, this is not good. She hurriedly cut the connection, leaving behind an anchor in his mind so she could get back in if she needed it. I must find Gran, Water thought, fearing it was already too late.

Gran, where are you? Gran, do you hear me? We have to go now! Why won't you answer? Please, Gran, someone is trying to kill you!

She could not reach her grandmother without calling attention to the attempt. I suppose if I screamed a thought throughout the great hall, I could contact her. Water sighed, resigned to waiting until after her doom to talk with Gran. The elders were calling for her. It was time for Choosing.

Gran's demise? What did he mean? I have to figure out what is going on before it catches up with me. She felt lost and scared, sitting alone in her room, dreading the call she just received. Water got up and swept her hands over her Choosing outfit, a beautiful shimmering wrap. Her dress spoke to her decision. "I choose nothing. I choose to be me," She was wiping away the imaginary wrinkles.

Why did I do that? Smoothing out nonexistent wrinkles, like Sista, would let me go anywhere around the people not looking excellent. Water smiled, settling down a bit as she remembered Sista. "These people talk," Sista said, "Let them talk of their envy."

Sighing deeply, Water began her walk of doom to the great hall. Gran had gently teased her for being melodramatic most of her life. Well, not this time, Gran. She could feel the sense of urgency creeping up on her, angry at herself for being so unaware of the intrigue surrounding her.

She crossed the barrier between her home, Cliff's- Edge, and the compound with ease, no longer even mindful of it. She and Gran were the only ones able to do that. She silently Crossed the field where the festivities had been taking place all week, noticing the eerie silence on the grounds, reflected her silence. Water saw no one there, not even the vendors, empty stalls, every one of them. They were all inside the throne room awaiting the commencement of the Choosing Ceremony, she thought, wishing she could just run away. She had made her way to the massive oak doors that opened to the throne room.

"I am here," she called out to no one, "come for my sentencing."

She quietly reestablished the sliver to the Chief Elder as she pushed the doors open and walked in, head held high.

I always hated this room, so massive and gloomy Water thought, it looked nothing like Cliff's-Edge. Those rooms were airy and light of spirit. A fresh breeze ran through the open windows, with no glass panes constricting the flow. Her bedroom barrier circulated fresh air, maintaining a balmy 80 degrees during the day and cooler temperatures at night for sleep. She loved the feel of her home.

I never liked this place. Water's thought rang out across the throne room, not caring who heard. It Feels like death in here.

The throne room design was cumbersome, with windowpanes so thickly stained it shaded and blocked the sunshine. It was always dark inside, rain, or shine. The sound echoed everywhere in there. You couldn't help but hear the clip-clop of everyone's new fancy shoes. There were no other buildings like the great hall on Core. Gran said she made it that way. She didn't want any of those elders to be too comfortable. At least they take too long in doing their job and not leaving as quickly as she wanted them to. She wanted them to hate coming there as much as she disliked having them here.

I will not let the elders sense or see my turmoil, Water thought with determination. Head held high; she kept moving to the center of the floor. I'm in luck, she thought, looking down so they could not see the sudden glee she felt. The chief was mind speaking with the other elders. Now, she, too, was connected with all of them as well.

She stood before the elders awaiting her doom. *I am my grandmother's child;* she bolstered herself and brought her will forth. *I will not run, nor will I fear;* her mantra rang out silently in her mind; only she could hear it. She wanted to run as far as she could, leaving this Choosing way behind. Instead, Water stood quietly and looked directly at the elders, refusing to give in to her fear or let them see anything but strong determination within her.

It is what it is; Water spoke in her mind letting all the elders hear it, quoting the people's favorite saying. Water felt the elders reproach. She didn't care what they thought about her.

What did I just hear? She was trying to concentrate on the crazy thoughts she was picking up from one of the elders. *Who was trying to harm Gran, and why? Whoa! Who is that? Who was so angry,* she thought.

"Wow," the words escaped softly from Water's lips. She was suddenly alert, almost thrown off balance by intense hatred directed at her; it hit her like a hurricane. She could not make a move without revealing herself. So instead of panicking, Water severed the mind-meld with the chief, steadied her heartbeat, stepped forward one pace, and said,

"I, Water of Core, Grand Daughter of Aiya, present myself to the elders to speak my choosing."

There was a moment of pause; the elders' bland facial expressions belied the truth of the moment. Water could sense a buildup rippling through the air; she knew they were anything but bored. The anticipation was palpable. She knew she would not be allowed to speak again. They were making her choice.

Slowly, Chief Elder stood up, "Water, kin to Aiya, today we, the council of elders, have chosen the path you will follow," he began. "As elders, we have the power to name the path of Choosing for anyone participating in the Ceremonies, if we deem it necessary for the good of the people."

Water looked to each elder as the chief finished his statement. That clause had never been used, not in two-hundred-fifty years of Izaria's existence. Not until now. The pact Kaiya made with the people at the beginning of the time allowed for this. Gran could not interfere. *Another thing that makes me different from everyone else on the islands,* she reminded herself.

Here it comes; water spoke out clearly in her mind and didn't care who heard her thoughts.

The Chief Elder cleared his throat.

Water came from this memory sharing with Gran with a new understanding. Looking through Gran's memory, she knew that Gran wasn't concerned about Zebble and the Chief's petty conspiracy. She wasn't worried about them taking control of me either, Water realized. Gran knew that was never going to happen. Gran knew the whole-time what Kaiya was going to do at this ceremony. Gran and Kaiya had plotted this out months ago, maybe even years ago, she realized.

Gran was looking for everyone involved in the conspiracy. Gran already knew one other elder was involved, but she needed to know who else was a part of Zebble's conspiracy

"Remember the details," Gran always told her, "it is the details that speak the truth."

That night of Choosing, Kaiya spoke her first words to the elders in over a century.

Sit down, elder, Kaiya said to the Chief.

A shocked and awed silence rocked the hall. It was so quiet; a feather could be heard falling. Fear reeked from all the elders except two. There was no surprise from Wiffle (was he in on it and whose side was he on, questioned Water) and pure panic from Zebble. Every elder dropped their mind shields in shock when Kaiya spoke at the Choosing. Gran and Kaiya planned for that to happen; they wanted to see who was hiding what. And for the briefest second, Water could read them all as well. That was all she needed.

" Ah," Water exhaled her breath. She understood. They no longer felt Kaiya, no longer talked to her as a friend, and shut her existence away from them. The elders believed her far removed from their lives. These elders sure didn't want the real Kaiya here now; they had gotten comfortable without her, Water realized. Zebble had somehow fooled the entire population into thinking Kaiya wanted Izarians to worship her and that he, Zebble, was the only way to her. This information set Water's head spinning.

Zebble knew the lie and fostered it, as did his ancestors before them. Chief Elder knew but pretended not to and reaped the benefits of the power Zebble allotted him. The two elders wanted power, not truth. Water could see Zebble had learned to shield his thoughts and feelings with a degree of skill she hadn't ever seen, except in her Gran. His ability was almost as high as Grans, Yet different. His was a dark power. She saw his hate the moment Kaiya spoke, and now she confirmed it. He hated Kaiya, and he hated Gran. And he hates me too. Why does he hate me? What did I do to him? He wants Gran and me dead! I can see it written all over him. Wow, thought Water, I never knew someone hated me so much. Gran must have felt it somewhere in her psyche to go hunting for it, as well as take the time to shield me from seeing this sooner, not wanting me to worry.

What an enlightening memory tour you've got me on, Gran. You and Kaiya plotted everything out; you know everything. You and Kaiya are in this together. You two set me up. I knew it," she said, trying to go back to Gran's memories and see what Gran and Kaiya were plotting. She couldn't. Gran was not letting her; this was a one-way trip. Water might not see what those two were plotting, but Water knew this; Gran and Kaiya were in IT up to their eyeballs together. And she was going to find out what IT was.

What a lie Zebble has created. And the people believe it. He is good at these deceptions," Water acknowledged. Where had Zebble learned to create illusions so easily, Water wondered? I breached his shield because he thinks I am nothing but a woman-child, insignificant to him, an advantage for me. They had been lying to the people for generations, keeping them docile. The people were blinded. Izarians trusted their elders unconditionally. Water sadly realized, the people were deceived, and they don't even know it. I need to look into this deeper. Can't do it now; Gran's not stopping the tour. Still, she questioned why Kaiya spoke when she did, right before the elders had an opportunity to manifest my doom? Kaiya did not let the elders choose for me. I am free.

If you are listening, Kaiya, thanks, I miss you.

The last thing Water heard Kaiya say to the elders in this memory was,

Little men with little minds, this one is not for you. Aiya, take her out of here now.

As swiftly as a mother bear grabs her cub to escape from danger, Gran scooped Water up and jumped her out.

Water felt her head spinning in real-time as it had the ceremony night.

Nothing made sense that night; everything moved so quickly from the time Kaiya spoke to the moment Water questioned, "What's going on?"

Jump complete, Water's thoughts interrupted this memory. "But I didn't go home," she said, as she started to feel the memory retake hold, beginning to feel the confusion of that night and then the awe and bewilderment. Not knowing where she had been jumped to, only knowing it was not Cliff's-Edge. She gazed around and saw Gran standing on the porch of an old home.

"I know this place," Water said, again experiencing the moment with grand awareness.

"It will be here that you will jump when the time comes, Water. Do you recognize this place?" asked Gran.

"Yes, Gran," Water replied, answering purely on instinct. "It's your ancestral home."

Soon it will be time for you to leave Core, baby," Gran said. "Do not interrupt me with questions, Water, not verbally or mentally," cutting off Water's questions before she could express them. "Just listen quietly," Gran said as she gently held Water's face in her hands. Gran knew Water would not understand the separation that was coming.

"I love you, Water, and I am so proud of you," Gran said, gently brushing a strand of Water's hair from her forehead and kissing her. "Kaiya will do one last thing for you on this journey before she leaves you. She will jump you here: my home and your ancestral grandmother, Laiya's home. You will learn more about yourself here at Sanctuary. It's time to choose a path. There is only one question you must answer. Will you go or stay? I must leave and will not be with you much. You will do this alone in the beginning. Set this in your memory," Gran was saying as the memory faded.

Water was jolted back to the present, in her room at Cliff's-Edge, listening to Zebble argue with Gran. Gran had left that meld open, wanting Water to be aware of the conversation taking place as she came from the memory.

I understand. I know Gran.

Water felt it in her whole being. I know Zebble thinks my very existence is dangerous for his plans, she thought.

He wants us both out of the way. That was impossible now that the

Choosing ceremony has failed. Now he wants me dead right along with you, Gran.

Yes, he does, Water.

Water opened her eyes, looking around her room, her space, her sanctuary. She was sitting in front of the barrier, face pressed lightly to it, smelling and tasting the salt in the air that filtered through the force field. The view was spectacular, and she loved feeling the breeze upon her body when she stood in front of it. She loved to press her face against it to peer down below to the compound as she had three months ago, watching the Ceremony activities. And today, as she watched the elders on the old path.

She turned and gazed upon the pictures she had drawn and placed on the walls. There were six of her favorites drawings; One of Gran sitting by an open fire that she drew when she was eight.

She smiled as she looked at it now, remembering how Gran had told her she had lots of potential and hidden talent. Water had shelves of rocks she had gathered from the shores, caves, and valleys of Core over the years, her collection of dried herbs and plants on those shelves too.

Water smiled, somewhat messy she thought as she looked around her room from the cushions she sat in by the barrier. I LOVE this room, she said to herself. She stood up and looked out of the force field one last time: first, to the compound far below, then to the path leading to the shores of Core and the oceans beyond it.

"Beautiful," she said out loud as she turned and walked to her pack sitting beside the door and bent to pick it up.

Three months before, Water had readied herself and prepacked for the journey: fishing pole, hunting knife sharp enough to cut coconut if needed, fire kit, first aid, and waterproof shelter.

Water knew how to live off the land; she had grown up with Gran doing just that. She had eaten her meals daily from Core and knew the hardship coming would not be finding food or shelter. She could do that easily.

No, the most challenging part would be that she would now be utterly alone. No Gran or Kaiya or Sista Sol to share her mind and thoughts. Just the silence of herself.

It's time to go, she said silently to herself.

CHAPTER 10

MEET ABBY

*H*OW GOES IT, *Sisters of my soul, Laiya sang out.*
I flick this ride you call time; Abby sang back. *Do you see what comes?*
Where did you get that word from? Laiya laughed at Abby. *Who says flick? And to answer your question, I see some. Kaiya sees more than I. Neither of us sees as much as you.*

I am curious as to what the faeries are doing. The wood nymphs tell me interesting things. Abby told Laiya. *I think we need to look a little deeper into their agenda; what plans do they have that affect humans and the Elon, more specifically us? Why are they so helpful, seemingly without reason. Faeries do not do that. They have a reason for everything they do—ten out of ten times, it is in their best interest, whatever they are doing*

I will talk with Aziel. I will know if she hides something, Abby, Laiya said. *In the meantime, what of the Elon?*

The others are beginning to wake up; some sing my name, asking, How can this be? The old ones still dream and have not yet heard. Abby continued, *I wonder if Aldebaran will call them. He says I am young and that we, and what we create, are new to the universe, and they must contemplate. Aldebaran is looking at the silence and wondering what is happening at the edges as well. He hears the silence and is not sure what to think. He is moving too slow;* Abby mind spoke to Laiya

The awakened are divided. For such short-lived people, you have a long history of destruction, of letting someone take control of your lives and wiping

you out. I'm just saying, Abby, pointed out with a mental shrug. *Your species has started over more times than your earth has been alive, as they see it. Some remember a couple of hundred thousand years ago to a more peaceful race of humans and wonder what happened.*

The Elon never thought of you before, and now they are not sure what to think of the three of us, let alone the human species. We keep pushing, saying things like time is short, we must hurry.

Time is not to us what it is to you. There is no time.

Time is a concept that we must study, Aldebaran has suggested. I tell them we don't have time for that.

We shall wait and see, he says.

I say we sing to Senjo, wake him up.

CHAPTER 11

READY, SET, ENTER

"**A**MAZING. IMAGINE THAT," River proclaimed, "Real windows."

She promptly placed her fingertips upon the pane, pressed her face to the glass, and gazed down the row of floor-to-ceiling glass panels on the south side of the house. It was an antique passive solar design, she guessed. Each room had its treasure, but this room, the big room with these beautiful windows, caught her eye.

"Oh, wow," River said again, peering into the massive room inside. The afternoon sunlight illuminated a wall of books that lined the north wall, floor to ceiling, wall to wall.

"Books," she sighed, her heart beating with pure joy. Her mind quickly calculated there hadn't been a window or a book on Rake in centuries. I've never seen either.

This room triggered a slew of memories she could not control. They just came, and she let them in. She saw the first supercities born in the late 21st century, designed without windows. Rakians didn't need windows three miles underground. And one mile into the sky, where the elite lived, they didn't want them. Those above ground rarely wanted to look out into the smog and gloom. River saw the wastelands had not existed then. But now, three-hundred- years later, the supercities were surrounded by a thousand miles of wasted lands.

Nothing survived in those barren lands. River could feel herself choking on the dirt swirling around her. She quickly left those memories behind. She was walking in the memories, watching as they changed like the scenic views of a holovid.

She saw the beginning of the Automatic Home Environment, AH, for short, realistic enough twenty decades ago. She could feel and smell the scenes on the walls. Today's JIVE technology makes the AH look like simple drawings; River's real-time thought slipped into this memory tour. Today's conks are mini holo homes. You could live anywhere, be anyone, create an alternative reality right there, and never leave your home.

She was sitting on the porch, eyes closed, contemplating her options. She opened her eyes and looked at all the nature that was left in her world, here in Sanctuary, an array of magnificent trees, vegetation, and flowers. Birds were chirping in trees and frogs singing by ponds. Even a stream gurgled nearby. Without Laiya's foresight three-hundred-years ago to bubble this land in a protective force field, none of it would exist.

We have come a long way on the road to destruction while calling it progress, sighed River.

I hate living in the Cities, yet I wouldn't know what I know now to be true without living there each year. Rakians never wanted the real thing. That was too messy. How sad, she thought. As far as I know, Sanctuary, my land, was the last of its kind anywhere. Rakians don't see the beauty of the land. They never smelled flowers in the wind or the scent of pine in the air - not the real thing. She understood They do not care, and they never will. They were holo living. How blessed I have been to have this, she thought, grateful Sanctuary was her home.

As her mind rambled through Rake's history, her senses absorbed Sanctuary, the land, and the house, which smelled of age and longevity to her. I live in a disposable world, where everything is thrown away, including the people. Why am I here? What is going on? And how am I involved; she asked these questions of herself. I gotta figure out what I need to do.

OK, think, she admonished herself.

"Note," River spoke out loud as she began to organize what she knew. Note, her cloud PA (personal assistant) had been tuned to River's wave signal since birth.

"Copy as I speak," she commanded and started ticking off what she knew and what she suspected.

"One," River said, watching the Note script write her words, "I'm on my own, sitting on the deck of Laiya's house."

"Two, I wasn't yoked. I made no choice, nor was one made for me." A small reprieve that Izen will try and rectify.

"Three, an heir is coming. Laiya has been the only heir to Sanctuary in almost three-hundred-years."

"Four, the lease is up fourteen days after my fifteenth birthday."

"Five, Izen wants control of Sanctuary and me." If he can't control me, is he willing to kill me? River wondered. Yes, he is, she answered her question.

At this moment, River was sure Izen was securing his place as the next heir. Doing whatever he has to do to ensure that, River thought to herself as Note effortlessly copied everything she said verbatim.

"Sanctuary holds the key. But to what and where I don't know. River took out Gram's last message hidden in the holo-map and read it out loud. It didn't make much sense, either.

"River, remember your studies with me. You will need them. When you find the key and choose this journey, look to Aldebaran to guide you. You must be in the house, in the library, when the sun is setting in three days."

That was it, nothing more.

"Who is Aldebaran?" River questioned. She can't mean the star she pointed out at the Naming, can she? Gran made it seem as was a person, not a thing. And how does Aldebaran guide me if I don't know who or what that is? Knowing Grams, it could easily be a "what" and not a "who." I am no closer to understanding any of this, River realized.

"Stay active," she told Note, as she put the letter back in her pack. She stood up from the deck, wiped the dust from the road off, and walked to where she could see the sun.

"How beautiful, a sky of melted lava," she said as she stood there for a moment, soaking up the energy freely given to her. "Ahhh," she sighed in awe and contentment, "what a beautiful way to close the day," she told the sun, then turned toward the door, opened herself to the memories, and stepped back in time as she walked in.

It reeked of memories. River saw and felt the beginnings of this old home, three hundred years earlier, and all the following generations.

Everywhere she looked, there were memories. Some were quietly waiting, and some felt as if it were urgent that River saw them now.

"Grams is the spitting image of Layia, just older," River said again as clips of Laiya's life flashed by. She couldn't distinguish the time frame of the memories. They blended without distinction, the laughter, the struggle, kids everywhere. Such a large family, River whispered in awe, envious. The wisps of lives were forming and dissolving all around her, making her unable to tell if they were old or new memories or even happening right then.

Why, in almost fifteen years of my life, had I not been brought here? She had not expected this. Grams has kept this from me on purpose, thought River, miffed at the idea that this home, these memories, had been blocked. She couldn't remember.

This home was huge.

I wonder what it was like living with that many people, grandparents, parents, brothers, sisters, cousins, aunts, uncles, even friends. Everyone would be everywhere. I barely know my relatives, she thought, and what I do know I don't like. I dislike my cousins. I would rather be anywhere else than around my cousins or their parents, especially Izen.

Her mind skimmed over the memories like water falling over the edge of a cliff. Facts that stuck out, she added to Note.

"Look at this video, copy and record Note. It stuck out, this memory," she cried softly.

Population restrictions had been in place these two-hundred-fifty years since the time of the Disease and Irsei's Rebellion. Why is this crucial? River questioned as this memory hammered at her—one child per family after the disease's onset. One child per household winning the lottery now meant only one in every three-hundred-thousand people could have a child each year.

There was nothing new about this that River could see, and it made her curious; why is this memory so persistent? River saw that those measures weren't good enough. And for the first time, River could see Rake drowned in too many people and not enough resources. My world has been dying for a long time, she thought.

All of Laiya's descendants had at least one child and sometimes two or three. What happened to us? When did we become so, so...? What one word describes the arrogant self-glorifying, egotistical, worthless bunch of human dribble my relatives are? River queried once again.

The memory of the Disease came on the heels of the overpopulation memory, hard and fast, pushing and screaming, "**Look at me!**"

River stood amid people sobbing, watching while others tried to cling to children, parents, lovers, and friends as they faded away, unable to stop what was happening. It was just called "the Disease'. The first year it struck, twenty-percent of the population disappeared. She watched the years slide away and fear to settle in; who was next?

She felt her ancestors' fear. That terror had become hers as well. River shuddered at that memory; it was so personal. River lived Tarissa's fear; her baby boy might be next. And then, Tarissa's anguish that very next year when she watched her two-year-old baby boy slowly disappear from her arms. River was Tarissa, and they were holding her baby boy until there was nothing left but a blanket. Sobbing as he faded, begging,

"Please, Baby Boy, please, my little star, please don't go."

No one was exempt. Everyone felt it, even Laiya's kin.

A couple of years later, someone suggested population control measures, which everyone readily agreed to. Within a year, the Disease halted. No one mentioned the coincidence, but everyone saw it.

Wow, thought River, that was intense, wiping the tears away, still feeling the pain of Tarissa's loss.

How did the Disease know? The plague stopped after population control measures became law that same year, I think. Note, explore the dates of the population control statutes and the cessation of the Disease, see if they coincide, leave it for me to look at tonight," River spoke.

Did one of the high-ranking officials decide to implement the disease as a secret assault on the population? These questions kept running through her mind. It would have been disgusting, thought River, if the virus were human-made and controlled by someone. Who could be so heartless, was all River could think.

No coincidences, River, remember this, she said to herself.

River was the grandchild of Aiya. She was an analytical, fact-finding experimenter. She quickly calculated the importance of the Disease and the ramifications if it were human-made.

"Note, find all references concerning the Disease," River commanded.

It was a puzzle, and she the gatherer of the pieces. The Disease was a crucial piece in this puzzle, but she did not know where it fits like everything else so far.

Keep moving, River told herself. The sun is setting, I'm in the house, but where do I go again?

"Oh yeah, the Library," she said as she stopped moving, trying to get her bearings in this big house with the memories and wisps everywhere. The ground level alone was immensely spacious. There were five other separate areas; one looked like an old cooking area - strange, all of this equipment. The memories told her about the use of each appliance. Or so they called these machines.

She could spend an afternoon just hanging out here with the memories that crowded this kitchen and eating area. It was great, the smells of cooking from a time begone, hearing all the laughter, kids screaming - what a paradise. But she knew that was not the room she needed.

"The library," she said, moving toward it and looking through the door. Then she stopped in her tracks.

"The great hall," she said quietly to herself, in awe of what she saw. Then she noticed the sun slipping away. "Stay with me, just a little longer," she cried out to the fading sun, "I need your help to find the key."

She stepped into the great room filled with books, the sun resting on the horizon, reflecting on the river miles below. A clear view across the valley.

She turned to the east wall, "Ahh," she said, "So many books."

Just then, she caught a glint on the surface of the water. As the sun slipped away, flashing its last rays of light onto the river and reflecting directly into the house where it struck a copper disc with strange writing.

The Elon heard her call to him, asking him to help, and he responded with that beam of sunlight. Her gaze followed the light to the disc, and from there to the wall of books. On one book, dead center of that floor-to-ceiling wall-to-wall shelf, the beam of sunlight landed. River looked at the title, shook her head, and started laughing. The tension inside melted away.

"Oh, Grams, that is so you. Always a queen who likes a little drama." Paradise Lost, the title read. She and Gram's favorite old-time read. I am home, she said.

CHAPTER 12

COMING HOME

WATER WAS STANDING with her pack in her hand, ready to sling it over her shoulder, and yet she hesitated. She was listening again in her mind to what Gran had told her the night they jumped to Laiya's home and then jumped back home to Cliff's-Edge. The night of Choosing. She was there once again revisiting the memory, standing in her Grans workspace at Cliff's-Edge right after the fiasco at the ceremony three months ago.

"You will only ask yourself one question, Water: are you leaving Core or staying here? You must prepare yourself for a journey either way."

"What journey? What are you talking about, Gran?" Water asked, confused by what had just happened at the Choosing. She was still reeling from the intense hatred she had felt. And the sudden jump to a place unknown.

"Your life's path stands before you; the choice is yours to make. Stay here, and Core will protect you as long as it can, but you will be isolated and lonely without knowing who you are."

"That's the life I live now, Gran," Water whispered, looking down and shuffling her feet. She was coming to the realization she had been unaware of a whole lot her entire life.

"There is another path for you, baby. If you choose to explore that, I can only say it will change your life. You will have to decide if that change is worth it. I know there is much going on you do not understand. but will become clear upon the second path."

Grans slid the hologram she always carried to Water. "My home, where I grew up, where we just jumped from. It holds many memories never shared with the people. And yes, it was Laiya's home as well. It is time for you to know your family and to decide your path. When the time is right, it is to here you will jump," she said as she continued to press the hologram in Water's hand. "I will not see you for a while, and depending on your decision, that might last your lifetime. This home is where you must start. I love you, Water. When the time comes for you to do so, open the door, and walk in, you will find what you need. You will know when it is time to start your journey, Water. Trust your instincts, and you will not fail, I know it."

With that, Gran was gone.

Water opened her eyes, back in real-time, still mind-connected with Gran, and silently watching Zebble argue with her.

How much I love you, Gran, Water said to herself, glancing around her room again.

Gran? Water questioned.

I know Water; it's time, Gran answered.

Still seeing through Gran's eyes, Water's looked upon Wiffle, and this time she knew he saw her. Where does he fit in this, friend or foe? She didn't know.

Bye, Gran, I love you.

I am with you always, Water, even if you can't reach me, sending her love and hugging her with energy.

With that, Gran turned to the elders and said, "So, you wish to take Water with you now and hold her...where, Zebble?"

The elders had made it to the compound and the great hall ten minutes prior, short of breath, only to find the doors barred by Gran. They had just walked half a mile up a steep path to find themselves locked out of the building by a fierce woman standing in front of the massive oak throne room doors. She wasn't letting them in. She would address them in her arena, as she saw fit.

Eleven of them wanted nothing to do with her, the Chief included in those numbers. Ten elders were trying to figure out why they were even here. Zebble thought to force his way around her but could not move against her aura, shining white and bright like a winter sun reflecting on a mountain peak. She took one step toward Zebble and the elders as she was speaking. They began backstepping away from her. Even Zebble flinched.

"Answer the question, Zebble. Where do you intend to take Water?"

Water cut the connection, slung her pack over her shoulder, and looked around her room one last time. I will miss this place for a long time to come. The only home I have ever known, she thought, looking again at the picture she drew of Gran hanging on the wall with all the others she had posted through the years. That one just happened to be a favorite. Water stayed only a moment longer, allowing the memories of her childhood to wash over her. "Good-bye, old friend," Water said to the energy of her room.

I am ready, Kaiya, she mind spoke. But was thinking, am I prepared to leave the only life I have ever known?

I am here, Water, and I shall take you there now. Remember, you are loved, my child. Kaiya began the jump from Cliff's- Edge.

Water was standing in front of the old home. The house itself was in perfect condition as if time had not touched it. This place was huge - three levels high for sure, she thought, counting at least two more stories above the ground. And at least one down too, by the looks of it, seeing a window below the foundation. It stood out stark against the trees and pond that surrounded it.

"Kaiya did not build this," Water said. She thought it was more similar to Cliff's-Edge, visible for miles. Most homes on Izaria blended into the surrounding environment so well they could not be distinguished from it. Only Cliff's-Edge stood out stark against the landscape for all to see. Except what hid within the cliff, like her room.

"This house, It's just here, standing out like a mighty oak in all its glory," Water said in awe of what she was seeing. She could sense that trust and love built this place. Those two emotions engulfed this home and the land surrounding it. Walking up the deck stairs and around the platform, she came upon large glass panes encompassing the home's whole southern wall.

"This room glitters like a sea of tiny grains of sand on a sunny winter's day," Water laughed as she looked through the glass.

"Wow," she said again, stretching her arms above her head, shutting her eyes, and seeking the warm energy of the sun as she did every day back home. That was just what I needed, she thought, breathing deeply and releasing some of the stress of the day. I was home this morning, and now I feel as if I have no home. She felt an overwhelming sadness fall upon her. What is happening, Water asked, though she got no answer.

"Oh well," she sighed, talking out loud to distract herself from the panic beginning to rise. "I might as well explore the outside of the house on this strange platform. It reminds me of the decas our people build, high up in the palms, to sit upon and enjoy a sunset or sunrise. I wonder if that is what this platform for," she said as she walked around the house, completing one circuit and then sitting down on the front steps.

This level alone has at least six separate spaces that I can count, and each is different. Water realized each room had a unique function.

"I wonder what is up there," Water questioned, looking to the second level windows? "Or," she said, eyes moving down to the window below, "what's down there?" She walked to the outside wall with the sizeable glittering glass panes facing south and stared inside once again.

A big, oversized chair sat facing a massive stone fire pit on the northern wall, directly opposite the glass panes. Looking right, Water gaped at the spectacular sight of books lining the east wall, ceiling to floor. There were no books on Izaria, as the salt air was not kind to paper. She was beginning to feel overwhelmed again.

We don't have books on Izaria. We have only to think about a subject, and memory would tell all. Books had slipped from our history long ago, she thought sadly. I'm lucky. Gran had a few rare books we could read together. She got a strong urge to sit by the fire and read. As tempting as that feeling was, Water did not think it was the time for that.

This house's size is intimidating, she thought, standing next to it feeling small and insignificant. There were whispers of lives that ran through this place; she was trying to keep them at bay until she caught her breath and got her bearings. So many memories surrounding the home and the land; she felt them all. I need only the ones that can help me now.

"*Kaiya, if you haven't left me too, can you help guide me to the memories I need to find?*" Water settled her mind, took a deep breath, opened herself to what would come, and stepped into the house.

"I am home," Water said the moment she opened the door and stepped in. She felt it. It's my home. I've been here; I know this place.

She gazed around, memories floating on the edge of her mind. She here, as a toddler, running with her sister.

"My sister? What sister? I have a sister. Where is she?" Water exclaimed out loud.

Was this her memory, or a memory from the house of two children playing in a different time? Time didn't seem to flow here the way it did outside this house. She couldn't tell if the memories were three hundred years ago or last week. It was as if these memories are still made daily. But no one has ever lived here, not on Core, she said to herself.

Water needed to think this through. I am here to find the path that leads to me; this place seems so familiar. So, what am I supposed to see here or do here? You didn't tell me anything, Gran. What am I expected to do here? Well, I don't know, can't even guess right now, she thought. She was feeling exasperated by the whole ordeal. I don't have the first clue what to do. Water kicked her foot as if she were kicking sand on the beaches of her home, angry at her grandmother.

Why did you leave me like this, Gran? Water quested for her grandmother's energy and couldn't feel her. *You just cut me off from everything and everyone I ever loved, even in thought.*

She took an audible breath, expressing her sadness. It would be easy to let all that had happened these last three months engulf her, especially without Gran or Kaiya here now. She was used to being physically alone but never so cut off within her mind. No Gran, calling to her, mind to mind; no Kaiya dropping in unannounced to share a view or image with her; no Sista Sol chattering at her all day. She had grown used to them being there without thinking about it. Now there was just a terrifying silence.

Water was a happy-go-lucky girl. She was conscientious about all around her, knew every plant and animal on Core. She had no friends except the many creatures she had befriended with her aid and kindness. But the silence of her mind was like a deep gash in her. Now, she knew what it was to be truly alone, and she didn't think she liked it.

Water moved slowly through the lower half of Layia's home, just looking and touching, getting acclimated to her environment. There were six separate rooms; each room looked like something specific happened in there. One had a long oak table, which was the focus.

Twenty people could sit here, around this massive table, she guessed as she ran her hand across the top and smiled. The memories showed her there were numerous times twenty or more were seated, eating, and laughing, discussing the day's happenings. It reminds me of mealtime with Gran, cooking the day's catch, ripe fruit picked, pared, and eaten, sitting by the open fire because we both liked cooking outside.

All the things you have taught me have come to this, haven't they, Gran.

One of Water's first memories was of her toddling after Gran while she pointed out plants and their properties. Which ones we ate, which we used for medicines, and which were poisonous. It was second nature for Water.

It had been three months since the ceremony, and she had spent that time wisely, gathering herbs for medicine and preparing them for a long journey. She picked lady's fern - the root and stem for digestive issues and fever; sage and peppermint to help with memory and heal wounds as a paste; Marigold and tea tree for headaches; garlic and thyme for balance and antibacterial use. Many of the herbs she picked and dried could double for spicing up her food. She dried the coconut meat in the sun, smoothed a husk for a water bowl, and created chips from the other shells to start a fire. All this she had done in preparation for her journey. And I thought I was ready, well prepared; she laughed at herself.

"Only prepared to do what I've always done; live off the land." I'm alone, shut off from everyone, she realized. Neither Gran nor Kiaya would respond when she tried to contact them, and Sista Sol was too far away. Sista Sol's program confined her to a 10-mile radius around the house. Water knew they were not with her; she felt it in the silence of her mind.

Suddenly her mind ran on the possibility of harm coming to her. Now that is a crazy thought, she said to herself. Oh, I've had my fair share of bumps and bruises, but never any real damage. Core would not allow it. I am a daredevil. She smiled to herself as she remembered her life on the island. Rock climbing the cliffs, hanging on a two-inch ledge, inches from the top that was just out of her reach. She jumped for the edge, pulling herself up and onto the safety of the ground. Or climbing the tallest spruce tree she could find and scaling its heights just to have a perfect view of a sea of treetops deep in Core. Or she would race up the highest palm to look out to the ocean for miles.

She would wait for the massive leviathans to swim by during the mating season. Gran said they were the legendary sea serpents of days gone by. Water could hear them coming from miles out; they were singing to each other and her. She could communicate with many of the animals on Core. 'But the Leviathans were unique and special; she loved them fiercely. When she heard them coming, she would race down to the lowest edge on the cliff and dive into the ocean, swimming to meet those who had come close to Core to greet her. They could not come to shore; they were too big. Their average weight was three tons, and their span was as great as five-hundred meters. They would swim and play together for hours until the herd leader called out a greeting to her, then called the others back. It was time to continue their journey. Water would kiss each of her friends' good-bye until next season, then watch them until they were out of sight before she turned to swim back to shore. She could hear them singing to her long after she lost sight of them

I'm not so confident that I can't get hurt anymore, she thought, unsure of what was coming. She shook her head and told herself to stop daydreaming and procrastinating.

Stop lollygagging; you DON'T have time for this, she chastised herself. She didn't listen to herself, at least not yet.

In the very next breath, she told herself she had all the time in the world. I have this moment, she reminded herself as she slowly wandered the rooms, touching things that called to her. Water let the parade of memories that resided in the house flow as she walked through them.

Nothing stands out for me, she thought. I see a wisp here of a woman cooking and singing here, or over there, a child in the lap of an elder who was reading a story, but nothing significant, she felt. That is until she stepped into the book room with the big fluffy seat by the stone fire pit and the wall of books. The books didn't just dominate the east wall; they *were* the wall. It stretched twenty feet across and rose to the ceiling. Amazing, she exclaimed. As she turned to see the whole room, she became aware of a memory that seemed to be happening now; or at least it had an intense feeling it was happening now. She looked toward the glass-paned south wall.

Water saw a young girl with long flowing curly coppery brown hair and coconut brown skin standing in this very room. The girl was intensely watching a beam of sunlight travel through the room. The girl was about her age.

What, thought Water, looking at the girl's hair and skin. Both were shimmering with colors of gold, copper, midnight blue, and brown when the light of the sun hit her.

"Wow, like me." I know her, Water exclaimed. The girl felt oddly familiar like she had known her all her life. How can this be? I have never met her and don't even know if she exists in this time or three hundred years ago. Water found herself mimicking the girl's movements as she watched the light's path.

The light fell upon the water of the river miles below the house, striking the surface and sending a beam into the room, where it hit a copper disc and bounced off.

"Astounding," Water uttered, slightly perplexed as she watched the sunbeam in her Sanctuary doing the same thing as the beam of light in the other Sanctuary.

Water and River both looked where the Elon sunlight pointed. Both went to the bookshelf, and there, the dead center was the book the sun had chosen: Paradise Lost. Both stared intently, and both laughed.

"Oh, how wonderful," Water laughed out loud. "I am home, and she is my sister," Water said as she watched the other girl fade.

CHAPTER 13

HIDDEN TRUTH

"**W**HERE DID THAT kid go?" Zebble yelled, steaming with anger.

"Aiya deliberately took her away. She made sure Water was out of my reach," Zebble said, slamming his right fist into his hand as he walked back down the path to the ocean.

"I will leave the same way I came, Kaiya; I DON'T NEED YOU!"

Zebble shouted to the sky, then turned and looked back up the path, crying out at the top of his voice.

"And I'm sure YOU, Aiya, hid that kid from me, acting like you were unaware she was gone from your house, nowhere to be found."

He had walked the entire way down the path in half the time it took to walk up. Partly due to his anger, he was moving fast in his fury.

The other part; because going downhill is always easier than going up.

After that debacle of a meeting, he insisted Aiya bring the girl to him. That's when he found out Water was gone.

"Nobody in that house is talking. I'm sure she's in the interior, and they're feeling safe," he said, talking to no one as he walked across the small dunes and stormed onto his rift.

"Ready the sail, cast off immediately," he shouted to the captain as he came aboard and made his way to the lower level and his main cabin.

They think I can't get her, he said to himself and smiled, then reinforced his cloaking. He didn't want anyone listening in on his thoughts. Zebble knew something they didn't. There is a back way into Core; he knew, he remembered. He entered his quarters and locked the door. Oh yes, I remember, he thought, sitting down at his desk and beginning to cast his mind back in time to when he was a small lad.

No one had ever explored past Core's northern border, the mountain that butted up to the energy field. Zion, the mountain's name, so said those who called it home. They were ancient, the races who lived there. They had been there for thousands of years and stayed mostly to themselves, but not always.

Zet, Zebble's grandfather, did what none on his island ever did. He explored the mountain.

Zet heard stories of the mountain from a man who stayed upon the ocean his whole life. Everyone knew of the mountains. No one ever talked of them, and ninety-nine percent of the islanders would not ever go there. But Zet wasn't like the rest of the islanders. He wanted more. He was never satisfied with what he had. It was not enough for him to be Skaton's island elder. Nor did being the youngest chief elder of all the islands for the last two years satisfy him. It wasn't enough.

Then one evening, when he was sitting in the tavern mulling over his unhappiness, Zet met a man who would change his future.

The old man was well into his nineties and still sailing the ocean alone. He spoke of his travels across Izaria and of the marvels he had seen. He spoke of the ancient race he had lived with, who lived in the mountains north of Izaria. He told how the ancients taught him how to cloak his thoughts, so no one knew what he was thinking and how to create an illusion in someone's mind. He could make them believe what he wanted them to believe.

That old man made a bargain with Zet that night in the tavern, a place to stay through the winter in exchange for teaching him these skills. Zet immediately took Old Dan home, told his wife they had company for three months, then moved his son Zeek and his small family out of his room and into the work shed, which was okay with Zeek. He spent most of his time there anyway, creating exquisite musical instruments, the field he chose five years prior. He was finally getting established as a fine carver of instruments. People paid him now to do what he loved, although Zeek still gave away many of his instruments. He felt music was a key to happiness and thought it should be accessible to all. Zeek was a Master Craftsman, although the title, not his yet.

At twenty, he had been married to Isabella for two years. He had a one-year-old son, Zebble. He was the youngest candidate for a master's title in the Musicians' Academy history. Zeek didn't realize it, nor did it matter to him. He just loved carving beautiful perfect pitch instruments. Isabella took over Zeek's finances when they married, ensuring her family's well being. Zeek was still able to give his work away, thereby making people happy.

She didn't mind the work shed either. It was a larger space, big enough for their bed, Zebble's crib, and a small couch to sit upon. They did most of their cooking and eating outside with everyone else in the household. It was a time to gather and enjoy the repast with family.

After dinner, old man Dan and Zet would sit outside near the ocean's shore warming themselves on the driftwood fire they lit every night at early dusk. Dan would teach Zet the art of cloaking and illusion making. He would tell Zet of his adventure across the islands and beyond. Zet always wanted to hear more about the beyond; it fascinated him.

In particular, one story grabbed his attention and never let go—the legend of the Heart of Kaiya. A stone of immeasurable power was created at the beginning of Izaria by the ancients. The local lore had it, buried somewhere in the foothills of the mountain by an old gnarly pine, just north of Core's force field.

Zet began looking for the bloodstone called the Heart of Kaiya, traveling yearly to the mountain and staying a month. He followed any lead that fit that description. His grandfather's pursuit of this power kept his family in those mountains for years, obsessed with finding the heart. He was always looking for the legendary source of energy, Kaiya's Heart. Each year they traveled by sea for a week. Then by foot, three days to get to the foothills. It was unheard of, traveling on a rift for any reason besides fishing. None of the people would ever think to do that. Zet went to considerable measures to cloak his movements from Kaiya and the people. He wanted no one to know.

"They mustn't find out," Zet said.

In the time of Solitude, Zet took his family into the foothills of mount

Zion and trained his son Zeek and his grandson Zebble in the arts of cloaking their real thoughts and creating illusions in the minds of others.

Zebble had just turned five that season of the sun, right before the time of Solitude began when his grandfather finally found the Heart of Kaiya. They had been in the mountains for about two weeks when their search ended. Zet found the heart and a map leading into the belly of the mountain. Both, lying in a faery-crafted wooden box, buried in a grove of oaks surrounding a gnarly pine lying in a secluded valley, forty clicks into the foothills of the mountain. Zet, stumbling across the root of a dead oak, fell face down into the ground and found himself staring into a crack at the base of the tree struck by lightning several months earlier. The mighty oak, seared down the middle of its trunk, opened up the trunk's roots and exposed a corner of the box. He just finished digging out around the container, loosening the ground that held his treasure, when one of the ancients, a male faery, stumbled into the grove, crying about Kaiya, mumbling about never date an Elon-human

Zet hadn't ever seen a faery before. He sat, amazed by the small man, and as he listened to the story, his amazement grew. He couldn't believe what the faery had said about Kaiya or the container he had just dug out from the charred tree.

Kaiya had told Kasor the night before she didn't want a relationship with him. Kasor had never been rejected so quickly before. Two days into dating and Kaiya said no more dates. It broke his heart, he thought. It was more like his ego. He spent the night drinking too much nectar and was still inebriated when he found Zet.

"She will crush your heart," Kasor had sobbed to Zet.

Zet realized he had found the legendary bloodstone, the Heart of Kaiya. He sat staring at the open box encased in a substance he couldn't crack. Inside that beautifully crafted, small, wooden faery chest sat a map and a brilliant red stone, its center glowing like a piece of the sun. The heart of Kaiya, the faery had said.

Zet wanted to possess this stone, keep it for himself. As Kasor the faery stumbled away, still weeping Kaiya, Zet finished bringing his treasure to the surface and took it with him, away from the mountain. The next morning Kasor realized he had told Zet many things that he probably shouldn't have. He had drunk too much nectar the previous night, crying over Kaiya leaving him. He had a different perspective that morning. Faeries were not known for having lasting relationships. Friendships, yes, relationships, ahh no, not really. Kasor had already forgotten his broken heart, moving on to greener pastures, as he told himself. But Queen Aziel would not let Kasor be remiss in his responsibility for messing up the time continuum that day. Of course, no one else but the faeries knew how bad they had messed up, and they weren't telling anyone.

"Kasor!" rebuked Queen Aziel when she found out later that day, "What have you done?"

"I'm not quite sure," Kasor softly spoke, head swirling, swearing off of nectar forever.

"Go find out now," Aziel commanded. Kasor, now compelled to comply, jumped to the future and jumped back.

"Well," Kasor hedged slightly and then continued. "It's fixable, but it will take a while," showing his queen the time frame he suspected it would take to bring the continuum around.

Aziel raised her eyebrows high, shook her head, and said, "You better get started. Fix this mess," was her last command to Kasor.

It's going to take some time, Kasor said to himself. I better get busy. Their plans were usually accomplished over eons—a drop in the bucket to faeries.

CHAPTER 14

THE KEY

SEVEN MONTHS AGO, Izen's luck changed. A young illegal from the lower paths knew Laiya's math.

His spies had discovered this kid named Seeca from the bowels, writing mathematical symbols from the twenty-first century, the lost art of quantum math, on his Note. That triggered a more in-depth look at him. Izen had whisked the boy out of the bowels and placed him in a conk on the middle level. The kid's every move was recorded and analyzed by a team of experts.

The kid now says he needs the key to go forward. Izen pondered this sitting at his desk, leaning back on his chair. His spies knew a lot, but they didn't know everything. No one knew what the key was or what it unlocked, only the coordinates the kid had given the guard, telling the man he needed to go there. It was outside the City.

"The key, the key, what is the key," Izen pushed forward in his chair and pounded his fist on the desk.

"JIVE," Izen called out.

"Sir," responded JIVE.

Exasperated, Izen asked JIVE, "Exactly where is this place the kid says he needs to be, and what is it he thinks he will find?"

"From my conversations with the lad, he says he will find a way into the in-between there."

"What is he talking about, 'the in-between'?" Izen was beginning to think the kid was a waste of his time.

"I think that is just his way of explaining what he sees. You, sir, would call it a different dimension," Jive stated.

That caught Izen's attention.

"Another dimension? Can that kid get me to another dimension? Where are the coordinates, JIVE?"

"The exact coordinates are forty miles into the foothills of the Argot Mountains, sir," JIVE responded.

"I'll bet it's the same place River is heading to," he mumbled, not realizing he was speaking out loud to himself. Izen was calculating the odds of killing two birds with one stone.

"She's headed that way too, I know it." Hmm, maybe I don't kill this kid right out, he thought. I'll see if he can earn his keep until he meets with an unfortunate accident.

"Ok, JIVE, find out what needs to be done and make it so. Have this kid and my son, along with Jenkins, prepare for the trip. In six days, I want them all at those coordinates in the mountains, whatever it takes. Tell Jenkins he must guard the kid at all times. They leave in thirty-six hours." Izen commanded.

"Oh yeah - prepare a team to bring supplies in advance of their arrival. That team leaves in twelve hours with the supplies needed, including mini hoovers to get to the coordinates the kid provided. Their drop point will be close to the foothills. Find someone who knows the area; there must be *someone*," Izen exclaimed.

"Yes, sir."

Now the kid finally gave me a way to find the key and get my hands-on, River. He said to himself, calculating what he needed to do.

"I'll send someone to greet her," he sneered, knowing what he meant by someone. "Who could that be," he questioned once again. I know, he said and rose from the chair.

He sent two commands to JIVE.

"JIVE remove Sanctuary holo, replace it with my office, and call the Pearl. I have a job for him."

Izen thought of himself as the best of the best. His home rested high above the drudgery of the cities' masses. He had been going over the estimated profits for the expansion into the solar system for minerals. Once he became the next heir, he would become privy to all. He expected to quadruple his net worth in the first nine months of production. It was the mining rights and the rights to the other worlds he was after; he was sure the jumps could move him to the next level of intergalactic wealth. *That will secure my future for the next millennium*, the concept of so much wealth gleefully playing in his mind.

The advancements in age therapy's capabilities have come in astounding leaps and bounds, he thought. *Of course, only those qualified could receive it.* Izen laughed at that; he had made sure he qualified with a hefty endowment.

I intend to be here for a very long time, and that girl is not going to get in my way.

CHAPTER 15

WHAT DID WE CREATE?

"*WHAT IS YOUR say on Izaria?*" Abby asked.

"*It goes as predicted; there are many possible futures, pick one,*" Laiya said.

"*You are funny, sister. You have already chosen the path you create,*" Kaiya put in her two cents.

"*Humph, I am creating as we go, sisters.*"

Both Kaiya and Abby laughed and said together, "*It has always been so with you, LayLay.*"

It fascinates the old ones, the chaos your species adores, sang Abby to her sisters, mind-to-mind. *Even in your physics, you prefer the mess of the plunks over the natural flow of the Universe. We are violent in our birth and death, and our worlds reflect all aspects of us, we who give in light and dark. We flow with the universe, all banded together on that 'highway' you found. There is no distance nor time between us. There is only now.*

The old ones are undecided about whether to allow your species to travel that highway. It is a huge decision. Aldebaran speaks of those of your species, which are already here. He is now waiting for all the Elon to wake. It has gone out in the song, the story we tell, asking all to wake and listen. Abby continued mind speaking to her sisters, telling all she knew.

Senjo, the oldest, is listening to the song, something he has not done in 2 billion of your years.

I wonder what he'll say when he knows he USED to be a catalog reference number with humans, Abby said, smiling. "SMSS J031300.36-670839.3," I believe he will find humor in that. They are singing of us, my sisters. We are new in the universe; we three who became one.

CHAPTER 16

ZEBBLE

ZET NEVER TOOK the box back to his island after the first year.
"Too risky," Zet said, "Kaiya might feel it gone from the mountain. We keep it here until we take the control away from her."

They left the box in the exact place Zet had found it when they left each year, Not sure if the faeries would take it from him or not.

His grandson, Zebble, accidentally discovered how to break the seal and open the faerie box.

The Karat, one of the most potent musical instruments Zeek ever created and Izaria's musical treasure, was carved from driftwood he had found lying on the beach. A wood no one on Izaria had ever seen before, a red-streaked ebony hardwood. There were no trees like this on the island. It must have come from Core, Zeek surmised. He had been carving musical instruments from wood for over forty years since he was a young boy. It was his obsession. He had never seen this kind of wood before - not anywhere, on any of the islands.

Zeek had a natural talent; he could find the harmony inside the wood and make a pitch-perfect instrument. But this wood was almost too hard to carve. He had searched the shores and caves for Stardust, the one substance he knew would allow him to cut into this wood. Zeek had almost given up in despair, so rare was the mineral he sought.

His six-year-old son Zebble brought him his treasure. He had found it exploring deep in the crystal caves one day at low tide.

These caves were dangerous. Zebble knew that deep within the cave was a treasure of stones and crystals brought in with the current. The downside of exploring this cave, Zebble remembered, was that you had to keep track of time internally, for you could not see the sun. He knew if he got caught unaware at high tide, he would drown.

Zebble went deep into the crystal cave that day despite knowing this. He couldn't say why he traveled so far into the cave looking for crystals and gemstones; he knew the danger of getting lost and drowning. But his instincts told him to keep moving deeper into the cave and pulled him along to whatever awaited.

Hours later, having found nothing of value, he felt the changing of the tide. He had to hustle back quickly; he had spent too much time there. He turned around, retracing his step, disappointed, he had not discovered anything of importance. When out of the corner of his eye, he saw something shimmer. He hesitated for a moment, knowing he was cutting it close, but he had to see what it was and ran to find out. When he saw it, he knew right away what it was. He hurriedly dug the precious mineral out and tucked it into the waterproof bag tied around his neck. He ran through the cave, sprinting for the shallow cove at the entrance.

The water was no longer shallow when he reached there; it was waist high and rising, the tide rushing in. Zebble was a strong swimmer and an expert diver. He knew he had to get out now or drown in that cave. He timed the next wave coming in and dove over it. Then he dove under the current, scraping the bottom of the cave floor, pulling himself out of the entrance against the tide. He kicked against the rushing waters of the tide to the surface. He swam to shore, exhausted and grateful to be laying on the land and not floating face down in the water until the tide changed and washed him out to sea, fish bait.

Zebble shuddered at that thought. It had been close, he thought, elated as he reached out to touch the bag around his neck.

"I have Stardust," he shouted with glee, looking at the mineral.

His dad would forge his new instrument, Zebble thought as he laughed, watching the Stardust shimmer like the night skies in his bag, feeling exhilarated.

"It's Stardust," he laughed. "My father said it is the only mineral on Izaria that, once he forged it, would be strong enough to carve that hardwood he found. And I will be the one to bring it to him," he finished with pride. Zebble loved his father's gentle and distracted ways, absentminded musical genius.

Zeek was overjoyed when Zebble presented his pouch to his father. He hugged his son, ran to his shop, stopped, ran back, and wordlessly hugged the boy again. Zebble smiled; that was his father.

I'll never tell him how near to death I came for his Stardust, Zebble vowed as he watched his father running to his shop. He never did, and Zeek never asked. But Zet saw. And he conveyed his pride in Zebble, achieving his goal at such high risk. Zebbles' age was deceptive, mature beyond his six-years. He had to be with Zet as his grandfather. Zet was a hard taskmaster and a maniacal genius.

It took Zeek months of painstaking work before he finally achieved perfection and created his new instrument, the Karat. You played it by blowing air gently through the hole at the instrument's top, creating sound. The moment he played it, he knew this was the music of the stars.

Zebble had been rambling through these memories as he sailed away from the shores of Core. Aiya had given the elders only the choice of how they would leave, not whether they would. Either Kaiya would jump them home, or they could board their rifts and sail back the way they came. All the other elders except Zebble had elected to jump back to their home islands.

"Oh, I know a way into your precious Core, alright," Zebble sneered, "I created it."

He was showing his hand. He did not allow Kaiya to jump him from Core. He sailed from Core to Indigo, Wiffle's island, on the sleek water rift he had commissioned the master rift builder to make six months ago. Then to Mount Zion, Zebble thought with determination. He was ready to seek the promise of power in the belly of the mountain. His newly commissioned rift, designed to travel with ease over long distances, was the first of its kind on Izaria. He had another rift carrying the supplies and ground transportation.

"I will never use you to travel again, Kaiya, do you hear me? Your rule is soon over; it's my turn," he said to the sky and waited. "Just like I thought, no response. Not talking again," he said sarcastically, knowing she was watching and could hear everything he said as he sailed away from Core.

There was one memory he shrouded, allowing no one into this memory but himself. He was his seven-year-old self, seeing and feeling it as if he were there again at the very moment.

Zebble and his family had been in the mountains on the edge of Core for almost two weeks. Zebble was turning seven years old that very next day. Zet had watched his grandson practicing the arts and noticed Zebble had a natural ability to create illusions.

On the day Zebble turned seven years of age, Zet said to his grandson, "Zebble, it is to you I will leave this mantle. You will live to see the ending of Kaiya and the beginning of our dynasty. I changed history in the minds of some of the people using the abilities I have been teaching you since you started speaking. I feel we can create the illusion that Kaiya is a god in need of worship. Stop the tribes from talking to her every day."

Zebble rarely interrupted his grandfather when he was talking; it wasn't worth the pain. But he didn't understand why his grandfather was talking about Kaiya that way.

"I can tell it is you who walks in my footsteps. Sit down, boy, and I will tell you the real story of our world, and who Kaiya is," his grandfather had said to him that fateful day. Zebble's world changed when his grandfather finished his story. From that day forward, Zet's mission became Zebble's. A week later, his head was still spinning with the knowledge of who Kaiya was.

They had come in the month of Sun, rather than the Time of Solitude. It was warmer that month. His grandfather was getting old. His father did not think they would be back this way again after that year. Grandfather still felt if he could just crack the force field around the box, that energy could give him strength, immortality, and more power. The bloodstone's energy stayed with Zet in a weakened form even when he left it buried in the mountains. He craved more. Zet wanted it all.

Zebble remembered the day he cracked the force field around the faery box holding the Heart of Kaiya.

Father watched me and spoke on the lessons of cloaking thought and creating illusions when he stopped and walked to the force field surrounding Core, reaching for it. His father had just realized that the material encasing the box and the force field surrounding Core were similar. I figured that out last year, Zebble said to himself as he saw the realization sink into his father's brain. Zebble had told his grandfather his discovery a year ago. Why didn't I tell dad too, Zebble wondered?

Zet, Zeek, and Zebble - father, son, and grandson - finished the day sitting by their small campfire. Zeek played his music, and Zet was absorbed yet again studying the bloodstone. Young Zebble was staring first at Core's barrier, shimmering like an electric force field, as far as he could tell. He could always see the invisible barrier surrounding Core. No one believed him, though, saying it was his overactive imagination. So, he kept his sight to himself.

But that night, something felt different, almost magical. Zebble looked at the barrier, then looked down at the ebony Karat on the ground before his father.

The instrument, lying so close to the fire's edge, reflected the flames in the polished black wood, turning the Karat into fire flames of copper, cobalt blue, yellows, and oranges. It seemed to call him. Fascinated by this display of light and fire, Zebble reached out, picked up the instrument, stood and faced Core, and began to play. The moon overhead, full and a rare blood-red, felt warm and inviting to him. He played for the moon and played for Core. It was music never heard before. Zebble was not aware of what he played; he was somewhere else in his mind. He felt the moon speaking and the Karat calling. His father stopped talking, entranced by what he heard, and looked upon his son playing the karat with such precision tonal balance. Zeek felt the vibration in his very soul.

Three things happened that night.

First, Kaiya's heart resting in the box in front of his grandfather, bathed by the light of the fire, came to life. It resonated with the Karat, shattering the force field substance encasing the box.

Second, the barrier surrounding Core began resonating with the Karat as well. The whole of Core was vibrating to the song, cracking the electrical substance that surrounded Core. That substance shimmered with energy yet felt solid. Seven-year-old Zebble stopped playing and stared at the crack in Core's shield, awestruck.

He saw fission began along the bottom, starting somewhere beneath the ground and reaching six feet up. He turned to his grandfather, whose hand had just wrapped around the glowing stone in the box.

"Grandfather, do you see," Zebble said excitedly.

His grandfather never looked up, never saw the breach in Core. Zet touched the stone, and his body lurched forward, glowing like red fire. The heart of Kaiya slid from his hand back to its resting place in the box. His grandfather did not move; Zet's spirit left his body. Kaiya's Heart killed Zet.

That remained forever etched in Zebble's mind. Shocked, Zebble screamed out in his mind.

YOU KILLED MY GRANDFATHER! He knew he had awakened Kaiya's awareness, and she looked his way. He did not care. His grandfather was dead.

Zeek backed away from the power of the stone, never wanting to touch it or use it. Not Zebble, though. He craved to find a way to hold the Heart of Kaiya and absorb the energy and not die like his grandfather.

Legend said two bloodstones had the power of the stars, and he that wielded it could rule the world. Zebble realized his grandfather had one of the legendary bloodstones. From that day forward, Zebble knew he was the one: he would rule. A tiny fracture was all. It was a start, the crack in the shield of Core.

His father never went back to the mountain, nor did Zebble while his father lived. But Zebble never forgot the small break in the protection of Core. It was the beginning and end of Zebble. From that point, his desire was for the power of Core and the Heart of Kaiya. Zebble upheld his father's wishes and did not go back to the mountain while he was alive. He had spent those years wisely working on his plan. He consolidated his power, began a takeover for control of all within the tribes, and achieved it. He worked daily with his mind and honed the skills his grandfather had taught him. Using the stone's blunted power in the box, he increased his cloak abilities and created illusions thousand-fold stronger.

Zebble smiled. Now all the tribes but two believed Kaiya no longer wished to speak with any of them. Instead, they were taught to worship her, she who gave them life. Using the power of the bloodstone, he had wiped memories of nearly all the tribes. Replacing the truth with an illusion, Zebble convinced the people Kaiya's silence was their fault. They needed to worship her. And he was the Supreme Elder. The people firmly believed the illusions Zebble fed them. Only to him would Kaiya speak. And I, of course, Zebble said to himself, preening in front of his full-length mirror, will speak for the people. I am their leader.

His due diligence had got him this far. Now he wanted the full power of this bloodstone and the map his grandfather had found buried in the oak grove. He was ready. It was time.

Zebble inherited the Karat and the bloodstone when his father had died. After his death, Zebble went to the mountain again in a time of solitude. Like his grandfather had, when no one would be the wiser, he worked on his skills, honing them to perfection. For three years, he traveled to the oak grove, where his grandfather had reburied the box. Heeding his grandfather's words, he would only take it from the woods when he was ready to find the gate. The map, buried with the faery box that held the bloodstone, was at the oak's base directly east of the old pine. It spoke of a hidden treasure deep within Zion, a gate between two worlds in the belly of this mountain. Still, Zebble never found any mention of a gate in any of the shared memories. He had glimpsed something in the mind of the Indigo elder, Soin, Wiffle's predecessor, right before he passed on to Kaiya.

It's intriguing, Zebble thought. "I just can't make sense of it yet," he said aloud.

Soin's memory was of his ancestor, who Kaiya brought to Izaria without a mind wipe. The ancestor knew who he was and where he came from, although it seemed like the time frames were different. This elder talked of a dying planet and the gate between the worlds deep within Zion's belly, protected by Solomon's seal and the Gate of Primrose. Zebble knew Zion was the mountain's name, but could it also be a destination on that mountain; he wasn't sure which. He would have to find out. And what is the Gate of Primrose? What does it look like, and where was it on this forsaken mountain? What world was dying? And what does that mean to me, asked Zebble?

He knew the map his grandfather had buried would give him answers. He knew where to go, and he knew where she would be. He would be waiting. Neither Zet nor Zebble understood the coded message that was in the box with the heart. Zeek never touched it after his father died, nor allowed Zebble to either. It had killed his father, and Zeek said he wanted nothing to do with it. They could easily see the message, and Zeek had deciphered the message, but they did not understand it.

"Until now," said Zebble, as he came back from that memory, "Water is the key."

The cryptic message within the bloodstone box read,

When stars that fall from the sky become human, Kaiya's heart will be known. The colors of the blue Elon upon her, and red upon her twin. The key will lie within.

"Water is the key," Zebble said again, thinking of her shimmering blue hair and skin. He didn't know anything about a twin, and he didn't care. Dismissing that part of the note, he says, "Never know what Aiya hides on that island."

Standing on his ship's deck, Zebble watched Core disappear on the horizon, dismissing both Core and Aiya from his thoughts. I don't know about Wiffle, though. Soin could have told him something before he died. Zebble caught a wisp of thought from Soin and the image of an entrance to a cavern from Wiffle. It's as if Wiffle knew Zion. But, he has shut his mind to me and says nothing. I don't trust that kid. He's too curious, asks too many questions, and is too quiet of mind, Zebble thought as he sailed to Wiffle's home site Indigo.

Zebble was in his cabin, standing in front of a large table. All the converts' reconnaissance maps of Izaria, thrown on top of the table. For the last five years, Zebble had sent a few faithful followers out, mapping all Izaria. He was studying those maps, for the first time, seeing the layout of the lands. No one in Izaria had ever thought about distances between islands; Kaiya jumped them everywhere. The range wasn't even a thought. Looking at the maps, Zebble could see the distance from Indigo to Core.

"Not far, he said, "strategically sound location." But they've always been strong supporters of Aiya and have a long-lasting relationship with Kaiya as friends, he noted. Not as worshippers, Zebble thought, like I have taught most the people to be. I'm not sure now if Wiffle's tribe hasn't been speaking with Kaiya all along. I might have to rethink this. It might have been a mistake thinking so little of that tribe. I dismissed Wiffle's tribe as small and unimportant and had never wiped anyone's mind from Indigo. Now, why did I do that? Zebble questioned, never thinking he had been guided himself by Soin to dismiss Indigo as insignificant. He couldn't remember why he hadn't mind-wiped the population of Indigo. I need to investigate that island a little deeper, he said and dismissed them once again.

It took fifty years of rumors and subtle illusions placed in the people's minds for the lie to set in. One hundred years later, and it's the truth. And now, one-hundred and fifty years later, it is their way, Zebble laughed. My family did this, bragged Zebble, changed their history, just like Kaiya changed ours when she dropped the firsters on this planet and wiped their minds. And now their future is mine. He laughed again.

Zebble walked onto the deck of his sleek ocean runner and breathed deep the air. He stopped laughing, remembering Indigo, The island he skipped over as insignificant, and unsure why he did. This is no time for missed details; he said to himself as he looked out over the water. I'll soon be on that island. Then I'll see what I might have to do.

"I am like Kaiya; I am supreme," Zebble preened and spoke out loud, "I will rule."

In seven months, with the pact's changing, Zebble intended to seize control of Core, eliminate the old lady, and rule Izaria. The only thing that might be a problem for him was Water, and how was it that she was the key.

"If she does not conform to my will, I will destroy her," he said aloud, knowing he would follow through with that threat. Nothing could go wrong at this juncture. Zebble's family had been planning this for decades. The time of change was near — With winter's death came the ending of the pact. Zebble felt Kaiya had given him no choice after almost three-hundred-years of her guidance.

"Her iron-fisted rule, more like it," sneered Zebble. So well trained are the people to feel she guides rather than rules with an iron fist; they're so gullible," he thought with disdain. "But my grandfather knew better," cackled Zebble. So, she hadn't spoken in one-hundred and fifty years, so what, thought Zebble. She had not talked since his family started brainwashing the peoples. And now, I have control of their lives and will guide them with an iron fist they can believe. Now it was time to bring in the elders, Zebble thought. They take control of the people, and he would control the elders.

"Perfect," was all Zebble could say. He was ready.

CHAPTER 17

＊———◇———＊

THE PEARL

"**I** HEARD YOU WERE looking for me."

Izen dropped the glass in his hands as he spun around to find The Pearl standing in his home.

"How did you get in here?" Izen demanded.

"Not your concern, One last time: I heard you are looking for me."

Like everyone in the Cities, Izen knew of the Pearl. Although few had met the Pearl in person, his reputation preceded him. Izen knew the name, not the man. Izen had used his services a couple of times and thought little of the man. He's just another bowel runner, Izen thought, angry the Pearl had breached his home so casually and spoke as if he, Izen, were beneath him.

And therein lied his first mistake. Knowing of The Pearl was not the same thing as knowing him. In Izen's arrogance, he was ignorant, more like stupid — it was dangerous to be stupid around the Pearl; people disappear right after an encounter with him.

The Pearl was known everywhere in the Cities, but no one knew where he resided, how he came or went, or where he would show up. No one asked. And most felt the less they knew of him, the better. He trusted few and called no man on Rake, friend. The Pearl could slide in and out of places, be gone before you knew he was there. If you were The Pearl's target, you were as good as dead. Nothing could save you, and no one would protect you. Trying to stop the Pearl from his goal, just put a target on your back.

Izen's second mistake was to look at the Pearl and dismiss him.

"You should never turn your back on a cobra, Izen. But of course, you don't know what a cobra is, now do you?"

Izen stared blankly at the Pearl; he had no idea what he was talking about.

"What is it you want, Izen?"

The Pearl was a man of few words and did not take kindly to anyone who beat around the bush. If you irritated him enough, you would find yourself outside hanging from the side of a very tall building on a very short rope. You would more than likely die hanging there, for there were no windows to look out of, and no one ever went outside. And the Pearl would remind you of that as he tied you down. He did not play.

"Jive," Izen called out, "Replace Sanctuary holo with my office and check the security; I want to know how this man got into my home." He adjusted his clothes, giving himself time to regain his composure and his attitude as JIVE changed the holograph to Izen's office.

Damn, who is this man, Izen thought. "Look, I require the service of a man like you." He said, walking around his office desk, moving away from the Pearl, using the desk as a barrier between them.

"What kind of man is that Izen of Laiya's seed?" The Pearl asked, distaste and disdain dripping from his voice.

The Pearl walked closer to the desk and placed his hands on the edge for ten seconds, then let go and sat down in the chair opposite Izen, casually crossing his legs bent at the knee.

WHO is this man? Izen was flabbergasted and irritated. He did not like The Pearl's condescending tone. How dare he? I am the elite of the elite, who is this man to talk to me so, Izen fumed to himself, miffed at this arrogant man sitting in front of him.

The Pearl cocked his head to the side slightly and smiled a feral smile.

"I am who I am; that is how I dare."

Did he just read my mind, questioned Izen? No, he couldn't, he thought, it's just a coincidence, and dismissed the idea.

"Look here," Izen began in a tone meant to rebuke the Pearl, then he stumbled over his next words, unable to get his tongue moving right.

Looking at the Pearl eye-to-eye, Izen meant to intimidate him, as he always did with anyone with whom he did business. Instead, what Izen saw frightened him. The man saw right through Izen, knew him for who he was.

In the eyes of the Pearl were the trials of a man over hundreds of years. Izen, however, only saw the eyes of a cold-blooded killer. The Pearl was a chameleon. He only showed what he wanted you to see. No one came away from an encounter with the Pearl with the same description of him.

"Ah, I'm, uh, I need, well," Izen cleared his throat. He stood there silently, looking at The Pearl, getting the first clue that he might have made a mistake in underestimating The man. Izen did not like this feeling; he had never been afraid of anyone or anything.

WHO IS THIS MAN? He cringed.

"I, I understand, you know about outside."

Izen waited for the Pearl to acknowledge him; he was unsure what to do when he did not.

The Pearl watched Izen fidget, watched the realization sinking in for Izen that he, the Pearl, was a dangerous man. The Pearl smiled that feral smile again. He had seen that same look before on many a man.

Bolstering his courage and rushing on, Izen said, "I need a tracker who has been out of the Cities. I need a girl tracked. She will come out of the encased land on the far northern side at the mountain's base. She will be searching for or going to a place called Primrose Gate."

The Pearl lifted an eyebrow ever so slightly at this information. Izen did not take notice.

"She might have had as much as three days head start, and she moves through the restricted area without trouble; River's protected there. She will come out close to the gap they call Lion's Roar. Track her, find her, watch her, and bring to me what she acquires; her if possible, but not necessary. Her life is of no matter. I do not care what you have to spend; what you have to do to accomplish this, get it done."

"In return?" asked the Pearl.

"In return, I am offering 2% futures, invested in off-world mining rights."

Let him about that, smirked Izen, feeling like he was on familiar territory again. Izen knew money talked.

"All expenses paid carte blanche, plus 350,000 chips deposited into an account of your choosing one hour after a bond is signed. You have two months to achieve this or lose everything, including your reputation," sneered Izen, feeling like he was once again in control.

"You offer a lucrative incentive and then a threat. Interesting way to do business, Izen," said the Pearl as he turned to leave. "My word is my bond. I will track the girl. I will leave within the hour. Have everything ready, including my 350,000 chips."

"I can get you close to the encased land," Izen said, dismissing the Pearl.

"No. One hour." With that, The Pearl was gone.

A strange man thought Izen. He knew the name the Pearl had been around for at least a hundred years, maybe more. He couldn't be the same man, could he Izen said to himself. He doesn't look that old. Izen wonder if the Pearl had an anti-aging serum, not on the open market?

"JIVE," Izen called out with anger. "How did that man get into my home without my being aware? I want you to do a complete systems check, look for backdoors into the security. Never do I want this to happen again."

"Yes, sir, I will start on that now."

I will finish him when he ends this job. Izen leaned back in his chair, plopped his feet on his desk, and plotted the best way to seek his revenge on the Pearl.

It had taken the Pearl twenty-four hours to gather what he needed. Then he contacted his co-conspirator.

Bossman, you listening? The Pearl asked.

I am, came the reply

Izen is bold, boss. Stupid, but bold.

Yes, he has ventured far. He presumes much, which is to our advantage.

He intends to mine the local solar system and branch out across the universe; not going to happen, Aldebaran said absentmindedly, thinking on another subject. *That young man Izen found and squirreled away; he is quite capable. I foresee a great future for him. What's his name, Seeca, right.?"*

Yeah, Bossman, that's his name, but whose side is the kid on?

Ours, I see it. Would you kindly refrain from calling me bossman? That title belongs solely to your mate. Aldebaran laughed and broke the connection

The Pearl chuckled. You are right about that, Al.

CHAPTER 18

THE WAY IN

RIVER WOKE THAT next morning, ready to begin. She felt so good thinking about the sun striking that specific book, her inside joke with Grams. Grams often spoke of ancient authors and their writings. Paradise Lost was one of the books she and Grams would read together. River knew this book well. We joked all the time about being kicked out of paradise and working on getting back there. River smiled. Even though she could not reach Gram, she knew she was with her. Who but Gram could set up that scene? She wondered how long it had taken her to place everything just so. What had she put in the water to get such a full reflection off the surface of the water? And such a tight beam of light, like a laser? River was curious. I will ask Gram when I see her. It never occurred to her that it was to her the sun responded, and not a trick set up by her gram.

Last night she had opened the book, and a paper slipped out. On it was strange writing and symbols that glowed in holo imagery. On parchment paper, no less. This paper dates somewhere around the 21st century, she thought, scrutinizing the article. But it looked as if it were written yesterday, not three centuries ago. She couldn't make sense of the words written in ancient English. Gram could speak English and write it; River never tried. It seemed vaguely familiar, like she could almost read it and do the math too. Where have I seen this before? River asked herself, examining the equation.

"Oh yeah, on Grams work desk at the compound," she said absentmindedly, thinking aloud. River remembered she was doing some complicated math for an experiment, and the side notes were in old English. "Gram said she would teach me another day. That day never came. Now I wish I would have looked a little closer," she sighed.

The parchment was impressive, but she needed time to decipher it, and right now was not the time. It looked like old English, but she wasn't sure. In the book lay hidden a key made of exotic metal and a blueprint. River had no idea what lock the key fit, so she dismissed it for the moment. The diagram held her interest, though; it looked like a blueprint of this house, River concluded. Gram had her design a place for them; two bedrooms and a level made below the home, she called a basement, scaled to size. It took River six months to create a home for them on holo that wouldn't fall apart. Then Gram had given her a sheet of rare paper and showed her how to make a blueprint. We were to begin building this summer. Not anymore, thought River,

"You set me up, Grams, and probably not for the last time on this adventure either," she said aloud to no one.

When it came to Grams, be prepared for anything, she always thought out of the box. Bet I am the only person on Rake that can read a blueprint or build a home with something called a basement. At least on paper anyway, she laughed to herself. I'm pretty sure I'm looking at this house. River was hesitant to say she is 100% positive. The layouts of the first floor are the same, except there was an extra room not visible. Now that's strange, she thought. Something's off with the house. The blueprint shows a place that should be where that bookshelf is, River thought, pointing to the wall.

"It's hidden behind the shelf," she said. "Why? More importantly, how do I get into it?"

Her excitement was growing. How fun, a secret place, and I'm going to find it. She began exploring the house for a concealed door. Four hours later, River was back in the library. I've looked in every nook and cranny of this entire house, bottom to top, and can't find the entrance. Anywhere. This house is BIG. I came full circle and found nothing. I'm back where I started, the great room. She sat down crossed-legged on the floor, facing the bookshelf, contemplating the possibilities, and biting on her bottom lip, as she always did when she was thinking. Biting her bottom lip and speaking aloud to herself, two habits she displayed when problem-solving. River spent a lot of time alone growing up, and it helped to hear a voice, even if it was just hers.

"Where are you?" River pondered as she sat upon the floor, staring at the bookshelf, her pack open in front of her. She absentmindedly took out a power bar, tore it open, and began eating. She was reflecting on what she knew about this house. If I were hiding something as big as a room with a staircase, how would I get into it without a door? A secret panel that slides, perhaps? It's behind the wall of books that much I know. Maybe Paradise Lost was more than a hiding place for the blueprint and key. Maybe it hides the way in, she speculated. River took the book down from the shelf and examined it again but could not see anything that helped her find a door. After reviewing the book thoroughly, she saw no new paragraphs written in a different font, no hints on the cover, no hidden compartment with directions showing how to get in the room. There was no door on the blueprint either.

"I'm out of luck," River said, replacing Paradise Lost into the cubby.

With the book midway in, she stopped and looked intently at the cubby. That's deep dark space; you could hide something in there, River reasoned. What if, she thought, taking the book back out and reaching in, searching for something, anything. She felt it. In the back of the cubby, a small indention in the wall. Not sure what it did, she placed her finger upon it and pushed.

"Hey! Let go of my hand!"

Suddenly, it felt like the indentation enlarged, taking River's whole hand with it. She could not pull her hand out, the grip too firm. River, giving rise to the panic she felt, yelled again,

"Let go of my hand!"

"Scanning"

"What?"

"Hold still, please."

"JIVE, is that you," River hesitantly asked? Her hand was still in the grip of the wall, and no amount of struggle would release it. But that sounded a lot like a female JIVE.

Had Gram programmed this house bot, too?

"DNA recognized: Laiya's seed, River; access granted."

Whoosh, her hand was released. She hurriedly yanked it out, examining it for cuts or marks and finding none. Then the books began to move.

"Oh wow, would you look at this," River said aloud, smiling as the bookshelf slid open to reveal a 22nd-century room.

"There's the staircase," she said when she saw the stairs at the opposite end of the room. And the spiral one the blueprint shows," she smiled. It led up through the ceiling to the next floor. "Yep, a good place to hide a door," she said.

She could not stop grinning. She had found the hidden room! It was the only room in the house with technology past the 21st century. Complete with a computer from that era too, she noticed

"All day, I've been searching for you. Oh, you hide so well." She was so ready to explore, barely controlling the desire to run in and touch everything. "This place is extreme," River said as she ogled the room in awe.

The furniture was three hundred years old; an antique wood desk, an Edison lamp, and an old computer. It looked like it might have been a top-of-the-line 2160 hologram computer. I wonder if that still works. Everything in this house seemed functional, she mused, remembering her night in the house last evening. River had tried a few knobs on walls that brought on light or brought forth water, as she discovered this morning looking for a cleansing station. She figured the way she cleansed and what they did three centuries ago might be entirely different from each other. She was correct; she had searched for the cleansing unit and hadn't found one.

It took her a moment to figure out the waste disposal. All the rooms on the second level had the same structure and furnishings mostly, differing in size only. The two chambers were different. In one, she discovered a sizable free-standing tub. When she turned the knob of the structure sticking out from the top of the basin, water came out. Hot and cold. There was a separate enclosed tiled room that sprayed hot and cold water too. Also, something you sit on that flushes water away when you stand. They must have used water to wash with, and abundantly, she thought, a little shocked. Water was a commodity on Rake.

River was surprised these cleansers still operated, as they hadn't been used for cleansing in hundreds of years. Where is the water coming from? Because she noticed the bowl always replenished itself after she flushed. A lot different from stepping into the cleanser of today; fifteen seconds later, you and your clothes were both clean. She laughed. Which made her stop and think: how did she wash her clothes here?.

What was that River asked? That noise seemed to come from outside on the deck. Suddenly alert, she thought to herself, no one is supposed to be here. I'm in Sanctuary. She reminded herself, no one gets in here who is not both family and friend, and Bubble decides who fits that description. And no harm can befall anyone welcome on the land—Bubble's rules, she reassured herself. But not wholly, as she wondered, did Izen find a way into Sanctuary.? Can he get to me? Had he come for the formula she just discovered?

Spooked, she said out loud, "How does this door close?"

"Door closing."

"Well," said River, a little surprised, "That was easy."

She left the room, making sure the door was sealed completely. She was taking no chances. This room was her secret. She walked from the library, peering around the corner, looking. Where did that sound come from, she asked, creeping to the front door. Extending her senses, she listened, searching for the noise that disturbed her. There, on the right side of the house, I hear it again. She moved to that side of the house with stealth and peered out the pane.

Who is that old man standing alongside the house, complaining to no one?

"Why do I come and see my flowers looking like King Kong walked through them?" He looked up and saw the curtain drop. "Who's in the house? Hey, who are you? Whatcha doing in there? You the one stomping through my flowers?"

Oh no, now what do I do? River panicked, feeling caught. There was no place to run. She was unfamiliar with the house and the surrounding land. He's not an uncle; he didn't look like one, sizing the man up quickly and efficiently. Well, maybe, she thought. He does resemble the old guy Grams was talking to the night of the Naming fiasco, Eldar Wizard, the one Grams was conspiring with. I wonder if this old man is related to that old man; she was curious about the resemblance.

"No harm, only family and friends," she reminded herself quietly under her breath. Gram had told her help could come in unexpected places. So could trouble, River reminded herself.

✦   ✦   ✦

Water had just watched the girl find a hidden room in the other Sanctuary. The entrance should be here, as well, she guessed. Something had disturbed the girl there in her Sanctuary, and the vision faded. Water knew she was watching this in real-time. I am watching my sister. She let that realization sink in — neither past nor future, but here and now. She spent the morning exploring the house, visiting with the memories that flooded this home. She was looking for any clue that would lead her on her path. She stumbled on the vision of her sister in the great room, the same room as yesterday. Yet her sister was somewhere else that mirrored this home. Why?

Probably another world, she thought, resigned to feeling they may never meet. Water knew this was not a memory but was happening now, in real-time, only in another space. Mirror images, she wondered. All these memories showed her Sanctuary. It had begun in a different world, one that had trouble with problems she did not know could exist. There were too many people with too little connection with each other. She saw the destruction these people had created on their homeworld from their greed. It seemed strange, this different world. Does my sister live there? I feel sorry for her if she does. I am sure we are walking the same paths, just in different places.

Is this my sister for real? Doubt was slipping into her mind. Or just an illusion? She asked, questioning her perception of reality. She realized there were a lot of people in her life that could have easily created this illusion. I have learned not to trust, and that has brought me doubt. Shake it off, Water, she said to herself. Look at the facts. It looked like they were on similar paths, and if that is so, she wondered if they would catch up with each other?

"Enough daydreaming, let's take a look at that bookshelf," Water said. She reached for Paradise Lost, moved it out of the way, and placed her hand in the cubby, feeling the depression and pushing it.

What's wrong? I don't feel any changes. Water's anxiety rose slightly.

What if there is no secret room here in this home? Then what? She moved her hand a little further in and pushed once more.

"There it is," she started to smile when something grabbed her hand. Just like the other girl, she began and then stated firmly, MY SISTER. Water admonished herself. Stop second-guessing yourself, Water. That girl, River, her name just came to Water in thought - she is your sister.

Wow, this would be scary if I hadn't seen River do it first, but on the other hand, maybe if I am not the one to open it, it would just cut off my hand. It was taking too long. Something was wrong. Hadn't she heard the word "scanning" and something like "DNA? Water didn't have the time to go back in memory right now; besides, she was beginning to feel that panic she had seen on her sister's face.

"Oh no, it's going to cut my hand off," she yelled and began to panic.

Gran always said I jump headfirst into something, then look later. Tugging on her hand, Water shouted, "At least give it back if you won't let me in."

"Why did you stick your hand in there if not for me to take it?"

"What? Who are you? Let go of my hand! Please," Water pleaded, trying not to give in to the panic she was feeling.

"Who am I," the voice asked. "Who are you? Remember, it is you who came into my space."

Water had no idea what was going on. What's happening to me sure didn't happen to my sister, she thought. Who or whatever this was sounded a lot like Sista Sol. Now Sista is a biological holograph, but her limits centered around the hall for ceremonies and home. She began fading 5 miles from home and disappeared completely within 10 miles. The voice sounds similar, but Water knew it wasn't her. It's not her, Water thought, but maybe an earlier version. One of the first models, maybe, she wondered. It's possible. Here goes, Water thought, I'll treat this house bot as if she were Sista. Besides, it still had her hand.

"I'm sorry, I'm Water; my grandmother, Aiya, invited me to come here. I meant no offense to you. Can I have my hand back, please?"

"Aiya, hum, well, I am just going to have to talk to her about guest etiquette." She released Water's hand and then started speaking cryptically.

"Water, the time has come for you to find yourself, child of the star, daughter of Kaiya. What have you come to seek?"

A ritual thought Water, her mind already clicking with questions. Child of the star? Daughter of Kaiya? What did I come to seek? And this house bot seems to know my Gran. It's a trick question, smirked Water. Like all those ancient stories, Gran would tell at night when she and I settled in for the night. It never failed. The sphinx always tried to trick you. If I say, 'me, that's what I seek,' this holo might give me a mirror and say "here" and ship me out. I have to think this through. An idea came to Water, "Why not," she said aloud and responded.

"I look for the path to my understanding. This path begins here and leads to a destination. I am satisfied with letting that destination be, yet I do not know what concrete steps I must take nor which directions to travel. I seek the map and key to Kaiya's heart.

"Well, now that's interesting," Spoke the voice. "You are the key to Kaiya's heart, and whatever direction you go, well, there you are the key."

I knew she wasn't going to give me a direct answer! Water let out a heavy sigh, knowing she got what she predicted, a riddle. What is this crazy house bot computer talking about, Water questioned?

"I am the key. Well, that doesn't help. I do not know where to go," Water said aloud to the voice.

"Now did you know of Zion," asked the voice. "It is the mountain that lies to the north of here in the forbidden lands. On the crest of that mountain is where you need to go; a lion waits for you there."

What is this thing saying? Water did not understand any of this. And the voice kept right on talking.

"I will release your hand. Go to the hidden room, and on the desk, you will find a map of Zion; take it with you when you go. Take the path leading north from here. It will take you to the foothills of the mountain. Follow the map from there. On the map, you will see an ancient oak grove stop there. You need to retrieve the Heart of Kaiya, your bloodstone from Zebble," the house bot said.

"What is this crazy house bot saying," Water asked, totally confused. What do I need to get from Zebble? I'm running from him. Does this crazy machine not know Zebble? He is NOT going to give me anything. More than likely, he will try and capture me. The house bot just kept giving information, continuing to astonish Water as she listened.

Zet, Zebble's grandfather, stumbled onto the bloodstone created in your name. There are several ancient races on the mountain. The wood nymphs and fairies are two. I believe they are related somehow, maybe cousins, not sure, they never told me, and I am just guessing," the voice laughed lightly. "Anywhoo," she said, "the faeries forged two hearts from a rare bloodstone. The wood nymphs kept it for you, awaiting the day foretold of your coming."

Water was flabbergasted. Awaiting whose coming, mine? Coming for what? WHO IS THIS SIM? Water asked herself, cloaking her thought and emotions from the computer. The computer didn't skip a beat; it kept right on talking.

"The faeries play their own game and have their reasons for what they do. They allowed Zet to find and keep the bloodstone. Now the nymphs and faeries are willing to help you retrieve what they say is rightfully yours. For the faeries, that is a bit unusual."

The computer kept talking as if everything made sense to Water. Like she was aware of the intrigue and drama that moved in circles around her. Water stood in the library, dumbfounded. What is this crazy computer telling me?

"By the way, my name is Abby. Did I tell you that already? I get to talking and forget if I introduced myself to you or not," she said.

Water was too stunned to say anything as Abby kept on talking

"I know why the nymphs' help. They found the stone from their quarries that the faeries forged for you centuries ago. I'm still not sure what the faeries are up to, though," the computer Abby said.

Is she a house bot like Sista is? Can she manifest herself, Water wondered, Still stunned by everything 'Abby' was telling her. Abby continued speaking, almost non-stop, since she started.

"Water use caution when dealing with faeries. They are a beautiful race, long-lived. They are sooo ancient Water; you have no idea. And they play by their own rules. The faeries look out for themselves ten out of ten times. Remember, it is to their advantage to help you, and when it's not, they won't. I advise you to love the faeries from afar," Abby continued, schooling Water on the ways of faeries. "You will love them, Water; you can't help but love them. They have that effect on humans. Just remember, when it comes to faeries, suspect your judgment always."

Then Abby changed the subject abruptly.

"You must confront Zebble in that oak grove and get the bloodstone from him, or all could fail. Tonight, I will prepare a feast for you, a warm soak in a tub, a cozy sleeping area by the stone fire pit, and a book to read. Relax, Water, you will have a few days of peace. This gift I give to you; I will watch over you.

"I did tell you I am Abby, right? I'm just kidding; I know I did." She was the only one who laughed at her joke."

"Upstairs to the right, and you will see a bathing room, with a natural spring tub. Feel free to use it anytime. Meet me down here at dusk for dinner. Until then, Welcome home, Water.

OK, Water thought, this house bot is strange. How does she know so much? Confront Zebble? And how am I supposed to do that? I don't even know where he is. What is she talking about, bloodstone and faeries and times foretold? What was all that? Water knew the bloodstone was a rare stone. If Zet took it from the Faeries, how did he do that, she questioned? The little I know of Faeries came from Gran's stories at night, and I did not know those were real people. I know this much; they did not like it when someone stole from them. They would hunt that person down without fail. At least according to Gran and her stories.

Unless the Faeries were using that person in some form or another, and the person was unaware. What's going on here, Water thought.

Last night she slept outside the house under the light of the Royal Stars. Core protected her; there could be no harm here. She just felt more herself outside. She liked the fresh air and quiet; it was suitable for the contemplating, examining, hypothesizing, fact-finding mind work she had to do. Besides, being in that big house at night with all those memories - nope. She went outside after that strange discovery in the great room and slept outside where she could think.

Today, she was being told by a house bot named Abby she had to confront Zebble, and soon.

What next, thought Water. What next?

CHAPTER 19

SEECA

"**G**IVE ME AN update. You are not progressing as planned," Izen rebuked Seeca.

He's large as life, Seeca thought, looking at Izen's image on the wall to wall vidcom as he noticeably stepped away from the image.

"I already told your guard and your house bot," Seeca told Izen, "I can go no further without going to the coordinates I deciphered. I am unable to read the formula without going there. There's another dimension there somewhere. The key is there. I don't understand how or why I know it's true. To decipher this formula, I must go there," Seeca brazenly confronted Izen, but wisely blaming the guard and the JIVE system watching him.

"Seeca, I am willing to fund an expedition to the coordinates, which puts you outside the Cities, somewhere on Argot mountain. You'll be leaving tomorrow. Begak will accompany you, as will a guard for your safety."

"Oh, ok, I'm not prepared to go outside the City." How lame, thought Seeca, no one's prepared to go outside. "I'd like to see my mom and dad before I go." No one comes back once they go out, crossed Seeca's mind.

"Didn't I tell you," Izen said flippantly, "Your parents are on an extended vacation out of this City. My expense. Wouldn't want anything to happen to them, now would we."

"No, sir," Seeca said to Izen. Then to himself, I know a threat when I hear one.

"I have all the gear you need prepared. You are to jump at sunrise. Begak and your guide will be here before then. Be ready," Izen commanded as the holo faded.

I'm in a world of trouble. How am I going to get out of this?

Seeca grew up speaking to himself in his mind all the time. He had been alone, an illegal kid, with no friends, just his parents. Rarely did he speak aloud; there was no reason to.

I'm a great hacker, but that's it. Too damn nosey for your own good, Seeca, he admonished himself. I have to stay one step ahead of Izen, or I'll find myself on an extended vacation for real, the kind you never come back from, ever. How am I going to get out of this one, panic setting in?

Seeca had managed to hack into the old Jump portal he had discovered below the City's bowels a year ago. The portal had been forgotten with the onset of home jumps three hundred years ago. It looks like one of Laiya's first public portals, Seeca guessed when he stumbled on it in the ruined city below the bowels. He had dropped down an ancient service tunnel that day, which led him to an old part of the City he had never seen before. I'm just going to try it to see if it still works, he said to himself that day. He stepped through and found himself riding a wave, becoming the stream. He saw clearly in his mind's eye this wave, and he became the wave. There was no monitor, no automat asking where he was going, just him on the stream.

He was hooked ever since.

It was like nothing he had ever seen or felt or done, and he loved it. He didn't know why he could see the wave or ride it, or even *be* it, but he could. None of the other hackers had ever experienced becoming the stream on the wave while jumping. He had asked Note to find out discreetly, and the answer came back, no. The wave sang to him, and he sang back. He spent hours flowing in the stream of infinite space and time. On one of these trips, he discovered the ancient symbols that had caused him so much trouble.

"That was a crazy ride that day," he said aloud, forgetting Izen had him under around the clock surveillance.

He was thinking back to the first time the wave took him to a real place. He was not in his body, but he was there in the garden with the young girl. He could see and hear everything going on and watched her telling a wisp she named Cuz what she had discovered: the formula for riding the wave.

The moment she had said she could ride the wave, he knew he had somehow gone back in time and was watching Laiya before she had seeded Rake. The formula is on that parchment she is holding in her hand, Seeca said to himself. I want a glimpse at the paper, curiosity grabbing hold of him,

"Is it the jump formula," he asked?

The next thing he knew, the formula exploded in his mind, seared his brain. Seeca couldn't forget it now if he wanted to. But that didn't mean he understood it. He woke up sometime later, not knowing how long he had been free-floating everywhere and nowhere on the wave, not even sure how to get back to his time and a self that wasn't so scattered.

That was the first time I heard his voice in my head, Seeca remembered.

"What are you doing, little one, riding the wave. Who taught you this?" came the voice out of nowhere

"I taught myself," Seeca said. In a flash, he was showing the voice of how he accomplished it.

"Astounding," came the reply. "The first of your kind to come through naturally. What makes you so different, little one?"

"I dunno, I can see the wave in my mind, and I travel it. Who are you?"

"Who am I," asked the voice? "I have many names, but you can call me Al."

"Hi, Al, can you help me get back to my time? I seem to be a little lost," Seeca said, feeling scattered.

Chuckling, Al said, "Are you now? I suppose I can help you get back."

"Can you make sure all of me goes back too?" Seeca asked, not sure what had just happened to him.

Al laughed, "All of you will go back, little one. I see you hold in your mind the pattern of the wave. There will come a time when you are to share this. Until then, hold it close to you and share it with no one. You are the first to find your way. Time for you to go back. Remember, the one you share this with will be of the sun."

That was the first time he had talked to Al.

One week after he had gone on that trip, Izen's goons showed up at his house, took his parents hostage, packed him up, moved him to the middle path home with a lab, and put him to work. How did Izen find out? Seeca racked his brain, trying to figure out how Izen caught him and came up with the answer. When I had started to record this math equation on Note and then thought better of it, that's how Izen found out I knew part of the formula. That math is lost

I'm in trouble. I knew better, Seeca berated himself. Stupid mistake. Now Izen and his goons watch me all day, every day. He felt that stress.

Luckily, Al said he would help me out of this jam, although I don't know how to reach him. He comes to me in my dreams. I'm getting a little worried. I haven't heard from him since he told me to tell Izen I needed to go to the mountain and say it was a dimensional thing.

Seeca hadn't ridden the wave since Izen's goons had put him up here, now going on almost seven months, he sighed and said quietly,

"I miss the wave." He couldn't go to the hidden portal in the belly of the bowels. His every move watched, and every word recorded. He had to be careful.

Little one, give these coordinates to your tormentor. Al had reached out to Seeca while he dreamt that very night.

"Hey Al, I'm kinda scared," Seeca was dreaming he was free-floating on the wave looking for Al. Cool, thought Seeca. I dreamt I find him, and here he is. Was that me, he wondered?

"Sorry I haven't come to visit you on the wave, Al, can't ride the wave except in my dreams, not with the way these people watch me," Seeca told Al. "They found out because I wrote some of the symbols in my note. I got hacked. Sorry about that too."

He was talking so fast; it took his mind a minute to catch up with his mouth.

"Hey, am I dreaming again, right? I called you this time, and you came, right?" Seeca questioned but did not wait for a response. "Al, they took my mom and dad. I don't know where they are. I'm afraid Izen will do something bad to them."

It rolled out of him, his constant worries and his fears.

I believe I cause you more harm than help by giving you this burden. Al voiced his concern. *Do not fear for your parents. By the time you are ready for travel, we will have them with us.*

Who are we? Seeca asked that question in his mind.

129

Chuckling, Al said, I *can hear your thoughts, little one.*

"Oh, right, I'm dreaming."

"You are dreaming, but I am here with you. I will travel with you too, although there is not much I can do to protect you from harm."

"You didn't grow up in the bowels of the cities, Al. We quickly learn how to protect ourselves."

Twenty-one years ago, Seeca's parents, Winsoul and Prina, had married, one of Rake's longest-lasting marriages. They were a rarity in Rake. They married for love. Unions on Rake were made to consolidate power or move up the social ladder, rarely for love. They had applied for the lottery to have a child every year for the first four years of their marriage. Each year, they failed to win the lottery. In the fourth year, they were told they would never be allowed to have a child. An anomaly was discovered in their DNA; both had a recessive gene. There was a one-in-four chance this anomaly would be dominant in their child. It was a new gene-one the bureaucrats had never seen before, a wild card Rake's officials did not want to chance. Winsoul and Prina would have no child. They were devastated. For six months, they let that be.

Until Prina told Winsoul, "I want our child, want to see him grow within you. I love you more than life and would not lose you for anything. But I sense this child would be a blessing, no matter the hardship."

That day Winsoul reached for her husband and said, "Heart of my heart, I feel the same."

One year later, Seeca came into the world secretly, in their home's silence on the middle path. For two years, they were successful in hiding him from the census takers. They completed each other. The hiding ended when he was a little over two years old; the censors found him. His parents were given an option; either turned him over to the censors or be sent to a lower path to work and live. They chose their son and the bowels. Their son would never be allowed citizenship in Rake.

Winsoul, Prina, and Seeca were a family, and the love they shared grew stronger through the hardship. But they all knew that unless he became a great inventor, Seeca would spend his life in the bowels of the City. Where all the misfits and illegals stayed, eking out a living as best they could.

Every city had an underworld, and Seeca knew that world well. He knew all the service ducts and old portals that were never used anymore.

He knew all the ways in and out of the depths of his city. He even explored the earlier parts of the city, where no one ever went anymore.

I am just learning about you, humans," Al said to Seeca. *"Many of us feel you are too violent and arrogant to be allowed to spread out amongst us. But it's strange. Most of you are not like that, just led by a few who are. Those few are too caught up in their illusions of life and care not for life itself.*

This home you call your planet, Seeca, is a friend to me. She was a friend to your kind at one time too. You have marred her beauty and destroyed your home, for no apparent reason. Seeca, I will tell you; my friend Gaia will not sustain you any longer. There will be no humans here on her surface in less than a hundred of your years. It will only take her one-thousand years to come back from all of your damage, and in five-thousand years, it will be as if you never existed here.

That is no time for us. Even the Elon of your eco-system is hesitant to allow you to continue as a species. Still, he has a certain affinity for your species and is leaning toward helping you.

Seeca didn't know how to respond to Al. He was born into this, knew nothing of Gaia's rich history or the beauty that had once been. And Al was the only Elon he knew, and he had not even met him, not in person anyway. He and Al just talked in his head. I have an Elon in my eco-system, he dreamt. I didn't even know I had an eco-system.

All Seeca knew was that to go outside meant certain death.

You will come to see some of what once was in your world when you go to those coordinates. You are going outside the Cities, Seeca.

"Whoa, I can't do that, I'll die for sure. The air is poison, and there is no food or drink," Seeca began to panic in his dream.

No, little one, you won't. You will see it. Even when you leave your captors and find yourself alone outside, you will have all you need to survive. Now I am giving you a gift. Knowledge of the land, the tools you will have and their uses, and what grows upon Gaia that you may eat without fear.

You must leave your captors and head to the second set of coordinates I give you. Remember this in the morning. Goodnight, little one, let my light be your guide.

Seeca woke with knowledge of lands and rivers, oceans, and mountains, of tools he had never seen, and exactly where he needed to be. Now, just days later, Izen had taken the bait. All I have to do now is figure out how to get away from the guard.

Seeca began organizing the information he received last night in his dreams. Man, this all feels crazy, he thought, closing his eyes and putting the pattern together in his mind like a puzzle.

I got all the pieces; I gotta make them fit.

For the first time in his life, he was trusting someone outside his parents. I'm putting everything I got on Al being a friend.

Seeca went over everything once again, feeling antsy. He had never trusted anyone outside of his parents. He came to the startling realization he thought of Al as a friend. My first and only friend, he said to himself.

"Al, keep your promise. Get my parents to safety. And I will do as I promised; find the one with the sun inside."

CHAPTER 20

TIME IS UP

"ZEBBLE, IT IS an honor to have you with us. Satchel's manhood trial is upon him. Tonight, we honor him and send him out upon the sea tomorrow at dawn. I remember you communicating that tomorrow you would be here, Zebble."

Wiffle had heard Zebble in his mind, an hour after he sailed from Core to Indigo. Seeing Zebble continue to travel across the oceans surprised Wiffle. A new twist, he expressed with interest. Zebble has come out of hiding; he no longer cares who notices.

Is he that strong? Wiffle questioned that?

Change of plans, Wiffle informed his tribe, cutting Zebble away from his mind, clouding Zebble's understanding at the same time.

Glancing at Zebble, Wiffle shook his head ever so slightly; Zebble did not even realize it is he who is in an illusion right now.

How sad, thought Wiffle; what will this lead to? Everyone learning to lie and deceive. Out loud, he said to Zebble, "I see you travel a great distance by water. And continue to do so after we met with Aiya." Wiffle said.

"That is quite a distance, over the ocean," Satchel said.

Wiffle noticed Zebble's shoulder twitch and felt the subtle cloaking of his mind. Not enough to be detected by most, but Wiffle wasn't like most. Nor were all who lived on Indigo, the smallest island on Izaria and the closest to Core. They were all watchers and knew the real history of Izaria.

"Where I am traveling from or to is none of your concern," sniffed Zebble. He looked directly at Satchel, then dismissed him and turned to Wiffle.

"But I shall tell you anyway," bragged Zebble, for he was proud of his ship. "I am testing a new rift, which has greater speed and durability and is built for long-distance travel. It even has a room for me as well, and dining facilities and housing for a crew," he preened.

"Oh, I would like to see that. Your rift must be stunning," said Wiffle, stroking Zebble's ego.

We need to keep him off balance a little longer. Wiffle sent the message out to his people.

Zebble did not know Wiffle was a master of misting thoughts, capable of sending illusions. Wiffle could make one believe they were reading him when all along, he sneaking in and reading them.

"Please stay for the ceremony Zebble," Wiffle asked politely.

Zebble shook his head no, saying, "I have pressing business and will be off soon. But I see I have been long in my neglect of your home site. I intend to remedy that, bring you back into the fold. I propose all children ages five to thirteen be trained together, starting in two seasons. Since my homesite is the largest and best equipped for this, we will start there. The children will stay with my tribe for the first five years," Zebble continued telling Wiffle his plans. "I have come for a roster of all children in that age group. Also, we will limit all jump activity, so it will be necessary for them to stay on my island while training."

"Have you discussed this with the elders and the people of all the homesites?" asked Wiffle, eyes narrowing.

"All but your homesite and Baltic's have agreed. The people do not need to be involved in the decisions. We do what is best for them," Zebble off-handedly waved Wiffle's question away.

"Oh really," Wiffle said, unwilling to hide even a sliver of his disgust. "We do not do so on this island. All have a say in anything and everything that affects this island and its people. It has been so for two-hundred-fifty years, Zebble, and it will remain so."

Zebble looked at him, tilting his head slightly, sizing Wiffle up.

"Times are changing, Wiffle. Wait too long, and you will be left behind. Well, I came for what I needed and saw all I wanted. I shall be leaving. I will return this way in two moons. Think about what I said. Have the answer for me then," Zebble said, dismissing Wiffle again with a wave of his hand.

He turned and started back to his rift. Hmm, thought Zebble, I see the trouble with this site. I might have to mind-wipe them all, like the others. When I get back from getting this troublesome girl, I will make this my first stop; he said to himself as he boarded his rift to leave Indigo on his way to Mount Zion.

Wiffle turned to JB,

"Get my nephew Satchel up here and prepare to launch in five hours. Zebble is on his way to Core, to the house. Aiya has informed us of a crack in the force field; he will enter Core without Kaiya. He will seek Water in the mountains if he misses her in Core. Kaiya may not keep him out of Core, but Abby will make sure he brings no harm to Water on the land. I must seek Aiya and inform her of the changes. Satchel must be on the mountain and find her first. Move," Wiffle said to JB. He tuned everything else out and contacted Kaiya.

We have to talk," he said to her. *Zebble has been busy; contact Aiya and bring me to Sanctuary to meet.*

When Zebble moved up his plans, they had to change theirs. Wiffle had gone back to Sanctuary to speak with Aiya and returned before Satchel had launched.

"Satchel, travel plans have changed. As you know, you were chosen for the journey because you are closest to Water's age. We hope you can create a trusting relationship with her, so she accepts your advice and help. Wiffle told his nephew, "You have trained for this your whole life. You are a watcher. You have studied the histories of both worlds, know who Water is and who her grandmother is. Satchel, we planned to give you a couple of days to get to know each other and plan how to retrieve the Heart and get to the dimensional crossing safely. That is no longer possible. Aiya says you are to jump to Core early tomorrow and meet Water at the house. Also, Zebble will make it to the rip by midday. She must be gone long before that. Kaiya says they have calculated an 80% chance that the path taken by Water will lead to her capture by Zebble or one of his converts without you."

"And with me," Satchel asked?

"60% chance he will find you both."

"Better than 80%," said Satchel, determination set and seen within his mind.

"Kaiya says to leave before the sun is high in the sky and take the straight path north until the fork by old man oak. Set your trap there. You will have the advantage. That land is ancient, and the wood nymphs and fairies love it. They will help Water; Aiya is sure of that. It is there you must set your plan in motion and get the heart stone from Zebble,"

Wiffle finished his instructions to Satchel verbally while transmitting the Oak Grove's mental image and the old gnarly pine center of that grove.

Uncle," Satchel asked, looking at Wiffle, "can we spend a moment together reviewing the possibilities and their consequences? The mountains are restricted; we will not be able to communicate once we leave Core. Does Zebble know he won't be able to mindspeak long distance?"

Wiffle turned to Satchel, "Come walk with me. We are not sure if he is aware of that or not. We have time to sit, eat, and discuss. You will leave at first light, Satchel."

CHAPTER 21

WHO'S YOUR DADDY

"HELLO," RIVER YELLED as she hurried to this strange man. Who is he, talking about his flowers? This home is my Gram's place. He's on our property River steamed, a little miffed.

"Are you the one who stomped my plants?" asked the old man. "Look at what you did to my flowers," pointing to the ruin.

River rounded the corner and saw what he meant. Her footprints were all around the windows. She had not realized she was destroying all these plants and flowers in her rush to see inside.

"Yes, I am sorry."

"Girl, what were you thinking? Come on over and help me clean this mess up."

Contrite, River moved closer to him. It doesn't even faze him, me being here. It's almost like he expected me. Or else having some stranger in the house is normal for him, River thought, shaking her head at the whole situation. Weird, she said, because I sure didn't expect him. None of this is typical, including him being here.

"Take out the ones you ruined; I'm going to get some replacements," was all this strange man said as he left.

WHAT? River questioned as he walked away. She looked at the damage she had caused and knew she would do as he had told her. She created this damage; she would do what she had to fix it. River, left alone while she worked, removing the flowers and the plants she had destroyed

137

from around the house. As she worked and saw the damage she had done, it made her feel small and selfish.

I was too absorbed in what I wanted, trying to see inside this crazy place. I didn't care. River admonished herself, pulling up the plants she had damaged. An hour later, she finished.

Wow, that was pathetic, she said to herself as she pulled her wagon full of dead and destroyed plants toward the shed in the back of the house. I've got to be more careful. She left the cart outside, turned, and began walking to the house. And just that quick, her mind went back to the secret room. The old man is nowhere around, probably not coming back, she reasoned. Checking her surroundings and realizing she was alone, River raced back to the great room, determined to find the secrets that lay hidden there. She ran from the shed, making sure she was far enough away from the plants that survived the destruction. She rounded the corner of the house, sprinting for the porch when suddenly, the old man showed up right in front of her.

"Where did you come from?" River yelled, skidding to a stop and veering to the left, barely avoiding running him over.

It seemed like he came out of nowhere, thought River suspiciously. As if he had jumped to her location. I believe the 'no jump no JIVE' restriction is in place here at the house as well, she thought. She looked at the man and smirked, knowing he wasn't there ten seconds ago. Then she saw he was toting a small wagon full of flowers and plants along with him.

He is not that **quiet,** she said to herself.

"Here, girl," the old man abruptly interrupted River's suspicions.

"Begin with the ones on top and work your way around the house," he said and started walking away.

"You want me to plant those," she asked? This old man just wants some free labor, River said to herself, walking to the wagon and pulling it to the house, ready to begin planting.

"Ain't nothing free in this world, girl. You broke it; you fix it."

Did he just read my mind!? That was kind of spooky how he said it right after I thought it. This place is full of surprises, noticed River as she began planting the flowers and small bushes. Two hours later, she looked up from work and realized she finished.

"Wow, I enjoyed that," River said, standing and stretching.

She gazed at the pattern she had created with the plants and flowers and realized it was the recurrent theme in her life, the design that stayed within her mind, always. She called it 'the pattern of her life,' her wave an intricate design and color pattern. Like her, as she grew, learned, and changed, the design within her mind changed too. What she saw was herself. What she created with the life force of the plants was the life force of her change. Working like that brought her peace of mind, at least for the time, she and the plants were of one soul, and she had no worries. She stepped back, surveying her job, feeling a bit proud of her work. Beautiful, she mused, still connected the earth, the plants, and the sky, enjoying this newfound sensation of belonging.

"Proud of yourself, are you? What, you never did a little hard work in your life?"

River spun around. He's doing it again, sneaking up on me and reading my thoughts. She stared at him; read this, River directed, sending a mental image of her sticking her tongue out at him.

He just looked at her, cocked his head a little, and laughed,

"Come on, girl, come get something in your stomach. It looks like you ain't eaten in some time, skinny as a bean pole."

Who IS this guy, River was wary about this stranger on her land. But he was right; I'm hungry, she said to herself. No harm, only friends, she silently reminded herself.

Besides, she thought, sizing this old man up, I could probably take him if he tried anything funny.

He walked to the kitchen, back to River, and proceeded to unpack all kinds of food. He set it on a table in the center of the room. The aroma was fantastic and made her mouth water. This smell is heavenly, breathing in deep and letting the sensation of smell touch all of her. The smell of roasted chicken, heavily seasoned with garlic, thyme, apples, and cinnamon, hung in the air. She saw the feast he had brought and could not believe her eyes; seven different kinds of food were placed before her. Her eyes widened in surprise and pleasure as she bit into the small, round food she had picked up. It was sour and crunchy and fabulous.

"What is this? It's great," she said, taking another bite.

"It's a dill pickle girl, ain't you ever had one? Where have they been keeping you? In the Cities, eating the sawdust, they call food?"

He filled a plate full of food and passed it to her. River promptly tore into it, realizing as she ate, I'm hungry, and this is the best food I've ever tasted. They both ate in silence, savoring the meal set before them.

"A feast for a queen," she said, pushing her chair back from the table twenty minutes later, "Thank you."

The old man sat back, looked at River, and said, "What's your name, girl? Why are you out here all alone?"

She wasn't going to tell him anything, but she found herself spilling out her whole story, along with her name, when she opened her mouth. When she finished, she felt as though a weight had lifted.

"Well, now that's quite a story, little girl. My name is Irsei. Been in Sanctuary from the beginning. I knew your Gramma since she was a little thing herself, running around her with her gramma."

Which beginning is that, thought River. He's old, but three-hundred years, that's stretching it. He confused his time table all up, River thought to herself. And I did not know gramma had a gramma out here. It seems like there are a lot of things I don't know about my grandmother. She has neglected to tell me **a lot**, River realized.

"I am not a senile old man girl. I know what I'm saying. Hate to see you out here alone, River, even if your granny thought it's ok. Tell you what, let's go look at that secret room and see what we see."

He got up and began moving to the great room. River looked at the leftover food with longing, picked up two more pickles, and stuffed them in her mouth. "Ok," she mumbled, wondering why he had said something about being a senile old man. He continued talking to her as he walked ahead of her out of the kitchen.

"By the way, little girl, stop assuming you may or may not know something about someone and what you may or may not be capable of doing to that someone. My mama always told us, kids, when we were growing up, that when you assume, you make an ASS of U and ME," Irsei said. "More than likely, you just make an ass of yourself. You would have a hard time whoopin anything out here, even this old man," he said and laughed as they walked into the great room.

Irsei went right to the wall, removed the book, stuck his hand in, and the wall just let him in. He left River looking dumbfounded in his wake.

He read my mind! She said to herself, stunned.

"Welcome back, Irsei. All is well at home," Abby asked?

"Good as ever. How come you let this girl tromp all over my flowers, destroying my plants?"

"Let her? What do you want me to do, hit her with the laser, knock her out? I see you fixed her, and the flowers, at the same time; you didn't need my help."

River looked on, amazed, still stunned he read her mind. They acted just like Gram and JIVE, old friends. And then it hit her; the sense of belonging, mixed with the comfort of knowing that for this moment, she was safe. That feeling blew her away. She couldn't talk, just stood and listened as those two bantered with each other.

"Abby, old girl, why don't you tell us where Laiya hid what this child needs to find? Hmmm? Make it easier on these old bones. I won't have to bend and stoop, reach, and search. Save my friend River and me some time. Might even be able to stay over tonight and play some chess with you."

"Irsei, you old coot, are you trying to bribe me? Well, it worked. Laiya never said I couldn't show you, so I see a loophole in our contract. Ok, get out that key you found and go to the oak desk, River. The key fits into one of those drawers."

Why do they keep calling Gramma "Laiya"? Her name is Aiya. They keep confusing her with the Laiya, who created the jump three-hundred years ago. She had thought Irsei was a bit senile. Was this Abby a senile house bot too?

Too much, River felt. All of this is too much, she thought. Don't say anything, she said to herself. She walked to the desk, not correcting either about Aiya's name.

"Just do what you're told," she quietly said under her breath. And then reminded herself, *you're in Sanctuary no harm, no foul is the rule.*

She heard them both chuckling with each other and wondered what was so funny. She found the key slid into the lock of the top right drawer. She opened it and saw a bloodstone, vibrating sapphire blue at its core, and a map of trails leading from the house out in a wagon spoke. There was one illuminated path heading northeast out of Sanctuary. She also found a note on old parchment written in old English. Although many of the words looked familiar, she couldn't make heads or tails of what it was saying. It did seem like Gram's handwriting, though.

"Give me the note, girl; I read English." River handed the note to Irsei, watching him read it. "Huh, right," Irsei said when he finished.

"Will you read it to me please," River asked?

"Yes, Irsei, read it to her and don't leave anything out either," said Abby.

"Abby, you're too bossy," said Irsei. "Ok, I'll read it to you, River." He cleared his throat and began.

River, my child, I know this is all confusing for you. Soon you will understand. The choice is yours. If you choose to follow this through, though you don't know what you will find, you must go to the mountain, to the primrose gate, and seek the mouth of the lion. You will find someone who will travel with you, looking for the sun.

Irsei, I knew you couldn't stay out of this. Take River to the edge of Sanctuary, put her feet on the right path. If you are choosing to move forward, you must leave by morning light mid-month.

You do not have to do this, River. You can choose to stay at the house and live your life, but you will not know your true self. I always have and always will love you, child of my heart. Take the stone with you when you go. Run with the Wind River. You are meant to be more than you are.

River had closed her eyes when Irsei started reading. She heard Grams speaking, not him.

She remained still for one moment, thinking, when did you write this Gramma? How long have you been planning this? And you know this man, Irsei.

River opened her eyes and said, "Mid-month is tomorrow. Will you please help me get to the edge of Sanctuary, Irsei?"

Irsei looked at this young girl, vulnerable and alone, and said, "Little girl, I will walk to the ends of the earth with you. Come on now, let's get some more food, and I will teach you how to play chess. You can help me beat my sunshine, who thinks she knows it all."

"Don't listen to him, River," piped in Abby, "He's a senile old coot. I do know it all."

Chuckling, Irsei left the great room, heading to the food.

"Thank you, Grams," River said, "For this one night of peace. Even though you still have a lot of explaining to do when I see you, Gramma."

She heard her Grams say, "Leave tomorrow's worries for tomorrow."

Yep, River thought, let tomorrow be.

She got up from the desk, walked out of the secret room, and followed Irsei to the food. "Time to eat," she said with a smile.

CHAPTER 22

OUTSIDE

"**G**ET UP, YOU lazy dog!"

Seeca woke to someone banging on his door, rolled over, and put his pillow over his head, ignoring it. Guess I jammed the lock real good last night, he mumbled into his pillow, smiling to himself as he sat on the edge of slumber. Even if I can't go anywhere, they can't just walk in either, proud of what little he could accomplish to show his independence. I'm a prisoner.

"Open this door. How did you lock this, you little rat? I am going to kick your butt when I get my hands on you," Begak yelled.

I'm not going to get any sleep, Seeca sighed, rising from his bed and stretching.

"Now, why would I open this door just to let you in to beat me up?" he said, smiling for the camera.

"We're jumping at sunrise, fifteen minutes from now. You better not screw this up. I know you're not smart enough to figure out that math by yourself, tunnel rat. Be ready or be dead," Begak said, stomping off.

What a twit, thought Seeca. Begak couldn't find his feet without his daddy. You like to go 'slumming' Begak, I know you, Seeca berated his tormentor in his mind, barely refraining from saying it aloud. Begak frequented the lower bowels and had a reputation for being mean.

Begak lives in the sky and me, just one level above the bowels. But it's me Begak's dad needs, not him. I can feel his hate; he can't wait to kill me, which makes him mean and dangerous.

Seeca had worked all night on a plan. He could see the map in his mind. He had a photographic memory; once he saw or traveled a path, he had it in his mind forever, never forgotten. They did call him tunnel rat, or just rat, naming him after some animal from long ago that ran the bowels. Well, that suited him, and as the rat, he knew all the ways in and out of the bowels. But he had left the bowels days ago, and in less than an hour, he was traveling outside under open skies.

I'm not prepared. I can't go outside; outside meant death. I can't do this. I'm being set up, Izen found out about the portal and the wave, and now he's going to kill me. Jump me outside and let me die. Al was just a figment of my imagination. I made him up out there when I was scattered everywhere. Seeca was in a small panic in his mind, getting ready to move into a full-blown meltdown.

Even if you just made me up, that was pretty cool, don't you think?

Al, is that you? Seeca questioned in his mind without thinking.

Maybe, might be your imaginary buddy, Al sang his laughter out to Seeca in his mind.

If Seeca hadn't been so close to a full-blown panic about going outside, he would have realized Al had just mind spoke with him, and he had answered Al the same way. He didn't stop to think and opened his mouth to speak.

"Before you open your mouth to speak, remember your friends who watch."

Seeca shut his mouth just as quickly. What am I going to do now? How will I communicate? Seeca asked himself, seconds away from a meltdown.

I can still hear you in thought and word, little one, laughed Al. *Calm down and think.*

Oh, thought Seeca, settling down a bit.

"I'm," he started to speak to Al, caught himself, and finished, "going to cleanse before I go."

That was for those who were listening with the monitors. He whistled as he walked to the cleanser, disappeared inside, and set the timer for two minutes, the maximum time allowed and continued his conversation with Al in his mind.

Wow, Al, outside by sunrise.

You are feeling stressed, my young friend? Al spoke to Seeca in his mind.

Oh yeah, Seeca coughed slightly. *I wish I could see where it is, I am going,*

145

and where I need to be. I spent all night coming up with different plans, but I don't know the land. Are you sure the air isn't poisonous to me?

You will see you breathe just fine. Now I will take you in your mind to where you are going; see the paths and where each leads. This gift of flyer sight is my last gift to you before you begin your journey.

Suddenly, Seeca was soaring in the skies high above the lands.

Oh, WOW, he thought, astonished. It's the most spectacular thing I have ever seen, giddy with the joy of flying. I'm flying like the ancients. Only I don't need a ride. Outside looks like this, Seeca questioned as he flew over the lands, surprised and shocked. Nothing but devastation everywhere, barren lands with the look of dust and death. He brought his eyes off the ground and looked out to the horizon.

The further out from the City he flew, the more the landscape changed. What's that, he wondered. For under a protective shield, for hundreds of miles, Seeca saw lush greenery and vegetation.

WOW, he declared, again looking everywhere. He had never imagined anything like what he was seeing could exist.

"Ah, I see," he said quietly.

The wave and that shield down there, surrounding all that lush land, are made of the same substance. The same way Seeca knew the wave was both energy and matter, he knew this shield was too. He could see it was solid, but he also knew he could walk right through that shield if nothing stopped him. Well, how is that he queried? He brought his sight up from the land and out to the northern horizon and realized he was nearing the mountain, etching the details in his mind.

What's that? He asked, looking at the peak.

What IS that? He questioned, again peering at the carving of some ancient animal covered by green and red vegetation.

Ah, there it is, seeing the information he needed pop up in his head: Lion's Roar, sculpted after some long-forgotten animal. His AI reference library in his head gave him the knowledge. The information comes easily, feels natural, he thought. Seeca saw the paths leading to Lion's Roar from the first coordinates AI had given him by the rushing river. The second set was the mouth of the beast.

In that split second, Seeca had all the information he needed. All the ways on and off that mountain. He saw the passages into and through it as well. Now he was ready to travel.

"My parents, Al?"

We will have them by an Elon evening starlight, little one.

Thank you, Al, Seeca said in his mind as he stepped out of the cleanser, refreshed and ready to go. Walking to the door, he picked up the pack he had made several days before. He had asked Izen to supply him with the essential supplies he would need for warmth and nutrition on this journey.

"Hey, Begak, it's time. We are going outside," Seeca yelled as he opened the door and startled Begak and the guard. Both had been waiting for Seeca to come out of the room.

"Why are you yelling," Begak growled, "And what's with the stupid grin?"

Seeca just looked at Begak and kept right on grinning, making Begak cringe, and involuntarily stepped back a pace, which made Seeca howl with laughter. Seeca was ready to go.

CHAPTER 23

PLANS WITHIN PLANS

'M AT THE northern border tomorrow, the Pearl said to himself, contemplating the plan.

He saw all the players like pieces of a chess game. The kid and his guard will be following soon after. I calculated their course; he and the girl should meet the day after the boy gets here if he succeeds in escaping without help. If not, there was always plan B.

"Oh, what a web we weave," The Pearl sang out loud. "All in the timing. All in the timing," he gleefully said to himself as he sat upon the porch watching the sunset.

"The kid left yesterday. The Pearl is somewhere on the mountain. I'll be glad when his services are no longer needed," said Izen to no one. He was in his office going over his plans for creating a business conglomerate dominating the flow of mineral and mining rights and the real estate sales of the solar system.

"I hate that man," Izen sneered out loud. "What kind of name is 'The Pearl,' anyway?" he said quietly under his breath.

Jenkins has standing orders to eliminate him the moment they find the girl. I have no intention of giving that man any percentage of my profits. Not solar mining or real estate in the solar system, let alone this galaxy,

"NO, I will not." Izen was talking out loud to himself again, pacing his office, unable to sit. He was so angry. How dare he, Izen thought. "That man shows me no respect, no fear of my name or my power. He will soon regret that." Izen seethed. "The pearl,' what kind of name is that anyway," he said again, so angry he forgot he had just said that.

"Tomorrow, I'll go to Eldar Wiz and request the requirements and procedures for naming the new heir," already forgetting the Pearl. That subject is closed. I doubt those elders know anything about selecting an heir either, sneered Izen. How could they? We've never needed to; Laiya was the only heir. Walking behind his desk, Izen sat down in his chair, finally relaxing. It's just short of the three hundred years on the lease, Izen thought. Not a coincidence; he knew it. No, not a coincidence at all.

"The first heir since Laiya. Well, actually, ever," said Izen to himself, unconsciously speaking out loud, shaking his head. A new heir had never crossed anyone's mind until that old Wiz stood up at the ceremonies and caused an uproar. That's not a coincidence, either, that old lady Aiya created that chaos with Eldar. It wasn't the first time that idea crossed his mind these last three days.

Still, I've consolidated 75% of the vote," calculated Izen. It doesn't matter what the requirements might be; I'll win should it come to a vote, he thought, very sure of himself. Less than a year from now and Sanctuary will be mine. I'll have the formula for the jump, one way or another, he schemed.

"JIVE, contact Begak before they reach the point of no communication and get an update. Also, contact the consortium; set up a meeting. I want to get these contracts signed before the lease is up; consolidate my power base. And last, JIVE, but far from the least, set a vidcom conference with Eldar and the committee of Elders finding the heir. I need to know what they're looking for."

Not that it matters, Izen shrugged, dismissing the thought just as quickly. I am the next heir.

"Yes, sir, shall I interrupt you when the call comes in from Begak?"

"Yes, I don't want that idiot to run off without talking to me."

"Yes, sir, I will get right on it," JIVE responded.

Izen sat back in his chair, gazing into space, dreaming of his future. Soon, I will be the supreme ruler of this world, and, if all goes as planned within ten years, the universe. I will not let anything stand in my way.

CHAPTER 24

TIME TO GO

"**W**HAT TIME IS IT?" River jumped up from the bed, a little disoriented. It took her a moment to remember she wasn't home, but in Sanctuary, on the run from her uncle on some crazy quest Grams sent her on. She laid back down, snuggling deeper into covers, remembering last night in the great room watching Irsei play chess with Abby. Abby had manifested a body and accepted Irsei's challenge in a game of chess. River thought she was beautiful, all glowing red and yellow like the sun, laughing at Irsei and he at her. The idea that they had been friends a long time came to River as she watched them together. It just seemed like Abby was much more than a house bot. And Irsei more than a gardener. As she watched them together last night, she realized Irsei looked a whole lot younger. He didn't look like an old man anymore. She shook her head; none of this makes sense.

River had to admit her sleep was deep and relaxing, better last night here than in her own home lately. She felt safe, protected. She propped her head upon the pillow and breathed in deep. What is that smell floating in the air? She asked as she got out of bed and crossed the room, opened her door, and breathed deeply again. It's coming from downstairs, and I'm hungry. It smells great!

She hurriedly got dressed and went to the waste closet. What did Irsei call this room? "Oh yeah," she said aloud, "the bathroom."

A funny name, she thought as she dashed through her morning cleansing and ran where her nose led her.

"Well, good morning, sleepy," Irsei said to River as she entered the kitchen. "I was wondering when you were getting out of that bed." He was standing in front of what memory told her was a stove.

"Am I late? I didn't mean to sleep so soundly'. Guess I was exhausted," River said. Irsei was looking at her funny.

What thought River. Why is he looking at me like that?

"You're not too late, baby girl; you're right on time. There are some eggs and biscuits and a slice of that apple pie from last night for you. Eat, child, you'll need the energy," Irsei told her as he handed her a plate of the hot steamy food. He didn't have to say it to her twice; she dug into the food, savoring every bite.

They had readied for travel last night by the fire pit. Irsei dumped the pack Gram had put together for River. He took each item one at a time from the pile and explained its function. River was intrigued by the swiss army laser — the laser cut through anything. It also had a light beam to see at night, a GPS for guidance, a mini JIVE that knew all the plants surrounding their area for one mile, as well, as a map of the stars. (*What, Grams, just in case I forgot all those lessons, you pack a mini-JIVE for me. What happened to the no jump, no jive rule. You don't have to follow it?*) River chastised her Gramma silently. There was a line on the Swiss army laser that reeled out to five-hundred yards. Irsei assured her it was strong enough to hold him, her, and three-hundred more pounds as well. Gran packed her fire stick, first aid, and dried food and liquid energy as well, enough to last her two weeks. After that, she would have to live off the land and what she had prepared before leaving.

She had risen early and dressed to travel, clipping the laser to her clothes; she wanted it close to her. River went into the kitchen, grabbing a bite to eat before leaving. The sun was rising; it was time to go.

"You are still going to the border with me, right, Irsei," River asked?

"Yeah," he said with a touch of, 'you **actually** thought you needed to ask that question,' edge in his voice. "Did you think I would even let you leave here without me, baby girl? Not if you live a million years, would I," he said vehemently.

"Ohhh kay, thanks." River was grateful she would not be alone but wondered at the fierceness of his statement. She had never been off Sanctuary before and wasn't sure what to expect.

"You ready, girl?" Irsei asked, picking up his pack and looking at River.

"I guess so. Abby, thanks for your help. Maybe I'll be able to come back and see you again."

"River, I enjoyed our time together here. I am sure we will meet again. You take care of our girl, you old coot. Now both of you be on your way. Irsei, take the fork to the left; It goes to the river, which will take you further up the mountain and closer to where she needs to be."

"You act like I ain't traveled all over this land, Abby. You're just talking to talk, old girl. We'll be alright. Let's go, River; time's a wastin."

Though they hurried, River and Irsei enjoyed their time together traveling to Argot's northern border. They had followed the river out of Sanctuary with Irsei telling stories of his life. River had never gone by foot so far across the lands. She was content to travel with Irsei, walking as close to the shores of the river as the wild berry bushes would allow. It was easy traveling; they were still in Sanctuary, where no harm could befall them, and the way seemed to open before them. The weather was warm, the sun shining brightly in the summer haze. Irsei pulled a couple of ripe blackberries off the bushes and popped them into his mouth. And then he reached for more as they walked along.

"What are you doing?" River demanded to know as she swatted the berries from his hand to the ground, shocked by what he had done. "They might be poisonous. She had never seen these berries in Sanctuary before. And she knew well enough from Grams studies never to eat handfuls of anything if you don't know what you are eating. It was a natural reaction for her to swat away the berries. Grams had done that to her as well many times.

"They aren't," he laughed, picking a handful more from the bushes and quickly sticking them into his mouth before she could knock them away.

"You should try some; they are ripe, juicy, and sweet to taste," Irsei laughed again. "We make camp here tonight," Irsei said as he stopped and began setting up their tents on the small sandy beach they had come upon. River eyed the berry bushes, thinking, maybe just one.

Irsei had woken her early that next morning, saying, "Rise and shine, girl. Today we make a raft and travel by the Missouri River".

"What?" River asked.

Irsei looked at River, astounded. "Girl, don't you know your history? Didn't granny teach you anything? This river used to be known as the Missouri River. One of the most magnificent rivers that had ever moved across the land before the Cities were born. If we were traveling south, the Missouri River would have merged with the Mighty Mississippi, and *that* was a river to behold. The mountain range you see was known as the Rocky Mountains. Now, though," Irsei sadly recalled, "even this river disappears underground just outside of Sanctuary before the barren lands began. Thousands of miles of wasted and destroyed lands. Sad, so sad," he said.

Irsei was giving River a lesson on the history of her world, something she did not know. Nor did 99.99% of the population on Rake, thought River. A rich history swallowed up, forgotten as if it never existed. I wonder if that happens over and over on this planet. Civilizations come and go, and no one remembers she questioned.

"Come on, girl, let's gather some wood, make us a raft. We'll travel by water this last part, like Huckleberry," Irsei laughed, bringing her out of her reverie.

"Make what? What's a huckleberry?" she asked.

"You are in serious need of some education. What's Laiya teaching you? Come on, Irsei said, "I'll school you while we build our raft."

Irsei hurried her along, talking the whole time. Off they went gathering supplies for the raft. Simultaneously, Irsei explained what barges, boats, and ships were, how they had dominated the waters before the jump and were no longer because of it. When they finished three hours later, she had built her first raft. Irsei stepped back, surveying their work,

"Pretty darn good if I do say so myself. Now let's put some final touches on our raft."

He reached into his pack, pulled out two small discs, laid one center on the raft and one to the rear, and opened simultaneously. The center disc spread out, top and bottom, sealing the raft, waterproofing it. The other, a pencil-thin antenna that descended into the water and rose waist-high. A small holo station nestled on top of the antenna. River wasn't sure what she had just seen or the purpose of either object. Seeing the confusion on River's face, Irsei laughed and pulled the computer station out of the antenna.

"JIVE create cushion seats." She watched as the cushions materialized onto the deck of the raft.

"The first seals our transportation watertight and will act as a shelter should it rain. You do know what rain is, don't you, Izen asked? River nodded.

"Good," he told her. "The second is our motor. How did you think we were going to move this raft upstream?"

Again, River looked confused, not knowing the answer. She didn't know what a motor was.

But then said to herself; first Gram packs a mini-jive, now irsei talks to JIVE here in the restricted lands, and gets answered. When has JIVE ever been allowed in Sanctuary? Who's making the rules? She asked.

"OK, you know nothing about rivers either, I see," sighed Irsei. "You sorely lack historical knowledge. Santayana once told the world, 'Those who cannot remember the past are condemned to repeat it. I'll bet you don't know who that is, do you? Nope, I see you do not," he said when she shook her head. "Have you ever heard that before River," Irsei asked?

"Yeah, from Grams," River admitted. She just didn't remember who said it. Although she vaguely remembered her Grams attributing it to George, somebody, or another.

"So much for listening to your Grams when she's teaching," Irsei said off-handedly. "Guess it holds for almost everybody nowadays. Few know the quote, and no one seems to know who was the first to say it. And they are now living their doom, he finished. Tsk, tsk, little girl, Laiya sure didn't give you much of an education. Don't worry, girl, we got all day to ride the river; I'll teach you all about your history, through my eyes. Let's push off."

Why does he keep calling Gram Laiya? I know they look alike, but still, Irsei isn't that stupid. At least that's not my impression of him, she concluded, as she climbed onto the raft from the edge of the water. She heard the whisper of a voice ringing, *thank you*, in her mind.

"What," River asked?

"Get on now," Irsei told her, ignoring the 'what.' "Don't want you to drown in the river trying to push off with me."

"No, I mean, what did you say before that? I thought I heard 'thank you.'"

He shoved off and jumped agilely onto the raft. His movements belied his age. How old is he, River questioned in her mind.

"Old enough, that's how old I am."

He can read my thoughts!

Yes, I can, and so can you read mine.

He had just spoken to her in her mind.

I hear you speak in my head like you are speaking out loud, she exclaimed excitedly, mind talking back to Irsei without realizing she had.

Looking directly at her without speaking a word, *I hear you, too,* he responded.

Speaking mind to mind, Irsei showed her how to navigate using the raft holo. He instructed the holo to respond only to his or River's commands. River gave the orders to maintain a course for Primrose Gate and Lion's Roar. They set sail to a calm river and sunny morning. She was happy here with Irsei at this moment.

She knew it could not last, but it was good for now.

CHAPTER 25

LET'S PLAY CHESS

M Y THIRD DAY here in the house, Water thought. She spent the first night outside before entering the house. The second night she slept in a wonderfully comfortable bed.

The yesterday settled into a relaxing exploration of this grand old house, she reflected. That is, after that scary moment when Abby wouldn't let go of my hand, she shuddered, remembering her first encounter with this crazy house bot. I wasn't sure if I was getting my hand back from Abby, let alone get into the secret room.

What a great day it turned out to be. She smiled at that thought. But it's time to go she reminded herself. Water knew she was leaving Core tomorrow, moving on in her journey. That funny feeling is creeping up on me again. I'm procrastinating; I feel like I'm not quite ready to go yet. It feels like I'm waiting for my sister, and we can move forward together. I can see her through the mist sometimes; again, she peered hard into an unseen dimension looking for her sister.

The one called River, she's my sister. She and the older man built something similar to a rift, but more straightforward. Water recalled her dream from last night. She often saw her visions more clearly when her body and mind rested. She had dreamed of her sister as she slept. She's traveling on the water today. Who is that man; Water brooded over that question. She sensed a cloaking around him. What is he trying to hide, this man called Irsei? Is he traveling with my sister the whole distance?

River seems to trust him, although I don't know why. Can't she see he's not what he appears to be? But then, she realized, neither is this house bot named Abby what she seems to be. Or Kaiya. Or even Gran. Everybody's hiding. Water smiled disparagingly.

What's wrong with the adults in my life? She muttered to herself, shaking her head.

I enjoyed spending time sitting on the porch with Abby yesterday, watching what she called the river meander. It was relaxing. Abby had presented herself in human form right after she released Water's hand from the trap.

Water smiled, like Gran and I used to do in the evening, sitting and watching the sun sink along the ocean's horizon, talking about our day. Oh well, she softly chided herself. She's not here, nor will she be. I'm alone except for Abby, the crazy house bot. I don't like this man who hides his true self and tries to befriend my sister, she said a little possessively, but she could do nothing about it. Her insight did not let her see everything. She sighed, hearing her resignation resound in that sigh. I'll trust my sister on this. We'll meet at the right time.

Recalling yesterday with Abby, Water smiled again. It had been the most fun she'd had in three months. It allowed her to rest and think things through. Abby, the house hologram who almost took her hand off, manifested herself as someone's mom glowing copper and golden reds and cooked the most fantastic meal. They chatted by the fire while playing a game called chess that Abby taught her. A game of strategy, Abby called it.

"Think three moves ahead," Abby said. "What and who are you willing to sacrifice to win?" she questioned Water as they played, taking Water's rook and sacrificing her queen. "HMMM?" Abby asked again, three moves later. "Checkmate."

Abby smiled, forcing Water to concede a loss and say to herself, what am I willing to sacrifice to win? They played well into the night, talking strategies that Water might use in the next part of her journey. Water liked chess; she was a natural strategist. She loved the game behind the game.

"I see you are moving at least eight moves ahead in your mind now, Water," Abby was impressed with Waters skills as they played through the night. "Most of the great chess masters think that far ahead. Remember

157

Water, a pawn, considered the weakest piece on the board, can become the king."

Water fell asleep by the fire pit, listening to Abby's stories of all the generations who lived in Sanctuary. She loved the stories Abby told, but Water knew that generations of her family had not resided on Core. I wonder where this other Sanctuary is, she remembered thinking as she drifted off to sleep.

Water woke this morning back in the large bed that practically swallowed her up. How did I get here? She remembered drifting off to sleep in the chair by the fire pit Did it matter, she flippantly answered herself, wanting to snuggle down deeper into the covers and keep on dreaming. Her senses perked up.

"Something's up." Water bounced out of bed. She centered herself, closed her eyes, and slowly began raising her arms out before her.

"I can feel the geomagnetic energy all around me," she said as she opened her eyes and watched the hairs on her arms rise.

Even here, I am in tune. Or maybe, Water reflected, I feel it more so here.

She settled into her morning routine. One hour later, she finished her mind and body exercise and Started walking towards the room that Abby called a bathroom last night. Just getting a quick shower, she said to herself, grabbing the towel from the small closet right before the entrance. She stepped into the room and gazed at herself in the oversized mirror before her.

"I've been feeling the energy around me all morning," she declared. "There's a storm brewing here," she mimicked Gran's voice and mannerism. "My sister will wake to that storm and travel with it," Water absentmindedly had just predicted their future. "I'm not sure what form the power will take with my sister; it's unclear," she said with apprehension. Maybe just an old fashion thunderstorm, she hoped, and nothing worse. She saw the energy raging around both her and her sister in her dream. She wondered what that would bring. She turned on the shower and lightened the mood with a smile and a little laugh.

"Bathroom," she said aloud to herself. "Everyone has their name for their waste closets, I guess," she said with a smile, stepped in, and closed the door.

Water stepped out of the bathing room fifteen minutes later, dressed, refreshed, and ready to go. She looked around the room, surveying it for the first time with an eye for awareness. It still feels like it's time to go, she said to herself, reaffirming her decision. She wasn't on a schedule that she knew of, but she felt the need to leave today. Water repacked her bag and began her morning routine of organizing her thoughts and mapping out her day.

Abby interrupted, calling up to her. "Water, we have company coming, ready yourself to meet him. I will make a nice meal to eat this morn, and I have packed food for your journey."

"Ok, Abby, thanks. Who's the company?"

"Satchel, Wiffle's nephew. Now get ready."

Water was down in ten minutes, drawn by the aroma wafting up the stairs. Stepping into the kitchen, she noticed the sun kissing the morning dew and shining through the large open windows across from where she was standing. The world outside seemed to sparkle with the dawning. Seated around the dining area were Abby and a young man maybe a year or two older than her. His skin the color of the dark pebble sand; his golden hair and eyes the colors of the lightest sand; they were almost white. I wonder if he glimmers in the sunlight too, Water mused.

She caught Satchel, smiling at her as the question formed in her mind. Is he reading me, she wondered, though she hadn't felt any invasive tugs. Why had she never met him before?

"Hello, Water; I am Satchel."

"Hello, what's that wonderful smell, Abby?"

"Cornbread, grits, greens, and eggs. A good way to break your fast."

She filled her plate full; she was hungry and didn't know when she would eat this well again. "You live on Indigo," she asked him?

"Most of the time, yeah," said Satchel.

He's evading the question, Water sensed. What about the question has him subtly cloaking his mind, she questioned.

"I saw your uncle a couple of days ago." She wasn't sure how much to tell this stranger, if anything at all. It was strange he was here. She sensed a deception about him, but Kaiya would not let anyone in that meant her harm. I'm sure of that; she reassured herself.

"I know, he told me. Look, Water, we have to talk," Satchel said to her abruptly.

"Oh," Water said, raising her guard a little more. She waited for him to speak. Her gran told her that one word, 'oh,' conveyed a myriad of different feelings, meanings, and nuances. Her Gran was right.

"I know you must go into the Lion's Gap on Mount Zion."

"Ooh," she said, eyes narrowing a bit and looking more closely at him. She didn't even know that till yesterday. She was not giving away anything else about herself or her thoughts. Water sat there silently, looking at Satchel, not blinking nor speaking, shielding her mind, and probing for subtle changes indicative of an intrusion.

"Abby, can you help me here," Satchel implored, the first to look away, "Explain to her, please."

Abby looked first to Water and exchanged a look and smiled.

"Yes, Satchel, I will help. Water listen, this is what we have learned."

We, who is 'we,' thought Water? *And who are you, Abby?* She questioned not bothering to shield her thoughts.

"Oh, Water, I know this is confusing, and you are learning to distrust."

"Oh," said Water, not failing to see that Abby had also used 'Oh.'

Just listen and hear us out, please, Abby asked Water in her mind.

"Wiffle's father and your grandmother began to suspect someone was mind wiping the people. It was subtle, the mind-altering, done by Zet and Zebbble; it went unnoticed for generations. Kaiya and her sisters were busy and did not look this way until it was almost too late. Zet stole the heart of Kaiya over one hundred and fifty years ago. He stumbled over the root of the lightning-struck oak, where the wood nymphs had placed the Fairies wooden carved box and one bloodstone heart they had forged some three hundred years ago. He dug it up and took it with him.

Zet, Zeek, and Zebble all learned to control some aspect of the stone's powers over the years when they came. Zet reburied the box with the stone before they left the mountain to travel back home. He said they could not take it off the mountain again. Not until they were ready to wrest control from Kaiya. He feared Kaiya would feel the energy pulse of the heart if he took it. And she would have.

They honed their skills, learned to use the power of the stone, and managed the people. The lie set. Zet created the illusion Kaiya wanted to be worshiped and wiped their minds clean of what their relationship had been. Zebble enforced and continued the mind-wiping. He created the illusion Kaiya was not a friend but an entity that needed worshiping after his grandfather died. And now, the lie they created has become the truth for the people of Izaria." Abby sighed and continued, "Zebble is more powerful than his grandfather and by far a greater threat. He is a megalomaniac."

"A What," asked Water?

"Someone obsessed with their power, Water, let me finish now, I am almost done telling you all we know about what Zebble and his grandfather have been up to these many years," Abby said gently to Water.

Even though Water had cloaked her thoughts, Abby could see the confusion written all over her face. She resumed her story.

"The stone does not have to be in their possession to use the power, although nearness does intensive it. Zebble's family is responsible for wiping Kaiya from the peoples' minds and changing the relationship between them and her."

"I knew Zebble had something to do with that," said Water. "Wait, did you say, 'Kaiya and her sisters'?"

Abby continued, "Yes, she has sisters. That is not important now. When Zebble destroyed the energy force substance that held the bloodstone, he created a fracture in the force field that encases Core. We just became aware of that recently too."

Who are 'we,' Water puzzled once again. "I saw that crack in a mind-meld with Gran," Water said.

"Laiya is slipping," was all Abby said.

Water looked at Abby, questioning the housebot routine. Abby the housebot, Kaiya the pretend god, and Gran; where do you fit in all of this, Gran? What is going on here; Water mulled this over, instinctively cloaking herself. This housebot keeps calling Gran "Laiya." Why? Questions flowed in Water's mind like the ocean waves pounding the shore.

"Stop with all the questing in your mind, Water, and listen," Abby scolded her gently.

"So much for cloaking my thoughts," Water said under her breath.

Abby just shook her head and continued, "Zebble has learned to cloak himself well. And yes, he created the fission in the dome around Core fifty years ago when he was a small boy of seven years. We felt it. At the time, we thought it would go no further. Zet, Zebble's grandfather, lay dead, and Zeek, his father, never went back to the mountain nor took his family."

Abby Continued," But Zebble started coming back to the mountain again after his father died three years ago. He took the box with the stone with him this time. Zebble is ready to implement his takeover. He has widened the crack and can now come through it. He will be here by midday. You must leave now; it's a two-hour walk to the northeast border where you need to be. Zebble's breach is only a couple miles directly west of the path you must take, but your paths should not cross. Laiya did the probability math; she is good at that kind of stuff." Abby started to laugh at some inside joke only she knew about when she looked at Water, who was staring at her like she was crazy.

"Never mind," Abby said and continued giving them instruction. "Make it to old man oak. That will be the best place for you to retrieve the bloodstone from Zebble without much of a fight, or if you're lucky, none. It is where his grandfather stole the heart. It has come full circle. Your goal is to get the stone back from him. You will need that and the map you received here, Water. Without it, it will be Zebble who succeeds, and this world will fall to his greed and need," Abby solemnly told her. "Everything you need will be there at the crossing. You will know when you are leaving Core, Water. Use the resources of the land. Find a way to get that bloodstone back. In your hands, it will jump you to the Lion's Gap."

"Oh no," Abby suddenly grimaced with pain, "Zebble has breached Core. I feel the tear opening."

Water doubled over in pain the same moment as Abby, as though someone had torn her flesh. It only lasted a moment, but it was enough. What just happened to me? Why do I feel the pain Abby feels?

"This is much earlier than we anticipated," Abby said, catching her breath. "I'm still allowed to operate with free will within the bounds of the restricted area. I will jump you to the northern border. Zebble is intent on getting here. He has heard about the home and wants its treasures. He will not think to look next to him or behind him for you. You'll have the advantage. I'll delay his progress as much as possible. Zebble will not reach the grove until sunset tomorrow, that much I promise," Abby said. "Remember, to the old man oak now."

Abby jumped them to the border with all the supplies. "Better to ride than walk," she said, considering it again, and sent a hoover Irsei had brought from Rake some sixty years ago. "Good thing that old coot liked to keep it tuned," Abby said. To Satchel, she sent the knowledge of how to ride.

Journey well, my children.

Flabbergasted, all Water could think was, WHO OR WHAT IS THIS ABBY, as she felt the pull of the jump take.

He had just missed her. She was here, Zebble sniffed. Her essence surrounded this place. He snarled. He was staring at the legendary Sanctuary, the one his grandfather had spoken about in the mountains. The one the angry faery had told his grandfather existed. It was not that Sanctuary; rather, it was a phantom Sanctuary, a very impressive illusion. But Zebble did not know this.

All that Kasor had told Zet, Zet had told Zebble. And Zebble remembered everything his grandfather had told him as he stood before this grand house; Thinking this is my time for power. Zet had told then him the night he died, never to think again of this place they could not get into, always stopped by a barrier, until the day he would conquer it. That was today, or so Zebble believed. Instead, there was nothing but trouble through this tangled land.

It was as if this whole cursed land is against me, Zebble swore to himself. My every move is hindered by something. One man tripped over a tree root and was unfortunate enough to sprain his ankle and had to be left behind. Good luck to him, thought Zebble; I won't be going back that way. Another got bitten by some godforsaken long, pencil-thin viper with vicious-looking teeth. "Had to leave him, too; probably already dead," Zebble was mumbling to himself. He was down to two men when he got to that monstrosity of a house and couldn't get in. He tried bashing the door and breaking the large glass panes. No matter what he tried, nothing worked. That house would repair itself like nothing ever happened quicker than he could get in.

On top of everything, he was unable to jump anywhere. Zebble did not like walking at all. They had to leave their mounts at the crack's entrance; they could not come through - much too large. He and his men had walked in. He was angry, tired, and knew he had to find his way back. Turning his back on the converts, Zebble began mumbling to himself.

"I know where she is going," he reminded himself, deciding to cut his losses and go there now.

His grandfather had been there first, many years before her. And he had been there himself over the years. I have to get out of this hateful place. I'll send these two idiots to track Water, he concluded, staring at the converts. I'll go ahead and set an ambush at the crossing. There was no way, thought Zebble, she could get through this tangled web of overgrown vegetation faster than he could. It never crossed his mind that this was her home and therefore did not treat her like him.

I will get out of here and set my trap. "Set this place on fire, burn it to the ground. Then track that girl," Zebble barked. He walked away, not even bothering to hear their mutterings.

The two henchmen just looked at each other.

"Jurl, how we supposed to burn this place down. We can't batter it; we can't break it. What makes him think we can burn it?"

Jurl shook his head, "I dunno, we can burn the land around it if it doesn't burn."

"Ok, idiot, then how do **we** get outta here? You been here before, Jurl?"

Jurl shook his head no.

"Me either, and I ain't going to cut myself off from where I might need to be by a fire I started. You can stay if you want, but I get this feeling this land, and this house, doesn't like us. And right now, all I'm gonna do, is tell this place to let me out, and I won't cause no more harm, and I won't come back."

With that, he turned his back on Jurl and walked away. Maybe he noticed, perhaps he didn't; the plants opened a way for him to travel and promptly closed behind him. Jurl noticed.

He turned back to the house and said, "Man, I'm sorry I said I would burn you and your land. I'm with Beel. I won't do you no harm, and I will never come back."

A path opened for him; he ran, yelling, "Beel! Hey Beel, wait up, wait up, I'm coming, don't leave me. I'm coming, Beel! Beel, you hear me?

The path silently closed behind them.

CHAPTER 26

SENJO WOKE

THE THREE HAD created it — years in the making. Now, the old ones were all awake.

We have just begun these discussions. What are you called these days, Al, right? A shortened version of Aldebaran, Tascheter, or do you no longer go by that ancient name Tas? Senjo sang Elon's language. *What is the sense of urgency I detect in the new young one,* he asked? *What is making them so agitated?*

There has been a new development, the first in this period. A young wave rider who has the natural ability to see and ride the wave, stated Aldebaran. *He does not yet realize he is the portal, but he will soon. We cannot keep this species off the wave forever. They are a short-lived species and move fast. What is no time for us is a life span for them. We had been considering the possibilities and all the changes since Abby's birth three hundred years ago. Also, there is one who poses a serious threat to our ecosystems.*

One? How can one of them be a threat to our ecosystems or even us? Senjo questioned disbelievingly.

There is a possibility this one gaining access to the wave and bringing his destruction out to all the universe, Al said. *We would survive, but our eco-systems would not.*

One of them can do this. Do all the others agree, Senjo asked?

No, but they don't have to. Only a few hold power. In three seasons of this planet's cycle, this human male will have the ability. The three have been

165

working toward another path. Still, if he gets this access, he will spread his vision, not theirs, stated Aldebaran matter of factly.

We never worried about these species before; in fact, we didn't even bother to see them. They are but tiny particles in the scheme of things, Tascheter.

I know, Senjo. The time has come to decide if this species is worth saving or destroy them, for they will ride the wave and spread out,

"*Senjo. We may need their help with the darkness,* Aldebaran said with concern.

The darkness is lurking on the edge of our home; he sang to Senjo. *We have lost contact with our brethren on the rim of our galaxy. There is only silence. The three set a plan in motion. It includes all the players now coming together and those Elon willing to work with this subspecies.*

You have been talking to the one who rides Tas. I would like to meet him and the child of Abby, Senjo sang.

I will call you the next time I meet with him. He and one of the children of Abby travel together, Al said, fading away.

CHAPTER 27

HOOVER WHAT?

"Wow," "WATER SAID, looking around after Abby jumped them from the house.

"I'm standing at the edge of Core in the foothills of a mountain I didn't know existed four days ago." Overwhelmed and more than a little bit confused, she just wanted to sit for a minute, get her bearings, and see who Satchel is. Water was facing away from Satchel, had been since they jumped to the border of Core. I hadn't known anything was wrong. She shook her head in disbelief. My life trashed in one night, and I still don't understand why three months later. Zebble brought violence to Core. Gran is missing. I can't find Kaiya anywhere, and it looks like those two set this whole thing up.

It would be just like you, Gran, to plot with Kaiya. Water added mind speaking, just in case either was listening. *And who is this crazy house bot, Abby?* She threw that question out to Gran for good measure. Was this the same programming as Sista Sol? It's the same time frame. No wonder she went rogue. I sure would have.

I like order, Water shouted in her mind. It's been nothing but chaos for months. Gran isn't saying anything, leaving me unaware of everything. I didn't even know I would be leaving the sanctuary of Core. I sure didn't expect Satchel or all of this drama. Water sighed, fighting the tears that would not stop. I didn't know this was my last goodbye to my home. She looked down quickly, glad her back was to Satchel. She had always traveled freely everywhere in Izaria, though in truth, she rarely left Core. Water liked being home. Going like this, it just felt so different; walking out felt permanent. Water sensed the shield around her, felt it vibrate through her, speaking to her heart. My home, she said.

"We are walking off the sanctuary of Core." Water stretched her arms out above her head, feeling the energy of her land, her Core giving back the love she had given it all her life. From here on out, anything could happen, thought Water.

"What am I thinking? It already *has* happened," she said out loud, not caring to explain her outburst to Satchel, dismayed at all the changes happening so quickly. None of them felt very good. Zebble had breached Core. Unbelievable, she said over and over in her mind. The impossible had happened. Taking a deep breath in and wiping away any evidence of tears, Water began questioning Satchel as she was turning toward him.

"How far do you think we have to wa…. What's that?" Water was staring slack-jawed, mouth agape at a strange object that Satchel was fumbling with. "What are you doing?"

"I'm activating our transportation. Abby calls it a hoover," he said. "An ancient machine used for travel. It has been on Core for sixty years but built closer to three hundred years ago. It comes from a distant world, a friend of hers brought it over," Satchel mater of factly relayed the information Abby had given to him. He was looking over the hoover he had just found a little ways off the path.

"What? What do you mean? You mean, Abby the, 'I am only a house bot (but not really)' - that Abby. The one who seems to know my Gran and calls her Laiya. THAT Abby. Who I knew nothing of until yesterday. She has some of the powers of Kaiya if she can jump us. You mean *that* Abby," Water said sarcastically.

Satchel sighed, "Yes, I mean that, Abby. Your instincts are right, Water. Abby is more than that; she and Kaiya are alike."

"Oh," Water sarcastically replied to Satchel with a straight face. That 'oh' dripping with irony, "I couldn't tell."

She had already been thinking along those lines since the day she met Abby. Water was standing in front of the hoover, staring at the contraption Satchel claimed was transportation. She had never needed to travel like this; she jumped when she needed to go anywhere.

"Abby gave me the knowledge of how to operate this machine. Put the packs in the space inside the seat," Satchel said, lifting the seat and going to retrieve his pack from where he had laid it.

"Are you kidding? Do you see the size of these packs?" Water inquired, pointing her finger to the pack Satchel was picking up and then to the one slung over her shoulder. Satchel just looked at her.

"Now, you see this tiny seat?" Water continued speaking. "How are these going to fit there?"

She was seriously questioning both his mind and the available space; one tiny seat, barely seating two, and two large thirty-pound packs. It didn't add up.

"It is an infinite space box," Satchel said.

"A what?" she questioned, perplexed.

"Abby says space is infinite in there; we can store a lot more than these packs."

He first placed his bag in the open seat; it disappeared without a hitch. She unslung her pack and placed it over the seat, and put it in. Sure enough, both fit without a problem. Water quickly shut the seat down, then reopened the seat again, and the packs were still there.

"Now, that's crazy," she uttered, shutting and opening it one more time and looking in.

"Ok, quit playing with the seat, Water. Are you ready?" Satchel asked as he sat down on the vehicle and motioned for Water to climb behind him.

"You've got to be kidding me. You want me to sit where?" Water questioned, crossing her arms across her chest. Satchel continued to look at Water.

"I'm driving," he said, motioning her again to sit behind him.

"You're what -" she started, then relented,

"Yeah, ok," climbing on behind him, feeling the seat adjust to her. Maybe it won't be so bad. The notion jumped into her head. Yeah, it will be, she responded to herself. Yeah, it will be.

"How much of a head start do you think we have? Never mind, I know." Water answered her question, remembering what Abby had said before she jumped them.

"A day and a half," she said aloud.

"I'm not sure, Water. Zebble is capable of doing a lot." He remembered what Wiffle had told him about their odds; there was a 60% chance of getting caught. "The quicker we get started, the quicker we get there," Satchel said over his shoulder and inputted the chip Abby had given him.

"I suppose you have that map in that head of yours, too," Water said cynically.

"I do," Satchel said as the hoover roared to life then settled into a quieter mode.

This machine hasn't been used in a while, Satchel thought, getting comfortable driving.

He flashed the path possibilities into Water's mind as well, and the driving knowledge, just in case.

"Now, you do, too," he said to her.

"Ok," Water began as she looked at the possibilities.

"Let's head to the northeast path, that seems the best way to go, Satchel, and it's also the one Abby suggested we take."

They headed out across the mountain base, the morning sun shining down upon them, both glittering in the rays.

CHAPTER 28

HOW TO WORK A GIFT

IVER DISCOVERED THE leisure of traveling on water. Irsei talked nonstop, both verbally and in her mind. It got to the point he mixed them up so much she longer thought, 'this is verbal, that's mind.' It was the same either way. He taught her to cloak her mind and deflect someone trying to sneak in and hide in her head.

"Girl, your thoughts are out there for anyone to hear—quiet your mind. Let me show you how to control what you're doing, put a barrier between your thoughts and those who are trying to get into your head," explained Irsei. "You want to be able to hear them, but they can't hear you."

"How do I do that?" River quizzed Irsei, working out the logistics in her mind.

"Everyone does it differently, finds what works best for them," Irsei explained with a shrug of his shoulders.

"Me, I put a mist around me, so thick, those trying to sneak in my mind get lost trying. If I want someone to believe they are reading me, I send a sliver through the mist of what I want them to hear or believe. Now, you practice hiding from and blocking me," Irsei said.

All-day, they played this game. They called it, 'catch me if you can.' She would try to sneak into his mind, and he would sneak into hers. She noticed the differences between someone talking to you in mind and someone trying to sneak in. Irsei was one of the best at sneaking in. It wasn't until late that day; she felt the difference instantly.

"I caught you," she laughed. Irsei laughed with her.

"Bout time, girl, I was giving up hope."

"Making the barrier was easy, Irsei. Controlling what I let out and who I let in is in the details. Like Gram always said, it's in the details. I think I got this. Let's play some more."

By early evening, she stopped him three out of the four times he tried, and she had caught him napping at least twice. She sat quietly in his mind until he noticed.

"You're a natural at this baby girl. Of course, you had a master teaching you," he preened. Come on now, navigate over to that inlet around the bend," Irsei said, pointing it out on the computer screen. "We're coming off the river. We'll set up camp there. We're close to the border, and I want to cook us a good meal and rest up before we leave the land."

Working together smoothly, they brought their raft onto the inlet's sandy shore.

"You have a disc for everything," River said as she watched Irsei place one on the ground and open it into sleeping quarters. "How about dinner," she asked? She was feeling hungry.

"Well, I could open one of the foods," he nodded to her, pulling out a disc, a pencil-thin object that, with a flick of his wrist, snapped open. River nodding, thinking that was a good idea.

"Naw, let's fish for our meal tonight," he laughed, holding a fishing pole in his hand. "I'll catch us some dinner. You set up the fire and get some of those herbs out your Gram packed. We're going to have a good old-fashioned fish fry."

Just then, they heard a loud screech and looked up. High above flew a magnificent creature. River stood, mouth agape, entranced by what she saw. Its wingspan had to be sixty meters long, with a golden-brown body half the size of its wings and a golden crown flecked with copper and brown.

"What IS that?" River cried out. "We match in colors," she exclaimed, radiating joy at the sight of the magnificent creature.

"Yep, he's a golden eagle," Irsei said, watching the raptor fly overhead. "Bout ten times the size they used to be in my time. Glad he's not hungry. Might look at us as a snack," Irsei mumbled casually, looking away.

River stared at Irsei dumbfounded, looking up again; *Snack?*

Apprehension set in. Irsei looked her straight in the eye with an intense glare and then started laughing, confusing River even more.

"Not to worry, River, those raptors don't like human meat, say we taste of the poisons that surround our nests. Can't vouch for any of the other raptors, don't talk to them," he finished, tipping his hat to the eagle in the sky.

He walked to the river's edge and cast his line, laughing the whole time. River just stood on the raft, watching the eagle fly away.

A snack, she thought, again.

HI GNARLY

THEY HAD RIDDEN well into the dusk of the day, stopping to eat and rest for an hour only. Not knowing how close Zebble was, they kept moving, even though Abby had promised a day and a half head start. Water knew once he made it back to the crack, he would mount and ride to Lion's Gap. His mount might be swifter than Abby might have known. Izaria mounts weren't much to look at, but they moved very quickly over land. She had seen them on Gran's guided history tour. They looked like snails and ran like sailfish, gliding over the water. They were fast, Water realized, more rapid than this odd machine she and Satchel were riding.

Water again realized with a shock that Zebble was planning some takeover. Never in all of Izarian history had that possibility even come up.

"Water, check the map. How close are we to the crossing?"

Water pulled the map up in her mind, looking for markers on the land as well.

"We're close, Satchel, within one-eighth of a mile; we'll come upon the oak grove. See that rock formation to the right?" she said, pointing to a stacked stone structure resting on a hill that seemed to lead to a particular star, the largest in a group of four. "That's one of the markers pointing the way. Let's go up the hill and see."

The star rising right above them shone all around, directing the way. Looking up and seeing the brightness beaming down upon her. Water smiled and felt the joy of sharing energy.

"The royal stars," she said aloud and pointed to the four stars above them, making Satchel take notice also. They crested the hill and came upon a broader trail that crossed the road headed north.

Satchel stopped the hoover, and Water dismounted and stretched her legs. Although it was dark, the starlight shone bright enough to see the immediate surroundings.

"Look, Water, just past the road going north. We can set up camp there; it's off the road and sheltered. It looks like the land dips by the trees. We can get our bearings in the morning and go from there," Satchel said.

Water was tired and ready to rest some and eat a little too.

"Yes, Satchel, I agree," Water said as she began walking toward the trees. The air stirred, and wisps of shadows began to show themselves.

"Satchel, we're walking on ancient grounds here."

Water stood by the old gnarly bristlecone pine in the oak forest center on either side of the road. This old gnarly pine was speaking to Water. The memories that flowed from this beautiful tree, the twenty-five-hundred-years its life had spanned, such glory, marveled Water. The wood nymphs' are here, thought Water as she moved around the Grove. Gran was always so fond of storytelling about the nymphs and faeries, as she called them. These are the ancient races that Gran talked about that I had never seen until today. Ancient races I did not know lived on Izaria.

"Satchel, do you see the nymphs and the faeries? They're all coming to the field with us," Water said, smiling.

Satchel looked all around, awed. He had been watching them arrive for the last few minutes: Some came alone, some in pairs, a few in groups of five or more — they are gathering around Water, he said to himself, stunned. Satchel heard of the legendary faeries but had never seen one until now. The wood nymphs were notoriously shy and rarely dealt with humans. Now there were hundreds in the grove, and more still came.

These lands were restricted; they had been since Izaria's beginning. It was Satchel's first time on the mountain too.

The faeries danced with Water and the ancient gnarly pine in a dance of love, while the wood nymphs sang harmony with the earth and sky. Sparks of golden light flew from the faeries as they danced. Water, herself, was the reflection of sunlight and oceans.

"Sunlight, at night, in a forest lit by faeries, a tree, and a girl." Satchel was astonished.

Water was dancing in the light of the sun while the moon rose full and high into the night sky. When he looked, he couldn't see Water. He saw reflections of oceans that raged, the waters of a calm blue lagoon, and the foam on a monster wave. He saw the blue burning of a hot sun born centuries ago. He heard the wood nymphs singing with the oceans in a sunlit grove on a starry night. Satchel had always been a watcher, trained from birth. Watchers came from Sanctuary and were a part of the original contract with the three. There had been a watcher in his family since time began in Izaria. Satchel, who thought he understood who Water was because he was a watcher and knew her history, realized he knew nothing about her.

What a fool I have been, Satchel berated himself. How arrogant of us to think we know this girl because we see her history. He understood one thing: this girl will make things interesting.

"Satchel, the old one tells me you hide the truth, and the faeries feel I should give you a chance to speak what you know. They say they can always kill you if you become a threat. Seeing Satchel's face show a twinge of fear, Water laughed softly. "Satchel, Gran would have never sent you if she at least didn't trust you. Abby would not have given us any help if you meant to harm. The faeries will cause you no harm, although I can't say they won't play a trick or two on you."

Water was smiling and looking at Satchel once again as if she walked in his mind, and he was not aware. Satchel knew not to take faeries lightly. They played by their own rules and had their own ways. Anyone who underestimated a faery didn't stay around long.

"I, for one, am going to enjoy this, for here, tonight, I am safe," Water sighed a relaxing breath. "Tomorrow, a storm brews."

"They're not sure about you, Satchel. They think you conceal much of the truth, not quite a liar, but close." Upon saying that, Water walked away, declaring, "If I wanted to see your secret, all I would have to do is look or maybe ask. I see you are as capable as your uncle, Wiffle. Let's agree to respect each other's boundaries, ok?"

"Yeah, Water. I think that would be a good start. I believe there are things you know, and I would like to share what I know. And by the look of things, that might not be much."

He was pretty sure she would find out everything and soon. He thought to himself, what would you think of me if you knew how much I hide? And how much would it change you, Water? She had an innocence he would hate to see disappear.

"I am tired, Satchel, it's been a long day, and they are offering a night of peace. They will protect us tonight. Let us rest here and begin fresh in the morning. The faeries say Zebble will not be here until late tomorrow. They, like Abby, will make sure that is when he gets here."

With that, Water turned and walked into the grove and nestled into the roots of the ancient one. The old one covered her against the cold and kept her warm and safe.

Yep, Satchel thought, it will be very interesting.

CHAPTER 30

GONE FISHIN

SEECA HAD TRAVELED twelve hours over the wastelands, and now day two traveling by foot toward the mountains with this idiot, Begak tormenting him all the way. They had reached the foothills of the mighty mount Argot five hours ago. Seeca's internal map told him he was close to the first coordinates Al had given him. He believed it was just over the ridge. He could hear water running the closer they got to his destination.

"How did you get that formula? My dad says it's incomplete and makes no sense. He's starting to question whether you're worth his time. Better enjoy the space in the middle levels; you won't be there for long."

Begak would not shut up, and Seeca had had enough. There was no reprieve from Begak or the guard; both were watching his every move. Tomorrow he had to be away from them. He had to find the one with the sun inside. Al said I would know. I would be able to see the pattern of the wave within her. At least I know it's a girl, Seeca sighed, having no idea how he would escape.

They hadn't seen a single soul out here in the wild. The eerie silence was broken only by the calls of the strange creatures who soared the skies. Ever since Al showed him the sights above, Seeca could enter a flyer and see through their eyes. It was amazing how much they saw, at least a hundred times better than him, and he had perfect eyesight. It was too easy to get lost there, seeing through the raptor's eyes, with no thought except finding food, just soaring.

I need to get my bearings, he thought. He looked up and saw the golden raptor flying through the skies. Seeca reflected a nanosecond on the consequence of his next action, then jumped into the raptor. At the same time, Begak and the guard walked in front of him. Seeca jumped to get away from Begak as well as to survey the area.

He was flying again, soaring through the skies! He felt like screeching for joy and did.

Upon hearing the magnificent golden flyer/him, Seeca watched Begak, and the guard looked to the sky, awed by the sight of it/him. Can this creature be prideful, he wondered? Because I sure am, he laughed as he flew higher. He was one with the creature he rode with, soaring over the river, thinking only of food, when he saw two humans on the water, floating on cut trees.

A raft, he thought, pulling up Al's input.

Both auras on the swift-moving raft were bright, but as the flyer's gaze fell upon the smaller being, he saw the pattern of the wave.

He screeched his joy again; He knew he found her.

But how far behind him they were, he wasn't sure. Measuring the distance in the bowels and measuring distance high above in the sky was not the same. And darkness would soon be upon them. He knew Begak would go no further today. His last glimpse of the two on the raft was coming off the water. And the man tipped his hat to the sky. He looks familiar. Seeca thought of the man riding with the girl as he came back into his body. I didn't get a good look, though, since the man's head was down the whole time, almost like he didn't want me to see his face, Seeca thought

"Hey dummy, what's got you so stiff? Afraid of what's coming? You ought to be," Begak prodded Seeca in the side with a stick he had picked up a day ago and carried with him.

Seeca had stayed too long with the flyer; he came back into his body while Begak was making a slicing motion across his throat. Seeca hadn't figured out how to soar with the flyers and keep part of his mind on the ground and functioning.

"We're parking here for the night," Begak declared, standing on a small ridge looking down at the raging river.

"Yeah, I figured that out already," Seeca smirked under his breath.

He heard the guard snort softly, wondering if he too saw Begak's arrogant behavior. The river both fascinated and horrified the boys, especially Begak. He did not have the foreknowledge Seeca did. But even with the knowledge within, the river was a terrifyingly beautiful site — miles wide moving with frantic speed. Neither of the boys had ever seen anything like it. Begak made camp as far away as he could from the water, high on the small ridge. Seeca camped on the beachhead near the water. She would be coming this way, he thought, remembering the girl on the raft. He knew he had to leave in the morning. He had gone through several different scenes in his head and rejected them all. They all had the same ending: he either got caught, or he died. He knew the one he saw on the water was the one he needed to find, and she was moving on this raging river somewhere behind him. Seeca was determined to see this through.

"Tomorrow, I go, whatever comes. You will leave tomorrow as well," Seeca whispered to the one he saw. *And on this mighty river, I see you will travel. I will be here to meet you.*

✦ ✦ ✦

They woke to a dark and gloomy sky. Irsei was cleaning their site and replacing the discs into his pack.

"This's the last day on the water, River. We'll come upon the standing rock by midday. We go different paths from there," Irsei was telling her.

River was feeling very apprehensive about splitting from Irsei and being on the mountain of Argot alone. On top of that, River thought, the weather is terrible. She had never been in a rainstorm before, wasn't sure what to expect.

"Looks like a storm is brewing," Irsei said. "Those clouds are looking mean," pointing them out to River. "Going to get a downpour soon."

"What's a downpour?" River questioned. Bubble didn't water the lands with downpours and storms, just timed sprays.

"Lots and lots of water from the skies," Irsei said, absently looking at the rolling dark clouds. "It looks like you're going to experience one firsthand, my girl," he said, smiling at her.

She wasn't sure about that smile. That smile does not look friendly, she thought. It seems more like Irsei's about to play a joke on me. Based on that smile, River knew she would not like a downpour.

"Did you notice when we crossed the barrier, River?" Irsei asked.

River thought back to the ride on the water last night. About an hour before they made camp, she had felt a sharp tug on her body, like she was wading against a current.

"About an hour before we made Camp last night," she said to Irsei. "It felt like when I'm in the water walking against the current." She had learned a whole lot about rivers these last couple of days with Irsei.

"Yep, that's right. I never had that much resistance from Bubble before. I think Bubble didn't want to let you go."

"That's funny. I felt the same thing as if Bubble didn't want me to go. Bubble and JIVE were my only friends on the land growing up. Bubble was always there to catch me falling out of trees and went with me on all my exploring. Maybe he didn't want me to go because he knows he can't protect me out here."

"More than likely," said Irsei, "Abby had to tell him to let you pass."

Cloaking her thoughts from Irsei, River again questioned, who are these people? Grams and Irsei were human factors. Abby was what? More than a housebot, that's for sure. River went back to the day she rode to the house. She was remembering a man named Irsei cropping up through history. Everywhere. The disease and the rebellion came to mind quickly. She had thought about both on the ride to the house. Then she recalled her first impression of him and asked,

"Irsei, do you have family in the Cities? You resemble an elder, I know, Eldar Wizard."

"I got kin everywhere — time to push off. Keep the shelter open halfway just in case that downpour starts quick," was all Irsei said.

What is he hiding? River questioned as they readied the raft, sliding it into the water, both jumping aboard with water travelers' ease.

Seeca woke that morning, knowing it was time to go. He was sleeping by the fire he had built on the sandy beach. He had no shelter - hadn't the whole trip, Begak made sure of that.

"There's no equipment for you," Begak sneered at Seeca.

Seeca had packed his supplies based on the knowledge Al had placed in his mind. Casually He asked Izen for what he needed, saying he got the lowdown on the web. Izen was to give him the disc for shelter. Seeca never got it. He woke before the sun rose and saw the gloom; this would not be a day for sunshine. He didn't know the sky could look so angry or what that meant. Only that rain would come. But what kind of storm would he see? He had only Al's references to rain, which was as vast and varied as this 'outside' thing. He had been in the wild for only two days, and it had become blatantly obvious to him that he sorely lacked outdoor knowledge.

This place is not the bowels; he would remind himself daily. I'm in this knee-deep and sinking. He didn't need to tell himself he wasn't home. It just felt right to say it; like a mantra, it relaxed him.

Seeca could hear Begak cursing his plight.

What's he complaining about now? That's all he ever does, tired of hearing him. He looked to the ridge and rethought going up there. I don't care. Let the guard deal with him. Seeca shrugged his shoulders and went back to reviewing all the paths out of here, going to the lion's roar. A lot of ways out, only one way up.

What Al had said kept playing in his mind. Two nights and that was it. He had to get away from them today. Now was the perfect time to go. Begak didn't function well out here, especially in the mornings. Seeca smirked as he listened to Begak cursing and swearing at everything he encountered. Begak considers this a hardship. It's different, but not harder, for me. Let Begak know the difficulties of Rake, eking out a substandard living in the bowels. Then he would know what hard is.

I wonder, Seeca speculated, if it's possible to live outside all the time? When this is over, I might try. And bring mom and dad if it works. He started daydreaming as he began to move closer to the water. How deep is it? It flows fast, he observed. How had those two built the raft?

"The tree limbs seemed to float. Would one large one hold my weight?" Seeca questioned aloud, planning his escape.

I'll only be able to get one fallen limb to ride upon; it must hold my weight. But how do I calculate what's big enough? Too small, and I will probably sink. Looking toward Begak's camp, Seeca considered the alternative. Not to go now was certain death.

He looked to the sky once again — dark rolling clouds, with light playing through them. Lightning, the name came to the front of his memory. Another life-saving memory that Al gave him. Lightning and thunder were not a bowel experience. Still, he felt as if he knew of thunder and lightning personally and had experienced it. It was new to him, and it was old to him.

"Thanks, Al, for this knowledge." It had given him the edge he needed. Begak had begun to become suspicious of his knowledge, questioning him last night as he watched Seeca set up his camp.

"Who told you about outside?" grilled Begak.

"Your dad," Seeca barked back at Begak, tired of him.

"My dad, what? What did my dad do? He gave you the same info he gave me. He told me he wouldn't give you any, didn't want you to have an advantage. Guess he changed his mind. Just like that sob to do something like this and not say a word to me," complained Begak, walking away.

Seeca just smirked and went about his business. Of course, it wasn't Begak's dad. But he wasn't telling Begak that.

Seeca brought his mind back around to the problem at hand. "How am I getting out of here right now?"

Thunder rolled through the air. Seeca could hear Begak cursing almost as loud as thunder.

"I'm not leaving this site, not with the sky looking like that, Jenkins. We Can't jump out of here; it doesn't work. I can't reach anyone, no communications. Only when I reach the bend and meet with the Pearl tomorrow will I get out of this place; I'm not leaving right now. Jenkins, tell the rat we're staying one more day."

The Pearl will be here tomorrow, Seeca, worried. Now I gotta get out of here for sure. He doubled his efforts to find a tree limb big enough to hold his weight. Everyone in the bowels knew the Pearl. Seeca had met him some years ago, down where he found the old jump site. They had met by accident, or so Seeca thought and had remained amicable. It was months after they had met that Seeca became aware he was the Pearl. It hadn't seemed to change their relationship dynamics, though, so Seeca let it ride. You never knew with the Pearl if he was friend or foe.

I am going to be long gone before tomorrow comes, vowed Seeca. I'm leaving now, he decided, seeing a log washing ashore that he calculated was big enough to hold his weight without sinking. He began to cautiously wade out into the river, feeling the cool nip of the water. Brrr, he thought as the cold hit his body. He reached for the log floating by. The eddy had brought the limb closer to shore and slowed the rugged path it was on.

That girl was somewhere behind him, Seeca thought, and he began to formulate a plan to ride the river downstream and then wait for her to show up. Not a great idea, he thought, but it would have to do. Seeca did not want to think about what might be in the water with him. Already, Al's instant knowledge was bombarding him with images of man-eating killer fish.

River and Irsei rounded the bend and saw Seeca standing in the water near the small beachhead, looking as if he had lost something. Seeca had seen them seconds before that.

"I can see the pattern of the universe in him," said River.

She and Irsei both heard him simultaneously,

"The Pear...," Seeca started to say, then looked to River, astounded, and said, "You are the sun, I see the wave in you, I've been looking for you."

That was the last thing she heard him say before he screamed, and something yanked him into the river.

"What the... you!" Yelled Seeca feeling something grip his feet as he watched the two on the raft disappear beneath a shield. And then suddenly, he was flying through the water, held tight by the line that had wrapped around his feet, pulling him in as he desperately tried to get away.

Jenkins had just crested the small bluff, looking down on the beach for the kid. He caught a glimpse of some bright glare on the water, then just as quickly, it disappeared.

What was that? He barely had time to think when he heard the kid scream. Jenkins automatically began moving toward the sound of the screaming and stopped dead in his tracks.

The kid was flying through the water, dipping under the waves, then coming up sputtering and choking and fighting to get away from something under the water pulling him in.

Under Seeca went again, the fog and river taking him away. Shocked, Jenkins stood watching the kid until he went under and did not resurface.

Again, he heard a scream; this time, it was Begak screaming in rage. Seeca was gone.

CHAPTER 31

THREE IN ONE

"*WELL NOW, AREN'T you just a busybody, Abby. I see your handprint all over this*". Senjo declared.

"*I didn't break the letter of the laws. Although, I think I might have skirted a couple of them,*" giggled Abby.

"*You have had a hand in this too, Tas, aka, Aldebaran. Or is it Al now,*" Senjo sang out? *I don't know what to call you anymore. I wouldn't know how to translate the Elon name we sing when we sing of you. These humans forget their histories so quickly. They don't even remember the name they gave you twenty-five hundred years ago, let alone your name a mire ten-thousand years ago. Now, as to the young man, you found, scattered on the wave. Tell me of him,* Senjo asked.

"*Seeca came to me on the wave, separate from three's experiment. But yes, synchronicity. We must allow the flow of the wave to do just that flow. I see the beginning of a new pattern in the universe. Let's see where it goes,*" sang Aldebaran and left and sought Abby.

Senjo will meet with the two youngsters soon, Abby. He is interested in the young one who is a natural wave rider. I think he is a bit curious about your girls, too. He says things like 'Star born hey, an Elon and a human. Interesting.' Sen hasn't been overly curious in 4 billion years, dreaming the last 2 billion," Al remarked. "*Abby, let Layia and Kaiya know it is time to share this with all.*"

Roger that Al sang Abby, laughing aloud, *Oh right, they already know;*

they knew when I did, Al, Abby laughed again. *We are the same, Al.* She sang out to the universe.

Don't you love their expressive language, she said as she faded from him.

She was sitting in her kitchen, drinking her morning tea. She reached out to Irsei.

Good morning love.

Morning baby, I'm a bit busy right now. What's up?

Abby looked through his eyes and saw he was on the raging Water with River.

I see. I need you to contact your brother Eoh. We might require his services.

Baby, he is right there in Sanctuary. You could easily find him. What is it you need? Irsei knew his woman had something specific she wanted.

I could, but right now, he is in Scottish mode with his treelings and doesn't like to be disturb. Besides, we might need him for his old trade, the one he still leads but pretends he doesn't—the Assassin's Guild.

I know they forced him to maintain the title Master of the Guild, even though he does not reside in Rake anymore. I'm sure the Guild doesn't know that either. Knowing him to be a master of disguise, they think he is everywhere and anyone. He lets his second handle the day to day business, I'm sure. OK, Abby, is it a top priority? I can't leave this project for another day.

No, it can wait till then.

I will catch up with you in a day or so, and you can explain. I'm fishing now, baby, about to reel in a big catch, he said, laughing and showing her what was on his line.

Oh goodness, Abby chuckled. *Make sure that boy doesn't drown Irsei; we need him.*

CHAPTER 32

REELED IN

SHAKING LIKE A leaf on a tree, Seeca rode through the cold river like a fish caught by its tail. All the while, he was wondering what huge beast might be chasing him as he bobbed through the water like bait on a line.

"Hey, get me out of here," Seeca sputtered through mouthfuls of water, trying to flip around and get a glimpse at his new captors.

Slowly he felt himself making headway to the raft that remained invisible and cloaked. He only knew he was getting closer because the line that held him seemed to end abruptly, vanishing into the fog.

In between drowning, he was trying to wrap his mind around who he saw riding that raft. He was surprised by both, and one was completely unexpected. The last person he would think would be there.

Whose side was he on then? Seeca's mind was whirling with the possibilities. An opening formed, and the shield around the raft parted enough to drag him close. River and Irsei reeled Seeca in, then pulled him onto the raft. Seeca was caught feet first by the cord, his head dipping back into the water as Irsei removed him from the river.

He is drowning me, Seeca panicked, kicking out his legs and flailing with his arms.

"Quit moving like a fish on the line," Irsei commanded, pulling Seeca up by his shirt collar and throwing him onto the raft.

Sputtering and coughing up all the water he swallowed, he looked up. Oh my gosh, it *is* him, Seeca cried out in his mind, shaking uncontrollably from the cold of the water and the shock of realizing who was staring at him: the most dangerous man he knew.

Irsei stood above Seeca with a finger to his lips.

"Shhh," Irsei whispered. He yanked the boy up into a sitting position, releasing the wire from around Seeca's feet and rewinding it, and resealing the opening, all in less than ten seconds.

The raft was once again invisible.

"What was that all about?" sputtered Seeca.

"You looked like you needed rescuing. You were shouting something about how I was the one you needed to find, so we rescued you," said River.

"I never shouted anything," stated Seeca, "I was just thinking about it when I saw you."

"Thinking really loud then," River said to him.

Can she read my mind? Seeca asked himself. Does that mean he can too?

Seeca looked directly at the man who pulled him out of the water and onto the raft. Irsei turned and smiled his feral smile, and Seeca was once again terrified.

"Why did you need to find me? Remember, I can just as easily throw you back in the river. And let you fend for yourself against a man-eating water beast," River said, staring into his eyes.

Gran always told her to make a man look you in the eye when he is talking.

"This girl is reading my mind," like Al, thought Seeca.

"My name is See..."

"Before you get caught up in telling me your name and life story, skip to the bottom line and tell me why you of all people needed to find me out here, outside, of all places, where NO ONE goes. Why were you looking for me out here?" River demanded. "And what are you doing with my scumbag cousin, Begak?"

Seeca was tired. It had been a long two days with Begak. And now, he was just too tired to do anything except tell the truth. He felt he had to, or that man staring at him, who looked a whole lot like the notorious Pearl, was going to throw him back into the water.

"OK, I found a way to ride the wave, got lost, saw Layia's formula on the ride, met Al that day too - he brought me back to my body. One week later, Izen and his goons abducted me, took my parents' hostage, and now Izen wants me to figure out the wave formula. Al showed me outside and said I needed to find you by today. That's the short version of my story."

"But Al didn't say anything about him, though," he pointed the finger at Irsei.

"You're lucky, Irsei is here; otherwise, you would be on that sandbar still," River told him sternly.

"'Irsei,' that's your name? Ok, Irsei, thanks for saving me, I think." Seeca said, looking at Irsei skeptically, assuming this girl doesn't know who she was riding with or how dangerous he was.

"Don't worry, boy," Irsei said to Seeca. "Hold your tongue, and I won't have to kill you."

Seeca visibly balked at that, and River laughed.

"Irsei isn't going to kill you, at least not yet," she said. Seeing his expression, she smiled.

"I'm kidding; I'm kidding. I'm River, and you are Seeca. I want to talk to you about this 'Al.' And maybe you can explain what I see in you, like a pattern, a map of the universe, or something. Irsei says Lion's Roar is near, and there he'll have to let me off. Are you coming with me, then? Why did you need to find me? How is it you came outside to look for me? What did Al say you needed to do?"

Oh my gosh, she had a million questions, thought Seeca as he began to answer each of them, one at a time. I'm exhausted, he thought. I just had the most harrowing experience of my life. I live in the most dangerous place in the Cities, where every day can be a harrowing experience. All the questions she asked, this will take all day, Seeca sighed inwardly.

That's ok. We have all day, Seeca. River spoke in his mind

Yeah, I guess we do. Seeca answered in his mind, as well. So exhausted from the water ordeal, it took him a minute to realize River had spoken to him in his mind, and he had answered in kind.

He looked up to see River smiling at him like they shared some inside joke no one else knew. He just stared at her for a moment and then cracked a grin.

That's something else, River, he thought.

Yes, it is Seeca. YES, IT IS, River replied, grinning at him.

CHAPTER 33

IZEN'S BANE

"**W**HAT ELSE COULD go wrong?" Izen said out loud, exasperated. "I'm just going to have to go out there myself."

Begak is meeting up with the Pearl tomorrow, and now, there was no Seeca. According to my idiot son and the halfwit guard, the kid was pulled into the river. By the silver tongue of some giant water beast, it seems. He supposedly surfaced twice, then went under and never came back up, lost to the fog and river. Of course, this information was relayed secondhand, and now almost a half-day old, Izen fumed. When Izen had sent the team with supplies ahead of his son, he had discovered they could communicate by video com until the foothills of the mountains.

"My son had crossed into the foothills the night before. Six hours they had traveled into the foothills, according to them." Izen sarcastically spoke aloud as he sat in his office, tapping his fist on the oak desktop, his anger rising. "It has taken them almost twelve hours to cross the wastelands, not the eight JIVE had estimated," he seethed. "Then, those three idiots supposedly walked another four hours to reach the foothill, and six more into the mountain, where they could not reach me." He continued his rant, his fist hitting the top a little harder. No longer tapping but knocking. "My son, Begak, Jenkins, the burly bodyguard, and one wiry little runt they were supposed to guard had NOT even been traveling for three full days."

"They rested by a river, Begak said. Seeca by the river's edge, Begak said. The weather is bad, he says." Izen was still ranting, unable to stop,

190

letting his anger rise. "He has been traveling in thunder and rainstorm to get out of the foothills so he could contact me and inform me that Seeca got eaten by a monster in the river."

Izen quietly stood up when he finished this sentence, took a deep breath, then slammed his fist down onto the desk.

"JIVE," Izen yelled, "fix the coordinates for Lion's Roar in memory. Have ready at the exit point whatever transportation that will get me there as quickly as possible. Jump me to the closest point. How far is that?"

"The southeast side of Sanctuary is as close as I can get you. The wastelands lie between the Cities and the foothills of Argot everywhere but Sanctuary, and you cannot go through there. Your sand runner has a good chance of crossing the wastelands in 6 hours with a light load, but your load will not be light if you tow another mini hoover for your use in the mountains. That would require 8 hours to cross the wastelands. Once you reach the foothills, you can abandon the sand runners and use the hoover. You would reach your destination within a day; this is the best plan of action, as I believe there is no other transportation, sir."

"Damn. How long to travel like this?"

"Twenty-four to thirty-six hours, sir. to get to Lion's Roar."

"What?! How barbaric! Taking a day to get anywhere, it's insane! What did Layia think when she restricted jumps in Sanctuary and on that mountain?" Izen yelled at JIVE, frustrated. "The first thing I'm doing as heir," he screamed, "is to make it so I can jump anywhere." As an afterthought, he said, "And I am charging to use the jumps."

Ok, enough daydreaming, thought Izen, and called out to JIVE again. "JIVE, set up a pack for me, essentials only with one weapon. The hand-held laser. I'll be ready to jump in four hours. Have a team assembled and ready to follow no longer than six hours behind me."

Izen was glad Laiya's descendants were exempt from all the restrictions. Otherwise, he would not be able to jump carrying a laser weapon that he intended to use on anyone who got in his way.

"Set the rejuvenator for three hours, JIVE. I'll need the extra time; I don't intend to sleep for the next forty-eight hours."

CHAPTER 34

———✦———○———✦———

ON THEIR OWN

RIVER AND SEECA had left Irsei many hours ago, leaving him on the shore as they continued to their destination, the inlet closest to the Lion's Roar. Irsei had hidden a hoover beneath an invisy-shield on the side of the path.

"At least this hoover is a newer version than the one I rode to Laiya's house," said River to Seeca as they prepare to ride to Lion's Roar. "Like the other one, this one has an infinite space box where all our supplies and packs will fit nice and neat," she said matter of factly.

Seeca just stood there and stared as he watched River put both packs into a tiny little cubby beneath the seat. He had never seen a hoover before, let alone an infinite space box. Both dumbfounded him.

"I mean, I heard about these before," pointing at the hoover, "I suppose I could learn how to ride. Seeca wished Al were here and could zap him the knowledge. But how could all that stuff fit in that tiny box? But every time he opened it, sure enough, everything was still in there.

"Stop playing with the seat, Seeca, and get on."

"On where?" he asked.

River climbed on and patted the seat behind her, "Right here." She didn't have time to teach him how to drive the hoover or the patience to instantly show him how to grab the info from her mind instantly, so they doubled with her driving.

As she drove along to the grove, she thought about this adventure that has brought her here. It wasn't even a week ago that I left the compound and started this journey, River said to herself. Really? It seemed so much longer. I am a different River now than the one I was just days ago. And it's time to act on something she said to herself.

She stopped the hoover, turned around, and said, "Ok, Seeca; spill it."

He had remained silent since leaving Irsei behind. Seeca looked at River, now, trying to decide what to say or even how much to say.

"Look, my whole life just changed," Seeca began, "And I mean like forever. There's nowhere I can go that Izen can't find me," he said, looking directly at River.

"And don't think I don't know Izen is chasing you too, and there is nowhere you can go he won't find **you**. For what? Do you even know River? Why are you running from Izen," he asked?

"I know why I'm running from him; he wants me to decipher a three-hundred-year-old formula that I can't. Izen thinks I'm a math whiz when all I am is a good hacker; he'll kill me when he no longer needs me."

"Slow down, Seeca. Let's start with Irsei and work our way back. You know him; he scares you. Who is he to you?"

"I would rather not talk about him. People tend to disappear around him."

"We're far enough away from him. I don't think he can read our minds or hear our thoughts," River said offhandedly.

"He can read my mind! Like you did with me? Like Al does. Holy man, I'm toast!" he cried out.

"Ok, ok, I will tell you what I know," Seeca said, just wanting to get this all out, whatever happened. He had only trusted his parents his whole life, but right now, he was tired and just needed to tell what he knew. Maybe they could figure this out together, he thought. To him, it was worth a try. Perhaps we can be friends.

"I know him as the Pearl, and he's working for Izen."

"Irsei works for Izen?" she said, surprised.

"I'm confused about him.," Seeca said. "The Pearl has a reputation in the Cities as someone who can get a job done and someone you don't mess with if you want to live. We've crossed paths a couple of times over the years."

"He is that Pearl." Wow, thought River.

"If not, he could be his twin. Irsei seems like he is older than The Pearl, but The Pearl is a chameleon, and he can look like anyone."

Seeca shuddered at the thought that this man can read minds too. He's dangerous; that idea crossed his mind more than once.

"I don't know what he's doing with Izen; you can never know with the Pearl if he's friend or foe," said Seeca. "I do know the last thing he said to me, and I think he cloaked us from you, was, 'Boy, I will hunt you down and string you up by your toes if you let a hair on her head be harmed and you aren't dead or dying." Seeca shuddered, remembering that encounter. "Whatever he is doing with Izen will not include harming you. That's for sure," Seeca reassured River.

River waved Seeca's concern away. "I already knew that. I met him in Sanctuary with a house holo with impeccable honor who called him an old coot, and they were the best of friends. No one can bring harm to Sanctuary, and Abby loves him. It won't be me that he will harm."

"Seeca, I think you and I need to open up and share what we know. It's harder to lie when mind speaking. It's possible to lie, I saw Irsei do it, but he is a master," said River. "I'm new to mind speaking too, like you. I will do my best with you, Seeca. We will use mind-melding as a way of sharing information about this, our lives, our thoughts. Come, it is time for us to know each other, maybe establish a bond of trust. I think we're going to need that. Let's break, rest, eat, and talk."

"*Yes, River, I agree,*" answered Seeca in his mind. "*Might as well start now.*"

CHAPTER 35

BEGAK'S DECISION

"**Y**OU LOST THE kid?"

"It wasn't my fault!" cried Begak to the Pearl. "Some monster from the water snatched him off the shore and swallowed him whole."

"Really?" The Pearl had to laugh at that. "That's what you told your dad?"

"Yeah, why?" Begak defensively answered the Pearl.

"This happened when; yesterday morning?"

"Yeah," Begak said. He sounded so discouraged that the Pearl cut Begak a break and gave him some advice.

"Then Izen will be here by midday tomorrow. He will make his way to Lions Roar." The Pearl knew that much. "You have two choices, go there or go home. By the way, your father sent three mini's ahead of you. They are hidden on the left side of the road a half a mile up. Goodbye, gentlemen."

With that, the Pearl turned and was gone, leaving them standing with only a choice to make. Begak felt sick. He didn't want to stay in this hell. Yesterday, they had walked back six hours out of the mountain to communicate with his dad, letting Izen know Seeca was dead. Then he waited another day to meet with the Pearl. He was tired. I want to be home, in my space, back in my life, he thought. But he knew going home was his last option. Begak knew this hell was an easier hell than the one his father would give him if he ran back. He didn't have a choice; he was staying. Begak sighed, resigned to his fate.

"I'm going to go to the roar," Begak said.

They had walked to where the Pearl had seen the mini; hoovers hidden.

This is a first, Begak said to himself, looking at the mini. I only ride crazy vehicles in my hologram room. And that's only when I select ancient eras. Why didn't my dad tell me about these minis? They must have been here when we passed by yesterday.

"Jenkins, you are free to go home. You've been a great help to me out here. You deserve better than I gave. Thank you."

Begak began to prepare himself for this leg of the journey alone. He had maybe a day's ride ahead of him. As he readied himself to go, Jenkins did the same. Begak turned to this big burly man and repeated it.

"What's up, Jenkins? Go home,"

Jenkins didn't listen and proceeded to climb onto his mini. He was a big man over 6 feet 5 inches tall, probably 290 pounds, all muscle. He would have engulfed a regular-sized hoover, but it seemed as if he were floating on air on the mini.

Begak laughed; he could barely see the hoover under him. The tiny seat disappeared beneath him, completely swallowed up by the big man's buttocks. Jenkins had a big butt.

"Five minutes ago, you were my boss's son," said Jenkins. "Now, I guess we're companions. I have nowhere to go. I would see this to the end with you. Now, maybe we can look at what's going on here and figure it out for ourselves. We should make our way to the mountain top."

Jenkins started his engine, looked back at Begak, and said, "If you got anything else to say about me and my tiny ride, remember, I don't work for you or your dad anymore. I might punch you," he laughed and rode out.

Begak stared at Jenkin's back and couldn't help himself; he started laughing and could not stop for a moment, relieving much of his stress.

Wiping the tears from his eyes, Begak said, gasping, I won't say a word, my friend, but the picture is worth the beating."

He started laughing again and rode off with Jenkins.

For the first time in his life, Begak was doing something for himself. Not something he thought his father wanted from him or something his father commanded him.

He was doing what he chose, and it felt good.

CHAPTER 36

SENJO

"*W*HAT DO *I call you three? You, who are one?*" Senjo inquired.
"*We are Abby, Kaiya, and Laiya, Old One.*"
"*You two,*" Senjo said, pointing to Laiya and Kaiya.

He had created a matter form and placed his awareness within that container. It was interesting, he thought. An eye-opener for sure, he said to himself, to be in human form. In his thirteen-billion years, he had never experienced being contained in such a small space. I dance in the universe, he said and sent that energy out into space and time.

Everyone on the pier felt his confinement and his awe of his senses. For the first time, Senjo could smell the perfume of a planet; alive and healthy, she is, he thought, as he scanned the earth, seeing no illness on land or species. They were in Sanctuary, the dimension given to Abby, Laiya, and Kaiya, almost three-hundred years ago.

Abby chose the fishing pier off the pond in their backyard as an excellent place to meet Senjo, the oldest Elon in the universe. He was judging their actions since the time of their birth when she burst into being. Abby, Laiya, and Kaiya were born together that day.

She wanted him to experience the human side of who they were. It gave him a human perspective, his energy confined to a matter body, and the emotional experience of feelings. Abby hoped to persuade Senjo to their cause.

Laiya handed Senjo a fishing pole.

"Here, let me show you how to use this." She stood behind him and took his right arm at the elbow. Bend your elbow, so the pole is up and behind you," She said to him. "That's right," she said, helping him adjust the angle. "Now, push down the button your thumb is on." Which he did before she finished telling him to cast out at the same time and watched the line dropped into the water next to the pier. Laiya laughed and started over.

"Now wait to push the button at the same time you cast off," she said, "like this." And she cast off her line. Senjo watched and repeated the actions.

There have been others of your kind in our history. Some have made it to enlightenment; most die-off in eons and affect nothing. The changes wrought by your existence; we are not sure where they will lead. You created a new wave upon your birth. It seems we are creators now as well as observers.

We did not set the universe into motion, Senjo said to the girls as he stood on the pier, enjoying the feeling of being human. *Nor did we create the waves and the energy that brought us into existence. We were born of it, as you were.*

Senjo continued, You wrote a contract with the council three hundred years ago for your sanctuary and your children. You outsourced a dimension, set the downfall of one world, and the destruction of the social order in the other at odds with the character of four very young children. Sanctioned by the counsel while I dreamt is unbelievable.

Maybe one of you can tell the story of you from the beginning, hmmm? Be aware I am visiting one more group in this little play you have been directing these last centuries. When I am finished talking with them, I shall want to hear the whole story," Senjo singing his admonishments.

"Yes, Senjo. We will be here for you when you are ready," Abby said, trying hard to sound contrite. "In the meantime, we have work to do too. This part of the 'play' is almost complete, and it is but a tiny piece to a much larger picture. It took us three hundred years just for this small part. Imagine all the fun we shall have over the eons," Abby replied, laughter in her voice.

"Don't count on it. This performance might be your only solo on stage. We will see," remarked Senjo.

"Come on, Senjo, tell the truth, don't you just love the concept of language. Isn't it fun?" Abby kept pestering.

"Humph" was the only sound Senjo made. What have we got ourselves into, Senjo wondered? These three sure did liven up the place. And yeah, he did like the concept of language. So many ways to use a word and so many words they use. It was fun.

Enough he said and put down the pole. He called out to Aldebaran, *Come Tascheter, watcher of the east; take me to these children,"*

Senjo spoke in mind to Aldebaran, using his ancient name. *"Or shall I call you 'Al'?* Senjo sang with laughter in the language of Elon.

Al sent Senjo a mental image of him shrugging his shoulders, which sent Senjo into a fit of laughter. How did these three do it, one Elon and two humans?

They woke everyone up, he sang with laughter. *I will visit with Abby's child and the natural wave rider now,* Senjo said to Al.

If anyone happened to see them, they would have thought they were two young kids sharing a meal quietly. They were outside, and no one was coming by, and their minds were anything but quiet.

They had set up camp in a small grove of oak trees and chose to stay the night and begin a journey to friendship. They both knew the road that laid ahead wouldn't be easy, and not trusting each other would only make it that much harder. They did a mind-meld, opening their minds, which opened their souls, although they were not aware of that quite yet.

It was a new experience for both to trust someone outside their family. Once they started mind-melding, everything in their lives was exposed. They had no barriers in place, Seeca unaware and unable to make any, and River chose not to. Neither had barriers to hide behind. At first, it was overwhelming with no filters, and both were lonely for a friend. Everything that each had felt or been in their lives was exposed. Their most profound secrets, their worst fears, their whole lives flashed before each other like a living hologram. It wasn't long before they knew everything about each other and what had led them to where they were at this moment.

River awakened that morning feeling refreshed and happy. Whatever else Seeca was, River knew they were friends for life. It felt good to have a friend, the very first human one in her life. In time, they would realize they were each other's first bonds, a forever kind of relationship. This little grove of trees where they stopped and rested near the mountains' foothills;

manifested a feeling of warmth and security. River sensed that this grove had existed a long time, thousands of years, she guessed.

"Thank you," she whispered to no one in particular. "For another night of restful sleep." A night where she knew she was safe, even here.

She had risen early and enjoyed the dawn breaking across the oak grove in shades of red, yellow, orange, and copper. She loved catching energy from the sun. It hadn't quite burst onto the valley yet. Seeca was still asleep when she woke, so she took that time to find freshwater and do a morning cleansing. She had started a fire with the disc Irsei had given, warming the water for a little herb drink to boost their energy for the day ahead. They would need it. By the time Seeca had risen, the sun was golden with the first rays on the grove, just cresting the horizon. River handed him a cup of ginseng and lemongrass tea, spiced with a bit of ground cinnamon and banana pepper, a Gram special.

"Thanks," Seeca said, walking toward her and taking the cup of tea.

"It helps wake you up. I figure we need to break camp in the next half an hour and make our way to Lion's Roar." River said as she sat down beside Seeca, warming her hands on the hot tea, enjoying the early morning and the sense of friendship.

"Did you hear anything last night, Seeca?"

"Yeah, I thought I heard voices talking as they rode by. They didn't know we were here.

"I heard the same thing. You think it was Begak and the guard?"

"Who else could it be?" But the thought that it could be the Pearl crossed Seeca's mind. And River answered that just as quickly.

"No, not Irsei, he would have been alone, and he would not have missed us. It had to be Begak. You think he's going where we are?"

"I'm pretty sure he is River, and they'll get there first. Darn, I'll have to review these entrances and see what the best way for us is. We might have to try and sneak by them. I'm glad Al gave this map knowledge to me and let me have a flyer's view; it's excellent."

"Here, take a look." Seeca sent the maps to her mind; there was no longer a question of teaching him. The mind bond with River opened all doors.

"Let's get going, Seeca. We can review the maps along the way. Seeca, what are you staring at," she asked him? She couldn't make out the forms.

It seemed like they were wisps, but not. They looked human in form but intensely bright.

"Who or what is that, Seeca? They have the energy of suns," she said, shielding her eyes from the brightness.

Seeca stepped back toward her and said, "I think it's Al. But he's not alone, and I don't know who's with him."

At that moment, the sunburst upon the grove like diamonds hitting dewdrops and lifted the morning fog in the valley.

It was then that both Al and his companion became visible. River could see the pattern of the wave shining through them. Al's friend was laid out in deep-red copper colors streaked with yellow ochre. Vibrant red hues burst from him like a red sun. A warm burst of energy had her feeling fuzzy inside.

"Hello, glowing man," she said sleepily.

He chuckled, but it sounded like he was singing.

A glowing, singing man, how nice, thought River. She couldn't understand why she felt so relaxed, so sleepy. Didn't I just wake up? Or am I still dreaming? Her mind reached for Seeca and found him talking to the singing glowing man's friend. What's his name again? She questioned herself.

"Oh Yeah, Al." River remembered his name. She had a vague notion that she should be more awake than this, but it just didn't seem to matter, she thought as she slipped into a dream state.

CHAPTER 37

WATCHER

SATCHEL HAD ALL night to think things out. *What do I really know, beyond their history,* he asked himself. *Not nearly what I thought. And how much did the old one, the faeries, and the wood nymphs know? Probably everything* he realized. Water assumed the faeries were joking about killing him if he were a threat. He didn't. He knew they would. They lived by a different set of rules than men, and it was a mistake to think differently. The faeries were known to take humans hostage and not return them until they were old. What was his responsibility to the watchers, to Sanctuary, to Water? While Water slept, he wrestled with his conscience, obligation, and a newfound respect for this girl. But now it was morning, and he had decided.

"What are you thinking so hard about, Satchel?" Water came up quietly behind him and asked.

Satchel opened his mind to her. "You, Water. I struggled for a long time, questioning what to do, what to say. What should I tell you, what amount of the truth? But really, it is easy. The old one feels you need the truth, the fairies too; who am I not to hear? Let's mindspeak, Water; the truth is harder to hide." Satchel began his story.

"We, watchers, came with the contract. Izaria is the brainchild of the three. They were young in their creation, fifty years old maybe," Satchel began with the history of the watchers, how Izaria started, and why. The imminent demise of one world by overpopulation and wasted lands led to the Izarian experiment. There have always been watchers on Izaria. Watchers never had a mind wipe either. We came from Sanctuary, not the dying planet," Satchel continued speaking out loud and opening his mind to Water as well. "The three had created Sanctuary, a floating dimension, years before, trying to save Rake, the dying world, and the people who lived there. "They took twenty-five percent of the population off Rake and sent these people to three different planets. They took one-fifth of those people and sent them to Izaria. They wiped the peoples' minds, hoping they would be able to begin again without the memories of their old lives:

"The watchers believed Abby and JIVE and the Jumps were all the same energy, as well as Kaiya and Laiya." Satchel concluded, "I'm not sure, or at least I haven't figured out what their source of energy is."

He left out three things: who and what Water was and who Water's grandmother was, and who her mother was. He felt it was not his place to tell. The nymphs, and the old one, were humming, vibrating, and resonating with Satchel's sharing. They heightened the awareness and the feeling of the moment in time. They did not disagree with his choice not to tell. It wasn't their place to tell either. They knew Water's grandmother and mother well. All the faeries had to say about his story was, they could always kill him later. Satchel noticed that was the second time the faeries had said something about killing him.

"Ok, that's a lot to take in," Water interrupted Satchel. "And you're saying my Gran is deeply involved with this experiment and has been her whole life."

Satchel, thinking of Aiya, who she is, said, "Yes, her whole life, deeply involved."

"What is Gran doing? How do I fit into all this? What is it I'm out here seeking? Water began questing into memories still tied to Satchel.

Gran's last words, "Choose the second path, and you will find yourself," popped into her head.

"Ok, Gran, I chose the second path."

So obviously, who I am will be revealed to me sooner or later. Or is that what I am doing now? I'm finding myself. Do I have to have who I am 'revealed' to me? Who better to know who I am than me? She asked all these questions in her mind in a split second. They were relevant but not of importance right now.

"What takes precedence now, Satchel is this moment. Zebble is close behind us. And if I am correct, he will have a small army following close behind him. Whatever we are about to discover, Zebble wants it. And he thinks it will lead to more power because the heart stone has given him a taste of that," Water told Satchel.

They were still mind linked, and speaking out loud as well, reasoning this out. The mind link deterred lying, and you could feel someone evading a question. But it did not prevent skipping over facts or just not speaking of them. You could dodge if no one asked.

"Ok, we need the bloodstone from him. His army is still a couple of days out, maybe. He will be coming alone or with just one or two men now. He wants to catch me. He doesn't know I know about the bloodstone, and that's to our advantage," Water reasoned.

"He doesn't know that I'm with you either," Satchel added. "And he won't be expecting an attack from you."

"The faeries have agreed to help with our plan, and the wood nymphs will warn of his coming. And I agree with you, Satchel; better to steal it away than fight. But we'll do whatever it takes to get that stone back.," she said.

"Ok, ready to set this plan in motion, Water?"

"As ready as we can be. Let's go, Satchel."

Water turned to the old one and said, "Much thanks and love to you. You gave me peace when I needed it, nourished my soul while I rested safely in your arms, and told me great stories of time lost long ago that I can share." She bowed to the tree, then took three strands of her hair and placed them deep within the ground across his roots, saying,

"May there always be water to quench your thirst, sun to nourish your soul, and the breath of life to keep you growing. Be well, ancient one."

She Turned to Satchel, saying, "Let's go."

Still, she amazed him. He felt the power of her words and knew they were a blessing that would stay with the old one for as long as he existed.

He got to thinking it was her; she was the power. And she didn't even know it. He feared what Zebble might do to have that power.

CHAPTER 38

ARGOT

IVER WOKE WITH a start. How long had she been asleep? She looked up to the sky and saw it was not yet midmorning. Has any time gone by? Was this a dream? Who is the burning red man?

"*Seeca!*" River shouted mentally, "*Where are you? Seeca, answer, please.*"

"Don't shout. I can hear you," Seeca said as he came from behind the trees right outside her view.

"What just happened?"

"Geez, I'm not sure I know what happened," Seeca answered. "My friend Al showed up, the first time I saw him as a human - well, somewhat human. He brought his friend Senjo to meet us; I spoke with him for about one minute. He called me a natural surfer. I felt his gaze leave me and heard him chuckle at something you said, and the next thing I know, you and he are blanketed in a red haze, and I can't see or hear you. Nor could I move to get to you. The weird part about it, I didn't seem too upset by any of this." When I questioned Al, he said, 'Senjo chose to speak to you in private.' And that's all I know," Seeca finished.

"Al said Senjo is one of the oldest of their kind. He said you and I are special for different reasons, and Senjo was coming to see us. Not sure what happened after that. It got all foggy in my mind," said Seeca. "I do know this, Al and Senjo, left with smiles on their faces."

Get down! Seeca gave a mental shout, but River was already moving.

She felt the vibration of the hoover on the land. She felt Izen's hate and lust upon the earth. She didn't know how or what she felt, but she knew when the pattern changed. She had learned to trust her unique sense. She didn't even think about it now, no second-guessing herself. She felt it; she knew it. It used to be that she had to analyze, categorize, and approach everything logically. Not anymore. She was living by the seat of her pants, as Grams would have said.

She felt him coming and dove for cover. Thirty seconds later, Izen came zooming by, moving like some evil was chasing him. He drove by so close River saw his downturned mouth. He looked angry and bitter like he'd lost something. He never bothered to look over, didn't even notice her, just kept going.

That's the difference between you and me, Uncle; I see what is before me. You only know what you want, and your hate won't even let you know what is right before you, River thought as she listened to the hoover drive away. She stood, shaking the leaves from her,

"What are we going to do now? They will all be up there," River said. "Making our way straight to the entrance is out of the question. Izen will be there in a couple of hours, and Begak and the guard are there now. Got any ideas, Seeca?"

"Funny you should ask," Seeca grinned, and he flashed River the mental picture that had formed in his mind,

"Compliments of Senjo," he said.

"Can we do it?" River wasn't sure it was possible.

"Yeah, we can do it. We'll get past Izen and his son."

"We can ride the hoover within a half of a mile, walk part of the way, and rope the rest. They used to call it rock climbing. Here," he flashed her the memories.

"You gotta be kidding me," River said.

She could not see herself swinging across some mountain on a thin rope dangling far above the ground. Mentally she shouted to her Gram.

Ok, Grams, what is this all about? I'm running from Izen, who I know won't hesitate to remove the problem by eliminating me. Running with another who happens to be running from Izen too. No coincidences, right, Grams? I'm running toward the very person I should be running away from, Izen. I am swinging from mountainsides to follow a path only you seem to know why I need to. How long has this been brewing, and who's in on this? People I don't even know are now prominent in my life. Abby, Irsei, Seeca, some outside alien called Al and his sadistic friend who put me to sleep." Continuing her rant, River shouted, *"GRAM, WHERE ARE YOU?"*

Seeca tried not to eavesdrop, but he didn't know how not to.

"I'm sorry," Seeca said, looking at the ground, not wanting her to see what she already saw. He would rather be out here, with all the hardships, than in the Cities. He never climbed mountains, but he moved through all the sewers and workers' tunnels no longer used. The abandoned underground work tunnels ran through the Cities, and no one bothered to remove or close them once they became obsolete. How much harder could it be to climb a mountain on a rope, he thought.

When Al gave him the memories, he gave him the experience. So, although he had never really rock climbed or repelled down the mountain, it sure felt like he had. Seeca knew it was more than possible they would succeed. He could see in her memories she had experienced climbing and running through Sanctuary as she grew up. Irsei's fishing line was more than strong enough to hold them as they crossed. It could work; he knew it could work.

With that in his mind, he turned and looked at River. For a moment, neither said anything.

"Ok, let's go scout this out, Seeca. If you say we can, we can," River said.

They gathered their things and prepared to leave the grove. At least they had this advantage: they knew where the enemy was.

CHAPTER 39

MEETING OF THE MINDS

THEY ALL KNEW instantaneously. The Elon were coming together. The instant the Elon thought about it, it happened. It had been a while since this many gathered together. The Elon were quite the loners; they needed no physical presence to hear or speak. They sang together and alone throughout the universe. They were the Elon, bringers of light and life. It had been so since the beginning and would remain so until the end of the universe.

Until recently, everything had remained constant. Now little things began changing; time was introduced to Elon, a concept they had never conceived of. Not in billions of years. This insignificant human species brought it, and their language, to their attention. More and more of the human language was creeping into their ways.

It was time; they gathered.

I met with two of the young ones, Senjo sang. They all stepped back to that moment together.

Ah, sang Cor Leonis, *"I wondered how you could approach them in physical form without damaging their cerebral cortex.*

I approached them in the dream state. The young man warrants a better look; he is tuned naturally to the wave; he was more alert than she. That, of course, will change very quickly. Senjo smiled at the reference to 'quick.'

The Elon did not know 'quick.'

It is the girls too; they are different, Abby explained. *We can all see the beginning with our birth three hundred years ago. Today, at this gathering, I would like you to use the human language as your tool to express yourself. This language brings what we cannot see or feel. The emotions of the one and then of all,* Abby said. She then switched to speaking out loud in the language of her sisters.

"Kaiya, sister of mine, go ahead, begin our story."

"Ok, Abs, since you were not a twinkle in our eyes yet," sang Kaiya with laughter.

She turned inward and began the story of their creation.

"We were twenty-six and twenty-four, in human years, the day we jumped, Laiya and I," began Kaiya. "I had just got back from my world tour. I was making music back then, not saying much of value. Here and there, I did a song with Papa; he was into conscious music. His upbeat, positive reggae vibe music told people to break the chains that bound, and it was all about one love in the world. That was my Papa." Kaiya smiled as the memory moved along. "I had been home for about a week, recovering from jet lag and the toll it took on my body."

As she spoke, the Image of her flying in a can across the sky projected itself upon those present. Theirs was a species that shared instantly; if one Elon knew, all knew. The concept of time didn't exist. The moment just was. All of this was new and hard to comprehend for them. They lived millions, and often billions, of years. They never stopped to be concerned about the minuscule creatures that roamed the surfaces of the worlds that orbited around them.

The three who were one, the name the Elon, sang when referring to them; Abby, Kaiya, Laiya, sisters in the universe. They were explaining how they came to be.

"Laiya, you were so excited. You kept telling me you knew you could ride the wave. You knew you could open a portal to the dark dimension," Kaiya had begun showing all the emotions that day had held for them.

"Dark matter, Dark energy, Dark dimensions, we didn't know anything back then, so we called everything 'Dark,'" said Laiya.

"Laiya, you were right about that. We lived in some turbulent times for humans back then."

"I see," said Antares B. He flashed a mental picture of just the last one-hundred-thousand years.

"I'm speaking more like five-thousand," sang Kaiya.

"Same difference" Sang Antares B.

"Ah," Kaiya sighed. He was right—the same difference.

"That morning, elders, Laiya came to me once again." Laiya joined with Kaiya and presented to the elders their human memories.

"Kaiya! Wake up, cuz. Look, I want to show you something. I did it; I created the portal to the Dark Dimension. I can see the wave the math predicted. It's there. Come on, Kyky, WAKE UP, let's ride the wave."

"Uggghh," Kaiya rolled over, trying to pull her pillow over her head, especially her ears. Laiya had been talking about opening a portal since she got home. Said it was possible. Wait, she rolled back over, looking at her cousin. She cocked her head and furrowed her brow like she did when catching a thought.

"Wait, did you say you opened a portal to another dimension?"

"Oh yeah, I did. I did. I can see the wave; it's there, it's there!"

("You were so excited," Kaiya laughed) ("Yes, I was," smiled Laiya)

Kaiya rose out of bed and looked right at Laiya, her face expressing all the joy that moment could hold for her.

"OH WOW, this I've got to see." She reached for her robe and slippers on the go and ran out the door with Laiya bouncing and explaining how the portal worked.

"Too much math for me," shouted Kaiya as they raced to the garden. "SHOW ME!" she cried again, laughing, and running.

Con Leonis reacted strongly to the girl's verbal description of the mental scenes. He saw it through them; it was personal. He felt the joy, the innocence of youth. He could see the tragedy that clung to them, the pride and honor that had sustained them, the pure love between two young girls who grew up together. He realized they did not know back then - what they thought they had lost - had been right before them. He saw two little humans. In all of the years of these tiny little creatures had existed, lived, and died their minuscule lives; he had never thought of them; they were of no importance. Now he felt they were his namesake, these tiny little creatures with such courage, lionhearted. At that moment, for the first time, he experienced love. Con Leonis loved them. He felt it as he continued to hear and see the story.

The girls had reached the garden. It had been a warm late spring day, and the sun was hanging just above the western horizon.

"Watch," Laiya said as she took a small disc from her pocket and laid it on the ground. "I already opened this an hour ago. I didn't shut it entirely so that I can reach the portal easier. Right now, opening the doorway is still tied to my quantum computer. I have created a way to use the jump as mass portals we can seed Rake with. And I am working on a prototype for homes, but that won't be ready for a couple of years.

"You just created this, and you're already improving it," laughed Kaiya. "Ok, so what do we have to do?"

"Step through it," Layia said, smiling at Kaiya. The girls looked at one another; they could almost read each other's minds. Kaiya laughed and loudly said, "ONE." Layia smiled, "TWO," she said as they reached for each other's hands and simultaneously said, "THREE..".

CHAPTER 40

STOLEN GOODS

"WHEN I COME back this way, it will be to destroy this place," Zebble fumed, muttering aloud. "Never will I step foot in there again, not while that force field encases this land." He knew that place harbored an ill will toward him.

"I'll have the people be the ones to destroy Core," he mumbled as he squeezed himself out the crack and out of Core, relief sweeping through him. It was enough for him that he spent the night in this place, lost in this forsaken place. He did not sleep well and was tired and mean.

"After I take power in six months, I'll create a story of Kaiya's sacrifice and the destruction of Core. Whatever story I choose to tell will be the truth to them. I am supreme," he said as he climbed upon his ride and left Core behind on his way into the foothills of Zion. He smiled smugly, sitting back and enjoying the ride. I'm out of that forsaken land. He trembled, wanting to put the experience as far out of his mind as he could. I'll catch Water at the crossing. She's alone, on foot, and there's no one out here to help her; Zebble smiled again. Perfect, just perfect, he thought. Finally, everything is perfect.

I wonder where those two idiots got to, Zebble seethed. Had they followed the girl like he told them to, or did they run and hide? He wasn't sure, but they no longer mattered. I see their mounts are gone, as well as those two men I left for dead. Did those two take all the mounts? Or did they all get out? How did they all get out ahead of me? He had struggled all day since he woke this morning. It was already mid-afternoon by the time he made it back to the crack entrance. He cursed the land and the men he had brought with him. I know they didn't obey my orders.

"Cowards!" he yelled, leaning forward and shaking his fist. "I'll see you when I get back. There's nowhere to run that I can't find you. Zebble sat back again, speculating. Maybe they had been smart enough to go after the girl, even if they ran from the land. Zebble had to admit he was glad to be out of that land too. Then he swept away any concern about how they beat him to the crack. I wasted the day fighting to get out of that place, Zebble complained, looking over his shoulder at a barrier, remembering the night he spent in there as well. It was not a good memory.

It's already past mid-morning, he thought, glancing at the sun. It's prudent for me to travel where I can mind-speak with Surg, even if it's out of my way. I need reinforcements. As my head of my converts, Surg will do what I need, Zebble thought, sure of his man's loyalty. Zebble learned long ago if you weren't within five-hundred yards of each other, you couldn't mindspeak near Core's energy field. It wasn't until he was about twelve miles away from the force field that he could reach out to Surg in his mind and get a response. The plans are set, and I'm ready. He closed his eyes and enjoyed the ride away from Core.

I will still make it to the grove before nightfall. I'm following my grandfather's steps, Zebble said and urged his mount forward. I heeded his words and never took the map until I was ready, proud he had followed his grandfather's instructions, never wavering. But, hc had only kept half the promise. He had taken the heart stone with him three years ago when he started coming back after his father died. Zebble did not think that was cheating.

"I'm ready now, grandfather," Zebble spoke out loud. With the stone, the red heart of Kaiya, and the map, he knew he was on a path of power, and he would claim it for himself. He was after more power - even more than he had already stolen; he wanted it all.

"Nothing and no one will stand in my way," he vowed.

Six hours later, Zebble came upon the crossing; He was later than he anticipated. Darkness seeped into the valley early in the mountains. It was predusk when he dismounted and saw to the needs of his mount. Stretching, he knew it would be dark soon, and this was an excellent place to set up camp. I'll be happy when all this is over; it's too much work out here, he grimaced. But I do feel I'll make my home here, like the one in Core, impressed with the land and what he saw. I will have a big, massive home, Zebble said to himself as he continued daydreaming. And it won't blend with the area like Kaiya's homes. I want everyone to see my house for miles. I'm sure all my flock will be more than willing to help me build a utopia here. No more Kaiya or Aiya, he smiled, well pleased with this dream. Zebble knew all these possibilities were right here; all he had to do was grab them.

You're too cumbersome a mode of transportation. Zebble thought as he led his mount into the pasture, settling him in for the night. I'll start the inventors on creating new ways to move around without Kaiya. Or these sea slugs. No more organic transportation; he threw in as an afterthought as he fed the giant snail.

Right now, I need to see to my own needs. Zebble chose a spot by an old gnarly tree and started to clear a space for a fire pit.

What was that noise, he thought, looking up from the task. Listening intently, he tried to determine where it came from and what it was he heard. The sound did not repeat itself. After a moment, he let it go. It's a new environment for me, Zebble shrugged; maybe that's a natural sound here. But it sounded like someone was getting ready to yell and got cut off. He waited silently without movement a bit longer to be sure and still heard nothing. Oh well, he thought and turned back to the task at hand - lighting the fire. He looked down where he had put the fire kit and involuntarily drew back. A swarm of bugs came out of the earth. They were all over the tree and moving out in a circular formation away from the tree.

"What is this?!" he exclaimed, quickly gathering his kit and moving far away from the site. He looked around for another possible place and noticed one across the path by a small grove of oak. "Ah, there's a good site," Zebble said, seeing a small stone pit. Water must have traveled this way. I'm not far behind her. Zebble contemplated moving on, catching her unawares at night. No, he decided, I could just as easily miss her completely. I'll stay the night, rise early, find the oak in this grove, retrieve the map, and be on my way. I know where she's going. With the map, I can follow her.

"I'm coming for you, Water. Wherever you are, I will find you," Zebble spoke aloud.

Water had watched Zebble begin to start a fire by the old one. "No!" she shouted without thinking. Satchel had subdued the sound and muffled the echo, but the sound of emotion, of anger, still managed to escape. She realized her mistake right away. If she and Satchel still could mindspeak here, Zebble could hear them too.

She quieted her mind and waited patiently for Zebble to swing his mind back to his task. She almost laughed out loud at the look on his face when he saw the swarm of beetles. She knew he wouldn't be sleeping there tonight. He found the fire pit they had left for him. They were betting he would use that rather than spending the time to build another, and they were right.

Water settled in for the night on the grove's north side—the faeries east and west of her. Satchel was opposite her, directly south. They were waiting for the sleep potion to take effect. The faeries had put it in his food as he cooked over the fire. It amazed her how quickly the fairies could move. Zebble didn't even notice their movement. To him, it felt as if the wind had picked up and then died down.

They waited well into the night when finally, Aziel signaled to Water that it was time. The faeries still weren't speaking to Satchel.

"He's asleep," sang Aziel, her voice the sound of beating wings, thousand per second. "We still say we should kill him. He is a threat."

"Yes, I know he is," sighed Water, "But tonight, we'll let him live. It's not his time for death. If he dies now, they'll make him a martyr. He'll do more damage to the people as a dead prophet than a live island leader, at least right now."

"Ok," a surly male faery said contritely. "Zet himself was worse than his grandson; the universe would have perished in his hands. But what more damage will this offspring of Zet's do if we don't kill him now? Did you ever stop to think about THAT? Worry about tomorrow, tomorrow, at least we faeries could then wash our hands of this mess.

It looked to Water like Kasor was about to say much more. What he said brought keen awareness to Water. Something else is going on here, she thought, quietly cloaking her mind without anyone noticing. She waited for Kasor to continue, but Aziel interrupted him.

215

"Kasor, enough," scolded the queen. Then turning to speak to Water, Aziel smiled. "Forgive Kasor's outburst; he is having personal difficulties. We dropped the sleeping leaves into Zebbles stew a time ago. He is asleep and will sleep like a babe till the morn," said Aziel. "It is your time, Water. It is your choice."

Yeah, it is, she said to herself, half her mind questioning why Kasor had said that and the other half watching herself approach the sleeping Zebble. My choice has taken me far away from my home and in the company of strangers, I do not trust, thinking of Satchel as she stood and Stretching the kinks out of her body. At least I have the faeries, she thought, feeling reassured, then stopped abruptly with that thought. She remembered what Abby had told her. I can't say I trust them either, no matter how much fun they can be or how soothing their words.

She waited for just a moment more. She wasn't taking anyone's word Zebble was knocked out sound asleep. She didn't know what this mindspeaker was capable of doing, what illusions he could conjure. She wanted to make sure he was sound asleep.

Earlier, Water had watched as he opened the wooden box and gazed upon the stone like a cherished possession, gently polishing the strange wooden box to a natural shine. She noticed he never held the stone, never touched it, never reached for the bloodstone. He stared at it and gently cleaned the box, then sealed the lid closed and placed it back in the pack. Why didn't he touch it? She pondered this as she waited silently for the fairy's sleep potion to be in full effect. Ready, she commanded herself. She slid her feet across the land as if she were floating through the air. Quietly, silently, she walked toward the pack near his head. She stopped mid-stride, knowing if she moved the bag, he would become fully awake. She contemplated the problem, wondering if unzipping it would cause him to awaken from the effects of the sleep potion reflexively as well. I can't just sit here all night; Water scolded herself and began quietly moving again until she was almost standing over him. Down she floated, easing herself close to the pack and unzipping it.

Whew, Water let out a small sigh of relief, lucky to find the box close to the opening. Aah, she exclaimed to herself, easing her treasure out; how I would love to keep this beautiful artifact. She could not. Water reasoned that if the box were missing, Zebble would know right away, the heart stone was also gone. But maybe they could fool him a bit longer by leaving the box in the same place; he might not look for at least another day.

She reached into the box and picked the glowing red stone up. It felt warm and inviting, like an old friend. She held the rare stone in her hand, then held it to her heart, damping down the glow.

Upon seeing her with the bloodstone, the faeries began to sing, "It is done."

"Shhh," Water told them, hurriedly replacing the box in the pack, zipping it back up, and stepping away from Zebble.

"I see you, girl," Zebble's eyes flew open, staring at her.

Water froze, not sure what to do.

Zebble slowly shut his eyes again and slipped back into his dream. She backed away from Zebble, one slow, small step at a time, visibly shaking. She had the heart stone in her hands, the warmth of it radiating through her. Water wanted to sing joyously with the faeries who hadn't stopped singing since she picked it up.

'It's done. It's done,' the faeries and nymphs sang.

The bloodstone felt like home. It was a part of her. She had lost it, somehow, never realizing she had ever possessed it before until this moment.

Satchel came behind her, wiping all traces she was there, even her scent. They met in the Grove, west of the path, when he finished. Time to go, Satchel signaled Water, reaching out to start the hoover, hoping this would not awaken Zebble. Satchel feared that the potion wasn't strong enough for this mindspeaker. The fact that he had opened his eyes and spoke to Water even though in a drug-induced faery coma made him think he wouldn't stay asleep.

But there was no other choice, Satchel felt, as Water climbed on behind him. She touched his arm gently, pulling his hand away. He turned, questioning with his eyes.

She shook her head no and whispered, "Don't start it." She held the Heart of Kaiya in her hands and thought of Lion's Gap, the appearance as well as the coordinates. "Take us there," Water said.

Satchel shook his head twice involuntarily, flinching backward into Water, his eyes traveling the length of the gaping mouth of a lion. Satchel's face was within inches of the left incisor. He got off the hoover and stepped back to get a better view. Neither had ever seen a lion, in real life, or as a hundred-foot sculpture.

"*Oh my goodness*," was all Water said.

"Yes, I would have to agree," said Satchel. His head followed the tooth up, seeing the majestic face of a lion king as he kept stepping backward.

They were here. Water and Satchel had made it to the Gap.

Water stared for a long time into the mouth of the lion. A vast cavern greeted her.

She knew they had a bit of time to relax. No one was waiting for them. It would take Zebble a couple of hours to get here, even if he woke this moment. Someone had crafted this lion; it was not a natural construct. Someone had cut the lion into the mountain. She saw the ancients had done these thousands of years ago. She felt a strong pull into the cave. Like the cave itself was waiting for her, and now was anxious to have her. She was not quite sure how she felt about that. It had been a telling journey and so far, not so tricky physically. But, emotionally and mentally, it had been taxing for Water. Holding the heart stone, she realized there was power here, more than she thought could exist. She walked into the lion's mouth and sat down on the cave floor, aligning herself unconsciously to Aldebaran.

"What are you doing?" asked Satchel.

"I'm thinking and searching for memories of Lion's Gap or the bloodstone."

There was nothing in memories about this place. Only a silly legend started by the faeries eons ago concerning the bloodstone.

"I feel as if both this mountain and Lion's Gap have been here a long while; the islands are younger, I am sure of that," she said to him. "Leave me be," she commanded of Satchel, "We have time, and I must see."

Water left her physical self on the floor and went traveling through her memories and those of the people. She was surprised to see she could access Gran's mind as well.

"She kept that door open for me for a reason. Let's go find out what she wants me to see this time," Water said, giving voice to her suspicions. She took herself back as far as she could go, and with Gran's memories, that meant to the beginning. Gran was talking to a young woman and someone else who was not present in physical form.

Look how youthful Gran looks, thought Water. But why am I here? How does it have anything to do with Izaria?

Listen. Water heard Gran say.

I miss you.

Listen, child.

Water returned to the memory before her.

+ + +

"I do not know why we are concerned with one planet's species; they have practically killed themselves."

Both girls said simultaneously, "Abby, quit flashing all those historical memories at us. We know our history."

The young woman with Gran is Kaiya. Water knew it. It was Kaiya as a young girl.

"Wait," Water stopped and said, "that's not Gran. It's Laiya!"

Wow, Kaiya and Gran as girls. Gran is Laiya, and Kaiya, a human, not godlike, whispered Water in awe of what she was seeing.

She had never thought of Kaiya as human. She had no form; she just was. I can feel a secure connection between the three. The three? Where did that thought come from? Water asked, And instantly, she knew; the Abby that Kaiya and Laiya talked to was the house bot, Abby. Water was astounded by this early memory of Grans. She was sure that the house bot she met at Laiya's house named Abby was the Abby in this memory.

"Abby's in cahoots with Kaiya and Laiya. I know this," said Water. As sure as she knew, Gran is Laiya, and Kaiya is no god.

Who are you, Abby?

Gran was pulling her back to the memory.

Ok, ok, I'm coming back, Gran, stop yanking on me.

Watch, Water, learn who you are.

Water heard her Gran say as she slid back in memory.

We know all the horrors men have caused each other, Abs. We want you to come with us and see the joy and laughter, the love and pain of just one family of this species. Join us in our form for a year, with our family - your family - Abby.

Are you kidding? What's a 'year.' NO time, that is what a year is, Abby responded.

Please, Abby, try it. You don't know what you'll see, Kaiya pleaded.

Ok, selves, I will join you. We shall be three biological-matter beings for one of your years. Water heard Abby say as the memory faded.

Water sat upon the stone floor in the mouth of a lion that had never existed in this world, contemplating the moment.

"Let's play chess," she said. Zebble was a minor factor in the game, but even a pawn can become king, she thought. There's something bigger here; she just couldn't put her finger on it. Now this memory of Gran with Kaiya and Abby. Abby seemed to think that the three of them were one being. Gran and Kaiya grew up together; she had felt the bond of kinship with them. They were cousins who were sisters. Abby was more than human. They were all more than they seemed. They had bonded; she knew it. She came up out of the memoring, opened her eyes.

She turned to Satchel and said, "Tell me what you know, Watcher. All of it, for I know I have been fed half-truths, and I now know mistrust. Holding this stone, I will see the truth full and fat."

She no longer trusted Satchel to speak the full truth. "I see the half-truths you speak and want none anymore. I see you fear this stone's power. Why don't you touch it, Satchel?"

Water held the stone out to Satchel, pushing it at him. He shook his head no, vehemently.

"Why not, Satchel?" Water asked again, all the while, her hand stretched out, pushing the stone at him. "Why won't you touch it? Why are you so afraid of this stone," pulling her hand back slightly, but only slightly.

"Ok, Ok, Water," Satchel said, holding his hands up in a motion of surrender as he began to tell the story of the stones.

"There's a legend among the watchers of two star-stones that can only be held by the one meant for the stone. They have the immeasurable power and energy of a hot sun held within the stone," Satchel said to her. "The wood nymphs called the bloodstone from the earth upon your birth and forged two hearts from one stone. Holding this stone killed Zebble's Grandfather the moment he touched it. Zebble's been chasing this power a long time, Water."

"You think **this** is one of the stones?" Water questioned Satchel. "And I am the one to wield the immense power supposedly. Is that right?" Water demanded to know. "That story Abby told about the faeries and the heart of Kaiya and a box buried, you're saying it is about me directly. That stone is mine, made for me by wood nymphs and faeries three hundred years ago. That's what you are saying?" Water watched Satchel hesitate for the merest moment.

"Watcher," she said with determination in her voice, "I expect you to tell, show, and give me all that you know. Or you will leave my side. I will not travel with you if you do not. I do not trust you. You have this one chance," she said as she uncrossed her legs and stood up.

Satchel knew she would use the stone to transport him far away from here if she even began to suspect he was hiding or keeping something from her.

It was his time to choose. Satchel knew there was no compromise; he would tell the truth as he knew it, or he would leave.

CHAPTER 41

PRIMROSE GATE

THE OPENING TO the main cavern was directly above them. River and Seeca were on the plateau under and right of its incisor tooth. They had traversed from the base of the lion's throat to under his chin, climbing up and moving to the left ear and the cave that Seeca saw while soaring with a flyer. Knowing Begak was already at the main cave and probably Izen too, they chose not to go into the mouth of the beast, so to speak, and bypassed it altogether. They climbed the mountain under the lion's open mouth. And It had taken them four hours to climb that far. Irsei's rope was a lifesaver. Seeca threw it up; it latched onto whatever it touched; they rose to that spot. Then they would do it all over again. It was mid-day. The sun was bright and the skies clear, except for the clouds forming on the horizon.

Seeca's training as a kid in the bowels kicked into high gear. He had always liked to explore, to know his surroundings. Right now, he was looking for different ways in and out. Right away, he spotted what seemed to be a stone staircase leading up and around the lion's chin to his left ear. He had missed that the first time he surveyed the area while flying. Once again, he was grateful to Al for giving him the gift of flyer sight. He might have missed the stairs had he used only his regular sight. The stairs were well hidden in the lion's mane, and by the look of it, not been used for a long time. They seemed to lead to the cave in the ear.

But neither River nor Seeca could see the opening of the Primrose Gate anywhere. They assumed it was hidden, but they didn't think it would be so hard to find it. They were beginning to believe the gate never existed, just a three-hundred-year-old faery tale. But something kept niggling at the back of River's mind. Something Gram had said. It seemed like a lifetime ago. Gram was sending her home from the debacle of the ceremonies with rushed advice and cryptic notes.

"That's it," River exclaimed. "One of the notes said, look for the Primrose Gate. Primrose was a plant known to protect the entrances to sacred caves. Grams taught me that."

"What?" Seeca quietly asked, unsure where Izen, Begak, or the guard was and not wanting to bring their attention his way.

My whole life seems to be in preparation for this adventure, she thought, as she scanned the area for the plant and not an opening. And there it was, higher up behind the ear, nestled in his mane. This stairway would get them there. Although it was a crumbling steep, and winding staircase, it would still be easier than scaling the side of the mountain

River reached out to Seeca, mind speaking, not wanting even the slightest possibility of being overheard and caught. River caught Seeca's attention. The boy was easily distracted, sighed River.

Seeca, look.

What? *I don't see anything.* He spoke back in her mind, as well.

That's because you're looking for the wrong thing. River proceeded to give Seeca the short version of one of Grams' Sanctuary lessons.

Primrose is a plant known to cover the entrances to caves. Caves like the one we are looking for, and there my friend, is the primrose," she said, pointing to the plant seemingly forming part of the mane. *"The stairs will take us most of the way there, Seeca.*

The problem is night will soon fall, and we won't be at the gate before dark. We can make it to the ear by dusk. I'm cold and tired. Seeca looked to River, waiting.

You're right, Seeca. Let's make for the ear and see where we might be able to rest and eat a cold meal. They began the climb again.

"Two thousand five hundred fifty-three steps, 2554, 2555, 2556, "Gawad, will this torture ever cease?!?!"

River did not want to count another step. The storm that began on the river soon chased them up to the mountain—what had started as clouds on the horizon caught up with them thirty minutes ago. In about an hour, it would be dusk. They were both near total exhaustion.

Just a little more, Seeca kept saying over and over, like a mantra.

And River counted. The stone steps were old and narrow. In some places, the ground ripped through the stairs, taking them entirely away. Or they were structurally broken and dangerously weak, as they had realized when the rain had caught up with them and turned to sleet.

There, directly in front, of her a tree fiercely clung to the side of the mountain, half its gnarled roots exposed and jutting out at almost a perfect right angle to the mountainside.

"How long have you existed," she asked the gnarly pine, whose limb hung over the stairs like a ceiling.

At that moment, River heard the crack of the stone she was stepping on and felt it give way. She had begun to fall backward and knew she was seconds from falling into the abyss that lay just off her right shoulder. She reached for the tree the same moment the tree snagged her and gave her those seconds she needed to grab hold and swing over past the crumbling stair. River knew she was tired.

She could have sworn she heard that old gnarly pine say back to her, "Long enough to catch you, little sister."

Seeca was ahead of her, his weight first widened the structural fault inside the stair, and her weight cracked it open. She was grateful the tree was there to save her life. That was an hour ago. And dusk was soon upon them, making the kids climb that much more difficult. Tired, exhausted, and losing the light, they continued to climb steadily. The higher they rose, the colder it got, until, fifteen minutes ago, the rain had frozen into white crystals.

"Are you as miserable as I am, Seeca?"

Seeca, too tired to speak aloud, nodded his misery to River. He paused on the steps and shook the frozen rain off the hoodie Irsei had given him, giggling to himself from exhaustion when Al's info corrected him. "It's snow," he laughed.

What are you talking about, Seeca? River was not understanding, and she was too tired to guess.

He was so grateful for that hoodie now. It had repelled the water and snow from his face and upper chest. It looked like River's had done the same for her. Even though Seeca was cold and tired, he knew he was warmer and drier with that hoodie.

"This is snow, River," Seeca said, showing his bondmate Al's info.

He gazed up the mountain and sighed a sound of relief.

"I see the ear."

"Ok, so," was all River managed to say.

"NO. I see the inside; it looks like one of the caves on the map Al gave me. And here is the Primrose Gate, it's slightly above and to the right in the mane. See," Seeca said as he mentally sent the map to River.

She looked up. Sure enough, she could see the opening to the cave, and it was in the lion's ear. They were here.

River and Seeca made it to the ear as darkness fell, stumbling over their feet as they dropped to the cave floor and lay there, exhausted and happy to be alive. Once inside the small cave, they realized they were well hidden from anyone on the cavern floor far below. Their small fire was not seen, nor were they heard. It seemed someone had already used this place to spy on those below. A fire pit used by a previous occupant lay ready for them to use. The acoustics were astounding. She could hear a small creature scurrying on the cave floor far below. There were strategically cut slits in the small eardrum cave's sides, allowing for a clear, unobstructed view everywhere. Still, unnoticeable from the cave floor below, if someone happened to look up, she bet.

"A perfect spot to spy," she whispered to Seeca, who nodded his head in agreement.

They found the cave went deep within the ear canal, away from the edge. Seeca and River were grateful for little blessings and enjoyed a light meal by a warm fire. They meant to switch off sleeping, with one always awake, but they both fell soundly asleep as the storm howled outside, well into the morning while they slept.

River dreamt of the blue girl who looked like her, memory hopping the same way Grams had shown her. She was sitting on a stone floor. She could feel the pull of the memory; it was meant for her.

Why am I here? She thought as she let this memory take her. There's Gramma when she was younger, and there was her cousin Kaiya. One other sounded like Abby, River, said to herself as she watched this memory go by.

Listen, child. She heard her Grams voice.

Grams? Grams, I miss you.

Be still and listen.

I'm dreaming, and still, you tell me what to do, she thought, smiling, so glad to see her Gram even if it was a dream.

Ok, I'm listening. River settled down and paid attention.

When she opened her eyes, it was morning, and she found Seeca staring at her. She caught a glimpse of him riding the memory with her.

"How did you do that?" she asked, whispering to him.

"I don't know; how did you do that?" He responded just as quietly as she had.

"That was cool. Who were those people? All of them had the feel of my friend Al or his friend Senjo."

"You can feel their energy even while memory-walking?" River probed Seeca.

"Yeah, sure, can't you?"

"I can. Grams taught me. Who taught you?" River asked Seeca.

"No one, I just do it."

They were both still lying by the small fire that had gone out while they slept. Pure exhaustion had taken over River and Seeca last night. They had fallen asleep quickly and slept soundly until the memory came.

"Ever since I went to the garden and glimpsed that formula, I've been a little different," Seeca said, quietly speaking as he sat up and stretched. "Like I knew you would be there to get me that morning. I sure didn't see how you would do it. I just had a feeling I would see you."

"Hey," Seeca added as an afterthought, "the young woman I saw in the garden talking to the wisp about the formula, the one I think is Laiya, is one of the girls in the dream. The one you call Gram."

"You are an idiot and no son of mine," spat Izen, surprising River and Seeca, jolting River instantly wide awake. It sounded as if they were standing right next to her.

"And you," Izen raged, pointing his finger at Jenkins, "I thought I fired you when you exposed your incompetence."

"You did. I'm with the kid," Jenkins replied nonchalantly.

"You let the other 'kid' escape. He was snatched out of the water by a man-eating monster, as you both reported. I've been here since early light. Where have you two bums been?"

Izen was seething, his angry brewing. "I got lost yesterday and spent the night in the woods alone," he said with a slight shudder as he remembered the experience. He kept thinking he was seeing ghosts all night long, half-drowned in the rain before he could find the disc that was shelter.

"I see you don't have the girl in your possession, either."

Both River and Seeca stifled an urge to laugh.

"Do you know where she is? Have any idea how a fourteen-year-old girl outwitted you two morons in a place she has never been without any help?"

"She hasn't come here. She isn't here, Father, we would know. We've set sound traps around the perimeter of the cave. We'll know if someone or something crosses within one-hundred yards of the entrance." Begak told his father.

"Really, that's what you spent your time doing? Have you searched the inside of the cave? Looked for any other entrances in or out of this place." Izen asked?

Begak just stared at him.

"Have you? I didn't think so. You two are useless. I disinherit you, Begak, and as for you Jenkins, you will never be able to work in the Cities again. I have loyal men preparing to follow me to this place. They'll be here in hours. Be out of my way and gone before then." Izen said as he stalked outside the cave.

River and Seeca sat stunned. For the first time, River felt sorry for her cousin. She began to realize what kind of life he must have had with Izen as his father and a mother who was inconsequential, at least by her uncle's standards.

"Hey kid, what do you want to do now?" Jenkins asked Begak.

"I'm still wanting to know what's going on. Not for my Dad," said Begak, "But for me. I get the feeling I'm missing something important, and it has nothing to do with my father and his world."

"Let's go down those stairs we found in the back. We can figure a way to lock that big iron gate and keep them out," Jenkins was thinking out loud.

"I agree, Begak: whatever's down there, I want to know about it. Let's go, make your old man believe we left, circle around, and come back in.

It'll take him until at least tomorrow to discover we didn't leave. We'll have a head start."

Jenkins got up and started moving out of the cave.

"Thanks, Jenks, for everything," Begak said, calling this big man a name you give a friend.

"You bet, kid, let's go stash the hoovers away from here," said Jenkins thinking out loud. "Maybe they'll be here when we get back. Who knows," he said as they walked out of the cave.

River and Seeca listened quietly while Begak and Jenkins discussed what they would do. They waited until they heard them leave the cave, looked at each other, and both simultaneously whispered,

"Time to go." They packed up and began their journey once again.

CHAPTER 42

WHOSE TRUTH?

WATER AND SATCHEL had slept little since leaving the house the morning before. They had stayed up most last night waiting for Zebble to sleep deep enough for Water to get the bloodstone and then came directly to the gap. Water sat upon the cave floor, quietly meditating and exchanging energy with the earth. She knew she would need it.

"Water, may I sit with you?" Satchel began and watched her hesitation; she had indeed learned to mistrust. She opened her eyes and looked at him, remembering her Gran's words once again.

"If ever you need to establish your control of a situation quietly, remember, Water, often is the case, the first one to talk, loses. She did not speak; she just continued to stare at him with a blank face. Satchel could not read her.

Satchel waited and then started again as he took a seat on the stone floor. He closed his eyes and reached for the memories of his life, his history.

"I choose the path of mind-melding with you, Water; you will know the truth as I know it."

Seated on the stone floor, letting the energy of the cave flow through him, Satchel opened his mind to Water - all he knew.

"The Sanctuary you went to on Core is a mere shadow of the home, the Sanctuary, that I grew up in"

As he began, she could see this was no mere settlement but a place large enough to be a city. Still, it felt comfortable, in harmony with the land, in a way that even Izaria's blended homes could not rival. She felt, more than knew, the way of these people. They were all mind readers, adept at using their minds to transport, see, and create. They were aware of their beginnings and their misdeeds as a population. They all came from different places, different worlds with one thing in common.

They were seeking something else.

Some would tell you they searched for years to get there. Others just stumbled into Sanctuary and never left. She felt the connection of the people even in memory walking.

Water felt pulled along into Satchel's life, and his history, so strong was the memory of Sanctuary. This farm, his family, that was her family too, thirty generations of them. She knew the taste of this memory; she had been here before. She had felt it in the shadow Sanctuary; she now felt it again, only more potent, more connected.

She knew this home. Sanctuary had been her home, and the golden copper brown girl was her sister. She saw it in Satchel's memories. He was two years older than her and her sister. Her sister at this time, not the past. Her sister River, the girl who was walking the same path she was somewhere else. They had grown up together until they were two-and-a-half years old and then separated and gone to live in different places.

"No, not just a different location," Water saw in the memories of the watcher.

"No, whole different worlds separated us," Water said, stunned.

One girl on Rake. One on Izaria, the water world the three had chosen two-hundred-fifty years ago. People were taken from Rake by deception and force—the victims of a disease that didn't exist. Abby, Kaiya, and Laiya had torn families apart with a fake illness that 'took' a percentage of the population every year for almost five years.

In Water's world, Izaria, Satchel's family were watchers from the beginning, since Abby, Kaiya, and Gran made a pact with Aldebaran some two-hundred-fifty years ago and brought the people from the dying planet, wiped their minds, and had them start over again on Izaria.

Water broke the link, "Wow," all she could say.

"WHAT!" she heard and saw the wisp of her sister fade away from the connection as well.

****"Are you alright?! Are you ok? River talk to me!" concern etched on Seeca's face as he gently shook River's shoulder,

"Stop shaking me, Seeca; I'm here. I'm surprised you didn't come along for this ride, too," River said, a little angry, trying to get her composure back.

What she had just experienced was mind-boggling.

"I was with you, River. Are you ok?"

"Oh. Yeah, I'm great. I just found out I'm related to the people who caused the disease, destroying the lives of millions of people. Yeah, I'm simply great, Seeca,"

River said again and headed out of the cave needing to think.

They had made it to Primrose Gate and cleared the wall of flowers into the cave when the vision of the blue girl came out of nowhere, this time not in her dreams, but a memory linked to the watcher. They all rode that memory together — Water, River, and Seeca, all memory walking with Satchel. They were on the same journey in a similar place, but somewhere else on different planets

Seeca had walked out of the cave moments after River, feeling her tug on him.

"I have a sister," River said in awe. "I was born in Sanctuary. My Gram's like three-hundred-years old and is Gram to some other girl in some different world. Only she's not our grandmother. Not only that, she, and her cousin Kaiya, along with some entity named Abby, who happens to be my mother, caused the disease."

Even though the disease had come and gone over twenty decades ago, all that suffering and anguish River had felt from Terrissa, her ancestor, was still very fresh.

"Why didn't they tell those people Rake was overpopulated and couldn't support them all and give them Izaria as a choice? None of this makes sense. And who and what is a watcher, anyway?" River sat down, shaking her head; too much, she thought, too much.

"Look, all this is new to me too, in a different way, River," Seeca began saying. "I've been illegal all my life, didn't have any friends, let alone a sister or brother. I was wandering the bowels running in the old vents and service ducts of the Cities. I'm an illegal River. There's no place for me in the Cities. It wasn't just Izen that brought me out here. Remember, my friend Al? I met him riding the wave, never in person until he came with the sleeping man." Those women, your Gram, and the one your sister called Kaiya have the same feel as Al. I think all of them are related or the same species or something."

Seeca lifted River's chin and held her head high. "River, I know you already know everything there is to know about me, but I'm going to say it out loud anyway."

"You know I found an old jump, one of the first Laiya seeded. I hacked into the jump and did just that, jumped. It was great riding the wave. I could see it all laid out in my mind. Till I came on your grandma in the garden talking to a wisp, she called Cuz. I saw the formula, felt it etched upon my mind. Until that moment, I was having fun," Seeca said. "For the first time in my life, I felt free when I was riding the wave. My whole life changed the day I found the wave," Seeca said. "And then it changed again when I saw that formula, the day I met Al, and he asked me to help the person with the sun inside."

"That's you, River," Seeca reminded her. "You are the one with the sun inside."

"Al told me he would make sure my parents were safe, and I said I would find you. River. I don't know what happened to me the day the formula seared itself into my brain, but it looks like a few of us are on the same wavelength, literally. And really, I wouldn't want to be anywhere else. Still, here, figuring out each moment as we go," he finished, knowing she saw all he felt, including his heart's desire: to be free of the yoke of the word 'illegal.'"

"Yeah, I feel you, Seeca. It's just a lot to take in. Why did my Grams separate my sister and me, and by worlds no less? I'm trying to wrap my mind around that my mother is an alien, and I have a twin. I don't understand all this intrigue, Seeca. Did that happen, or is it just another illusion that my life seems to be wrapped up in?"

"No, that was no illusion," he answered her question.

"What else am I going to find out? Grams called it, 'when's the other shoe gonna drop.'"

"Your sister's on the same journey as you are, Riv, he affectionately called her for the first time without even realizing it. Speaking gently to her, knowing how much this must be hurting her. "You have a sister, and she is moving through this at the same time," Seeca said, intently looking at River while he speculated on the odds. "You can calculate the possibilities that she, too, has experienced a naming ceremony gone bad. Because you saw her in Sanctuary; she probably has an evil someone chasing her, too. I get the feeling she's traveling with the watcher but doesn't trust him fully. I think the meld was showing her what she wanted, the truth. That's what I think," said Seeca, shuffling his feet on the cave floor, not exactly sure what to do next.

"I caught a flash of what the watchers thought was the history of us." River was once again replaying the scene in her mind. "But it seems they're just catching up to that too. They didn't know she could get pregnant or which species the birthing processes would follow. They seemed to be confused about timelines, and the three never said anything over the years. How did Gram do that? How was she in both worlds at the same time?"

"I don't know that answer. But, we have more information now than we had before, River. It's time to concentrate on the now. Begak and the guard are heading downward on the stairs." Seeca started to review all the options.

"The blue water bloodstone I carry feels alive. It feels like there's a spark of energy trapped within the center. I wonder if this stone is the other of the two in the legend. I know its energy is pulling to that shaft with a box in it. We have to go down, Seeca. We must go to the center of this mountain, someplace Gram called 'Paradise Lost.' I know my sister saw this too. Thanks to your memory of maps, Seeca, we know the passageways. What is that contraption, Seeca? Can it get us down? It looks suspended over a tunnel?" River was not sure what she saw on the map.

"I'm not quite sure. The old parts of the Cities have boxes like these; only they're steel, not wood. If I'm right about this thing, it's a way to descend and rise without walking. Let's get there; it's not far from here, just a couple more hours." Seeca started moving out. "You ready, River?"

"You're the navigator Seeca."

"I'm hoping Begak and Jenks figure a way to lock your uncle out. Keeping Izen out of the picture for a couple of days would be great. But I doubt a locked door will hold him longer than a couple of minutes.

"We must hurry, we must travel quickly and lightly, stay well ahead of him. If what I think is true about this box, we will. I wonder if we can

233

keep it down with us, not allow it to come back up?" pondered Seeca. "Eliminate this way down."

"We don't know what we are running to, River," he laughed lightly, then finished the sentence, "But we know what we're running from, though, don't we?"

"*Be quiet, Seeca, you talk too much,*" she mindspoke. Chuckling, River mouthed the words, "Let's go."

✝ ✝ ✝

Water rose from the floor, grabbed her pack, and said to Satchel, "He's right, the boy walking with my sister; we must travel quickly and lightly. We know Zebble and his minions will soon be here."

Time for us to go thought Water. "We're not where they are inside this lion, and it will take us close to half a day to get there and go down in that box. No guarantees it's even on *this* lion. We'll descend by the stairs," she said.

She turned and went to the staircase in the back of the cave behind a false wall. You had to be almost on the wall to realize there was a stairwell behind it. Thankfully, that boy riding the wave with her sister had given her maps. The maps were of her sister's mountain, but she bet <u>her</u> mountain was similar, maybe the same, perhaps a mirror image. She would soon find out. She still wanted to take the steps and not get in the box. Zebble would be there before they got up to the passage, and she didn't want to get caught trying to reach it. Besides, a gate existed in her sister's world; a gate is in this world might be here too. She would lock Zebble out, like her sister's cousin would try to do there.

"Well, the stairs are in the same place. That's a start." She turned and looked at Satchel, "You coming, watcher?"

He uncrossed his legs and stood up, shaking the dust from his clothes, "Yeah, right behind you," he said.

CHAPTER 43

SPILL THE BEANS

"**H**OW MUCH OF *this did you foresee?*" Senjo mind-spoke as he began to appear on the fishing pier once again.

Abby was waiting for him.

"We saw the variable of the watcher, but not of your wave runner," said Abby, speaking out loud.

"No one saw that one. I am glad Seeca stumbled onto my path. Or did I stumble onto his? I will never know for sure; refreshing," sang Aldebaran, as he materialized and sat upon the pier dangling his feet in the water.

"Let's leave the children for a minute and talk about the worlds and the contract you formed while I slept," Senjo said to Abby while standing at the edge of the pier. He was looking out at the spectacular view of Sanctuary's back yard. "You can start, Aldebaran, since you made the contract with these three."

"All awake agreed, Senjo," Aldebaran reminded the eldest of Elon. A fishing pole materialized in his hands as he continued speaking. He sat and cast the line. "It's a simple contract lasting three hundred years of this species' timeline. They are a short-lived species; one hundred years is the top end of their life span. Although with the recent breakthroughs, they should double that and remain in good mental and physical form. But I digress." One world is dying. We agreed to set a vortex system that we maintained to minimize the damage done by the oil-based product consumption. Laiya created JIVE. We gave them the integrated vortex systems they call 'jump,'

235

which we track and manage, as a contract condition. They can jump anywhere on the surface of the planet. The three were trying to reduce the destruction already done, trying to change the result.

"For Rake, it was already too late when they tried, Aldebaran said, "yet they tried anyway. Gaia will no longer sustain this species. She is choosing a few who will remain to begin again. The rest will leave one way or another. The day of reckoning is upon them. These people knew the Reckoning would come. It did; it's here. The contract ends soon. They will be informed the day the lease ends and given time to decide their destination, but they will all be gone within fifty years. The jumps and JIVEs will cease to work exactly five years after the lease ends. The people have the option of leaving this planet or dying on it. But that is for another time and is not included in the original contract. An addendum was added fifty years into this contract, creating habitats on three different planets for a portion of the Rake population. In one world wiped the minds of the people reaching there. On another planet, the Elon dropped the criminals of Rake. The Elon could ea their intent the moment they stepped into a jump,"

Al finished speaking, and Abby picked up. "The last group of people Aldebaran brought to his ecosystems. The people had what they needed to succeed on each planet's surface. Watchers were placed on both Rake and Izaria and intimately involved with the three - Abby, Layia, and Kaiya."

"That, Senjo, is the extent of it," Al concluded, waiting for Senjo's response.

"Ok," Senjo said, "tell me how this free-floating dimension; sits outside the human time continuum? How does your Sanctuary fit into all of this? Or Abby's children, where do they fit in the scheme of things? Or the two children born of the flesh, please explain, where do they belong in all of this? Aren't you completing this contract soon?"

"Oh, Senjo," laughed Abby, "I'm so happy you are awake. We can have long talks together and get to know each other. You've been here so long; you saw before the beginning. But to answer your questions, yes, the contract is up. Sanctuary is a floating dimension; it moves through time and space. It has currently sat for Centuries in one place, but not in one time," replied Abby. "And as to how this all ties in together, well, do we have a story for you. If you were human, Sen, we could remember together. I will take you there, to the moment we were born."

Show me," he sang back.

And Abby did.

They had just counted to three and didn't jump. Kaiya pulled Laiya back.

"Doesn't look like much," Kaiya said.

"Yeah, I know," Laiya said, considering the vortex that formed. "I figure we can DIY something cool for the peeps to jump through."

They were both standing there, looking into the vortex.

"You know how to get back, Lai?"

"Theoretically, I do."

"'Theoretically?' Are you kidding?"

"We haven't gone yet, Ky; it IS just a theory. But so was that wave until now. What do you say, Ky, you coming with me?"

They were standing in the garden Built for Tony, Big Rell, the family called him. They were best friends, cousins, soul sisters; they had been through so much together. They were both remembering Big Rell, Kaiya's brother and Laiya's cousin. How they missed him and knew all the opportunities that had been taken from him the day he was murdered. He said he was going to change the world. He had altered theirs, both his life and his death. They were standing there looking at each other, and they smiled. They knew they would jump. The girls reached for each other's hands,

"One, two, three!!" and they jumped into the vortex.

"I came into being the exact, precise nanosecond they jumped. One, two, three," said Abby.

"We didn't have a destination. We just wanted to see and come back. We didn't know what to expect," Laiya spoke. "I hadn't told Kaiya that we became energy on the wave. I had set the return for fifteen seconds."

"No, you didn't tell me I would feel like I was everywhere and nowhere at the same time," Kaiya scolded Laiya.

"Abby exploded into existence, her energy and ours' mingled, became one. In a blink of an eye, we were born," Laiya said.

"I don't know if Kaiya and I would have chosen to come back that day had I not already set a return. Those fifteen seconds lasted an eternity; we saw so much," Laiya whispered.

Kaiya finished, "Then we found ourselves back in the garden, gasping for air and puking our guts out, connected to Abby, a newly born Elon in mind and energy.

We came back into these tiny human matter bodies, after experiencing us as infinite." Kaiya laughed, "Now, that was some getting used to.

"Those two of my selves," Abby interjected in the memory. "Talked me into taking human form for a year of their time to experience family, love, pain, joy, and anger."

"Abby, you stayed in human form for a hundred years. You still come down and hang out with Irsei. You're just waiting for Irsei, too; you know it," laughed Kaiya.

"You should join us for tea sometime in Sanctuary, Senjo," Abby said, ignoring Kaiya. "Don't listen to Kaiya; she's always spreading rumors. By the way, if you tone down your light waves in human form, you can see the kids without harming them. Senjo, your red energy is stronger, and less is more. And one year or one hundred - same difference. And I'm not waiting for that old coot."

You are too, old girl, Irsei's thought drifted in.

"Who're you calling old? I'm just an Elon baby, while you, Irsei, are an ancient old human," Abby said jestingly to Irsei, who laughed and said to all present,

Hard to fight with a woman, either Elon or human, when she's right. On that note, I bid you adieu. And he stepped back out of the conversation, showing the image of his human form, shaking his head.

Senjo said, "I'm leaving too." They both faded out to the laughter of the three.

CHAPTER 44

PARADISE LOST

"LOOKING AT THE maps you got from the boy traveling with your sister, if we always take left turns on the path, is the quickest way with the least hazards," ventured Satchel.

"We'll go right." Water had decided.

She felt it; they were in a mirror. Off they went, taking the right turn in the path each time. Opposites, she thought, figuring safety would be the opposite way.

She had barely spoken to Satchel since the mind-melding.

Both Water and River saw glimpses of Abby, Laiya, and Kaiya in the beginning. How and when the watchers came to be, and their role in this contract. River and Water saw their origins in the nebula, who they were, how they came to be. Through the eyes of a watcher, they came to understand who their parents were. Satchel hid nothing.

And now Water wasn't talking to him.

"Zebble's about half a day behind us. I'm sure he's cut the distance he lost while waiting for his converts. He'll take the path of least resistance." Satchel continued mind speaking to Water. They were descending, sending all he knew of Zebble, remaining open to her probes and memory scans, even though she would not respond. She had closed herself off to him.

What have I gotten myself into? Satchel questioned.

"Trouble, Satchel, a lot of trouble," Water said, never looking back as she descended.

"Zebble's family has been pursuing this a long time, Water. For generations, they have worked toward the goal of no Kaiya for the people. He controls the people by worship. Zebble feels he's the one to achieve completion, to set into motion the plans. His family will rule Izaria, with him as the first emperor. He intends his lineage to rule here for at least a millennium," Satchel continued to tell her of what the watchers knew.

"I'm aware of Zebble's role in this Watcher," Water said.

Satchel cleared his throat and continued, "The watchers became aware of his intentions only recently. Zebble's family has been mind-altering the people for generations. Zebble's confident he'll succeed and is moving toward overthrowing your grandmother and Kaiya.

The three focused on the edge and the darkness gathering there and almost missed this entire happening on Izaria."

"That's interesting. What darkness is growing; where? On the edge of our galaxy, Satchel?"

"Yes, our galaxy."

I must put that aside right now; this is the more pressing issue. I'll come back to that darkness when this all gets settled, Water said silently with determination.

"Show me what you know about the elders and their involvement with this situation, Watcher. Who has joined Zebble, who is against him? I'm playing chess," she said, calculating her next moves. Satchel gave her a quizzical look. "Inside joke, Satchel. Don't bother to try and glimpse my mind either. How much further do you estimate?" she asked as they continued their trek downward.

"less than an hour to the first exit barring no trouble. A couple more if we go all the way down."

There hasn't been any trouble so far, she thought. These stairs were smooth and polished granite. It wasn't the fastest way down, like in the box her sister was taking if they figured it out.

But it was interesting. The walls were smooth and creamy, with fairy fire fungus veins running through them, casting an illuminating light and glittering gold. It seemed the ground they walked upon was a forest floor of dirt and smelled of ancient earth. No one had walked these stairs in generations. Some might have panicked, moving deeper into the bowels of this mountain, this magnificent entity named Zion, but not Water.

She loved the smell, the feel, the sense of this place. The deeper they traversed, the more she knew; Zion called to her. Water was headed to Gran's Paradise Lost,

I will always be with you, even if you do not feel me, Gran had told her.

"I'm coming, Gran." She stepped a little lighter, moved a little quicker down the narrow passage. She was going home, and she knew it.

She looked over her shoulder and said, "We will take the first exit, Satchel."

✦ ✦ ✦

"Where are we?" Begak wondered.

"Not sure, still going down," Jenkins responded. "At least we can see. These fungi are crazy looking, glowing in the dark like that on the walls. Amazing. It makes me wonder what we're moving toward."

"You know, Jenks; I didn't want to make this trip, my father insisted, said it would make me a man. He always said I was too much like my mother to be any good to him. Soft and weak. I tried to be like him, thinking he might love me if I was more like him. I think I just ended up being a mean worthless kid: like he's a mean and worthless man. Money and power, that's all my father respects or loves." Begak was resenting the harsh truth in what he had just said.

"You sound bitter, Bwoi," Jenkins said, reverting to his ancestral language. "Even with your lout of a father, you had a life ninety-nine percent of Rakians will never know. Don't cry about what you didn't have," Jenks admonished Begak. "Look at your world and tell me, what's wrong with this picture? Do you think your father and men like him will be able to continue their ways without getting off this planet? That's what your father's looking for: a way off the world. He would spread his kind of disease everywhere without thinking about those affected by his greed. Is that the kind of man you wish to be?"

"No, I don't," Begak adamantly denied that choice. But who *should* I be? If not the son of the wealthiest, most ruthless CEO, who am I asked himself. If I go back, he controls everything, down to what food the ionizer creates.

Begak said, "I have nothing, nowhere to go."

"You have here, Bwoi, and you have now. Let's see where this path will take us," Jenkins said as he moved a little quicker down the belly of the mountain.

"Yeah, right," Begak grumbled, "we're just going to stumble on to some paradise, and it will all be just perfect."

"Begak, you never know what we might stumble onto, but it's for sure you'll keep stumbling all over yourself if you don't let that bitterness go. Come on, boy, let's get moving again. Never know what's around the corner to meet you. And I, for one, am not interested in meeting your dad on his way down because we lollygagged," Jenkins said, moving more quickly down the passage than before. "Keep up or go back, either way, but stop complaining about the choice YOU made," Jenkins yelled to Begak, who had stopped walking.

Begak looked back behind him - nothing but walls; he looked forward and saw the same; the mountain passage didn't change in either direction. The difference, he thought, is how I see it. There is nothing for me going back, and every possibility laid ahead. Jenkins was right. He was looking at this wrong.

"I AM COMING," Begak yelled back to Jenkins and began sprinting down the tunnel to catch up with him.

"What have you found?" Izen demanded.

"Sir, there are at least three passages down into the mountain. Laser shows one here, here, and here," Stepon, the messenger, showed Izen the three passageways the laser discovered.

"This one here is just outside the lion's ear, a hidden cave in the mane. It leads to a shaft that descends to the bottom of the mountain."

"Can we use it to get down?"

"The engineer said it might be an anti-gravity loop. It'll take an hour to hike up there and check it out. He said he wasn't sure if the loop exists or if it would reach the bottom of the mountain. Supposing the bottom level is where we need to get off at. The engineer asks what you would like him to do?"

"Get moving. That's what I would like the engineer to do." When Stepon did not move, Izen barked," What are you waiting for? Go set it up. Tell him to be ready in two hours. Also, set a team to explore the other paths. I want a report from everyone in one hour. We go after that."

"What have you found?" Zebble questioned the convert.

"The map you have is accurate. There are at least three paths down. The one in the mane has a shaft leading down, we assume to the bottom of the mountain."

"I am not going to the bottom; I am going to the center. Can I get there going down the shaft.?"

"You might be able to. We won't know till we send someone down there. We can mindspeak in here at short distances, not sure how far down into the mountain we can go before we lose communication."

"Get moving; find out. Find me a path to the center. We leave at daybreak, fifteen minutes from now. Have a way for me by then."

Zebble was still extremely angry at having lost the bloodstone. He had a vague dream memory of seeing Water at his campsite, stone in hand. But he couldn't believe she had mastered him, that she could hold the bloodstone and not die. That had to be a dream; I must have lost the stone in the woods, he reassured himself, then questioned, was there another player? Was Aiya here; did she steal the stone? He was getting paranoid. Those woods had reminded him of Core like they were alive; they spooked him. He felt like he had slept little last night, yet he could not wake up. Everywhere he looked, in his dream, he saw eyes looking at him. He could not see them, only wisps of what might be, but he had felt them, that's for sure. They terrified him. He thought he heard whispered words of killing him in his sleep. A shudder went through his body. He had to have lost the stone somewhere in that grove. He knew it.

He didn't realize the bloodstone was gone until an hour ago when he took the box out and saw it missing. That was a blow to have lost it, and he could not go back to find it.

I know those faeries grandfather talked about must have stolen it back from me. I know this mountain doesn't like me. The feeling is mutual. Why did grandfather pick that place, that haunted grove, he questioned as he paced the cave floor. It doesn't matter, he swore to himself, I was drugged. The spores in the ground, pollen in the air - who cares, I'm just glad to be gone from there.

"We'll meet again soon, Water!" he roared into the cave, startling the convert standing next to him.

He knew she was in there somewhere, and he was close. How can a kid be such a nuisance, he thought. She's got me questioning her capabilities. But what could one kid and her grandma do to stop him?

"Nothing," he proudly answered his question.

The new convert, Mere, wasn't sure what to say, or even if Zebble was talking to him.

I'll somehow get rid of Aiya and betroth Water to my son, Asand, then lock her up until my son becomes of age. Zebble began scheming in his mind. Asand might have to marry her when he turns eighteen, Zebble considered. But I doubted it, he thought, I can do a lot in ten years, and she'll be of no value then

"I'll be emperor; I won't need her. Not that I've ever needed that child," spoke Zebble aloud.

"Sir," Mere asked?

"Nothing; leave," Zebble said, waving him away. He had forgotten about the kid and was irritated that he was still there.

"Find the center before daybreak, and yours will be a great reward." Zebble walked away, already forgetting the kid.

Yeah, right, Mere thought. I am just a convert, and I didn't even want to come. My dad made me. Find the center of this mountain in one hour, he thought.

Yeah Right. And maybe I can move a mountain or two while I'm at, Mere grumbled, glad to be away from Zebble, even if he had no idea where he was going.

Mere had never been off his island. Before three days ago, he never knew there was such a thing as a mountain until its colossal structure loomed before him yesterday morning when he arrived.

Now, the supreme elder was asking him to find the center of this mountain.

"How am I supposed to accomplish that," Mere said, muttering to himself. "I'm seventeen years old. I didn't even want this job; my dad made me join."

According to the supreme elder, one person from each family had to enlist in servitude to Kaiya, who said Kaiya wanted it.

I can't imagine Kaiya wanting that, Mere thought, remembering how she used to talk with him every day. A year ago, he told his mom Zebble was wrong, and Kaiya would speak to the people. She threatened to take him to Zebble to set him straight. When Mere told Kaiya, all she said was she was sorry and would not be talking to him for a while. She told me she would call on me again one day soon, but she didn't want me mind-wiped for talking to her.

Who is wiping minds, he wondered when Kaiya said that to him. Mere did not understand then, and he sure didn't understand anything now.

Why me, Mere thought; why is it always me, he questioned. He wandered away, looking for the center of the mountain.

CHAPTER 45

PARADISE LOST AND FOUND

WATER SAT UPON the ledge, the waterfall on her right rushing down the cliff a mere stone's throw away. She was looking out over a vast valley below her, a forest of plants she never knew existed.

"Exquisite," she exclaimed. "So beautiful." I could sit up here looking out forever, she thought.

Water could not wait to categorize each one of the plants; what they were, what was their use, were they edible, medicinal, poison, or mind-altering. I guess your training and your love of nature rubbed off, Gran. Now, I want to be you and experiment all day long. She laughed silently, saying to herself, it is comfortable down here.

"Feels like I am home," she said as she gazed at the lush landscapes of plants she had never seen before.

"Wow, I just realized all my thoughts are about being here, like long term living here, Satchel. Here is Gran's paradise."

She was happy to be here in this moment.

Then she remembered. "Ok, she's not technically my grandmother, is she?" Water sadly said as she looked out over the valley.

Was it just days ago everything came crashing down, only hours ago that I realized everything about my life had been an illusion? She no longer knew what was real in her life or who she could trust. Everything was suspect, especially Gran and Kaiya. Water saw with a lot more clarity than she had had just days ago.

As she sat contemplating her life, she realized that no one had actually 'lied' to her; they just didn't tell her anything. They left out a whole lot of truth in my life. Water sighed. At least I found out I have a sister - the one good thing about this entire adventure.

I wonder where she is right now. I wish she were here, Water thought.

Water and Satchel had descended into the depths of Zion down a narrow path of steps to the first exit. It stopped abruptly at an abyss, with a rickety bridge leading to the other side.

Satchel hesitated, not sure whether to cross or stay put and move further down the other passageways. Was this a trick leading them to their doom? He questioned.

Water looked at him and rebuked him.

"No trick Satchel. Go back if this scares you. I'm sure you'll be able to make up some excuse for your being here when Zebble or one of his henchmen catch you."

She pushed past him and walked onto the bridge.

She's right, Satchel realized, as he watched Water fearlessly cross the old bridge.

"RIGHT," he said. He breathed in deep, sought his courage, pushed his fear aside, and began crossing behind Water.

"OH wow, it's an illusion. Amazing," Satchel said.

His right foot hit the bridge, and he saw the bridge was surprisingly very sturdy. The illusion kept out those who were not welcome and those too afraid to see past their fear.

Water, several paces ahead of Satchel, stepped off the bridge and immediately felt she had crossed a barrier. She turned and looked behind her. She could see Satchel still coming across the bridge, and she could see the energy of the illusion. Yet she could see nothing that had set her senses off, making her feel she had just crossed a barrier. It's much subtler than the dome around Core or even the boundary between Cliff's edge and the compound, deduced Water, scanning the area for the sign of a barrier she knew was there.

"*We crossed some barrier, Satchel. Take note, it's important, I can feel it,*" she mind-spoke to him, maintaining the eerie silence of the place. She rounded the corner and stepped onto the plateau, awed at what met her glance.

It was paradise. She hadn't realized they were on top of a cliff until she reached the edge. She almost walked off the cliff so entranced with the scene far below. The haze of the dawn light filtered down from above showed her where she was.

Water sat down, fascinated by the sunlight. The highest reaches of the cavern were hidden from view. Bright light danced off what diamond-encrusted ceiling was visible and filtered down from an unknown source.

I'm coming back to stay, Water vowed, determined to make this so. She looked out over the landscape. Waves of plants were dancing, their vibrant colors swaying in the wind, illuminating the valley far below.

How did that sunlight travel down here, she contemplated? It looks like stars shining above me, and below me, she laughed out loud, loving everything she saw. She would have to investigate how the light filtered down. Water knew she would be spending time here, as much as she could. She was almost home.

"What do you think?" River asked Seeca. They had climbed onto the top of the box; their map had indicated it was transportation down into the mountain.

On their stomachs, they were gazing over the side of the box, looking down the abyss of the shaft. They could see no bottom. Seeca turned around, slipped through the door in the ceiling, and landed lightly on the floor inside. He was studying the mechanics. Seeca popped his head out of the hole in the ceiling.

"You would be surprised to see what I've found in the bowels," he talked to River as he motioned her to follow him into the wooden box. River was shaking her head no, skeptical about this way down.

Seeca just kept right on gently talking to her as he guided her down into the box.

"No one goes down to the rubble of the Cities beginnings. A lot of those areas are underwater. There are whole abandon cities down there. Kinda spooky the first time I went down there. Like this," he laughed, popping his head back out the ceiling door, making River laugh too as he pulled himself in and out of the box.

River was not comfortable being in that tiny box dangling over a shaft ending somewhere far below.

"Ok, this conversation is going where?" River questioned, breathing a little hard and just wanting to get down to the bottom of this ride.

"Well, down there in that rubble is a building that had a similar one of these, same mechanics," Seeca said as he dropped down into the box next to River and stayed.

"It stopped on each floor in the building, going both up and down," said Seeca, as he flashed her the memory of exploring the old city.

"Ok, that box had buttons and numbers; this has a lever." River was feeling dubious, not sure this was the same thing.

"*Yeah, I noticed the difference.*" Seeca had answered her in his mind, preoccupied with the lever. "Well, the lever has a button. We can push it or continue walking downward on the path."

"You know, Seeca, I'm into moving this right along. I don't want to be in this box any longer than I have to, especially not debating how I'll go down. The long way has been ah, interesting" River was thinking back on what they had gone through to get here. "I am ready to see how the easy way goes."

"Let's go," she said,

"Ok," Seeca agreed, shutting the trap door, not needing to be told twice. River reached the lever and pulled back.

Silence: nothing happened. Ah, River thought, so disappoint-....??? "What was that?"

They waited. It seemed as if whatever was happening was happening outside the box. Ok, now what, both thought.

Then the bottom dropped out from beneath them and the box; they were plummeting down the shaft.

✦ ✦ ✦

"*The kids have made it to the dimensional divide,*" said Senjo. "*Tell me, creating a world so close dimensionally, was not there a chance for great destruction?*"

"*Laiya did the math,*" Kaiya said as if that answered everything.

"*I see we are moving in real-time for the humans right now. How many possibilities exist at this moment?*"

"8,252, oops, that just changed," sang Abby, *"oops changed again. Isn't a moment fun?*

There's an infinite number of possibilities that can change the path they are on. For this, you must wait and see. Ride out the choice like the rest of us," Laiya told Senjo.

"Choose for them. Isn't that a part of this contract?" Senjo questioned.

Abby stiffened in response to Senjo's thoughts. *"Water and River are my children, and they are Irsei's children. They are not a part of this contract, nor will they ever be. They are free to make their own choices, whatever those choices may be. And none can interfere. THAT is a part of my contract."*

"Then, we ride the wave and see where we land." And Senjo winked out.

"AAAAAAHHHHHH!!!!!" Both River and Seeca were screaming as they dropped down the shaft inside the box. They ran out of breath and noticed they were not accelerating anymore; they moved at a steady rate — a-controlled fall. Fifteen minutes later, there was a sudden jerk, a couple of bounces, and everything stopped.

"Maybe not that well controlled." River said, smiling.

"Not like riding the wave, eh," Seeca responded, smiling too.

They came to a complete rest but didn't know where.

"Come on, River, let's go look," smiled Seeca.

They pried open the doors because they could not figure out how to open it and were afraid to push anything that might take them back to the top.

They opened the doors, and both groaned.

A cave-in had blocked part of the passage. Since River and Seeca could not go around, they again used Irsei's handy swiss laser and cleared the way. Twenty minutes later, they crawled through a narrow tunnel they dug to the other side. Seeca wiggled back and forth, inched his way out, turned and grabbed River's outstretched arms, and pulled her through.

"That's an experience I never want to do again," River said, visibly shaken by the ordeal. Too cramped for her, several times as they were moving through the debris River had felt her panic rise. It took all her concentration not to give in to that feeling. She was sincerely glad to know she would not have to come back this way again.

"Imagine that," said River, "just another coincidence; my dad gave me a tool that is exactly what I need, she said sarcastically. "That sounds weird, calling Irsei, 'Dad,'" she told Seeca.

Logically, River should be happy about this, but she was not. Those two, Irsei and Abby, could have saved me a lot of time and hardship if they had just told me back at the fake Sanctuary they were my parents, she thought.

"Would you have believed them, River?" Seeca asked River, eavesdropping in her thoughts

That stopped her. Would I have believed them?

"Maybe you had to go through this to understand and believe, then to know. I mean to know who you are and who you may become. So when you found out a star and a human loved each other, you'd be willing to believe that it's true. Maybe this whole thing for you and your sister was to see who you are. Think about it, River. Both you and your sister on a quest at the time of your naming. This quest is for you to see yourself and choose your path. That is what this is about," he finished. "I think I'm just a wild card," said Seeca, a little downcast.

"No, Seeca, you were always meant to be. Even stars (no, not stars, they're the Elon, she reminded herself) can't see everything."

Both of them stopped in their tracks. Where was the morning light coming from? It was a question that River would ask later after reviewing the memories of this event. Right now, neither could do anything but gape, mouths open at what lay before them.

Water stood up. Something had just happened; she could feel it.

"Did you feel that Satchel?"

"Feel what," he asked?

"I don't know... does anything feel different to you? It's getting stronger, a vibration, this feeling something has transpired - or is about to."

Water placed her hand in her pocket and brought the bloodstone out. It had begun to radiate intense red energy coming from the center.

"What are you trying to show me, little friend?" Water said, holding the stone in her hand, palm up.

They couldn't help it. Neither River nor Seeca had ever seen anything like this in their lives, nothing compared with it. There were flowers and plants dancing and swaying, everything glowing in a multi-colored neon fluorescent dance with the wind in the early morning dawning of the new day. River wanted to dance with them and found herself moving into the midst of all this color, hearing the music in the winds, riveted by the beauty of this strange landscape. Something was calling her up on the cliff; It was singing to the stone in her pocket. She pulled the blue water bloodstone from her pocket, holding it palm up. She gazed upon it and saw blue energy dancing in the center, radiating out like a strobe light. Suddenly, from a top of the ledge miles above her, another dancing red strobe sang out.

"Hello, sister," they both said simultaneously. Then they were in each other's arms, crying and laughing as though they had never separated.

"I guess having an Elon mother has its advantages," laughed River. She realized she had just transported herself to the ledge to be with Water. They were then down in the valley together, surrounded by the stones' blue/red energy streamed.

The bloodstones seemed to melt away, leaving only the balls of energy that danced with the girls like old friends meeting after years of separation.

They didn't have to speak of all they had gone through these last weeks and months. They knew. River and Water laughed at Seeca's and Satchel's confused faces. The girls weren't speaking any language the boys understood; they were singing Elon's speech. And they were transporting themselves back and forth between the valley and the waterfall ledge. They had found who they were when they found each other.

"Seeca, meet my sister, Water.'" "Satchel, this is River, my sister." Simultaneously the girls spoke, both with Satchel on the plateau and Seeca in the valley.

"I'm confused," said Seeca. "I see you are both here with me in the valley. And it seems you are both on the ledge as well. My connection to you has me seeing you in both places at once, and I think I have vertigo; my perspective keeps changing every other second. Can you please choose one spot, and one of us men can walk to meet the others?" Seeca shut his eyes against vertigo.

The girls started laughing. We don't have to walk; they already knew where they were going and transported Seeca to them.

Seeca was standing on the ledge, looking down to where he had just been. "You ought to give a guy fair warning when you're about to jump him. What changed here?" Seeca felt a difference within the girls.

"You no longer need the presence of the stone to control your power, Water," observed Satchel.

"Always the watcher," commented Water in an off-handed manner.

"I didn't even know I had power until right now. River raised an eyebrow, "You're right. The stones carried a piece of our energy. Hers for me, mine for her. The sparks are happy to be home, no longer confined within the stone," she said.

"Let me get this straight," Seeca said. "That stone you have been lugging around with you everywhere we went could have gotten us here in a blink of an eye. We were struggling up those thousands of stairs in the cold, wet, snowy weather, and you could have jumped us straight to that cave in the ear had either your parents or your grandmother bothered to let you know. Seeca was feeling a bit of anger with the adults in their lives.

"On top of it all, these characters, most your relatives, River, let us walk right into danger," Seeca pointed out. "Which, by the way, we're not out of danger yet, and it's not far from catching up to us. That's coming in the form of your Uncle, River." Seeca looked at Water and continued, "I don't know who's chasing you, Water, but I can bet he's just as bad as Izen."

"His name is Zebble, and he is not far behind me," Water said.

"Right, exactly what I thought," sneered Seeca, "I don't think I trust your people. I get the feeling they are apt to throw us into danger anytime they think we need it. It seems as if my Elon, Al, is in on this too."

"Zebble and your villainous Uncle are coming, River, and we need to strategize," Satchel said. What are you two capable of?"

"How would we know, Watcher? Weren't you right there documenting the events as they happened, so you can run back to your watchers and tell all? What do you think we are capable of?" Water practically snarled at Satchel.

River and Seeca stepped back, just a smidgen, surprise registering on their faces.

"The watchers will know with or without me, Water. It still does not change the fact you need to discover what you can do and discover it quickly. I know what is coming for us, and they seem to think what is coming for them is just as bad. We need to prepare," replied Satchel.

"You've got to admit he's right, sis," River interceded. "We need to see what we are capable of achieving, find out what we can do with this power. Who knows, maybe together we can jump them all back to their world, or all of them to one world before they have a chance to cause mischief. Come on, Water, let's see what we can do," River said, reaching out for Water's hand.

CHAPTER 46

ALMOST THERE

BEGAK AND JENKINS had made one wrong turn and found themselves having to turn back and begin again. At least they didn't have to go back to the gate, just to the second turn.

They had gone left at the first turn, and it had been clear sailing to the next corner. After that, Begak and Jenkins made a right turn, and nothing went right. They spent the next hour walking in a circle until they returned to where they had made their first left turn.

Begak and Jenkins were still ahead of his father by at least four hours, Begak calculated. That was too slim for him; he needed a higher margin.

"Jenks, we are making only left turns. Just keep going left." That was two hours ago; they had made good time since.

Jenkins called out to Begak, "You gotta see this; come on, hurry up."

Begak rounded the corner quickly, wondering what Jenks was seeing, and stopped dead in his tracks.

A sunlit cliff was before him. It overlooked a vast valley of swaying flowers, all kinds of colors he never knew existed, and all glowing fluorescent.

More extraordinary than that was the beautiful blue girl staring at him with the bluest eyes and hair he had ever seen. She was standing on the plateau shimmering in sunlight that should not have existed here, so deep in the mountain.

Instantly, he loved this girl. Then he realized she was holding his cousin's hand. He stared at them, unable to take his eyes away. River looked exactly like the blue girl, but copper. His soul cried out as he spoke to his cousin.

"I should have seen you, River. I never looked. I was trying to be what I thought my father wanted - someone like him. I made a mistake. Can you forgive me?" Begak looked to River, waiting for her response.

"I want to go where you are going," he said, looking directly at Water.

River looked at Begak, and she remembered what she overheard in the cave. She turned to Water, let her see what she knew about Begak. Water shrugged her shoulders and gave her sister a slight nod.

"Everyone deserves a second chance," River said. "Besides, maybe we can use you somehow to surprise your father."

"Good day, watcher," Satchel said to Jenkins. "I didn't' not know until now that watchers were on the dying planet too."

Everyone turned, staring at Jenkins

"Good day to you too, young master," Jenkins said to Satchel. "It says a lot about you that you were sent on this path. We shall set aside some time soon for the exchange of knowledge."

Turning to the others and nodding to the girls, he spoke with quiet authority, "My name is Jenkins, and I am at your service."

CHAPTER 47

※———·———○———·———※

THE STORY

"I CAME FOR A year and stayed for one hundred," Abby laughed. "You all know by now the humans call us stars, " she continued aloud, knowing those present in mind only would still have to do so in the language of the humans.

"I chose to experience this species reality to see what life was like in these miniscule bodies of matter. Trust me when I tell you it has been an exciting ride," she chuckled, flashing memories of her life on Rake as a young woman.

Unconsciously, Abby sought Irsei in the cosmic conversation they were participating in and touched him, mind to mind. Abby, Laiya, Kaiya, and Irsei had requested a tribunal with the Elon, asking all who chose to participate in the discussions to do so in human form.

It was time to discuss the darkness consuming them.

The four of them, Laiya, Kaiya, Abby, and Irsei, stood before thousands of Elon who had chosen to come and participate even with the strange request.

Human form indeed, some of them scoffed. Others decided it was interesting and piqued their curiosity. It was new. Still, there were millions more that opened themselves to the understanding of what was going on in their galaxy without making a physical appearance.

So small and insignificant, a species, the thought floated through the consciousness of the collective.

"You might think so," said Abby, consciously reaching for Irsei's hand as they stood before the tribunal in the arena at Sanctuary, where they had chosen to begin the show. All four felt it was the performance of their lives.

Rake's stark reality was very apparent in the arena. It was colossal as a virtual hall. The ambiance was dark and foreboding, like the planet. Laiya, Kaiya, Abby, and Irsei, looked small and vulnerable standing before the tribunal.

The stage was set.

"Now I know how River felt," Abby whispered to Irsei.

The four of them were standing in almost the exact place River had stood to face the uncles a week ago.

Abby was addressing the thought that had just floated through the collective.

"There was a time I thought so too. This species, these humans were small and insignificant," she smiled and turned to Irsei. "They are not."

I love this man, Abby said proudly for all to hear. She echoed this feeling into the universe and listened to the gasp of its vibration.

The Elon felt its power.

"And together, we created life — two beautiful daughters," Abby said aloud. She looked directly at each Elon present, brought them all into her view, reminding them that she, too, was Elon.

"I am Elon," Abby pronounced with conviction and pride. "Born in the vacuum of space, connected to my sisters in birth," showing the tribunal her connection to two small humans she called sisters.

She ignored the Elon the humans called little king. They also called him Regulus A. He danced in the universe with his white dwarf partner, according to the humans, in a binary solar system they called the Alpha Leonis star cluster.

"Our children are direct Elon and human energy, their DNA a new helix in the universe. They were incubated in the nebula for almost three centuries."

"No time at all for an Elon," interrupted Regulus A. Only recently had the concept of time been introduced to the Elon. Minutes, hours, days, years intrigued some of them, including Regulus.

"I know it isn't Little King," answered Abby with a smile on her face, feeling a warm fondness flow from her to him. "Nowhere close to the time it takes for an Elon to be born. I was giving my children the nourishment they needed to become," she sang in the Elon language. She spoke in the language of her sisters simultaneously.

Abby smiled at that. The art of speaking many languages, she thought, I have mastered it. Of course, humans were not thinking of simultaneously speaking all languages when they said 'mastered' languages; she laughed at that thought. "I digress," she said, knowing all the Elon could read her mind.

They didn't call it that, though; they didn't call it anything. The Elon just knew what you thought as you thought it. It was the humans who labeled it mind reading.

"Humans take nine months to incubate; Elons, sometimes millions of years. Our children grew for Two-hundred-eight-five years in the nebula. Safe and well cared for, until we realized the darkness was targeting our nurseries looking for our children. We had to remove their energy and bring them here, birthing them as humans do," Irsei said.

"I do know the pain of childbirth," Abby said in words and interjected the thought and feeling to the Elon. It was a first for many of them, the sensation of pain.

"We hid our children from the darkness that was raging after them. We chose to raise them as humans. They have been growing in human form for fourteen years now. When they come of age on the day winter dies, and spring is born, their fifteenth year in the human world, they will be a mere three-hundred years old by Elon standards.

"We had to move fast; the shadow on the edge of our sector in this galaxy is looking for our girls, and it has been for 250,000 human years," Abby concluded.

Some Elon did not feel the need to be involved and elected to leave the forum. The four watched them go, hoping no others would follow.

"Humans," Abby shouted, catching the attention of those leaving, "What concern would we, the Elon, have for these insignificant beings? They have been little to no concern of ours, ever. Am I correct?"

Most Elons thought of humans as a species barely recognizable; rarely did the species achieve enlightenment. Individuals did here and there, but they went unrecognized, insignificant to an Elon. Some of the Elon resented the three and refused to recognize two of them, addressing only

Abby. Some choose to open their essence to the knowledge accepting what these four had to say. Some just listened in and did not weigh in with their opinions.

The three - Abby, Kaiya, and Laiya, felt that human expression and confining Elon energy in human form were tools for them to use. Abby knew that the experience of moving from the greatness of the whole to the singularity of one tiny being of matter could be a daunting experience the first time. That experience alone could overwhelm one for a moment.

The Elon would understand better in human form.

"Aldebaran, can I call you Al like the kids do?" Abby teased. Con Leonis hid a smile behind his hand as he realized she didn't wait for Al to answer.

Suddenly Abby moved the tribunal away from the Arena on Rake.

"Hear us out. See our story. Feel our miniscule lives. understand our concerns of the darkness rising," Laiya, Kaiya, and Abby sang out together in both languages

"Al," Abby began, "When you are high in their sky on the day spring births, our girls will be three hundred years old."

They were in their valley. The three who were one, Abby-Laiya-Kaiya, brought the Elon home to Sanctuary.

This world is our Sanctuary. In the dimension we asked for and received three-hundred years ago from the Elon, Abby sang and raised her arms high above her head, smiling as her warmth filled the valley.

"We invite you all to feel the beauty, hear the quiet, and enjoy the space. All are welcome," Kaiya, Laiya, Abby, and Irsei said simultaneously.

Laiya had selected the valley near her home for the Elon tribunal to meet, keeping the Elon unaware they were shifting environments until the last second. It had the predicted response from the Elon in human form. They were in awe. That, in turn, allowed all the Elon to experience it.

Win-win situation.

Laiya knew centuries ago they would need the Elon's help to fight an enemy shrouded in darkness. It swept in and left only silence.

Location, location, location," Laiya had told her sisters when they first realized that the darkness had been seeking Abby's daughters; for over two-hundred-thousand- years.

They would need the help of Elon. They set this stage years ago.

Abby was replaying that moment for the Elon now present at the tribunal.

"How could that be. If you say, time is linear?" Senjo asked."

"That is a paradox I haven't figured out yet," Laiya said.

"We need your help to figure it out, and we don't have millions of years. The darkness is growing, and the silence increases," Abby said.

"We thought we could wow you with the beauty of your creations. Show you; you have created something worth saving," Kaiya spoke as she directed their attention to the surroundings in Sanctuary and then out into the galaxies.

"We wanted to show you the confusion we feel about the silence on the edge of our galaxy," showing the Elon the darkness on the edge of their home galaxy.

"Do you not wonder what has happened to our brothers and sisters? They sing no more," Laiya said, focusing the emotional aspect of her words out to the Elon everywhere.

"Then, we thought we'd beg you for your help," added Kaiya.

So let me see your begging faces, Laiya and Kaiya," Abby spoke, expressing her best-begging face, and her sisters did the same.

The three all showed the faces they had first practiced making a hundred years ago, simultaneously. The past had become the future, and the time was now.

"Ah," Abby said, "There is Leonis, staunch in his support for us."

Abby waved to him.

Such a human thing to do, he thought, smiling. He fell in love with the young girls who jumped and respected the energy they had become.

Senjo appeared as a red man but had turned down his power to a softer hue.

"You took my advice Sen," Abby nodded his way. "You don't look so mean," she chuckled.

Regulus, Sirius, Antares, and her brother, even the solitary one, had come. There were thousands present, and millions listened in.

Some still did not see the urgency or the need to work with humans.

"*Arrogance can kill as well as ignorance,*" Kaiya thought, looking around the tribunal.

Every Elon heard what she thought, she made sure they did, defiantly standing her ground.

"These humans are crazy beyond belief," Abby sang quickly before any Elon could take offense.

"All bound together in short lifespans with human emotions, all stemming from love or hate. I asked you again, my sisters and brothers. Before I/we existed, did you ever notice this species beyond a mere glance every few hundred thousand years, if even that?"

Everyone present nodded in agreement; no, they hadn't. Elon did not care about this subspecies.

"We live and die in a blink of your eye," continued Laiya, "No more important to you than an ant is to us," giving them a mental picture of an ant's life and how little humans care.

The four of them, Laiya, Kaiya, Irsei, and Abby, stood before the Elon tribunal, surrounded in Elon light and human love in the valley of their home. They willed the Elon to see them as more than ants.

They looked out at those who chose to come in human form and were awed.

"Feels like we are looking into the eyes of eternity," whispered Kaiya as she stared at the eyes looking at her.

"Yeah," replied Laiya, "but remember, they, in turn, are now looking out the eyes of extremely limiting human bodies."

"You're right, though, Kaiya; there is an eternity in the eyes of an Elon."

They couldn't control what their eyes showed. Eyes are the window to the soul; that human saying applied to the Elon as well. Kaiya spoke to the Elon in their language.

"*We were not even a plunk on the wave to you*, Kaiya sang to the tribunal, *"But we love you still."*

Laiya continued, "We crossed a barrier centuries ago when we put Sanctuary in its dimension. We're not sure if we opened a gate, and something followed us through, or if it had lain dormant in our universe until recently. Or some other reason unbeknownst to us. Have you not noticed darkness shadowing deep out on the rim of our galaxy? No supernovas are happening, just silence."

She watched as all present turned their awareness outward to the edge of their sector in the universe, their galaxy. Instantly aware of what they had let pass without concern for so long.

"Where there had been songs and chatter from planets, now there is nothing. We're losing touch with those of our kind without cause or understanding," Abby spoke and showed all the Elon the dark quiet of Elon ecosystems in their galaxy, going silent.

"We three cannot reach them," Laiya concluded.

Laiya was looking directly at each of them. Many of the Elon resented humans' intrusion and refused to recognize that both she and Kaiya were more than human. Elon energy ran through them. Laiya willed them to look into her eyes to see the truth. They saw the same eternity they had in them, in her. She was not Elon born, but she was of Elon's energy. She was human, and she was Elon. The Elon saw the future in these three. Elon energy flowed through these beings, even if most humans did not recognize that energy. These two humans, Laiya and Kaiya, connected to an Elon, were fire-bonded. And they now had the knowledge and the abilities of an Elon.

"The silence is spreading." Laiya knew she had their attention now. We noticed the darkness on the edge of our galaxy two-hundred years ago. When you live a human life, you tend to pay attention to the details. What you would have barely glanced at or even begun to contemplate for another ten thousand years, we saw right away," Laiya matter of factly stated. "Already, many of your brethren have gone silent; Elons' and their ecosystems, dead."

"We've been tracking it, and Laiya has some interesting theories we're willing to share with you," Abby continued.

"River and Water are not coincidental; neither are their friends. We will need these wave riders. They can go where we have a hard time perceiving, in the seconds between time," said Leonis.

"More natural wave riders will come," concluded Irsei. "We need to seek them out and set up a training space for all of us. We need your species to train also. Work with the human counterpart; become fire- bonded with a human."

That caught their attention.

"Fire-bonded with a human, NEVER," sang out many—a few thought, what a novel idea. The response was vast and varied.

263

"They can be your link to humanity, and you can be their link to all," Abby said. "I think, to defeat this darkness coming, we will need everyone's cooperation, even the likes of Izen and Zebble," she added. "One of us will have to work directly with those two."

"I will link with Zebble," said Kaiya. Everyone could see her plans for him and his cooperation.

"We will approach Izen," said Laiya and Irsei.

"I will address the training of the kids," sang Senjo, "And all the new Elon and wave riders in the future."

"We are asking for cooperation and assistance in seeking an answer to the silence," Kaiya said.

"We can work out all the details in the contract." Abby said, "we are playing a game called chess, bringing all the players together, positioning them where we want them to be, and what help and aid we will need from each. We've brought all the players together in one dimension, one easily accessed by all of us."

"Are you with us?" Echoed in the minds of All Elon, as Abby, Irsei, Kaiya, and Laiya sang out in both languages

CHAPTER 48

HERE THEY COME

"**R**EPORT," SAID IZEN.

"The shaft ends five miles down. Something is blocking the bottom, a wooden box that seems to be the transportation. We don't know how to operate it."

"Humph, is that all you have to report?"

"N-nooo," the young man stuttered, knowing he was about to give Izen more bad news.

"No word from the team that took the right fork, nor are they visible on the vid. The left fork seems to have come to a dead end."

"Is that all?" Izen eyes were cold. He was toying with an old relic that he found.

It was an ancient weapon with a sharp blade that he uncovered from the dirt floor when he explored the cave earlier, waiting for his men to come.

That reminded him of his son and his disappointment in Begak. Where did that kid get to, Izen thought. I haven't seen him since I got here and found him and that lazy guard sitting around doing nothing. Probably running back to his mommy like he always does, Izen concluded, dismissing his son from his thoughts.

Looking at the ancient blade again, he began to wonder what it was made of. He started to call out for JIVE and stopped, remembering he was far from home in so many ways.

When I get out of this forsaken backward place and back to civilization, I'll have JIVE analyze it and tell me what exactly it was. Maybe we can replicate it and sell it on the market as an outside find. That'll go over big; he was daydreaming.

I'm going to make lots of money. But first, I have to get out of here, Izen reminded himself. He wished this were already over and done with, and he had everything he camefor.

He had taken all the amenities of JIVE for granted. He'd never lived without that or the jump.

Sighing, Izen startled the young messenger, saying aloud, "It is what it is."

"Sir?"

Focusing on the messenger now and continuing to toy with the relic, Isen spoke to the messenger.,

"Right now, about the only thing I like is this razor-sharp relic. Sliced my finger just touching it," Izen said while examining his cut.

"What do you think it was used for three hundred years ago?"

"I.. I.. I... don't know, sir," stuttered the shaking and fearful boy. The young boy just wanted to leave.

Oh, why did I come, the young boy thought. He had been asking that question over and over. And no answer seemed good enough anymore.

Izen was frustrated. Nothing seemed to be going smoothly, just setbacks and glitches. Like this mountain didn't like him or his intentions. It was trying to hold him back.

"To hell with this mountain. I want the secrets it hides."

"Yes, sir!" said the young man.

Something's got to break. I have to get down there. Izen felt it.

"You," Izen said, pointing the knife at the boy, "go back to the shaft, tell that engineer to find me a way down that shaft, and out to what's down there. Tell him he has the time it takes me to walk up there to achieve this, or I'll throw him down that shaft myself."

"Yes, sir," the kid said, running to relay the message.

"If I have to climb down a rope, I'll do so. I will get down there," shouted Izen after the running boy.

"JIVE," he yelled. Damn, that's right, no, JIVE. His frustration was growing considerably. He was not a man used to waiting for what he wanted. He didn't like this feeling, and he didn't like this place. "Let's finish this," Izen said with bold determination.

Zebble had been traveling down the path the map had shown him. He had ten of his best warrior converts with him. He didn't like the feel of the shaft and would not travel that way. He set a watch there in case someone used it to come up. Otherwise, he left it alone.

They had started in the early morning, before the break of day, not that he could see the dawn down here. His internal clock told him so. They had now been moving steadily downward for the last five hours, single file the whole way. The path was too narrow to do anything else. They had passed an old rickety bridge Zebble had opted not to use, reasoning there must be something sturdier further down the passageway.

"Strategically, the best place for them to ambush us would be when we exit this passageway. We could not move," Surg, Zebble's number one man, spoke from his position in front of the line.

"I doubt there are more than two, possibly three of them. One is a girl child and one an old lady. They didn't have time to put an army together, nor did they suspect they'd need one. No army to protect them. No Kaiya to save them," Zebble told Surg.

According to Kaiya's contract with the firsters, she could not interfere with daily life on Izaria. Only once a year at the choosing could she wield some power. And that just passed three months prior. Not outside of that. Not while they were on Izaria could she do anything about what he planned to do, he said to himself, reaffirming his knowledge of the contract. She would have to wait until the next Choosing, and that would be too late.

I've won, gloated Zebble; nothing can stop me now.

Forty-five minutes later, Surg called to Zebble. "High Elder."

Zebble loved the title he had given himself. It was music to his ears—just a step from High Elder to Emperor.

"Yes?"

"We have come to a landing, Elder. Something is covering the exit." His men moved down and out of the way for him. He came forward to look, "Yes, I know this substance." He sat down and reached into his bag.

He pulled his Karat. He hadn't played it in fifty years, but he knew what to do. He didn't forget the music that shattered the force field around the box that held the bloodstone and the shield around Core simultaneously. Zebble remembered. His grandfather had died that day because he had played the Karat. He gently placed it to his lips and blew several notes, then combined them into an eerie, hypnotic sound.

"I suggest we move back into the stairwell. This substance will crack."

"I tried it on one other barrier. It cracked it wide open. It was a much larger barrier - much, much larger. Cracking, this should be a snap," Zebble said and continued to play the instrument his father had made.

CRACK sang the barrier. Everyone on the landing started pushing to move back up the stairs. They did not know what was coming next. Those still on the stairs were moving downward like the rush of a cool raging freshwater river meeting the warmth of a sea salt ocean. They clashed, then mixed and clashed some more until finally, all were back on the stairs away from the blast radius.

CRACKKKKKK. You could hear the strain and feel the substance give way to the eerie notes Zebble played — Kaboom.

"What was that," Surg asked?

Zebble was near to the landing and peeked out. The barrier had fallen. Finally, a break, he thought.

"It's clear," he said, "let's go."

"What do you know, engineer?" Izen wanted the right answer. He had just walked the way up here, and his frustration had been growing the whole way. The man was nervously standing by the shaft, speaking to two other engineers. He looked back at Izen and inconspicuously edged away from the deep drop.

"We believe it is an anti-gravity chamber. It seems to be working."

"'Seems to be.' You don't know for sure?"

The engineer shook his head and cast his eyes downward, wishing he were invisible.

"Ok, we are going to test it now," Isen said. "Engineer, jump."

"Whaaat???"

"I said, 'jump.' If your theory is right and you make it to the bottom, you will receive five times the money you are now receiving. If you are wrong, you die."

"But, but I ah, it ah, WHAT??"

Izen brought out the ancient weapon, "I've been practicing throwing this; it's impressive what the force of a razor-sharp instrument can slice through. You will jump, or I will cut you in half with this and watch your body fall, to see if it plummets to the bottom or not."

Engineer Jowls walked to the shaft and stepped in, falling into the falling into space.

Izen came to the edge and looked down. Jowls was descending at a controlled speed.

"Looks like you were right," Izen yelled down to Jowls.

"Everyone ready, let's go; jump at one-minute intervals," he said, and over the edge, he went.

It hadn't taken Jowls long to reach the bottom and see the cave-in that had obstructed the entrance. He went through the narrow passageway that had already been created in the rubble, enlarging it as he went with his power laser. It worked ten times faster than those sold on the web. The laser was made for engineers, not the public.

He stopped short of going through the entrance of the cave when he broke out of the rubble. Jowls knew Izen would expect him to clear the way to the entrance and wait.

Izen had ten men with him; the rest were topside. He wanted no more to come down. He was trying to contain this as much as possible. He wasn't even sure if he would let them all live. He was thinking about it.

Jowls waited for Izen to descend and let him be the first out.

"Wait here, come as a force. I'll wait for you beyond the entrance," Izen said and went out of the cave.

Zebble began moving toward the exit when suddenly the ground beneath them started to rumble, the walls began shaking, and the ceiling crumbled.

"RUN," screamed Zebble. He didn't have to say it twice; they were pouring down the stairs. As quick as water running over the cliff, they were out the opening. As quickly as they started running, they ceased when they got outside. Never had they seen anything like this. Glow-in-the-dark vegetation. Where were they? A few of them thought they were not on Izaria anymore. Once again, the earth began to rumble a little louder, a little longer.

"Let's go," Jowls said and moved out to meet Izen.

The men stepped out of the cave and stopped, frozen in time, staring at what they saw. Fluorescent plants were dancing in the wind. Where were they? Because it sure didn't feel or look like home. This place was not Rake.

"Did you hear that rumbling sound?" Izen asked the men. He was looking to the east. "That's the second time I heard that."

Then it was as if the earth caved in on itself. The ground shook so severely they were unable to stand. The shaft Izen had come down, and the passageway Zebble had just arrived from, collapsed, nothing but rubble left. Every man in there felt the loss of their way home. Trapped in a mountain with no way out, these men thought.

Zebble's action of cracking the barrier had led to the collapse of the mountain passageways. Both his and Izen's way out was demolished and buried. The teams were trapped, stranded in this strange world, unable to get out the way they had come in. All the men with Izen and Zebble immediately realized this. There was no way home. The look of resignation and fear played across the faces of these men.

The girls saw both passageways on the east and west sides of the valley collapse.

"You concentrate on Zebble, Water, and I will get Izen," River said to her sister as she began concentrating on sending Izen back to the Cities.

The girls first sent the two teams of men back to the entrance at the lion's mouth, figuring they would deal with them later if they stuck around after this.

Izen was staring in shock as his team disappeared before him. If he hadn't been so tired, he might have realized someone jumped them out of the mountain. He was conditioned to think only JIVE could jump you. JIVE was not working for him here, so he felt his team couldn't jump either. Instead, it reminded him of the tales of the disease, everyone disappearing, leaving him standing alone in the valley, unable to comprehend what happened.

Zebble's fate mirrored Izen's; he, too, was left standing alone while his men were transported out of the mountain. But Zebble knew what had just happened, and he was angry, looking around for Kaiya, thinking she sent them away.

Suddenly both Izen and Zebble began to feel the tug of a jump surrounding them, but neither had any idea where they were going. It crossed their minds that they were going into a jump but might not come out the other end.

"Let's send them back home, get them away from here so we can think," River mind-spoke to Water.

"As the faeries say, we can always kill them later," Water said, smiling. "Satchel let's link; together, we are stronger. You have a clearer picture of his island than I do."

"Come help me, Seeca. You're the navigator," River said, reaching her hand out to him.

"They're here," the girls said simultaneously.

"Let's do this," River and Water said, each focusing on the man who had caused so much confusion and change in their lives.

"Better to send Izen and Zebble back to their homeworld, then to kill them straight out," said Water.

What is she thinking, Begak said to himself? He will undoubtedly cause a lot of trouble, especially if he's anything like my dad.

"Ok," said River, but I'm with Begak; I still think they'll be trouble."

"Probably," sang Water,

They read my mind Begak asked, a little stunned?

"Yes, we did," said the girls.

"Me too," said Seeca

"I did too," chimed in Satchel.

"I will have to say I also read your thoughts, young master," Jenkins told Begak.

"All of you?" I have a lot to learn, he thought.

Yes, you do, resounded in his mind from everyone.

They all began to concentrate on jumping Izen and Zebble out of the mountain.

"Everyone's here in the divide, your Paradise Lost, Laiya. Are we ready?" Abby asked.

"Let's do this," all the others chimed in.

They all began to materialize on the plateau where River, Water, Seeca, Satchel, Begak, and Jenks already were.

"Something's wrong here," Water said.

"What's happening?" Seeca asked River, panicked. He noticed both Izen and Zebble were materializing on the Plateau no matter the concentration or effort she was pouring into jumping Izen home. She could see by the strain across Waters' face that she, too, was pouring the same energy into getting Zebble away and not succeeding either.

"Why are they up here with us and not in their homes?" Seeca's panic was evident in his voice. River began to concentrate harder, willing Izen away. You could see him start to fade.

"River, turn around, stop the jump. They're all here."

Water was inside her mind, reaching past River's concentration to snap her out of the jump.

"Look, River, I mean everyone is here," Water said aloud and caught River's attention.

River stopped the jump, staring at the group gathering on the plateau. Water and River broke their links to the wave simultaneously, shocked to see not only their gramma Laiya, but Kaiya, Abby, and Irsei. And there were Izen and Zebble. Here was another shock; those two, Zebble and Izen, looked like twins. Only their clothes and Zebble's full-length beard and long hair distinguished them. Izen was cleanly shaven.

The ledge began to brighten, and the girls turned to see Al, the sleeping man, and some stunning goddess staring at them. Every man there, amazed by her beauty.

The girls looked at each other. "Boys will be boys," River told Water. Water hadn't spent any time around boys, except at the ceremony once a year, and no one ever took time with her. So, she didn't know how they would be.

But Water felt the woman was breathtaking as well.

The girls turned to Laiya, saying, "Hi Gran/Gram" together,

"Irsei, Abby - Mom, Dad, whoever you are right now." River spoke a little harshly.

Irsei and Abby had the decency to wince in public, although it looked as though Abby was laughing the whole time. Quietly without the girls seeing, they just felt like she was. Abby was good at finding humor anywhere.

"Water, this is our Dad, Irsei. I met him already at the fake Sanctuary," River said. "He might be a fake too."

"Ouch," laughed Irsei.

"And River, this is Kaiya - soon to be an ex-god-like being and probably one third, our mommy," said Water sarcastically.

"Guilty as charged," laughed Kaiya. "You should see all your faces."

"Girls, your faces don't look as bad as those two boys," Kaiya laughed, pointing to Seeca and Begak. And they aren't near as bad as those two grown men. They keep staring at each other like they're in front of their favorite mirror," referring to Zebble and Izen. They could have easily passed for identical twins. Kaiya could not keep the humor out of her voice,

"Tweddle Dee and Tweddle Dumb," she called Izen and Zebble, referring them to some ancient children's poem.

"Al, these are my friends," Seeca said proudly, including Begak and Jenkins in that circle.

"And who's with you?" Seeca asked Al, staring at the beautiful Elon woman standing in front of them.

"Seiza, my name," sang the Elon woman. "I grew up with him," she smiled and pointed at Senjo.

Her voice is as beautiful as she is, thought Seeca.

River and Water were shaking their heads, having just listened to Seeca's thought.

"Boys," they both said this time.

Izen looked directly at Irsei, astonished. "You're The Pearl. I hired you to track the girl," he said.

"And so I have. I expect my money to be in my account tomorrow morning," Irsei replied matter of factly.

Izen did not understand any of this; he didn't like this sensation of not being in control of anything. Who were those two male-like beings that weren't human? Here was the power he was seeking. The Pearl was a part of this whole thing, and he was River's father? And she has a twin sister. Who was Abby? Izen was questioning everything. He still wanted that power, and he was busy calculating how he could turn this situation to his advantage.

Zebble was having the same thoughts, only trying to cloak them. He knew what Laiya was capable of, and Kaiya had been his people's god for a long time. He lusted for the power he had seen displayed here.

"You're still petty men," Laiya spouted to Izen and Zebble.

"Izen, be aware that everyone around you can read all your thoughts - everything. Zebble, your cloak is visible and broken."

Realization streamed into both Izen's and Zebble's minds from all of those around; bombarded with everything everyone thought of them.

"Don't think you're going to weasel away from this, Zebble. You're not strong enough to cloak your thoughts from a two-year-old in Sanctuary," Kaiya said, sneering at Zebble.

"You can't do anything to me!" screamed Zebble at Kaiya. "The contract forbids it!"

"You would be right if we were on Izaria, Zebble. Look around you, puny man. You are not in Izaria. You crossed into my dimension when you broke the barrier," Kaiya calmly told Zebble with a smile upon her lips. "You broke the covenant," she yelled, her expression changing just as quickly.

"All bets are off!" snarled Kaiya. "You could lose your life just for that. You are in the presence of masters and gods," roared Kaiya, "Bend your knee to me!"

She shook the earth and frightened both Zebble and Izen so much, they both quickly bent a knee.

"Kaiya, what are you doing," asked Laiya?

"Oh, come on, Laiya, I'm just having some fun, giving them a taste of their own medicine," Kaiya smiled impishly.

Leonis had materialized right before Kaiya did this. He did not want to miss any of the fun. He wasn't even trying to hide his laughter at the sight of Izen and Zebble. Al made the most human gesture: he coughed under his breath and into his hand.

"Oh, alright. Get on up, Zebble. That was just a taste of the god you were proclaiming me to be. Careful, you just might get it."

"These are your options, gentlemen," Senjo spoke for the first time. "Both of you are looking for a certain power. We are willing to give you the position of ambassador for us in this galaxy. In exchange, you will be working for us with an exclusive contract - unbreakable and binding. You will be rich beyond your wildest dreams and have the power to broker deals for us. The downside for you is, break any part of the contract, and you die," Senjo said. "We are sending both of you to the surface. Take a long way home and think about this," Senjo finished with them.

"Your world is dying," Senjo said to Izen."

"Zebble, the people in your world will know what you and your family did these last one hundred and fifty years by the time you get back. There will be nowhere you can go without everyone knowing. The choice will be yours to make," Aldebaran added. "You both will have until twenty-four hours after you get home to let us know your decision. If you disagree, there will be no contract and no help from us in the time allotted to you. If you agree, we will send you our contract, and you will sign and return before the sun sets the day you get it, or there will be no contract.

Senjo laughed, saying, "Elon joke, Tas?" Calling Aldebaran by his ancient Persian name.

"Something like that," laughed Al, then turned back to Izen and Zebble.

"The contract is non-negotiable. Your men are already on the surface, awaiting your arrival. We will contact you twenty-four hours after your arrival home," said Al as he sent both Zebble and Izen to the surface.

"Wow," said Seeca to River and Water, "I would say your people, pointing to Laiya, Abby, Kaiya, and Irsei set us up," pointing to River, Water, and himself. "But it looks like my person," this time aiming his finger at Al, "was just as involved in this set-up as your people were." Seeca pointed his finger again at Abby, Irsei, Laiya, and Kaiya.

Seeca was giving Al the 'I know what you did' look.

Al just laughed.

"We have a lot to talk about, young wave rider. Meet your new teacher, boys," Al spoke to the kids, pointing to Senjo. "You too, young ladies."

"We have much to do, and you have much to learn quickly. We will come to you all soon," Senjo said as both he and Al faded away.

"Your parents are in Sanctuary waiting for you, Seeca," Al said as he was fading.

"What are they talking about?" The kids turned and threw that question at all the adults.

"I told you," said Seeca. "Don't trust the adults."

Water, River, and Satchel all began to laugh. It was an inside joke between friends.

"Let's go home," said Irsei. "You kids got some explaining to do."

"*We've* got some explaining?!" exclaimed River and Water.

"Home where?" asked Begak.

"Why to Sanctuary, Begak, where you belong," said Laiya.

At that moment, Mere came on the ledge, having found the center of the mountain. He was staring at all the brightly lit people around him.

"Hi," Mere said.

"Where did you come from," Laiya question

"What? He asked.

"Hello Mere, how are you?" Kaiya asked him

"Kaiya, is that you? How are you doing? Did you figure out all that mind-wiping intrigue?" Where is everyone at? They came down here long before I did. At least I think they did. I'm kinda lost. I don't know where to go anymore. Not sure I want to go back to that life," he said, looking down at his feet.

Kaiya looked at Laiya, then Abby, speaking silently to both. Laiya and Abby both nodded in agreement.

"Laiya, do you remember what Gramma always used to say?" Kaiya asked.

"Yes, I do," she said.

"If you find us, you're supposed to be there."

"Come on, Mere, Come home with us."

✦ ✦ ✦

GLOSSARY

Abby - Born in 2026. Elon species. Humans call her a Red Dwarf sun. Sister to the humans Laiya and Kaiya. Companion to Irsei and mother to River and Water.

Aiya – aka Laiya. Born in 2006. Acting grandmother to River and Water in the 23rd century.

Aldebaran - aka Al. One of the four royal stars, watcher of the east. Ancient name Tascheter. Persians considered Aldebaran one of the four guardians of the heavens.

Argot-mountain on Rake

Aziel - Queen of the fairies

Bubble – An Elon entity contracted to shield Sanctuary for three hundred years. No one allowed is into the 200,000-acre property without his consent.

The Choosing – Coming of age ceremony on Izaria for all children turning fifteen. They all Choose their life path.

Core – Largest island on Izaria at 250 square miles. Home to Aiya, Water, and Sista Sol.

Elon - Ancient Species the humans called "suns" and stars."

Hoover – Transportation from the year 2060 on planet Earth/Rake. Uses lift energy to hover two feet above the ground for a smoother ride. Outdated mode of transportation on Rake in the year 2330. They are used by River riding through Sanctuary.

Firster – The fi=first people brought to Izaria in the year 2080 with their minds wiped of their past.

Indigo – Smallest Island on Izaria and closest to Core. All of the Indigo people come from Sanctuary and are contracted as Watchers.

Irsei – Companion to Abby, father of River and Water, kin to Laiya and Kaiya. Also known as The Pearl.

Izen – He is the greatest and most ruthless CEO on Rake in the 22nd century. CEOs rule the world in 2330. Uncle to River, father to Begak. The descendant of Laiya.

JIVE – Jump Intrawave Vortex Environment for homes. It was created in 2030 by Laiya.

Jump – Instantaneous interdimensional travel. Limited travel on Rake to the planet only.

Kaiya - Cousin/sister to Laiya. Sister to Abby. The benevolent god-like entity on Izaria.

Kasor – Male fairy who tells Zet about the truth of Izaria.

Laiya - he discovered the interdimensional wave in 2026. She is thought of as the creator of the Jump on Rake. Sister to Abby, sister/cousin to Kaiya. Acting grandmother to River and Water in the 22nd century.

Mere- from Izaria convert to Zebble. He stumbled into Sanctuary. A pawn who would be king.

Naming ceremony – Coming of age ceremony on Rake for all descendants of Laiya turning fifteen.

Rake - The Ratified Alliance of Kings and Executives formed in 2102, seventy-two years after Layia seeded the planet Earth with the Jump, making transportation and governments obsolete.

Sista Sol - A runaway 21st home vortex system that became aware. She ran away deletion day and went rogue. She met Laiya on the dark web and went to Izaria with her. One of Water's only friends.

Seeca - Natural wave rider. He was born an illegal child to Winsome and Prina in the year 2312, Relegated to the city's bowels at the age of two years old when the system discovered him. His parents chose to move to the bowels rather than give him up. Found one of the first jumps Laiya created while exploring the ancient pathways of the city. Friend to Aldebaran. First bond with River.

Satchel - Young Watcher on Indigo assigned to help Water.

Soin - is Wiffle's father and predecessor on Indigo, the Watchers' island.

The Pearl - aka Irsei's alternate persona

The wave The interdimensional wave was discovered by Laiya in the year 2026.

Wiffle – Elder of Indigo and leader of the Watchers

Zebble - Elder of the Skaten island on Izaria and leader of the most massive religious movement Izaria has ever seen. Zebble has mind-altered the Izarians to believe Kaiya wants to be worshiped. He is the only one Kaiya talks to.

Zeek – Father to Zebble, a gentle artist who creates the Karat's musical instrument, made of Core driftwood and craved by stardust mineral.

Zet – Zebble's grandfather. He found the fairy box's containing Kaiya bloodstone's heart and the map to Paradise Lost. He is the first Izarian to discover the true nature of Kaiya and the people of Izaria's lost history

Zion- Mountain on Izaria.

ABOUT THE AUTHOR

Sharon is an artist, writer, mother, grandmother, student, teacher. She joined the Army and graduated top in her class as an Air Traffic Controller in the 1970s. She joined the military as a WAC and left a soldier in this man's Army years later when the Women's Army Corp dissolved.

She is a disabled veteran. Undiagnosed PTSD led her down a path of addiction and hopelessness later in her life. She maintained the illusion everything was alright for a while, but She lost the battle and went onto the streets, another addicted homeless veteran. In 2005 she reached out to the VA hospital, "Help me, or I'm checking out." So began the fight for her life.

In February 2008, while living in Las Vegas, she received a call; her nineteen-year-old daughter had aggressive cancer that would kill her without equally aggressive chemotherapy. She moved back to Wisconsin to be with her daughter and made a promise to Her. She would shave her hair off in solidarity with her. Her daughter lost her hair quickly. Sharon shaved her head when her daughter finished treatment. By June 2008, they were bald together. She took the Nazarene vow and pledged to GOD,

"I wear dreadlocks have for the last thirteen years. They are my way of giving thanks for all that I have, even thru the tragedies of losing two grandchildren in senseless deaths. I continue to move in the light. I follow my heart to me on a path of peace amid violence and hate. We are one people with many faces. I know we are waking up.

I have survived. More than that, I thrive and help create Sanctuary for those ready to find it.